THE BIG TIMER

THE 4TH HIDDEN GOTHAM NOVEL

CHRIS HOLCOMBE

**BOOKS
LIKE US**

Published by Books Like Us.

This is a work of fiction. Names, characters, businesses, places, events, locales, and incidents are either the products of the author's imagination or used in a fictitious manner. Any resemblance to actual persons, living or dead, or actual events is purely coincidental.

"Cecilia," words by Herman Ruby, music by Dave Dreyer, ©1925 Published by Irving Berlin Music. Public domain.

"Bluenoses Get Blue," words by Chris Holcombe, ©2025 Original work.

"Prove It On Me Blues," words and music by Gertrude Rainey, ©1928 Publisher Unknown. Originally released by Paramount Records. Public domain.

"I'll See You In My Dreams," words by Gus Kahn, music by Isham Jones, ©1924 Published by Leo Feist. Public domain.

Print ISBN: 978-1-7364458-6-0

ebook ISBN: 978-1-7364458-7-7

ALSO BY CHRIS HOLCOMBE

HIDDEN GOTHAM NOVELS:

The Double Vice

The Blind Tiger

The Devil Card

The Big Timer

HIDDEN GOTHAM STORIES:

The Red Fox

The Naughty List

CONTENT INFORMATION

This is a noir wrongfully accused murder mystery, so there are some elements in the story to be aware of:

Violence, death of a spouse, verbal threats from police and prison guards (used sparingly), family estrangement, sexism (used sparingly), reference to conversion therapy (used sparingly), spousal gaslighting, and extortion over homosexuality.

On the flip side, there's also lesbian flirtations, sexual innuendo, irreverent, bawdy, (and dare I say it?), hilarious song lyrics, some big "Sisters Are Doin' It For Themselves" energy, and profanity.

What's *not* in here are racial slurs. We don't need that nonsense.

ACKNOWLEDGMENTS

No book is produced by one person, so the author wishes to thank the following beautiful humans for their support, guidance, expertise, and for otherwise putting up with his "bushwa":

My huzzband David Bishop, for once again weathering the storm of another book; I swear, love, I'll try to stress less on the next one; my sensitivity reader Erica Joy, for her insightful comments and enthusiasm; my editor Mary Louise Mooney, for her continued editing guidance and love for this series (chin chin!); Robin Vuchnich, for once again creating a fabulous cover that is worthy of El; the "boys" aka Rob, Ricky, and Peter, thank you for cheering me on; John Mainieri, aka "John with the Pugs," for being a fabulous neighbor and theater buddy; April Rodriquez, aka "Fierce," for the laughs, the "champs," and the love; Wendy Gross Alexander, for giving this one more read-through; and to all the readers I've met along this journey—your words remind me of why I do this. Thank you.

P.S.: I did not write this book with A.I. The plot, the characters, the dialogue, the descriptions, all of it, (the good, the bad, the clunky), came from my brain. Yes, there are em dashes in here. A.I. stole em dashes from us writers and I refuse to—wait for it—give 'em up. :)

For Alberta Hardison,

the kind of friend who
drives out to you in the middle of the night,
no questions asked,
hits you with the truth,
holds you with love,
and asks for nothing in return.

1

The stairs never looked so steep or felt more dangerous than they did the night El Train found herself arrested for murder.

"Don't break my neck, now!" she said as they rushed her down the stairwell of her building.

The elevator had broken down again and her greedy, lazy landlord hadn't bothered himself to fix it. 'Course, he hadn't bothered himself to fix the stairs either, given their uneven slants and leaning banisters and groans of protest.

Two white NYPD pounders flanked her on either side, their grip iron, their pace insistent, practically carrying her as they spiraled down, down, down. No small feat given that she often described herself as "built like a locomotive."

One of them, a spindly weasel of a man half her size with a pockmarked face, growled, "It would save the city the trouble."

El replied he was nothing but a cat-licking potato-eater, which prompted the other pounder, a taller, heavier fella with dull eyes and sagging jowls, to say in a bored voice, "Quit it, you two."

They continued their way down the stairwell, their heavy shoes thudding against the creaking wood like hammers beating on rusty nails. Nails to her coffin. How the hell was she going to get out of this? And when she was so close too!

"What's the evidence against me?" she said.

The pounders didn't answer.

"I demand to hear it! I've got rights!"

The pockmarked weasel sneered. "People like you don't *have* any rights, and you best remember that."

Above them, El heard the taps of another set of shoes, moving fast and gaining ground. Flo Russell. Somehow, that gave El comfort. What Flo could do to help, El didn't know, but she wanted—no, she *needed*—her friend by her side.

She turned her head to the pockmarked weasel. "You think you can just railroad me? You best think again! I'm going to have the best defense this city has ever seen." Which, she sincerely hoped, would be true.

The weaselly pounder abruptly stopped, causing all three of them to almost take a tumble down the rickety, rotting stairs. "Why you—"

"Morton!" called the heavier pounder. "Stop antagonizing the prisoner!"

His weaselly partner blushed.

El couldn't help herself. "Morton? What kind of name is that?"

"The one my mother gave me."

"She didn't like you from the start, did she?"

Morton's ugly sneer opened wider but before it could let loose with an indignant reply, his partner said, "And you, miss? You need to *stop* talking if you know what's good for ya. I mean it. Not another peep."

He glared at her.

The tapping of Flo's feet above them wound closer and closer, a strange, urgent metronome counting out these tense measures of rest.

El swallowed her pride—not quite a Herculean feat but close enough—and nodded.

He grunted in approval, and they continued down the stairs.

She and the pounders soon hit the ground floor and flew through the lobby. When they opened the front doors, they were greeted by a roar of male voices shouting sharply and incomprehensibly. What the hell?

Newshawks.

Of course, they'd be here. They wouldn't miss this for the world. The dramatic dénouement to the Alice Holloway murder case, the most baffling and violent murder to hit Harlem this month. Although give it time. November was just about to be five days old.

Cold air stung her skin. She didn't have on her usual white tuxedo jacket, much less her coat and top hat to ward off the frigid autumn night. All she wore were her white shoes, a pair of white men's trousers, a white shirt, and an unbuttoned white vest. Her matching bowtie hung loose around her undone collar. Had she known she was going to be seen by every reporter in Harlem, she'd have spruced up a little.

"El! El!" called the newshawks. Their questions came fast and furious.

"Why'd ya do it?"

"Did you think you'd get away with it?"

"What would you say to young girls wanting to be in the speakeasy life?"

"Was it liquor and jazz that caused you to murder Alice Holloway?"

El couldn't help herself. "I didn't kill her, you dumb Doras! I was trying to—"

The heavier pounder said, "What was unclear about 'not another peep'?"

El clenched her jaw so hard, she almost cracked a tooth. "Not a thing, Officer."

"Good. Let's go."

The two pounders dragged her through the throng of people. Behind the newshawks stood gawkers and onlookers resembling a Broadway chorus. The gawkers tittered with guilty pleasure and the onlookers clicked their tongues in disapproval. She could read their minds:

"The bulldagger finally got what was coming to her."

"A life of sin gets a life of consequences."

"God punishing the wicked," and so on and so on.

Well, as far she was concerned, they could go chase themselves into next week.

Two figures stood off to the side, away from everyone. El squinted. Was that . . . ? Was that Reverend Elijah Blackburn and his wife Constance? If so, she knew without a doubt what they were thinking: "I told you so."

Ahead of her stood the wagon, dark and silent. The opened door revealed a bottomless pit, a shadowy grave. A point of no return. Her mouth dried out at the sight of it, and she swallowed sandpaper.

Oh, babe . . . we're in it deep now.

The two pounders hoisted her up and into the back, slamming shut the door so hard, its echo sounded like a gunshot.

Like the gunshot that killed Alice Holloway.

El turned and peered out the barred rectangular window at the top. Her hands gripped the bars, her eyes searching the crowd. She saw Flo Russell pushing people out of her way. A tiny woman with incredible strength. She had to be to land lead dancer at Connie's Inn, where she laid down some serious iron six nights a week. She possessed the flexibility of a ballerina and the speed of a sprinter, which served her well now, El saw, as she ducked under and twirled around the bodies of the notebook scribbling newshawks, and forced the gawkers and onlookers out of the way to get to the door of the wagon.

El locked eyes with her.

An unspoken plea passed between them.

Flo called, "I'll get help!"

"Madam Watkins!" El replied. "She'll know what to do!"

The pockmark-faced Morton yelled at Flo to get back. His heftier partner pounded a meaty fist on the side of the wagon, and with the squeal of gears and the stubborn whine of the engine, the wagon lurched forward. El watched as the reporters surged after them, like a nest of ants chasing after picnic food being carried away.

She closed her eyes and forced her mind to focus. She had to think, had to plan. Because truth be told, it wasn't a complete surprise they arrested her. A part of her expected it ever since they found Alice Holloway's lifeless body. She'd been shot in the chest, indicating to the coroner and to the detectives that she'd been facing her killer.

She knew them.

El swallowed more sandpaper.

Which means I know them too.

"You best lay low for a while," Flo had told her.

El had just shaken her head. "You know I can't do that."

"El—"

"Don't 'El' me, sis. You know I've got to do this. I've *got* to."

And El saw that Flo understood. She didn't approve, mind you, but then again, Flo hardly ever approved of what El did, Alice Holloway being first among them.

"Well, then," Flo had said. "We best get a move on. We're on borrowed time."

And here they were a couple of nights later. El's time had most definitely run out.

I was almost there! It was just about to come to me!

It being the answer to the question that haunted her. That teased and toyed with her during the long days and kept her up during the even longer nights. That drove her to do things she'd never, in a hundred years, ever do. And discover things she'd wished she'd never learned.

Because Alice Holloway wasn't just a random white woman shot and killed in New York City.

She was El's secret wife.

BEFORE THE MURDER

2

"*Weeeelllllll shit!*" crowed El Train.

"*Weeeelllllll shit!*" replied the crowd.

El stood at the lip of the stage, hands on her hips, face flushed and wet. It was the first thing she said when she stepped on, and it was the last thing she said before she sang her final song and leapt off. Both instances, she'd stand like this, assessing her audience and seeing if they met up to her standards. And ever since she took this gig at Chez J.A., a club in the Blacks-only Watkins Hotel on West 145th Street and Lenox Avenue, the crowds always exceeded them.

Even on a Monday night.

Catching her breath after nearly two hours of performing, she squinted under those bright stage lights and smiled at the shadows gathered around those ghostly white tablecloths stretching out as far as she could see.

"Look at you! Clapping on the two and the four the way the good Lord intended. Made my job so much easier."

"I've got a job for ya," yelled out a male voice.

The crowd giggled.

"You do now?" El said. "Does it pay by the second? 'Cause you're not gonna last even a minute with me, mister!"

The room filled with laughter.

"What about me now?" called out a female voice.

A nervous *oooo* snaked its way through the room. Chez J.A. was a safe space for people like El—usually—but that didn't mean those out-of-towners visiting Harlem for the week or the weekend couldn't be scandalized.

She cupped a hand behind her ear. "What was that? Do I hear the light chirp of a sweet bird?"

The female voice replied, "Tell me where your nest is, and I'll be sure to lay your eggs!"

The crowd lost it.

Even El couldn't keep it together. She fanned herself with one hand while patting her chest with the other. She waited for the crowd to die down before replying, "You think you can keep up with me, sweet bird? Alright, let's see how you sing. Let's see how you *all* sing. You want to hear about Cecilia?"

"*Yeah!*" said the crowd.

El made her way to the upright brown piano set center-stage. "I *said,* do you want to hear about Cecilia?"

"*Hell, yeah!*"

"Hell, yeah is right."

El flipped her tuxedo tails back and perched on the piano's bench. She cracked her knuckles before placing her hands on the keys. Her foot stomped out the count-off and just like that, music unleashed from that wellspring deep inside her. Spilling out her fingertips and drenching those piano keys. It didn't matter what song she played (or how she was supposed to play it). When she started, she couldn't help but tinge those notes with all the shades of the blues: sweet cerulean, sparkling sapphire, moody indigo.

But with the song "Cecilia," El used passionate periwinkle, the color of the silk negligee belonging to her very first lover. Closing her eyes, El pictured the candlelit room in that Philadelphia flophouse. The smooth fabric slowly falling away from the woman's skin and dropping to the floor. The sweet smell of jasmine perfume tinging the air. The arms wrapping around her as hands caressed in a way that felt so right, so right, so right.

Without being conscious of it, El leaned her head back and opened her mouth wide. She belted:

> *Little Miss Cecilia Green*
> *Little over sweet sixteen*
> *But the cutest flapper that you've ever seen.*
>
> *When the fellows pass her by*
> *She will always wink her eye*
> *When she talks to them*
> *When she walks with them*
> *This is what they'll cry.*

El abruptly stopped her playing, turned her head, and said to the crowd, "You ready to sing?"

"*Hell, yeah!*"

"Alright, now."

And the crowd sang along with El:

> *Does your mother know you're out, Cecilia?*
> *Does she know that I'm about to steal ya?*
> *Oh my, when I look in your eyes*
> *Something tells me you and I should get together!*

"We gettin' together with Cecilia tonight?" El called.

The crowd responded that they, indeed, were and with gusto too.

El laughed before launching into the next verse, exhilaration flooding her body. Whenever she sang, it felt like *flying*. Nothing and no one could stop her or hold her back, not with her voice soaring around this room sounding bigger than life and driving this glorious music.

When she got to the end of the song, she slid her fingers down the keys in a trilled finish. The entire room erupted in shouted cheers and ear-piercing whistles. A few fists even pounded the tables.

She kicked back the piano bench, knocking it to its side, and strolled to the edge of the stage. She took off her top hat and bowed, waited, soaking in the applause before bowing again. She returned the hat to its usual place, bid the crowd good night, and jumped off the stage.

Temporarily, she was blind. Those stage lights were so bright, she usually needed a few moments for her eyes to adjust. Tonight, though, the lingering tempo of the music and the energy of the crowd pushed her forward into the darkness. Thankfully, she didn't trip or otherwise make a fool of herself.

She made her way to the backstage door, stopping to let a few shadowy strangers shake her hand. Opening the door, she entered a long hallway where the eight-piece band that played after her stood at the ready, dressed in shiny black tuxes.

Madam J.A. Watkins, Harlem's own woman millionaire and the owner of this hotel, kept pushing for El to work with the band and expand her show. And though El initially balked at the suggestion ("I'm a solo act, Madam!"), lately she'd been considering it. She wondered what an El

Train show would look like with a full band behind her. Could she get them to do what she wanted? All the band members were men and men didn't always like taking direction from her. Bad enough she was a woman, but a woman who dressed and acted like them? They'd be downright insolent. Most had in the past.

Although two nights ago, she'd played with an all-male trio down in Greenwich for a special Mischief Night gig. They listened to her fine—and one of those boys was even white! So, it was possible.

Rare, but possible.

(Of course, the club was almost raided, which annoyed her to no end, but the less said about that, the better.)

She nodded to the band as she passed and strolled to the end of the hallway. Her chest swelled with pride seeing her name emblazoned in gold on the green-painted door. A sign she made good. No, better than good. She had *arrived*. And if she could achieve all this by herself, then what else could she accomplish with a bigger cast, a bigger sound, a bigger show?

Maybe I should do it, she thought. *Maybe it's time for El Train to be an entire production. A band, dancers, everything!*

She smiled. Yeah. Now wouldn't that be something?

Still smiling, she opened her dressing room door and stopped abruptly.

There, lounging on the loveseat catty-corner to her dressing table, was Alice Holloway.

El felt a jump in her chest. Her smile instantly disappeared.

She's not supposed to be here!

Alice held a glass of whiskey in one hand and a lit cigar smoldering in the other. The window to the side alley stood open behind her, letting in the cool autumn air. Must've been how she got inside. A black masquerade mask and white gloves were tucked in next to her, which would've covered most of her pale skin and allowed her to walk the streets around the hotel without earning a second glance. The blue velour overcoat that El bought for her, which featured a fur collar and lining, had been tossed over the arm of the loveseat.

"Evening, El," Alice said in her low, husky voice.

El glared at her in response, though Alice made it difficult not to ogle her instead. Her dark brunette hair curled just below her earlobe, bringing out the amber whiskey of her eyes. She'd painted her lips red tonight, a deep ruby that shimmered whenever she spoke, and she'd brushed a hint of rouge on her cheeks. One would think Alice was your typical flapper, but then they'd notice, along with the glass of whiskey and the cigar, the black tuxedo she donned, complete with bow tie and tails.

A counterpoint to El's all-white tux.

That was the story of the two of them right there: similar, yet opposite ends of the spectrum. Both had broad shoulders, (though El's were much broader), and both had curves, (though El's curves were definitely wider). And while Alice may have been the smaller of the two, she more than made up for it in nerve. Like sneaking into El's dressing room when she knew good and well that El would be furious with her.

El quickly closed the door behind her and locked it.

"What are you doing?" she said, her voice coming out in a hoarse whisper. "You know you're not allowed inside the Hotel! It's *our* space, dammit, and you have no right, I said, no right to be here!"

"I know, I know, but listen, El, we need to talk."

El struggled to keep her voice down so as not to advertise their business to the entire hallway outside. "We got nothing to talk about. And where did you get that whiskey? You better not have ordered that from outside."

"Relax. I got it from your own personal bar. I'd never step foot inside the main club."

"You aren't supposed to step inside the *Ho-tel*, period, but it seems you've forgotten that rule."

"C'mon, El. You know I like to break rules."

"You like to break hearts too."

Alice flinched. She averted her eyes as she took a sip of whiskey. The hand that held the cigar gestured to their surroundings, swirling smoke into large loops.

"I gotta say, this is a definite upgrade from Leslie's place. You've got space to move around in here."

She wasn't wrong. El's old venue, the Oyster House, was a dive in the worst sense of the word. A piano that needed tuning after nearly every song. A cramped, drafty closet for a dressing room that leaked whenever it rained. And an owner, Leslie Charles, who pocketed all the sugar instead of paying his staff. Or fixing up the place. (He was also making trouble because she left him and his jalopy club for Chez J.A., but that was another problem for another time.)

Now El had what Madam Watkins called "a suite." Two large rooms, all done up in the colors of the hotel: lush green and shimmering gold.

The first room boasted a dressing area with a lit table so she could admire her short hair, round face, and wide grin with a snaggletooth dead in the center; a lounge area, where Alice currently sat, with end tables holding brass lamps capped by emerald-green shades lined with gold fringe; and a silver bar fully stocked with the best liquor one could find in Harlem.

The second room held a chaise lounge for naps, if El so desired, and a wardrobe full of stage tuxedos and day suits and all their usual accouterments: handkerchiefs, ties, canes, and an impressive collection of hats. Only one dress, in case they were raided, but the pounders didn't bother with the Watkins. Madam made certain of that.

"Uh huh," El replied. "I done told you this already. Look, if anyone from the hotel staff sees you and reports you, I'm gonna get in big trouble. And that is *not* something I need right now. Not with Les pulling his bushwa."

"It's just—you haven't given me a chance to explain."

"Explain what? Your engagement to some French frog? Or the fact that I had to find out about it in the *New York Times*? Sitting in a downtowner's speak, of all places!"

El could still see herself inside Pinstripes, the tiny Village club owned by her friend Dash Parker and hidden behind a tailor shop. She was there rehearsing for that Mischief Night gig. She and his band had just taken five when she grabbed Dash's omnipresent copy of the *Times*—Lord, that boy loved his newspapers—and flipped through it to see what was new about the Hall-Mills murder trial. Instead of some good old-fashioned scandal, she found in the top right corner of the society page the engagement announcement written big as life: Lucien Laurent and Alice Holloway. El vaguely remembered cussing, tearing out the corner, and racing out of Pinstripes, intending to have it out with Alice.

Only Alice remained locked up tight in that family townhouse of hers. The townhouse El couldn't enter on account of—well—everything about her. It'd been days since and not once did Alice answer the telephone when El called nor did Alice reach out to her.

Until now.

Alice puffed on her cigar; her face crestfallen. "You read about it at Dash's place?"

"Yes, I did. At a rehearsal, to boot. Do you have any idea what it's like to find out your relationship is over like that? All them engagements being announced and there you are, Alice Holloway betrothed to French aristocrat Lucien Laurent."

"El—"

"A French snob? Really, Alice? Didn't think you liked crusty, old baguettes."

"El—"

"I trusted you, despite what everyone else in my life had to say about it. And girl, they said plenty. Earfuls about how you were trouble with a capital T. Turns out they were right. And you *know* what I hate more than anything else in the world is to admit that somebody else was right."

"Would you just *listen*—"

El pounded her chest with her hand. "I felt like a fool! A common, goddamn fool, and nobody and I mean *nobody* makes me feel that way. You understand? So you better say what you need to say and get gone. Or else I'll—"

"It's not true, El."

El took a breath. "What's not true?"

"The engagement."

"Well, the *Times* seems to think so! So do the rest of the papers."

Alice fidgeted in her seat, crossing her legs in a huff. "Jesus, El, you gonna listen to me or you gonna yell?"

"I'm gonna yell, dammit!"

"Fine! Then yell!"

And that stopped El. Her tongue suddenly tied itself into knots, her mouth froze open. Her voice decided to leave the room altogether. She stood there, mouth agape like a goldfish as she struggled to continue the speech she had well-rehearsed (or so she thought).

The rhythms of the band on stage thumped through the walls, matching the pounding of her own heart.

"Go on," Alice said. "Let me have it. God knows I deserve it."

El closed her mouth and shook her finger. "Don't—don't you do that."

"Do what?"

"Do—I don't know! That *thing* you just did."

A silence settled between them.

El glared hard at Alice, who didn't blink. "Fine," she said. "You want to talk?" She pulled out the chair from her dressing table and sat down. "Talk." When Alice didn't reply, she gestured irritably, "Go on, now. But make it fast and make it good, *Lady Lucien Laurent*."

Alice frowned. "Don't call me that."

"That's gonna be your new name, isn't it?"

"Not if I . . ." She trailed off.

El crossed her arms. "You're wasting time."

Alice took a deep drag on her cigar and replied with a mouth full of smoke: "I was forced into it. Okay? You satisfied? I was a dumb Dora and got caught by a grifter who's threatening to tell my brother and all the city papers that I'm a lesbian."

El stared at her. "He *extorted* you into an engagement?"

"That's right," Alice said. "The bastard is coercing me into holy matrimony."

3

El shook her head in disbelief. "How did this come about?"

Alice found an ashtray on the side table and flicked off a huge chunk of ash from her cigar. "He found me at Pearlie's playing the tables one night."

She meant Pearlie Taylor, a prominent billiard hall owner who hosted secret games for anyone who could afford to play in his private upstairs parlor. Black, white, or any other shade, he didn't care. As long as you had the greens. He called them the Midnight Games. El knew him from when she first arrived in New York. She and Alice used to go there together on a date night when they needed to blow off some steam. Most of the time, though, Alice liked to have private meetings in that room, discussing business and other items that, frankly, bored El to tears, while winning game after game.

El shifted in her chair. "When was this?"

"A week ago. I'd never seen him before, but he must've been a regular on the nights I wasn't there, 'cause he and Pearlie seemed to know each other. They got into an argument when Lucien first walked in. I didn't hear what it was about, but it upset Lucien. I thought he was gonna leave, but then he handed Pearlie a handful of lettuce and Pearlie let him in."

"Pearlie does like his greens."

"A regular rabbit, that boy. It was spitting ice and rain that night 'cause of that strange cold snap, so Lucien and I were the only ones who showed up to the Midnight Game. He did most of the talking. You know how men are. Love to hear the sound of their voice. He told me his sob story: born and raised in Paris, his family died in the war, either on the battlefield or from the influenza that came afterward. Distraught, he took the boat over with his inheritance looking for something big to invest in and for a chance to start anew. He'd just bought an automobile, a brand new Cadillac coupe. In maroon with spotless black fenders, for your information, with magenta pleated and buttoned mohair seats."

"Uh huh. And how much sugar does this frog have, if he's buying brand new Cadillacs in maroon and mohair?"

"He didn't give numbers—surprisingly—but he did say he's staying at the Hotel Eudora."

El whistled. "That place takes some heavy sugar."

"And I took some of that off him. I beat him three games in a row."

That's my girl, El thought before she remembered she was supposed to be angry at her. She cleared her throat. "Go on."

"I hardly told him anything about myself, El, I swear. I couldn't believe it when I saw him again the next night coming out of a speak. One of *our* speaks."

"Which one?"

"Where we first met. Ironically enough."

El squinted. "The Drip Dry?" It was a lesbian speak

hidden behind a laundry that was nothing more than barstools and a literal hole in the wall where liquor bottles were passed over from the building next door.

"Somehow he learned who I am, or rather, who my family is. He must've followed me after the Midnight Game. He suggested we have a conversation. I told him we had nothing to discuss. He said"—Alice began mimicking a French accent. —"*Mademoiselle*, I am here to make an offer. A marriage of the utmost convenience. You can continue to date who you like, as will I. You will be protected by the state of marriage, I will have the means to stay in this country, and we both will be seen as respectable members of society.'"

Alice returned her voice to normal. "Respectable members of society. Whatever the hell that means. I told him to get lost."

"But he didn't."

"Persistent little bugger. Then I thought I could buy him off, but it was clear he was after a bigger payday."

"I thought he wanted citizenship? Oh. Your family's sugar." El frowned. "That doesn't make any sense, babe. If he's buying brand new motorcars and staying at expensive hotels, what does he need more for?"

"C'mon, El. You know how rich men are. They get a little money, they suddenly want more of it. *All* of it."

"That, or he spent all of his."

Alice sighed with disgust. "You could practically see the dollar signs in his eyes. He approached me one more time the following morning as I was leaving the house. Luckily Rich wasn't around and I told Lucien to go chase himself."

"I take it your response didn't go over very well."

"You saw what happened next. I opened the paper Thursday morning and there I am, engaged to French aristocrat Lucien Laurent. The bastard put the announcement in every paper in town! And before I could do anything about it, he shows up at the house, when Rich is there, of course. He's all smiles, greeting me as his '*amour*,' calling Rich whatever the French word is for brother-in-law. When I pulled him aside and asked him just what the hell he thought he was doing, he said, 'Securing a better future for the two of us.' A bunch of bushwa and I told him so. Only then he explained that if I didn't play along, he'd tell Rich and anybody else who would listen—cops, newspapers, tabloids, whoever—that I was a lesbian. Apparently, he didn't just see me coming out of the Drip Dry; he took photographs."

"Shit."

"My sentiments exactly."

"What does ol' Richie have to say about this engagement? Can he help us call it off?"

Alice scoffed. "Are you kidding? He's thrilled! Said it was high time I turned respectable—"

"There's that damn word again."

"—and got out from underfoot. Don't get me wrong. He's not exactly happy about me marrying a Frenchman. But a man's a man and a marriage is a marriage. Meanwhile, Lucien says we shouldn't have a long engagement and to get married as soon as possible. I mean, my God, he wanted to skip the ceremony and go straight to the courthouse! Took everything I had to steer him clear of that. 'Course, it also took every ounce of my self-control not to shoot him." Alice glanced off to the side. "Perhaps I should have."

It wasn't an empty threat. Alice kept a pistol, a .32 Colt, with her at all times.

El said, "Then you'd have a different problem on your hands." She hesitated, not wanting to ask the question but knew she had to. "Why didn't you tell me about this earlier? Not the engagement. Him harassing and following you. I'm your *wife*. I could've helped you. Or at the very least, dumped his body into the East River."

"You'd just started playing Madam Watkins's place and I didn't want to distract you from the gig of a lifetime. Besides, I thought I could handle him. And by the time the engagement notices came out, I couldn't risk leading his extortionate ass to you. To us. God only knows what he'd do with this kind of information."

"So you waited until tonight to lead him here?"

Alice waved off El's concerns. "He and Rich are at a masquerade ball. It's how I got these," she said, gesturing to the mask and gloves laying beside her. "I feigned womanly cramps and a very heavy flow to get out of it." A fiendish grin tickled her lips. "They couldn't leave me behind fast enough. They have no idea I'm gone, much less where I've gone to."

She dropped her head and stared at her lap. "I had to see you, El," she said in a small voice. "It's been the hardest thing not being with you. Not being able to explain all this to you. I knew you'd see those announcements and be hurt."

El let loose a long sigh. "Not gonna lie, babe, it's been hard. I thought you did a number on me. I thought all those things we said to each other meant nothing. That the *promise* we made meant nothing."

Alice looked up, those whiskey eyes big and round. "I meant every word, El. I made a promise I intend to keep. You and me. Against the world."

El felt an invisible hand tugging her forward, that gravitational pull Alice always managed to have over her. Her pride dug in its heels a bit. She couldn't let Alice off the hook *that* easy.

"You still should've come to me earlier. If we're truly going up against the world, then there can't be any secrets between us."

"I wasn't keeping secrets—"

El gave her a look.

Alice bit her lip. "You're right. I was keeping it to myself and that wasn't right nor fair to you."

"Thank you."

Alice took a shaky breath. "Forgive me?"

El closed her eyes before opening them again. "Yes. God help me, yes, I do. But from now on, you keep me in the know. I don't care if you think the news will ruin my entire year, much less my day, you tell me what's going on."

"Well, in that spirit, we have something else to contend with."

"You mean there's more than an extorting French fiancé?"

"Yup," Alice said. "And we both know what it is."

"What?" Then El knew. "Oh, no. Oh, babe. You mean—"

"If Lucien tells Rich knows about me, then my brother will use that as an excuse to scour through everything of mine. Including my trust." Alice finished off the last of her whiskey. "More importantly, what I've been doing with it."

4

El rubbed her forehead and pinched her brow. "I knew you getting involved in that stuff was dangerous. Didn't I tell you?"

"It's a worthy cause, El. I couldn't stand idly by and watch more people get hurt. And not just get hurt, but injured under my family name."

"I understand that, babe, and I sympathize, I really do. But using your trust to help fund a strike against your own family's business?"

And not just any business. The goddamn Holloway Paper Box Factory. Since its founding in 1910 by Alice's father, it's been the largest industrial employer in all of Harlem—and the cause of those dollar signs Alice said she saw in Lucien's eyes.

Alice lifted her chin slightly. "Not only ours. It's a city-wide strike against all the paper box factories in Manhattan."

"Somehow I don't think your brother, who let's not forget is the acting president, is going to be interested in the finer points."

"Who only got the role when Father died three years ago," Alice replied bitterly. "I should've inherited it over Rich. Our competitors are running circles around us, our customers are getting angry, and Rich is sitting there, like a Yale pretty boy in a boat who doesn't know how to row. It's his own damn fault the union had to strike in the first place. If he weren't so blinded by greed, he'd have followed Father's lead and continued his fair, humane policies. And then our factory wouldn't be responsible for so much harm."

Alice began ticking off the list of the factory's sins. Sins El knew by heart at this point.

"Children losing fingers. Women getting glue burns. Men savagely sliced. My God, what happened to Sam Willing is nothing short of horrific! Maimed for life! When I demanded that Rich do something, he laughed in my face and banned me from setting foot on the factory property ever again. I had to step in then. I had to get involved. Then I learned that all of them have been inhaling poisonous fumes and working fourteen-hour shifts six days a week. For less than fifteen dollars a week. Fifteen dollars! That was the pay nearly five years ago! And with the rising cost of living, not to mention inflation—"

El held up a hand. "Babe, you're preaching to the choir here."

"Thank God our parents aren't alive to see the utter selfishness of their only son. Mother, in particular, would be heartbroken. I mean, what kind of world are we living in where the misery and injury of human beings is acceptable because it makes a few rich men richer?"

El couldn't help it. She cocked an eyebrow and gave Alice a baleful look. "Girl, look at me. My people know *all* about rich men thinking they own others and can treat them however they want. Especially if it lines their pockets with more and more sugar. Hell, my ancestors *built* this country, and most of their descendants hardly have anything to show for it. And when we finally *do* get piles of sugar of our own, they take it away. Do I need to remind you of what those white folks did to us in Tulsa? Mansions, girl. We had *mansions* that they *burned* because they couldn't stand to see us more successful than them. So don't ask such a foolish question. You're smarter than that."

Alice was immediately chastened. "I'm sorry, El. I didn't mean—"

"Look, I know why you're doing what you're doing. I even support it . . . to a certain extent. But you've got to admit that this is risky as all get out."

"Sometimes we have to put ourselves at great personal risk for a worthy cause."

"That a Malek saying?" El meant Malek Polowski, the head of the Holloway strike, and one of only four union workers who knew of Alice's involvement.

"Never mind," Alice replied. "The point is, Lucien is a bigger threat than to just my personal freedom. There's one of two scenarios that'll play out here. One, the marriage goes through and he puts a stop to my weekly withdrawals. He may or may not know what they are. He may not care. What he *will* want is those withdrawals to go directly to him."

"Causing the strikers to lose their wealthy benefactor."

"Exactly. Or two, the marriage doesn't happen, Lucien blabs to Rich. Rich needs to put me on a leash, which means seizing control of my accounts to prevent me from further 'deviant behavior.' A judge may or may not get involved. He finds the withdrawals in an audit he's certain to conduct, tracks them down, and eventually learns where the Holloway money has been going for the past six months.

Forget what he'll do to me, he'll make it ten times worse for the union. Especially those leading the strike against our factory. Booker, Ferrin, Ramona. They'll never find another job in the city again. And Malek? I shudder to think."

"Your brother is vindictive when he thinks he's been betrayed," El admitted. "Babe, this is a righteous mess."

"I know," Alice moaned.

El got up and poured herself a glass of whiskey from the silver bar. She topped Alice off before returning to her chair at the dressing table.

"So what do we do?" Alice asked.

El took a healthy sip before replying, "I still say we drop Lucien into the East River."

Alice gave her a look. "El."

"Alright, alright." El thought for a moment. "I'll ask around my corners of town, see if there's some dirt I can dig up. If we can find out something about Lucien to discredit him, maybe even get him arrested—or better yet, give him the *threat* of being arrested—then he'll keep his photographs and his stories about the Drip Dry to himself. And hopefully get out of town."

Alice smirked a smile. "We're thinking alike. I did manage to sneak away from him and Rich and send a telegram to the Paris police department. Perhaps our little extortionist is already wanted for crimes. And since we're expelling immigrants as fast as we're barring them from our shores—thank you Johnson-Reed" —she added with an eye roll, referencing the racist sponsors of the Immigration Act of 1924— "our boy will likely be put on the first boat out of the harbor."

El grinned. "That's my clever girl."

"Problem is, God knows how long it'll take for the police department to respond. And Lucien's moving fast—"

"—which means we've got to move faster. I'll see what I can do."

Alice smiled. "Thank you, El. I'm sorry I didn't come to you sooner. I—"

"No need. We'll fix this. I promise."

Alice set her whiskey glass down, stood up, and walked over to lay the softest kiss on El's lips. "Maybe we can spend some quality time with each other soon?"

"At our usual place?" El referred to a discreet hotel on 150th that catered to people of their kind.

"Yes," Alice purred, straightening El's bow tie. "It's been so long since we've shared a bed."

"Too long."

"And I *have* been bad lately. You might need to teach me a lesson, Miss El."

El recognized that look in her eye. "Don't you start. We may have made up, but I'm still a little mad at you."

"Oh? What can I do to make it up to you, Miss El?"

"I said quit that."

"Do I need to stay after class, Miss El?"

"Girl, behave yourself."

Alice shrugged, unbothered. "Guess I'll have to get a few spanks then. You've got a paddle, Miss El?"

"Don't you dare—"

"I really need to learn my lesson."

"Alice, I swear—"

"My fanny stings just thinking about your big, strong, hard paddle."

It didn't happen often, but Alice struck El speechless. And she'd done it twice in one evening!

The air around them crackled with electricity, and the hairs on El's arms stood up. Behind her, the muffled moan of a trombone suggested moans of another sort, and she felt her body begin to respond.

Before she could grab Alice into an embrace, Alice pulled away and slinked towards the window.

"You little flirt," El growled.

Alice feigned innocence. "Who, me?" She winked while sliding into the blue velour overcoat, the fur of the collar bringing out the brown of her hair. She picked up her masquerade mask and gloves from the loveseat. "Besides," she said, "I don't think your new boss would appreciate you, ahem, 'entertaining' a fan in your dressing room."

"The door's got a good lock," El offered.

"I'm certain it does. But Rich and Lucien will be returning from the ball soon, so I better head home."

Alice threw one leg over the window's ledge, then the other, gracefully dropping down the three and a half feet to the alleyway floor below. She turned, the windowsill framing her chest and face like a painting, and said, "Hey, El?"

"What?"

"You know?"

Their code. Out in public, they couldn't be affectionate, much less say "I love you" before they parted. So they devised this exchange, one that if someone were to overhear, they wouldn't give two thoughts about. Got to be they did it so often, they'd use it even when they were alone.

Like now.

El stared straight into Alice's whiskey eyes. Lord, how they sparkled. "Yeah," she said. "I know."

"Good. And the next time I see you, you better bring your paddle." Alice blew her a kiss and then, she was gone.

"You tease," El muttered before laughing to herself.

How in the hell did she end up falling for such a stubborn, fearless woman?

Because she's a stubborn, fearless woman, a voice in her head replied.

And the only one who could keep up with El's own insubordination.

She sat for a few more moments, listening to the band thump through the walls while she sipped the rest of her whiskey, lit a cigar, and ruminated on everything Alice told her. She knew good and well that sleep wasn't going to be an easy option tonight. She felt the need to do something, anything to get Alice out of this predicament, but what?

The answer came when her whiskey was almost gone and her cigar had burned out. Pearlie Taylor. That fateful night when Alice first met this Lucien Laurent, she saw him in an argument with Pearlie. An argument that could only be settled by an exchange of money. El wanted to know what that was about—and if she and Alice could use it as leverage.

5

Pearlie's Parlor took up two floors of a three-story row house on 127th and Seventh Avenue. The first floor featured the billiard hall proper while the second floor hosted the private parlor, home to the Midnight Game. The third floor held Pearlie's apartment.

El pulled open the door and stepped inside the dark vestibule. To her left was the parlor filled with clusters of men smoking cigarettes, talking and laughing, pacing around the billiard tables looking for their shot. Straight ahead was a set of stairs guarded by a tall, broad man in a dark suit. He stood entirely motionless, his face hard as stone, his hands folded in front. A griffin holding court.

She said, "Is Pearlie in?"

The statue barely moved his lips as he replied, "Who wants to know?"

"Tell him El's here to see him."

"He's busy right now."

"Then he better hurry up. I don't have time to waste."

The guard didn't respond.

El crossed her arms over her chest. "Fine. I'll just wait here then."

The guard glared at her for a few seconds, then rightly realized she wasn't going anywhere. He sighed, turned, and stomped up the stairs like a petulant child.

While she waited, she glanced in on the parlor. Glass lamps hung over the half dozen tables, the green felt looking brand new, as rich and bright as spring grass. Shadowy players gathered around, their attention focused on the games at hand. She heard the simultaneous smacks of the cue balls followed by a rattle (one man made his shot) and a groan (the other man missed). Good-natured banter followed, with one man saying, "Whoo-wee. You make a deal with the devil or something?" and another replying, "No deal necessary. You just love giving me your sugar."

There was an odd, asymmetrical rhythm to their play. The dull thud of the stick on the cue ball. A measure or two of rest. The crack of contact and the rattling of one or more of the object balls going into the pockets. A pause. Some admiration, some teasing. Repeat.

Heavy feet descended the stairs, and the griffin slowly came into view. "Mr. Taylor will see you now."

"I figured he might."

As she passed by, the griffin eyed her with barely disguised disdain. She ignored him and climbed the steps. At the top, she saw two doors. The first one led to Pearlie's office. The second one down the hall led to the Midnight Game.

On Pearlie's door, she knocked once and entered.

The place had been spruced up since she last saw it. Black and gold wallpaper replaced the bare white walls of old, lit dramatically by big brass lamps like spotlights on Broadway. Boxy end tables surrounded two dark green leather chairs that sat across from one another. They looked more appropriate for a rich man's study, and she half expected there to be a fireplace next to them crackling with flames. Instead, there was a brass metal bar stacked with filled bottles and empty glasses. Beyond that was a large rectangular desk with a floor-to-ceiling bookshelf behind it and the owner standing in front, watching the office door expectantly.

Pearlie Taylor was as short as she was tall, his narrow shoulders holding up his balding head, where the remaining strands too stubborn to join their fled brethren had begun prematurely turning gray. His face was a perfect oval. A few wrinkles tucked in around his eyes, but his forehead and cheeks remained remarkably unlined. He wore a bright blue suit with a fiery red tie, the pops of color matching the incandescence of his forming smile, which eventually turned bright and wide as she sauntered in.

"El!" he said. "It's been an age. I hear you've been making quite a name for yourself."

"It seems so have you. I don't remember your office being this classy."

"I've made a few improvements. Did the same for the downstairs and the secret parlor."

"Business been good?"

Pearlie beamed. "Never been better. In fact, I got enough to make a second Pearlie's Parlor."

"I'm impressed."

"You'll be even more impressed when I show you my motorcar. It's silver and chrome and the sunlight sparks off it like a firework."

"Now you're just bragging."

He laughed. "You're right. I am. May I offer you something to drink?"

"That is mighty kind of you. Whiskey, if you have it. The good stuff," she added quickly. "Not that panther sweat that's been going around lately."

Pearlie looked mildly insulted. "I will have you know that I *only* carry the good stuff. No panther sweat or horse liniment at Pearlie's. I've made certain of that." He went over to the bar and set about pouring her drink as well as one for himself.

El slowly paced around the office as if she were admiring it, when really, she was thinking about how to play this conversation. She and Pearlie had a history. Not like that, thank you very much, but one when they were both new to the city, new to Harlem, and hell-bent on making a name for themselves. They met in the summer of 1925 at a tailor shop that rented suits. Pearlie needed one for a bank interview to get the loan for this parlor. El needed one for her audition at the Oyster House. They exchanged a few words—hilarious, profane ones, if you must know—and vowed to become good friends.

They didn't—become good friends, that is. Hard to keep that up in a city as big and fast as this one. But they remained acquaintances, seeing each other at social whist parties or at a new club. El came to the opening of his parlor and played the occasional game with Alice in his secret room, but that was about the extent of it. She hadn't seen him in a few months, by her estimation.

The drinks now poured, Pearlie motioned for her to sit in one of the green leather chairs. She took one and he took the other.

He crossed his legs and leaned back. "To what do I owe the pleasure of having the infamous El Train's company?"

"A week ago, you hosted one of your Midnight Games, and I need to know about one of the players."

"Why? They owe you money?"

"They owe me an apology and a way to make amends."

Pearlie snorted. "Anyone fool enough to cross you deserves what they get."

"Glad we're in agreement on that."

"Hold on. That's about all we're in agreement on. My Midnight Game is popular because it is exactly that. Secret. My Midnight Players depend on my discretion, so whatever you're after, you're barking up the wrong tree."

"Aw, don't be like that, Pearlie. After all, I've helped you out plenty."

"Helped me out how?"

"I didn't tell Corrine about Lovella. Or Lovella about Jocelyn. Or Jocelyn about—"

"Alright, alright. I get your point."

"I sure hope so. Corrine's a nice girl but she's got a pistol she'll use if she finds out about the Russian doll of girl-friends you carry around in your back pocket. And Lovella? Her best friend slept with her boyfriend once, and I heard she grabbed a rolling pin—"

"Jesus, El!" Pearlie took a hasty sip of whiskey. "I can't believe you'd do me like this. You yourself used to have several girls, if I recall."

El grinned. "Yeah, but I didn't hide them from each other. That's the difference. Girls don't like deceit. When are you men gonna realize that?"

"Insulting me isn't going to get you what you want."

"That wasn't me being insulting, only speaking facts. Lucien Laurent. A Frenchie. His name ring any bells? The game would've been on Monday night, October 25."

Pearlie paused, stroking his chin as if he were thinking hard. "Lucien Laurent," he repeated, rolling around the consonants in his mouth as if they were an expensive wine.

"Oh, come on," she said, impatient. "You don't get that many frogs in here."

"How would you know? Pearlie's is the most famous billiard parlor in all of Harlem. Why wouldn't we be an international sensation?"

El leveled her gaze at him.

Pearlie waited a beat and replied, "*Monsieur* Laurent. Now that you mention it, the name does sound familiar. That night sounds familiar too. What are you willing to trade for it?"

"My goodwill and patience."

Pearlie scoffed. "That ain't worth nothing."

"You have no idea how rare a resource my patience is. Worth more than gold and silver combined. Now tell me about this fella."

"Why are you so interested in him? This about his engagement to your girl—what's her name?—Alice?" His grin was smug. He must've read about it in the papers.

El replied, "That is none of your business."

"Just like my Midnight Game and my Midnight Players are none of *your* business. Look, you got your heart broken by a white girl. You're not the first and you won't be the last. Find yourself another one and move on with your life."

"Alright, then. I guess I'm having a conversation with Corrine."

They stared at one another for a moment.

Pearlie sighed and shook his head at her. "I'm only telling you this 'cause I like you."

"Uh huh."

"Lucien Laurent is a somewhat regular customer. He plays lousy, tends to lose a lot, but he always seems to come up with the entry fee. He's staying at the Hotel Eudora. I asked him once why he wasn't playing in their billiard room. You know what he told me? He said it's too dull in there."

"That, I can believe."

"One thing we have at Pearlie's is atmosphere."

"How'd he find out about this place? Seems a bit off a white man's radar, much less a Frenchie's."

Pearlie grinned. "I got a porter who works at the Eudora. Anyone who expresses interest in some billiards, he sends 'em my way."

"A nice little network you got there."

"Gotta pull the right strings to get what you want. As for your Frenchie, I don't know much else about him other than some sob story of losing his family in the war and its aftermath. Common as mud. Who didn't go through something like that?"

"Your sympathy knows no bounds. What did you two argue about?"

Pearlie furrowed his brow at the sudden change in subject. "Argue?"

"Hmmhmm. Alice said she saw the two of you going at it. Apparently, you said something to Lucien that made him quite upset. What was it? You said he always paid so it wasn't that he owed you sugar."

"No, it wasn't." Pearlie took a healthy sip of his whiskey. "A couple of tough guys visited me the Saturday before asking about him."

"Tough guys?"

"Yeah, real scrappers. Two of 'em. I didn't like the looks of them and said they needed to leave my establishment."

"And that was when? October 23?"

"Yup."

El sat forward in her chair. "Did they have names?"

"They didn't share them with me."

"What about who they were working for?"

"Didn't share that either. And to be honest, I didn't want to press too hard. The less I know, the better."

"I'm guessing you told Lucien."

"I did," Pearlie said. "That night, the 25th, when your girl was playing. And he was none too happy about it. Asked me all the same questions you're asking. When I didn't have the answers, it seemed to make him more disagreeable."

"What did he pay you for?"

"The entry fee to the game."

"Oh, Pearlie. Don't lie to me now. We've been having a lovely conversation. Just two big timers swapping stories over surprisingly good whiskey. I'd hate to see it ruined by falsehoods."

Pearlie frowned at her.

El batted her eyelashes.

"Shit," he muttered. "He did pay the entry fee, plus a little extra in case those fellas came back to say I haven't seen good ol' Lucien and that he was banned from my parlor."

"And did those tough guys come back around?"

"Only once. Last Friday, the 29th. I did what I said I'd do, because I'm a man of my word."

"Especially if you've been paid."

Pearlie shrugged. "Nothing's free in this life."

"Ain't that the truth. Did they believe you?"

"They haven't been back, so I assume they did."

El didn't like this turn of events, and Pearlie could see that.

"Look, El, I don't know what this fella is up to or what he's involved in. And like I said, I don't care because the less I know—"

"—the better, right."

"But you outta tell your girl, her fiancé might be putting her in danger." He paused to look straight into El's eyes. "They didn't look like the types who spare women and children, know what I mean?"

El studied him. "Yeah. Yeah, I know what you mean." She set down her empty whiskey glass and stood up.

Pearlie followed suit.

"One more favor," she said.

He held up a hand. "That's it. I'm all out of favors. If you want any more from me, you'll need to speak my language."

El glared at him.

He mimicked her move earlier by batting his eyelashes in response.

You little shit.

El sighed and made a big show of reaching into her pockets to pull out a wad of fews and twos. She handed them over to Pearlie, who quickly slid them into his own pockets, as if someone was going to swoop down from the air and snatch them from his hands.

"Now," El said, "tell me where I can find this Hotel Eudora porter. The one who sent *Monsieur* Lucien Laurent your way . . . "

6

Shrill bells ringing rudely roused El from sleep.

She groaned, "What the hell—?"

Something soft brushed against her face. Alice?

She opened her eyes.

No, only the pristine white sheets she slept in. Damn. She'd rather have woken up with Alice curled beside her, snoring softly like a purring cat.

She slapped the alarm clock off and sat up, rubbing the sleep from her eyes. Wobbly legs, not much more awake than the rest of her, somehow got her out of bed and carried her to the window, where she parted the curtains to let in the morning light. She looked down at the street below. Lenox Avenue filled with people walking, driving, or riding their way to work. She yawned. Felt like she'd just fallen asleep. How did other people do this every day? She usually slept until the late morning; early afternoon, if the night was good enough. But Pearlie told her that Isaiah Scott, the Hotel Eudora porter, received a shave at Jordi's every morning before his nine o'clock shift. Which meant that if El wanted to catch him, she needed to be at the barber shop on 143rd Street by eight-fifteen at the latest.

"Mr. Scott is nothing if not punctual," Pearlie said.

She turned and padded around her apartment where she lived all by herself on the top floor, of an elevator building, no less, with no roommates or hot beds. Another sign she made good in this city. True, the walls needed painting to cover the cracks in the plaster, and the floors were warped. The windows let in too much cold or hot air, depending on the season. But it was all hers and that's all that mattered.

It was a typical "buffet flat" in a five-story building on 135th and Lenox. Her bedroom and water closet stood in the back, followed by the kitchen (though she never cooked anything on that stove), and then the front room and the front door. Heavy ruby red curtains hung by the windows, pale pink shades with fringe topped the lamps, and a collection of dark wood furniture filled the rooms. All under the tallest ceiling she'd ever seen—until she saw the lobby of the Watkins Hotel, that is.

She dressed herself in a tweed suit with a red and gold paisley tie before pulling on her overcoat with the fur collar and a dark ruby cloche hat, her only two concessions to the so-called decency laws enacted and enforced on women walking the streets. With her lips painted a dark plum, she'd just picked up her cane with the brass handle when there was a forceful knock on her door. Now who could that be at this hour?

El paused to pick up her pistol from her nightstand, a 1922 Browning model from her Uncle Jim, the only one of her family to truly accept her. He gave her the pistol when he also gave her the money to leave that Philadelphia flophouse and come to New York.

She walked to the front door, finger on the trigger. "What do you want?" she called.

"El," a familiar female voice said. "El, you up?"

"Flo?" El slipped the Browning into her pocket and opened the front door. There stood her best friend, Flo Russell. And she looked exhausted.

"Oh thank the sweet Lord," she said, walking into the apartment. "I need your sofa."

"What's wrong with your place?"

"The girl renting my bed who's supposed to be at work got the flu and is currently sweating and sneezing up a storm in there." Unlike El's situation, Flo's apartment *was* a hot bed, a necessity when the landlords jacked her rent by more than five dollars a month this year.

"Tell her to take herself to the doctor," El replied. "You danced all night, you need your rest."

Flo flopped down onto the plush burgundy cushions of El's sofa with a sputtered sigh. "I know that. And you know that. But this girl? She's got this bug something awful and I can't send her out into the world when she's shivering all over."

"Why? You sweet on her?"

"Please. She's not my type. She keeps bumping gums about some guy named Rodney. What kind of name is Rodney? Sounds like a man with a cinderblock head and concrete for brains."

El regarded her friend splayed out on her sofa. Flo Russell was everything she was not: short, thin, bony, though her legs were pure muscle. Her black hair was cut straight and short, stopping right at her ear lobes. She'd outlined her dark eyes in the popular Egyptian style with thin black lines. She wore a brown fur coat and a matching cloche hat. Her burgundy shoes matched the color of the sofa she collapsed on.

"You best get outta all that before you melt," El warned.

"I'll do it in a minute. I needed to set myself down. Gracious, my feet hurt so bad."

"Uh huh. This wouldn't have happened if you asked those Connie brothers for a raise like I told you too."

"I'm getting around to it! You don't just walk up to your boss and say, 'pour more sugar into my bowl.'"

"Yes, you can! Add a little 'please' and 'thank you' to it and you're good as gold."

Flo fixed a look on her. "Let me ask you something. Did you say that to good ol' Les when you worked for him?"

"You know I did."

"And did you get the raise?"

"That's beside the point."

"No, that *is* the point. These club guys know if I don't accept their pay, they'll find someone else who does. And they *always* find someone else. Beauty of America: somebody somewhere will do something for cheap, or worse, for free. And then futz it up for the rest of us."

Flo paused and patted her pockets until El heard the crinkle and crunch of paper. Flo brought up what looked like a flyer and handed it over to El.

"Found this in your lobby."

El glanced down at the wrinkled piece of paper. She read aloud, "'Keep Harlem respectable!' That word again. 'Say no to shows that promote sinful, unnatural acts!'" El looked at Flo. "What the hell is this?"

Flo leaned her head back on the sofa, her face turned toward the ceiling, eyes closed. "Keep reading."

El did. "This is a flyer asking people to boycott any establishment that puts an invert on its stage."

"Uh huh."

"Who's the fella who wrote this? This Reverend Elijah Blackburn?"

"Only the reverend to the fastest growing church in Harlem. Given how many weekly tithes he must be receiving, he might actually get a building that's all his own instead of being in the basement of a tenement."

El pointed at Flo with the flyer. "Whatever happened to judge not lest ye be judged? See, this is why I don't hold with preachers."

"Not all of them are bad, El."

"Psht! You didn't know the one my family wanted to send me to. To 'cure' me of my affliction. Thank the heavens I left before they could."

"That preacher wasn't a good one, I'll admit it. But," Flo said, "churches can help build communities. And you've had plenty of church ladies help you."

"Yeah, and I've had plenty of them give me the evil eye."

"Well, that's humanity for ya."

El wadded up the flyer and placed it in a wastepaper bin where it belonged. "On the upside, I guess that means I've truly made it in the world if people want to boycott me."

"I'm not so sure this is something to celebrate."

"Of course, it is! There's no such thing as bad publicity."

Flo sat up, eyes opened but narrowed with suspicion. "You're in an unusually cheerful mood for a woman whose wife left her for a Frenchie." By virtue of being El's best friend, Flo was the only one who knew about her and Alice.

"About that," El said. "I saw Alice last night. She explained everything."

"Did she? What excuse did she use? He covered himself with leaves and she tripped and fell on top of him?"

"Careful now. That's my wife you're talking about."

Flo held up a hand. "I apologize. It's the delirium talking."

"It better be. I know you don't approve of me and Alice—"

"It's not that, El." Flo paused to get her words together. "I didn't want you to get hurt. Plenty of white girls have broken many a Black girl's heart once the novelty wears off and they realize how hard it is to love us in this world. And just like I feared, Alice did you wrong. You can't deny that."

"Yeah, well, it wasn't her so much as the lying conman who forced her into the engagement."

"Say what again?"

El repeated it.

Flo shook her head. "Yeah, that doesn't make any more sense the second time around." Agitated, she took off her cloche hat and stood up to unbutton her fur coat. Underneath she wore a wine-colored dress with a drop waist and long sleeves. "Woo! That's better."

"Told ya you'd melt. Now with Alice—"

"Hold up, El, hold up. Is this an overly long explanation?"

"Sort of."

"Tell me later. Right now, I need to curl up on this here sofa and sleep until the sun goes down." Flo settled back down onto the cushions, tucking her arms underneath her head. "Glad you got everything sorted. Night, El."

"Night, Flo. Use my spare keys to lock up."

Flo was already snoring by the time El turned to leave.

7

Opening the door of Jordi's Barber Shop, El caught raucous laughter. One male voice said, "You lie!" Another said, "It's the Bible, I swear it!"

Two of the four white chairs with tan cushions and metal footrests were occupied. One man was getting his hair cut with scissors while the other man was leaned back horizontal for a shave. Looked like they'd just started, given the amount of cream on the man's face. Two other men sat in white wooden chairs opposite the barbers, waiting for their turn.

The air smelled of woodsy cologne mixed with some kind of chemical and burnt hair, as if a hot comb had been in recent use. Mirrors assigned to every chair showcased El's reflection at four different angles as she walked inside.

All the men stopped talking and looked at her. She felt the weight of their silent stares. She'd learned over the years to feel out these silences and read them like how spiritualists and housewives read tea leaves. Friendly? Curious? Hateful? What would her future hold? This silent stare fell more into the curiosity realm.

The barber shaving the man El presumed to be Isaiah said, "Excuse me, but this establishment isn't for ladies."

El smiled. "Good thing I'm not one then."

Another awkward silence while they tried to sort her out.

"Well," the second barber said as he went back to using his scissors. "You need a cut or a trim?"

"Thank you, no, I'm good, sir. I'm looking for Isaiah Scott."

"Who's looking for him?"

"A friend of Pearlie Taylor's. He said I might find him here."

The second barber nodded. "Pearlie Taylor's a good man. Successful too. That's what I keep trying to tell those two knuckleheads over there." He jerked his chin to the two men waiting their turns. "You gotta work hard, take chances when life gives 'em, and get back up when life inevitably knocks you down."

One of the waiting men replied, "Hey, Pops. We've heard this sermon before."

"Yeah, and you ain't listened yet."

The first barber shaving the man said, "This gentleman here is Isaiah Scott. He would've introduced himself on account there's a straight razor near his mouth right now."

The man in the chair raised a hand in greeting.

El studied him. Kinda hard to figure his height, with him lying back in the chair, but she guessed him decently tall. Not taller than her, though. On the older side of forty but wearing it well. She could tell from the soles of his shoes that he'd walked more than a few miles in them, but the leather was well cared for and spotless.

He aimed his eyes at her, a stunning shade of green

she'd only really seen on someone Irish. He raised his hand again, indicating to the his barber to pause.

Once the razor was safely away from his skin, Isaiah said in a stately voice, "Who might you be?"

"I'm El Train."

"How do you know Mr. Taylor?"

"We both needed suits and went to the same shop. Been acquaintances ever since."

"And why did he send you to me?"

El noticed the place got suspiciously quiet. She cleared her throat. "Well, you see, sir, a friend of mine is . . . seeing someone who's staying at the Hotel Eudora. And I've got a bad feeling about him. She's always had rotten luck with men, especially with, uh, white men."

Muttering, murmuring, and rustling rippled their way through the barber shop.

The man getting his hair cut said, "Man, why is it the ladies don't go for one of us? What's wrong with a good, strong Black man?"

The first man in the waiting chairs replied, "Don't be a dumb Dora. He's staying at the Hotel Eudora. That means he's got bowls full of sugar."

"Trunk fulls," commented the man waiting next to him.

Isaiah hushed everyone and said to El, "What do you want from me exactly?"

"I'd like to know if my fears are unfounded. Or if you've seen, or heard, anything that might persuade her to dump his white behind and maybe date one of these fine gentlemen in here." That got a better reaction from the customers and barbers alike. "And Pearlie suggested I talk with you."

Isaiah Scott considered her story before replying, "Do

you know what makes or breaks the hotel game, Miss . . . uh . . . Train?"

"El's fine. And—I don't know—linen sheets and room service?"

A few chuckles from the barbers and knowing smiles from the customers. They apparently already knew the answer. Probably heard it from Isaiah more than once, given their smugness.

"Discretion," he answered. "Nobody wants to check in and have their business blabbed all over town."

"But my friend—"

"She's a grown woman. And if she can't spot a grifter, then she's going to learn a grown-up lesson. Thank you kindly for stopping by, but I don't talk about our guests."

The barber giving the haircut stopped using his scissors and said, "Oh that's the biggest bunch of bushwa I ever heard. You do *nothing* but talk about who's staying there."

"Yeah," added Isaiah's barber. "The only reason we allow you in here is so we can hear the latest gossip."

The man getting his hair cut said, "Tell her the story about the man who got into a fight with his wife and she locked him naked outside of their room."

The two men waiting for their turn chuckled from their seats and encouraged Isaiah to tell it again.

Isaiah raised his voice. "That's enough now." He pushed himself into a sitting position so he could look at El in the eye. "A lot of people at the Hotel Eudora. I probably don't even know his name."

"Let's give it a try. Lucien Laurent."

Isaiah winced as the whole barbershop came alive once more.

"Settle down, settle down," he said, frowning. Once the

other men quieted themselves, he sighed. "Your friend has lousy taste in menfolk."

"He made that good of an impression, huh?"

"He's hard to forget."

The barber who had been shaving Isaiah said, "Tell her about the eye thing."

El looked from the barber back to Isaiah. "Eye thing?"

Isaiah nodded. "It's the strangest thing I ever saw. He's got two different-colored irises. One eye is blue, like sky blue; but the other is emerald green."

The first man waiting his turn said, "I saw a cat like that once."

El took a seat next to the waiting man so she could be level with Isaiah. "What else about Lucien?"

Isaiah studied her intently. "You planning to hurt him?"

"Not if he doesn't ask for it."

A respectful muttering and tittering moved its way around the shop, ending with the man sitting next to El saying, "Okay, sis—I mean, sir."

Isaiah's gaze was unwavering. "If anything happens to him, I'm leading the police straight to your door."

"Understood."

He pressed his lips together, as if he already regretted what he was about to do. "Lucien Laurent is one of the most demanding guests I've ever had the misfortune of tending to."

"Tell her, Isaiah," quipped his barber.

"Nothing is good enough. The champagne isn't chilled properly. The food isn't rich with flavor. The baths aren't piping hot. I tell you one thing, if ever there was a grown man who needed to be bent over his mother's knee and schooled with a ruler, it'd be him."

"Take us to church now," said the waiting man next to El.

"Hallelujah!" shouted the second barber.

"And the way he spends money?" Isaiah made a face as if he smelled something awful. "I've never seen such waste. And mind you, the Hotel Eudora has some serious big-timers but him? He acts like he can just pull money out of the air."

"Testify!" called out the man getting his hair cut.

"Treats everyone as if they're dirt, including some of the other white guests. No one is as good as the French, according to him. Takes everything I have not to say, 'Then get your ass back to Paris.' 'Excuse my language."

"Trust me, sir, I've used worse," El said. "Does he have a job?"

Isaiah sputtered out a laugh. "Does he have a job? Good grief, no! He's some kind of aristocrat living on his dead parents' money. Never had to lift a finger, I can tell you that much. I'm surprised he knows how to tie his own shoes."

"Does he go out at night? Have visitors? Late-night friends, if you know what I mean?"

"All he does is go out. But dig this: he doesn't go out to the hoity-toity places. As much as he acts like a high hat, he don't like to hang out with other high-hats. Ha! Probably 'cause he sees himself in them and it's too ugly a picture reflecting back. No, he goes slumming."

"Ah."

'Slumming' meant white folks going to Black or invert clubs either down in Greenwich Village or up here in Harlem.

"Yeah. He asks me, 'Where do *your* people go for a good time?' My people. Pfft! But there's a dollar in his hand so I smile real big and give him a few names. Lately, though, he's been asking me about that Holloway Factory strike. What I thought of it—a mistake, if you ask me; they're asking to be unemployed and making things worse for the next people coming in—when it would end, what Mr. Holloway was willing to do to end it."

"When did he start becoming interested in the strike?"

"When he proposed to your friend, his fiancé," Isaiah replied with a shrewd glint in his eye. He apparently read the papers like Pearlie did.

El said wryly, "You don't miss a thing, Mr. Scott."

"Indeed not. I also didn't miss what he told me yesterday. Said he found out something that Mr. Holloway ought to know."

A coldness pressed its clammy hands against the back of her neck. "What did he find out?"

Isaiah shrugged. "I don't know, but he said he was going to tell Mr. Holloway at the factory this morning when it opens at nine." He glanced up at the clock on the wall. "If you hurry, you might be able to catch him."

8

The Holloway Paper Box Factory took a good chunk of the block on 125th between Seventh and Lenox. It was shaped like the products it made: a boxy, brown-bricked building with minimal ornamentation but a lot of tiny windows. Four stories; three of them, according to Alice, were work floors with the top floor belonging to the executives, where Alice's brother held court. Everything functioned from the top down. Orders came in to the fourth floor, which were printed and cut by the men on the third floor, which were then glued together by the women and children on the second floor, before being sent to the first floor, where the remaining men would pack up the orders into the trucks. The filled trucks would exit through the front gate to make their deliveries to shops across New York City and parts of New Jersey.

But now, the iron gate was locked up tight, and men, women, and children paced back and forth holding signs and chanting slogans. The picketers, a mix of white, Black, and eastern European, wore ratty coats over patchwork clothes. Dusty hats hardly clung to their heads in the sharp wind and threadbare gloves barely warmed their hands as they shouted, "Fair wage! Safe conditions! We will stand with the union!"

The signs written in big capital letters said: "UNION WORKERS ARE PROTECTED WORKERS," "LABOR ARE HUMAN BEINGS TOO," and "WORKERS WAGES NOT A PENNY TAX ON FOOD." The last bit referenced a line justifying low wages repeated, almost verbatim, by every businessman El had seen quoted in the newspapers. Raising wages would raise the cost of goods. Yet wages stayed down and the costs went up anyway.

Children held up signs too. One of them said: "LESS LABOR, MORE SCHOOL." That tugged at her heart. These little boys and girls should be learning to read, not toiling all day in an airless factory.

El pulled up the fur collar of her coat to ward off the chill. The November sky above them was its usual monotonous gray, the wind filled with its usual teeth. She searched the sidewalks for a French-looking man with two different-colored irises.

What exactly does *a Frenchman look like?*

Hell if she knew. Luckily, Isaiah Scott gave her a more detailed description: tall, trim, with a beak-like nose and an often grim, determined expression on his face. Dark brown hair with a slight curl near the forehead, which served in great contrast to his white skin. He had long limbs that made sharp angles and walked in a haughty gait.

"A dandy in every sense of the word," Isaiah had said.

And, of course, the eyes: one blue and one green.

She stood with the crowd watching the picketers and scanned for any sign of a man matching Isaiah's description. Idly she wondered if the other union leads were here, the ones that Alice partnered with. She thought she saw a

Polish-looking man standing in the center of the picketers that could've been Malek Polowski. The others were just names to her—Ferrin Thomas, Booker Freeman, Ramona Westfall—so they could've been any one of the picketers marching.

More than an hour passed and still no sign of any man matching Lucien's description.

The rattle of a big black motorcar caught the crowd's attention. They all turned their heads and watched it pull up to the entrance of the factory. Judging by the frowning faces of the picketers, they knew its occupants. Behind the black motorcar followed a truck of sorts. Looked to El like a paddy wagon. Both stopped and idled for a moment.

The back door of the wagon eventually opened and young Black girls, aged eighteen or less, stepped out. They were greeted immediately by boos from the picketers. One man holding up a sign that read "BUSINESS IS JUST ANOTHER WORD FOR TYRANNY" screamed, "Scabs!"

That prompted the others to join in a chant of "No scabs! No scabs!"

The picketers formed a line and blocked the entrance of the factory, preventing the young girls from entering. The girls looked around, fear widening their eyes.

The back door of the black motorcar opened and out stepped a man in a dark gray fedora and overcoat. His brown hair tinged slightly red, his facial features a familiar set of whiskey-colored eyes and thick lips. The male version of Alice.

Rich Holloway.

He said something to the crowd that El couldn't hear over the jeers and boos. From the corner of her eye, she saw a maroon painted car—a Chrysler coupe, by the look of it—park on the opposite side of 125th. A man in a dark gray suit got out and started towards the front gate. Intuition told her this was Lucien Laurent.

He called out Rich's name, but he wasn't heard any more than Rich was over the shouting picketers. The man tried to get close to Rich, but a crowd was forming around the factory owner, and they pushed the man away. Tension was building and El wondered if a fight would break out.

Suddenly, she saw Rich reach into his overcoat and pull out a pistol. He raised it into the air and fired.

The sound of the shot echoed so loudly, everyone jumped.

A few people even screamed.

But then everything got deathly quiet.

All eyes were on Rich Holloway.

He said in a loud voice, "You will let them through or the next time I pull this trigger, one of you will get a bullet! Do I make myself clear?!"

Now the picketers eyed each other with the same level of confused alarm as the young Black girls did mere seconds before.

"*Do I make myself clear?!*" Rich shouted again.

A man stepped out from the picketers. Ghostly skin, unkempt black hair, smudges like soot underneath swollen eyelids. His sallow cheeks revealed sharp cheekbones. A thin mustache arched over a humorless mouth. He wore a muddy brown overcoat, a dirty white shirt visible above the collar. A flat cap covered his ink-black hair. When he spoke, his words were tinged with a strange accent.

"There is no need for violence," the man said.

Is this the union lead Malek Polowski? El wondered.

She murmured her question to the people surrounding her. One fella muttered back, "Yep, that's him. Trouble-maker extraordinaire."

Rich replied, "There won't be if you move out of the way. You're trespassing on my property, and I have the right to defend myself."

"The sidewalks are public property, Mr. Holloway."

"But my gate isn't. And you're currently blocking it." Rich aimed his pistol at Malek, prompting many picketers to gasp. "Get out of my way, Mr. Polowski."

"Will you hear our terms?"

"I said—"

"Will you hear our terms?" Malek repeated.

Rich's mouth went through a series of twitches before his voice cleared his lips. "Are they reasonable?"

"More than reasonable, sir."

Rich stared at Malek for a tense minute more. "I'll consent to a meeting. But you will get out of these girls' way. They are not afraid of hard work." He glanced around to the other picketers. "Unlike the rest of you!"

Malek's face never wavered throughout this exchange with Rich. Never showed fear, concern. But now, it slowly morphed into a detached bemusement.

"Very well," he eventually replied. He looked to his fellow strikers. "Stand back. It's alright. Stand back."

The picketers grumbled but did as they were told.

Rich motioned with his pistol for the young Black girls to enter the factory, which they did in haste.

El hadn't realized she'd been holding her breath, and she exhaled and inhaled deeply. She knew Alice's brother was ruthless, but she had no idea the level of violence he was willing to inflict.

Babe, you better have covered your tracks. I mean it.

Because if Alice hadn't, well, El didn't want to think about what Rich would do.

Which prompted her to find the man she thought was

Lucien Laurent. She spotted him again, standing in the middle of the street, trying to get Rich's attention. His mouth moved fast, his long arms waving, but Rich focused more on getting the scabs into the factory. Once the last girl passed through the gate, he followed after them, locking the gate behind him. The picketers crowded around it, shouting incomprehensibly.

The man slapped his thigh in frustration at being thwarted by the picketers. He tried once more to get through to no avail. He scratched the back of his head, apparently unsure of what to do next. A truck trying to go down 125th helped him make the decision by honking its horn and the driver yelling out the window to "get the fuck outta the road, you crazy loon!"

The man waved the driver off and went over to the corner where there was a clear expanse of sidewalk. The truck rattled by and continued on its way down 125th.

Here goes nothing.

El crossed the street going towards the man, calling out, "Mr. Laurent!"

Confused, the man turned around. "*Oui?*" Picketers milled about behind him, having intense conversations about the scabs.

El walked until she was about three feet from him and stopped. She pointed to the factory gates. "I see you were trying to talk with Mr. Holloway. May I ask what it's about?"

"What business is it of yours?" he said, his accent thick, almost comical in its "Frenchness." Nothing funny about his eyes though. Isaiah was right. The sight was unlike anything she'd ever seen before: the bluest of blues in his right eye, a sparkling, shimmering green in his left.

"What business is it of mine?" she said. "I'm a

concerned citizen, Mr. Laurent. I heard from another concerned citizen that you have information that's important to Mr. Holloway concerning this strike."

"Who told you that?"

"Doesn't matter. What does matter is what you were going to tell Mr. Holloway."

Her question got the attention of some of the picketers. She saw them shuffle closer to where they were standing. One of them said, "Hey, what were you gonna blab to Rich?"

Another added, "You a spy? You betraying the union?"

"I saw you try to cross that picket line."

El saw Lucien quickly ascertain that these picketers, the men especially, wanted to express their anger over the scabs, and he did not want to be on the receiving end of their ire.

He held up his hands. "Gentlemen, gentlemen. The lady is mistaken. I didn't want to speak with him. I have no business with him whatsoever."

"That's a lie!" a picketer growled. "I heard him say Rich's name clear as day!"

El felt the men close in on them. She heard a bottle break, and she didn't think it was by accident. They started circling her and Lucien, cutting them off from a clear getaway to his Chrysler coupe. She tried to gently push some of the picketers back.

"Alright, everyone. No need to crowd the man. He and I are having a conversation, that's all."

"Who is he? One of the suits upstairs?"

"He a cop?"

"Nah, too well-dressed for that."

"I bet he works for the mayor's office."

"The mayor ain't on our side."

"No, shit. The mayor wants us all chained to our machines."

"Whattaya here for? You trying to sabotage us, fella?"

Lucien's eyes widened in panic as the picketers pressed up against him. He glanced over to El.

Dammit, she thought. *We gotta get outta here or they're gonna rip us to pieces.*

At that moment, El saw a cab round the corner of 125th and Seventh, heading their way.

"Mr. Laurent!" she called and then jerked her thumb over to the approaching vehicle.

Lucien thankfully caught the hint, pushed his way through two distracted male picketers, and leapt into the street, his arms raised.

For her part, El put her fingers between her teeth and let forth an ear-piercing whistle.

The cab stopped.

She told Lucien, "Run!"

He was gone.

El followed, taking advantage of the men's heads being turned and distracted by Lucien's leap into the street.

Lucien opened the cab and practically dove into the backseat. Before he could shut the door on her, El had crossed the street and grabbed the door handle, angling her way inside. She slammed the door and told the cabbie to step on it.

For once, a man didn't argue with her. They sped away from the mob of angry picketers, their fists raised in the air, shouting curses at them.

Lucien breathed heavily. A thick sheen of sweat covered his cheeks and forehead. He reached into the breast pocket of his suit and pulled out a handkerchief, which he used to wipe his face and brow.

"*Merci, mademoiselle*," he said. "As you Yanks would say, you really saved my bacon."

The cabbie—a small Black man who barely saw over the steering wheel—asked where they were going.

Lucien looked over his shoulder. "*Merde*. I suppose I can't claim my motorcar right now."

"You better hope they don't realize that's yours and burn it."

The cabbie asked one more time their destination.

Lucien replied the Hotel Eudora on Seventh Avenue between 124th and 125th Streets and then closed his eyes, trying to calm himself.

"You drove a block?" El said. "Why couldn't you walk it?"

"I drove to the Holloway house first and missed Mr. Holloway. Then I came here."

"I see." They didn't have far to go, so El picked up the pace. "Alright, I did you a favor. Now you're going to do one for me."

Lucien groaned.

"Don't give me that. You said it yourself: I saved your bacon. And little piggy, you're gonna tell me what you were gonna squeal to Mr. Holloway. Every. Last. Bit. of it."

9

Lucien pinched his brow. "How do you even know my name?"

"I'm a spiritualist," El replied. "This morning, I had a vision of a man with two different colored eyes who needed to be rescued at the Holloway Paper Box Factory."

"That true, ma'am?" the cabbie said.

El said, "Son, don't call me ma'am," at the same time Lucien said, "Of course, it's not true."

Lucien looked over at El. "You're lying, *mademoiselle*."

"And you're not answering my question, *monsieur*."

"You're asking a dangerous question."

"What's so dangerous about it?" She leaned in close. "This anything to do with those tough guys coming after you?"

Lucien said to the driver, "Please pull over, *monsieur*. I'd like to get out."

"Keep driving, *monsieur*. In fact, let's take a scenic route around Harlem, because the gentleman and I haven't finished our conversation yet."

The cabbie, bless him, didn't know who to listen to. "You getting out, sir?"

"Yes."

"No," countered El.

Lucien flashed an angry look at her. "Who are you? Why are you keeping me hostage?"

"Because you owe me some answers."

"Owe you? I've never seen you before in my life!"

The cabbie said, "If you two are going to fight, I'm pulling over."

"*Merci beaucoup.*"

"Baby," El said to the cabbie. "If you pull this cab over, you'll be aiding and abetting the escape of a criminal."

Lucien's mouth dropped open. "I'm not a criminal!"

"Then prove it! Or I'll have this cab go directly to the police station." El shut her mouth and let Lucien work out his response. They passed the Hotel Eudora and the cabbie kept going.

"I can't," Lucien murmured. "Not here."

"Why not?"

"Because the driver, no offense my good sir, will overhear everything we say. He'll tell on me."

"Cabbies don't do that. A taxi in this city is as confidential as a Catholic confessional." It wasn't remotely true but El hoped he didn't know that.

Lucien frowned. "But you Americans are not Catholic. Mostly not Catholic. Isn't that why you're afraid of most people from Europe?"

"I think it was mostly the job and housing shortages."

Lucien pointed to the cabbie. "Is he Catholic? If he is, then he can be my priest and then I will confess all."

The cabbie, bless his soul, said, "I'm Baptist."

Lucien looked over to El, a forced sad expression on his

face. "See? He is not Catholic. This taxi is not a confessional."

"Aren't you a regular trickster." El flipped a nickel that landed in the cabbie's lap. "Temporarily convert, if you don't mind."

The cabbie looked down at the coin and grinned. "You got it. Hey, mister? I'm Catholic. Hail Mother Mary and all the saints."

El said to Lucien, "You're safe now."

"I don't know," Lucien replied. "I think he'd still tell."

El turned to the cabbie. "Do you swear on the Bible to close your ears and not breathe a word this man says to anyone, now and forever until the day you're called to Glory?"

"Yes, ma'am."

"I'll allow the ma'am just this once 'cause you became a Catholic on my account." El smiled at Lucien. "Ready?"

Lucien crossed his arms over his chest. "Only if you tell me who you are."

"I'm El Train."

A blank expression greeted her. "And?" he said.

The cabbie couldn't help himself. "And? She's just the heppest piano player and singer in all of Harlem." He turned to look over his shoulder at her. "I thought that was you but didn't want to say anything in case I was wrong. I can't believe I'm driving *the* El Train."

She gestured towards the windshield. "Keep your eyes on the road, baby."

He faced forward again, turning them north, the numbered streets counting upwards.

Lucien wasn't impressed. "You're a celebrity, I take it. You Americans. You love your rich and famous."

"And you love not answering my question. I got the

cabbie to go Catholic. I told you who I am. Now you tell me what you wanted with Richard Holloway."

Those queer blue and green eyes watched her for an entire block. She thought she'd have to push him again, but to her surprise, he spoke.

"I found out something about the union strike leads."

Oh, no.

"And what's that?" she asked, her stomach queasy.

Lucien stalled some more, but eventually replied, "They're going to hire a—what do you call it?—a 'damage squad.'"

"Damage squad?" His response was so unexpected, El's voice rang true with surprise.

"*Oui, oui*, a group of them are planning to set fire to the factory trucks."

"Why on earth would they do that?"

Lucien shrugged. "I don't know. Maybe so *Monsieur* Holloway feels threatened and will be more amenable to the union's demands? It is a crude tactic. My fellow countrymen have been known to use it. It can be effective."

"But that's vandalism and—" El caught herself in time before she finished the thought, *and Alice would never condone that.* She cleared her throat. "How did you find this out?"

"I would rather not say."

El glared at him.

"Alright, *mademoiselle*, alright. I was walking through a park to, uh, clear my head."

"At night?"

"*Oui.* I find it relaxing."

"I find it stupid. That's a surefire way to get mugged in this city."

A bemused twitch of his lips. "The park was named

after Saint Nicholas; I figure the good Lord above would protect me. I also carry around with me a pistol. When I first came to America, I was told you are all, I believe the phrase is, 'armed to the teeth.'"

"Do you even know how to shoot a gun, mister?"

"Oh, yes. And not to brag, but my aim is quite good."

El didn't want to hear any more self-aggrandizement. "Go on. You're traipsing through Saint Nicholas Park like a dumb Dora. Then what?"

The cabbie made another turn, heading back across town and towards Seventh Avenue.

Lucien said, "I come to a bench and take a seat. I was trying to light a cigarette when I heard voices in the trees behind me. It was a group of men talking about the strike. Since I am marrying into the Holloway family, naturally I listened in."

"Naturally."

"And they discussed the best way to set the trucks on fire. They mentioned a lot of chemical names I couldn't repeat to you, but they all agreed it was the best way to get attention and to end the strike."

El thought Lucien's story was a tad too convenient, one coincidence meeting another. "You hear any names?"

He shook his head.

"Of course, you didn't. Did you get a look at this group of fellas? You recognize any of them today at the factory?"

"No, *mademoiselle*. I didn't move for fear of them discovering me."

"I thought you could protect yourself."

A wan smile. "I may have good aim, but I am not stupid. Multiple men against one? A gambler would say those are not good odds."

They turned onto Seventh and rode in silence, El

processing what Lucien said as the numbered streets counted back down towards 125th.

Once they reached it, he leaned forward and said to the cabbie, "Just up here, *mon ami*."

El glanced out the window. The Hotel Eudora, a thirteen-story, white-brick, terra-cotta wonder with reportedly over three hundred rooms, stood before them.

When the cab rolled to a stop in front of the lobby doors, Lucien thanked El for the ride and for saving him once again. "Though I must confess, I do not understand your interest in me or Mr. Holloway."

"You don't have to," El replied.

Lucien said to the cabbie, "Thank you for your conversion and for your discretion." He stepped out of the cab and almost walked away without paying his fair share.

"Excuse me," El called. "You forgot something?"

Lucien spun around. "Hmm? Oh. My apologies." He then made a show of patting his pockets. "I seem to have left my cab fare in my hotel room."

"Uh huh. You may have a fancy new motorcar, but I wasn't born yesterday."

"I normally don't walk around with much money. In case I'm robbed, *n'est pas*? I can simply go up and grab—"

"Nope. Search your pockets again."

Lucien smirked. He patted his pockets once again and raised his eyebrows at a sudden discovery. "Ahhh."

El mimicked his response. "Ahhh."

"Look at what we have here?" Lucien held up a quarter. "Will this do, *mademoiselle*?"

"Rub that quarter between your fingers and see if it comes up deuces."

Lucien's eyebrows fell. "If you weren't so kind, I'd say you were taking advantage of me."

"Perish the thought."

Lucien patted his trouser pocket and wouldn't you know it? He came up with a second quarter. He dropped them into El's outstretched hand.

"Thank you kindly," she said.

Lucien touched the brim of his hat. "*Au revoir*." And with that, he sauntered into the hotel lobby.

"He's a funny fella," the cabbie said.

"Yeah," El replied, watching Lucien disappear from view. "That's one word for him. Alright, son. Take me home." She gave him her address.

"Can-do," he said. "Only . . . Miss El, can I stop being Catholic now?"

10

"Come on, come on, pick up," El muttered as she waited for the Holloway household to answer.

She stood in the telephone booth on the corner of 134th Street and Lenox Avenue, the big box being buffeted by the wind. After the cabbie dropped her off, she gave him a healthy tip and went straight there. She had to tell Alice what Lucien said.

Damage squads? Babe, please tell me you're not funding shit like that.

A maid finally answered. Irish, by the sound of her.

El used her most polished downtowner voice. "Oh, hullo. I was wondering if Miss Alice Holloway was available."

"She is. Whom may I say is calling?"

El replied "Miriam King," which was a code name she and Alice agreed upon. "Of the Ladies' Auxiliary. I need to speak with her about the forthcoming ladies' luncheon."

Never mind that Alice never attended a ladies' luncheon in her life. The maids never seemed to catch on, or if they did, they were privately amused at the lifestyles of the abject rich.

The maid replied, "I'll see if she's available."

Plunk.

The maid dropped the receiver onto a table, from the sound of it. El massaged her bruised ear and waited. A sudden gust of wind shook the telephone booth. She turned her head and saw through the glass a man lose his fedora, as if yanked by an invisible wire. He chased it down the sidewalk, cursing as he went. The fedora blew into the avenue, where a large delivery truck was barreling down towards the intersection. The chasing man's eyes were only on the hat, not his surroundings, and given the speed he was moving, it was obvious he didn't see the truck.

"Oh no," El breathed.

She was about to leave the booth to warn the man when the truck suddenly blared its horn, jolting him out of his trance. He skidded to a stop on the corner a half second before the truck roared by. The force of the displaced air whipped up the tails of his coat. Once the vehicle was gone, the man walked slowly into the avenue and retrieved his poor crumpled, flattened fedora.

El blew out a long exhale of relief. "That was a close one," she muttered to herself.

The line was picked back up again and she heard Alice's voice. "Hullo, Mrs. King."

"Hullo, Miss Holloway. How are you?"

They kept up the charade because they never knew who was listening in on the party line.

"I'm well," Alice replied, her voice smooth as ever. "What news have you about the luncheon?"

"In a very roundabout way, which doesn't bear repeating, I ran into *Lucy* this afternoon."

Alice hesitated. "Oh?"

"Don't worry. I didn't let on about our little soirée."

Alice sighed. "That's good. She'd make things very difficult for us if she knew."

"I know, dear, that's why I was the utmost soul of discretion. But I did learn something *most* distressing. It appears *Lucy* heard that—that—" Oh, what name should she use for Malek? "—Merrick and the others might be hiring . . . *fire* starters for the luncheon."

"Fire starters?" Alice didn't get that one.

"Yes. They're going to—to—light little pieces of paper on fire. She said it would be very dramatic as they burned up in the air and disappeared. Like a magic trick, I suppose."

"Light paper on fire?" El heard the realization dawn in Alice's voice. "You don't mean—"

"I do and I must say, I'm quite disappointed that you'd approve of such an act."

The fact they could keep up this high-hat charade while discussing something so dangerous felt so absurd and yet, that's what life was like for them most of the time. If only the world would let them be who they were and love who they loved. Then again, the world was full of "if only's."

"Mrs. King," Alice said. "I promise you, I'd never approve anything of the sort."

"I'm certainly glad to hear that."

"You're quite right, though. This is most, most distressing." Silence while Alice thought. "I must call an emergency meeting tonight. This must be squashed at once. I cannot let this stand."

"Good." El paused. "Do you still have . . . that wonderful purse you carry around? The one with the ivory handle." She meant Alice's .32 Colt.

"The purse? Oh, the purse! Yes, yes I do. I never leave the house without it."

"Good. Make sure it's . . . *filled* with the right things." *Like bullets.* "Are you meeting at the usual place?"

The usual place being the basement art studio of Augusta Wilde, an up-and-coming sculptor who supported the union's cause.

"I plan on it, yes," Alice replied. "The usual time too." She meant eleven o'clock at night.

"Perhaps I should swing by there afterwards. See how the conversation went."

"Oh, no. You don't have to do that. I'm sure it'll be fine."

"Are you positive?"

"One-hundred percent. I've got to have a separate conversation with someone anyway. Nothing serious," she added quickly for El's benefit. "Just a confusing matter I need clearing up." A voice sounded in the distance on Alice's side of the line. "I must be going, you know?"

Their code.

El smiled. "I know. I must be going as well. Take care, Miss Holloway."

"You as well, Mrs. King."

After El hung up the receiver, she stayed in the shelter of the telephone booth thinking of her next move and couldn't come up with one. Lord, the morning felt like four weeks instead of four hours.

It was then she realized she was famished. Another realization: she'd yet to put in her numbers! She checked her wristwatch. It was now near her usual waking time. She could still put them in with her usual runner.

She left the comfort of the booth and was immediately accosted by the aggressive wind and the cacophony of noise from Lenox Avenue. Trolleys clanged up and down while newspaper stands barked the latest headlines. Sidewalks were filled to the brim with their usual hustle and bustle of men and women, swinging briefcases, carrying groceries, and pushing baby strollers. New arrivals with fat suitcases gazed around in wonder while girls and boys too young for school played on stoop steps, squealing with pleasure. Every last one of 'em Black and beautiful. The sight brought a smile to El's face.

As did the thought of placing her numbers.

Though she was making good sugar these days, she never stopped putting in her guesses. Not only was she supporting the largest Black-owned and -operated business in Harlem, but the ritual also kept her connected. The best neighborhood gossip—who was doing what and, most importantly, with *whom*—came from the runners. Last week, she learned a ladies' makeup salesmen had been caught painting rouge on a married woman's knees, and El wanted to know what the woman's husband decided to do about the situation.

When she arrived on the corner of 135th and Lenox, she found her usual runner gone. Instead, there was a young boy that couldn't have been more than eight years old, maybe ten, if he had a baby face. He wore pale gray dungarees and a dark gray jacket that belonged to a bigger, taller man. Same for the brown leather shoes.

Standing in front of the boy flailing his arms in argument was a man of about fifty wearing a ratty overcoat and a hat one size too big. When El got closer, she recognized the old man's voice. She steeled herself and strolled over.

"Hey, Terrence," she said to the old man. "What's good?"

The old man turned, his lips locked in a downward grimace. His bushy eyebrows were knit so close together, they looked like a hairy scarf draped over his toffee-colored eyes.

"Not a damn thing," he said. "Didn't get the right number, or so this boy says." He nodded his gray-whiskered chin to the nervous little gent, the gesture causing the brown trilby to slip down on his forehead. He pushed it back with annoyance.

"Oh, good grief. Leave that boy alone. He's just doing what he's told."

"Yeah, well, I had a dream the night before last that I was on 135th Street, and in my dream, I got real liquor, two women, and a five-course meal that included a *whole chicken*. Now if that wasn't a sign, I don't know what is."

You and your damn signs.

El looked down at the boy. "Where's Lucky?" she asked. His real name was William Something-or-other but everyone called him Lucky. God knew why. He rarely called the numbers they gave him.

The boy stammered, "H-he's out with the flu."

"I hear it's going around."

"That's bushwa," Terrence said. "He's at home counting all that money that should be going into *my* pocket."

El ignored Terrence's grumblings. "Sorry to hear about Lucky. You his boy?"

The boy nodded.

"Well, you're doing a good job covering for your daddy. No matter what *some* people say," she added, glaring over at Terrence.

"Don't you be giving me any looks now," Terrence replied. "That boy's lying, and he knows it!"

She asked Lucky's son, "What's your name?"

"Lenny."

El smiled. "Lenny. And what was yesterday's winning number?"

"As I told the gentleman here, yesterday's number was four-seventy-three." He held up the square piece of paper that every numbers runner received from the clearing house, otherwise known as the policy bank, where the bets were placed and the payouts distributed.

El peered down and saw the number matched what Lenny said. She tapped her cane on the ground and said to the old man, "You lost, Terrence. That's all there is to it."

"I couldn't have! Two women, El! And a whole chicken!"

"Just a dream, baby, just a dream. And you know as well as I that the numbers are selected from the day's papers. You can look it up." She turned back to Lenny. "What's today's number pulled from, baby?"

"The Exchange."

"The New York Stock Exchange?"

"Yes, 'em. The last three digits of the total Exchange from yesterday."

She whirled around to Terrence. "See? I bet if I grab that paper over there and look up the Exchange total, I'll find those last three digits."

"He's cheating me, El!"

"How? He sneaking down to Wall Street and seeing what they're putting up? C'mon! Now quit scaring the boy and pick a new number and fast. It's cold and windy as hell out here."

"Yeah, yeah." Terrence reached into his pocket and pulled out a dime. "Now listen. Last night, I dreamt I was on a train and that train took me to Venice. I don't know how. Didn't think they have tracks under the ocean but there I was, in Venice, drinking wine, chatting up all the womenfolk in gondolas. I could even speak Italian!"

El motioned with her hand for him to get on with it.

Terrence frowned at her before continuing. "And the train I was on left on track ten. Ain't that something? Track ten and I'm living the high life in Venice, so that's what I'm laying down." He handed Lenny his dime. "But I want a combo of two, three, and five. Ya got it?"

Lenny placed the coin in a burlap sack where it pinged against the others inside before pulling out a notepad and pencil. He scribbled Terrence's name and bet into it.

He looked over at El. "And you?"

She handed him a nickel. "Five, but I want a combo as well: three and two."

Lenny took her money and made his notation. Once done, he then ran towards a group of women, shouting, "Numbers! Numbers! Get your numbers!"

Terrence smirked. "That better work this time. Or else."

El turned to him. "Or else what? You gonna scare that kid into giving you ill-gotten gains? Listen to me carefully. If you do that and I hear about it—or worse, see it?—I'm gonna take this here cane and shove it somewhere that'll change the way you walk. Permanently. You understand me?"

Terrence's trilby slipped down his forehead again and he forced it back. The wind almost stole it from his head, and he clamped down on the brim with a scowl. "Why you women gotta be so mean?"

"Why do women gotta be nice? Nobody's nice to us."

Terrence muttered an incomprehensible response and shuffled off, holding his hat against the wind.

El sighed. Some men were just too tiresome for their own good.

11

"I would like to dedicate this next song to the wonderful folks over at the Committee of Fourteen."

El grinned as the crowd groaned and booed the organization that spent its time and money raiding speaks and publishing its reports about the "widespread degeneracy" that had overtaken the city.

She held up her hand. "Hold up, hold up. They're doing the Lord's work, I hear. Heaven knows their wives sure are. But even a group of people as pure and righteous as the Committee of Fourteen gets a little lonely sometimes."

A few giggles flitted through the air as tonight's patrons anticipated what the brave and profane El Train would do.

She trilled a chord and held it for maximum effect before launching into a stomping, greasy blues shuffle. The lyrics were inspired by the flyers being left all over town by Reverend Blackburn. A few had even been dumped in the lobby of the Watkins Hotel, as a matter of fact. He was poking his head into her business, and she wasn't going to stand for it.

She sang:

Believe me, baby, those bluenoses sure get blue
Believe me, baby, those bluenoses sure get blue
They coming to my back door, asking for my homemade stew

See, my stew's so hot and juicy, it dribbles down their chin
My stew's so hot and juicy, it dribbles on down their chin
I watch them gobble it all up with the biggest goddamn grin

The crowd gasped and roared with delight as every word seemed to get dirtier and dirtier, like the cocktails being poured in the back.

She continued:

He slips his spoon into my pot, and he stirs it up real good
He slips his spoon into my pot, and he stirs it up real good
Who knew my stew would bubble with such a
puny piece of wood?

She was whipping everyone into a frenzy with each shocking verse. Shrieks, guffaws, banging tables, stamping floors, the works.

The next verse about ended them:

I lift my fanny in the air and ask her to clean my plate
I lift my fanny in the air and ask her to clean my plate
She licks it 'til it's spotless 'cause good girls never waste

"You got that right, El!" shouted a woman from the crowd, followed by more exclamations from the audience.

"Go on now!"

"Sing it!"

"Teach them bluenoses!"

The room fully scandalized, she ended with:

God bless those bluenoses, don't they sure look blue?
They eat no home cooking, and they get so hungry too
Now it's my God-given duty
to feed them my homemade stew!

She finished with a slide down the keys, laughing as she did so.

"Whoo!" she said as the room applauded, cheered, and whistled. "I do believe I might have outdone myself with that one!" She paused to wipe her forehead with her handkerchief. "Oh, my. Those bluenoses, babies. They are something else, aren't they?"

"You're something else!" another woman shouted.

"Damn right, I am. I am the incredible El Train and I'll ride your rails from New York City to Chicago. All the way to the Pacific Ocean. If you can stand it, that is.

"Now. Here's a little number by our Empress, Miss Bessie Smith. You know Bessie? You don't futz with her. She'll rip your hair out by its roots, especially if you're feeding stew to one of her lovers. Hell hath no fury, babies. But I'm gonna do this song in honor of Bessie, who's being played on the radio all over the country. People are buying her record like it's real gin. I'm proud of our Empress, and you should be too, so sing along if you know it."

She launched into a version of "Down Hearted Blues." El was pleased to hear many of the audience members knew the words and the melody. A few more numbers followed before she took her final bows.

Back in her dressing room, she took off her tuxedo that was drenched with sweat and changed into a silk robe. She sprawled on her chaise lounge to nurse a whiskey and smoke a cigar, thinking about her conversation with Flo earlier. She spilled all the details, of course, about Lucien Laurent and the predicament she and Alice found themselves in.

"I told you that girl was trouble," Flo had said as they sat in El's front room. "Didn't I tell you she was trouble?"

"Yes, yes you did," El had replied.

"Gets extorted into an engagement by a fiancé who's got tough guys looking for him. I mean, how much trouble can one girl get into?" Flo paused. "You sure this love is worth it? I'm being serious, El. What does she give you that no one else does?"

El had sat there for a moment, thinking. How could she impart something so vast and deep into just a few sentences? "You know how long we've been together?"

"About six months."

"And married for two. But it feels . . . longer somehow. Not in a bad way. As if I've known her my whole life." El laughed self-consciously. "I can't remember much of my life before her. Like there was a missing piece in the puzzle and she snapped into place, completing the picture. Alice and El, El and Alice. Two sides, one coin. She's tough, so she can handle me on my worst days; but she's got a gentleness that brings out a softness in me on my better days. Always up for a good time, an adventure. Living life to the fullest, which I love. She's passionate about helping others and doing the right thing, a rare occurrence in this city. And she inspires me to be better, to do better. And in turn, I want all the good things life can bring for her—success, safety, freedom, fun. I find lately I want them more for her than I do myself, sometimes." El rubbed her brow. "I don't know if I'm making any sense."

"You are," Flo admitted. "She makes you want to be the best version of yourself. I get it. I really do. But she's *still* trouble."

"And nobody does it better. Look, Flo, you can gloat later. Right now, I need to help my wife."

El could tell Flo wanted to have a few more "I told you so's," but thankfully resisted the urge.

"Any idea who the tough guys work for?" she asked instead.

"Maybe from his past life in Paris? Owes somebody some money there?"

"Long way to go to collect a debt. What do you make of this truck sabotage business?"

El sighed. "I don't know. It came from Lucien's mouth and we know he's a no-good, two-faced liar. But on the other hand, he *was* at the factory and he really did try to talk to Rich. Desperately too, I might add."

"You think the union would set fire to those trucks?"

"I sincerely hope not. Alice swore they'd never. And I know she wouldn't sign off on that."

"But she is a woman," Flo countered. "And men only listen to women for so long. Even women with money. What do you know about the union leads?"

"Not much," El replied. "There's a Booker Freeman who represents the Black union workers. Alice said he's a stand-up fellow. His brother's a Pullman Porter helping out on their unionization."

"Lotta that going around these days."

"Lotta bosses pulling bushwa."

"I know that's right."

"There's Ramona Westfall who represents the women and children. She and Alice don't get along too well, though Alice wouldn't say why. Then there's Ferrin Thomas. He's their accountant. Alice works with him some, for obvious reasons. But mostly she partners with Malek Polowski, who is the lead and heads up all the negotiations with Rich, which, I'm sure you'll be surprised to learn, haven't been going well."

Flo opened her eyes wide, placing a hand on her chest, and said with an over-dramatic flourish, "Richard Holloway give in to a bunch of foreign-borns and non-whites? Why, he'd die first. He'd absolutely die!"

El chuckled. "My thoughts exactly."

"So that's the answer. The negotiations have netted nothing. They have Alice's money but eventually they'll run out, or she'll see it's fruitless and stop writing checks. And if Rich is hiring scabs now . . . ?"

"Desperate men make for dangerous men. Maybe I should stop by Augusta Wilde's studio after my show tonight. Make sure she's okay."

"Not a bad idea."

And that's what El intended to do after tonight's show. Only there was a knock on her dressing room door before she could do it.

"Hold up!" she said. "I'm not decent!"

A muffled male voice replied, "Madam Watkins would like to see you."

"Madam Watkins?" Then she muttered the answer to herself, "Leslie." She called to the man on the other side of her door, "Can it wait?"

"Madam says it's urgent."

El cursed under her breath. "I'll be ready in five minutes!"

She sighed into her whiskey and placed her cigar on the lip of an ashtray. Alice wasn't the only one having trouble with menfolk these days. El and Madam Watkins were trying to solve The Leslie Charles Problem.

See, Les had hired El in the summer of 1925 on the condition that she sign a contract that guaranteed him a number of shows per year at the Oyster House. In September of 1926, Madam Watkins visited the Oyster House and caught El's show. She loved it so much, she returned on another night and afterwards, offered El a spot at Chez J.A. El didn't think twice about it. She resigned soon after, foolishly thinking Les would do the gentlemanly thing and let her go gracefully.

She should've known better.

He was going to hold her to her contract, come hell or high water. Madam Watkins and her lawyers had spent the past month looking through it to see if there was any technicality they could use as leverage. El hoped this meeting tonight meant they found it.

She also hoped this meeting would be quick, so she could check on Alice.

"Apologies for keeping you waiting," El said as she sat in one of the two plush leather chairs in front of the large cherrywood desk.

She'd just changed into a fresh white tux and walked through the classy club and the impressive, opulent lobby, where she got on a private elevator that ascended straight to Madam Watkins's penthouse suite. The male secretary—inspired, El was told, from when Madam Watkins walked in on her and Dash Parker in the Oyster House office arguing about some dead flapper and they both pretended

Dash was El's secretary—led her to Madam's equally stylish office.

Much like the lobby, the club, and El's own dressing room below, heavy green drapes and shades, gold thread and fringe, and multiple shiny silver end tables dominated the space. The one big difference? The African silhouettes that danced on the walls. According to Madam Watkins, they were painted by Richard Bruce Nugent, a newcomer to Harlem currently under the wings of Wallace Thurman, Zora Neale Hurston, and Langston Hughes. Pretty hep company, El thought. And pretty hep work. The silhouettes struck her as regal, royal even, yet slyly sensual.

Madam Watkins nodded politely from behind her desk. "Not a problem," she said. "I know how crazy things get after a show. Good crowd tonight?"

"They're good *every* night, Madam, but tonight especially."

"And how's the stage, dressing room, etcetera? Everything copacetic?"

"As copacetic as it gets."

"Great to hear."

El sat back, admiring her new boss for a moment. Tall and trim with arched brows, high cheekbones, and a sharp nose and chin, Madam Watkins painted a stunning picture. She wore a purple chiffon number with a high front and a low back. A small beret with a thin veil adorned her head. For garnish, she'd decided on long white silk gloves, a double strand of pearls, and a pair of diamond drop earrings. Not bad for a former hotel maid who learned how to invest by overhearing the stockbrokers and bankers she cleaned up after.

"So," El said. "Any news from your lawyers about the contract?"

"I recently received word from them."

"And?"

A squawk turned her head as did the strange voice.

"Bitch, bitch, goddamn bitch!"

There, in a brass cage stuck in the far corner and almost hidden by the drapes, perched a blue parrot whose head tilted from side to side, regarding her with—what? Interest? Amusement?

El pointed to it. "What the hell is that? Excuse my language, Madam."

Madam Watkins sighed. "That is . . . a friend's parrot. He's out of town for the next two weeks and his staff apparently do not like his pet. One of them calls it a 'devil bird,' I believe."

"Bitch, bitch, goddamn bitch," the bird replied.

El said, "I can see why." She turned to face Madam Watkins. "What's its name?"

"Mac."

Mac the parrot immediately said, "Hello, Rosie, how's tricks?"

"You should take him to Coney Island," El offered. "He'd make some good sugar on the boardwalk."

"No doubt. Before . . . my friend . . . got him, he used to live on the docks. Don't sailors have the most colorful vocabulary?"

"That's one way to put it."

El noticed the pauses when Madam Watkins said "my friend." She knew what kind of friend he was. Ah, so Madam Watkins had a love life. A *secret* love life. Now El wasn't the only one. Not that El intended on keeping Alice a secret from her boss. It's just that she didn't quite know how to tell her she illegally married a white woman. Madam

Watkins was a modern woman through and through, but who knew if she was *that* understanding?

"I'm trying to teach him better manners," Madam Watkins continued. "But it seems the sailor influence is too strong on him. Isn't that right, Mac?"

Mac squawked and ruffled his feathers.

Madam Watkins smiled. "We'll do our best to ignore him." She pulled out a stack of papers from the top drawer of her desk, pausing to do a quick scan, as if the contents might've magically changed from what they were before. Satisfied, she gave a single nod to herself and laid them on the desk. "Unfortunately, my lawyers couldn't find a legal loophole to break Mr. Charles's contract."

El cursed worse than the bird. "I don't believe this! That slimy little worm is gonna ruin my career!"

"Hold on, El, hold on. That's just the contract. We tried to break it and we can't. But that *doesn't* mean we don't have any options." She tapped the paper in front of her. "That's what this is."

"An option?"

"A proposal. Men like Les want two things: money and power. They'll take both, and usually do, but when push comes to shove, money by itself will do just nicely."

El put two and two together. "You're gonna buy me out of the contract."

"In a way." Madam Watkins slid the papers across the desk to El. "You are to do two weekends of farewell shows, from which Mr. Charles will receive all the profits."

El waited for more. When there wasn't, she said, "That's it?"

"That's it. I've crunched the numbers, and with a handful of special farewell events, he'll make nearly triple the money he would've made had he kept you for the year's remaining shows."

El flipped through the pages seeing columns of numbers and dollar signs. None of which made any sense to her. But she did understand the proposal and what it meant.

"I do all the work and he gets all the reward," she said.

Madam Watkins shifted in her seat. "That's one view. The other is that you play eight shows versus thirty and are free of that man forever."

"But why this way?"

"Because a woman buying a man out is an ego blow. And men? They're fragile. Like eggs. Can't jostle them too much or they'll crack."

"Yeah, and then their yolk goes everywhere."

"This is a form of buying you out of the contract in a way that lets him keep his dignity intact. And he gets a public relations moment, which if he's smart, he'll use to his advantage." She pointed to the papers in El's hand. "Take that to him tomorrow afternoon. He's expecting a response from us then."

"Why wouldn't you send one of the lawyers?"

"He requested you specifically."

El rolled her eyes. "Probably so he can gloat."

"Oh, most definitely. But let him. Let him crow and strut around with his chest puffed out like Mac over there. What matters in the end is you get what you want. Look, I had to do it too. As a woman—much less a Black woman—I couldn't own property. My late husband had to purchase it and later on, I inherited it. Even though it was *my* investments that enabled the buy. On paper, he got all the credit. I could've fought it. Could've said 'why does Pembrose get to sign the deed?' But then I asked myself, 'J.A., what do you want?' And I wanted this hotel."

"And your husband bought the property with your money before turning it over to you."

"Unofficially in life and officially in death, yes. Is it pride-wounding? A little. But what do *you* want, El? To have Mr. Charles admit he was wrong to force you to sign that contract? Or to have the freedom to play here?"

"Here." El said it without hesitation.

"Well, then. Sometimes we gotta swallow a tiny bit of our pride so we can get the full-course meal we deserve."

El glanced down at the contract. "It's what I want. Freedom." She folded the papers and slid them into her inside coat pocket. "I appreciate you negotiating this on my behalf."

"Happy to do it. We sisters must stick together."

Mac then squawked from his cage, "She'll ruin us! She'll ruin us! Bitch, bitch, goddamn bitch!"

Madam Watkins gazed wearily at the birdcage. "Mac, I'm gonna wash that beak out with a bar of soap."

12

It was almost one o'clock in the morning when El finally got to Augusta Wilde's studio. An obscene hour for most, but Alice had told El Augusta stayed up all night working on her sculptures. El doubted the union meeting would still be in progress—unless things had truly gone off the rails—but this way she could see for herself nothing bad at happened. Threadbare reasoning, she realized, but worry never made any sense.

Augusta Wilde lived on West 143rd Street in a building that looked like so many others in Harlem. Brown brick. Brown roof. Three stories tall. Half the windows lit, the other half dark. No one sat on the fire escape but the weather was getting a little too cold for that these days, especially after the sun went down.

El watched the building while she smoked her cigar, wondering if this was wise.

What if she's fine? What if I make a fool of myself?

Or worse: *what if this Wilde woman tells Alice I woke her up in the dead of night for no reason at all? And Alice thinks I don't trust her?*

But did she? Yes, she trusted Alice. It was the others she was uncertain of.

Still tittering on the knife's edge of indecision, a couple brushed past her and went up to the front door, the man and woman chatting amicably and paying her no attention. The man unlocked the door while the woman laughed. He held the door open for her and followed in after her.

El acted on impulse. She dropped her cigar and ran up the stairs to the door, catching it just in time before it slammed shut. She stepped into the building's entryway looking for the basement door.

At the end of the hallway, she found it and went down a flight of stairs as rickety as her own. Once she got to the bottom, she found a closed door. She bent slightly at the waist and placed her ear against it.

Silence.

Alright, El. It's now or never.

She raised her hand and gave a gentle knock.

She held her breath while she waited.

After a spell, there was a rattling of a chain being secured to the door and the turning of locks. The door opened a crack, revealing a Black woman's face. Freckled skin. Dark eyes. Dark brows.

"Yes?" she said.

"Miss Augusta Wilde?"

"Mrs. I was married . . . unfortunately."

El gave what she hoped was a pleasant smile. "My apologies, Mrs. Wilde. My name is El Train and—"

"I know who you are."

"You do?"

Alice told you?

Augusta nodded. "You're the new act at the Watkins Hotel that everybody's talking about."

El relaxed. "Yes, yes that's me."

"I've been meaning to catch your show, but unfortunately, the muse strikes me at late hours such as this." She furrowed her brow. "What are you doing here?"

The trickiest of questions.

"I'm here," El said, "because my good friend is Alice Holloway. She was supposed to have a meeting and I wanted to catch her before she left to see how it went. Unfortunately, I got a little tied up at the hotel and couldn't get here sooner."

"I see," Augusta said in a tone that revealed she didn't. "The meeting ended about an hour ago. Around midnight. If you're worried about Miss Holloway, she left the meeting fine. They all did."

"You mean, Malek, Booker, Ferrin, and Ramona?"

"What is it you want again?" The question was pointed but the tone was mild.

El forced a smile. "I suppose to make sure my friend is okay."

"Miss Holloway seemed to be. There was a lively discussion amongst the five of them, but they often are. Workers' rights are a sensitive business and for these folks, it's a passion."

"A passion you're supportive of."

"Of course. We're all human beings. Shouldn't we be treated as such? Even at work?"

"Perhaps especially. Well," El said. "I suppose I should let you get back to *your* business. Good night, Mrs. Wilde."

"Good night, El."

El didn't sleep very well. She kept tossing and turning, never quite getting comfortable enough to fall into that sweet oblivion. Didn't help that the wind kept battering at the windows and rattling the glass panes in their frames. Just when she thought it subsided, another gust would beat the side of the building. They'd had a nor'easter a week or so ago; were they having another one?

When light finally peeked through her curtains, she gave up trying to doze. She dressed in a houndstooth jacket and brown slacks and shoes, tying a yellow polka-dot tie around her neck and stuffing a matching handkerchief into the front breast pocket. She grabbed the proposal Madam Watkins had given her and placed it in her inside coat pocket.

A knock on the door turned her head. "Flo?"

"Yes, it's me," said the muffled voice.

El opened the door to see her friend, tired and put-out. "I take it your hot bedmate is still sick."

"Even worse than yesterday. I tried to sleep on the floor but all her sneezing and coughing and choking kept me up. I had no idea the human body could make that much snot."

El gestured to the sofa. "It's all yours. Or the bed, if you want it."

Flo was already walking towards the bedroom, waving over her shoulder. "Thank you, sis."

"Any time."

Cane in hand, cloche hat on head, El left the apartment, finding the elevator broken.

Sighing, she trudged down the rickety stairs and found the nearest diner to get coffee and a big breakfast. In the back, she found a telephone booth and asked the operator to connect her with the Holloway extension. After four tries, the operator claimed rather curtly they weren't home.

"Huh," El said to herself. That was strange. There was always somebody there, even if it was just a maid.

She sat back down at her table and drank more coffee, trying to shake off the fuzziness of no sleep. She read and reread the terms of Madam Watkins's proposal, making sure she knew every detail. At noon, she ordered lunch and afterwards, tried the Holloway extension again. This time, the operator only attempted twice.

"The residence appears not to be answering. Another attempt means another deposit."

El hung up. Where the hell was everyone? Why was there nobody at the Holloway house?

She glanced at her wristwatch and groaned. Time to meet Leslie. She shook off her confusion and concern, so she could focus on the task at hand. Madam Watkins's plan hinged on El's delivery of the proposal. And Leslie Charles would be no picnic.

"Oh my goodness, I can't believe my eyes. Come over here and give me a hug!"

El laughed as she embraced Horace Henderson, the Oyster House's doorman. He was the only person in New York who could make El feel small and dainty. He stood at almost six foot five, and his wide shoulders and chest threatened to tear the seams of the gray suit he wore. Only his fey voice betrayed any softness to him.

"I miss you, Horace," she said into his ear.

"I miss you too."

They parted and he folded his arms across his chest, those meaty paws peeking out from underneath his elbows. His face was brightened by a grin he normally never let the customers waiting in line see. Small, observant eyes took in El, not missing a thing, and liking what they saw.

He whistled. "You looking good. Madam Watkins must be treating you well."

"Like a king, Horace, like a king. Why are you here this early? Les isn't opening the club during the day, is he?"

Horace's grin fell into a frown. "No, but he's got me watching the door anyway. Closed rehearsals, he calls it. Trying out new acts to replace you and let me tell you, El, none of them are any good."

"Of course not. I was the best talent this club has ever seen. But why does he care if someone comes in while they're auditioning? He should be thrilled anyone wants to visit his place now that I'm gone."

"He's worried someone's gonna hear an act, a good one, and then steal it from him. Much like Madam Watkins did."

El rolled her eyes. "She didn't *steal* me."

"I know, I know, but that's the way Les sees it. Done wrong by a couple of women. You're all Eves and Delilahs and Jezebels, according to him."

"Of course. The so-called superior sex always blames the so-called inferior sex for their shortcomings, of which there are many, no offense. I'm sorry you got stuck with this. Everything else copacetic?"

Horace shrugged. "I can't complain, though my wife sure does. Not about me," he quickly amended. "My brother, Ambrose."

"That's the youngest, right?"

"He never did turn out right. Always got into trouble, and I don't mean the kind we all get into when we're young and dumb. I'm talking real trouble. Used to work for some nasty bootleggers before I threatened to kick his ass to

Timbuktu. I told him, 'You will not break our mama's heart by getting yourself killed in some shoot-out over bathtub gin.' Got him out of that mess before he went too deep."

"What did ol' Ambrose do that's upset your woman?"

"His girlfriend kicked him out for having a wife."

El rubbed her forehead. "Oh, Lord."

"And the wife kicked him out for not paying the rent. Strange enough, she didn't care about the girlfriend. She told me she could actually get some sleep at night and that Ambrose was lousy at it anyway." Horace shuddered. "I did not need to know that."

"I take it he's living with you now?"

"Temporarily, we hope. He's got a job, though, so as long as he doesn't spend his money everywhere, he'll be able to save up for a place of his own."

"Where's he working?"

"Lehane Family Mortuary. Funeral parlor that caters to white folks. He's the janitor who comes in after hours. I hope he doesn't futz it up and get fired. My wife's about to pull her hair out as it is."

"Speaking of men making women want to pull their hair out"—El put on an exaggerated British accent—"I have an offer for his lordship and I shan't keep him waiting."

Horace touched her shoulder. "Don't kill him now."

"Hey, now. I'm reformed." She patted her coat where the new contract was folded up. "As long as he accepts this deal, there won't be any problems."

"And if he doesn't take the deal?"

"Then get a shovel, 'cause we're burying him in the basement."

She left Horace and entered her old haunt.

The inside of the club looked the same. Silver tin ceiling, bordello-red walls, crowded clusters of round tables and chairs. A postage stamp–sized stage with a beat-up brown piano stood at the far end. On it was an awkward boy of about ten, maybe eleven, trying, and failing, to play a hep new jazz song. His fingers stumbled on the keys, while his voice was too reedy and thin to be heard over the reverberating chords. His bored eyes screamed that he'd rather be anywhere but here.

You poor boy, El thought. *Who's making you do this?*

The answer came swift and harsh. An older woman done up in her finest glad rags turned to face El and said in an accusatory voice, "Excuse me. This is a closed rehearsal."

El was startled as she registered the woman's face. This *had* to be Leslie Charles's sister. The family resemblance was too strong to ignore. The same sparkling sapphire eyes, the same short stature they compensated with heeled buckle shoes (for her) and lifts in the soles (for him). The same high-coifed hair over a window display of a face.

Same temperament, too.

El glanced at the boy on the stage. The woman's son, given the fierce protective energy radiating from her.

El replied, "Apologies, ma'am. I need to speak with Les. Mr. Charles."

The woman's sigh came out in a hiss, like a steam engine opening a valve to relieve the pressure. "He said we would not be disturbed. Well, he and I are gonna have words later."

"I promise I'll be out of your way in two shakes."

That didn't mollify the woman. El ignored her glare and made her way through the narrow club to the closed door by the side of the stage. Les' office.

El knocked and heard Les shout, "I'm busy, Aurora! Goddamn!"

"Les? It's me. El."

A pause.

"Well, well, well," Les replied. "Come on in."

13

The office hadn't changed at all. Same desk El used to kick back and place her feet upon, an act that annoyed Les to no end. Same telephone that only *he* was allowed to use. Same window overlooking the back alley.

And Les himself remained frozen in time. He wore his usual tan pinstriped suit with paisley tie and freshly shined brown leather shoes. A regular Joe Brooks—if a Joe Brooks could also be a rotten, no-good, double-crossing bastard.

He leaned on the windowsill, his hands drumming the ledge. "Do my eyes deceive me? Or is this the infamous El Train returning to where she belongs?"

El smiled so big, she thought her cheeks would burst. "Les. You look good."

"As do you. What? You surprised I can be cordial?"

"I was expecting your usual commentary on my mannish dress. You know. Calling me he-she, and the like."

"Well, I do apologize. That wasn't very kind of me."

"Indeed, it wasn't. But I appreciate your ability to keep this professional."

Les held out his hands. "Why wouldn't I? After all, this

is a professional meeting about a professional agreement *you* signed. Don't you remember that day? How you were tired of playing rent parties? Singing for chicken scratch? Competing with Tubs Walker for the best gigs?"

That name took her back. Tubs Walker was infamous on the rent party circuit. Like her, he was broad-shouldered, his wide frame clad in suits and tuxedos. Used to be if you couldn't get Tubs, you'd get El. And El got so tired of being everyone's second choice. When she auditioned for the Oyster House, she'd have done anything to get top billing. And Les exploited that.

"Excuse me," she said. "But don't *you* remember my audition, when you said you didn't want a woman, much less a woman dressed like a man, and I bet you that once I started singing and playing that anybody walking by your club would be drawn in?"

Les shifted his weight. "Yeah? What of it?"

"You remember how many people were in here before I started?"

"I don't see how—"

She held up her hand. "Five people. Only five people in this dive. And do you remember how many people were in here by the end of my little set?"

"We're getting off track—"

"Every chair and barstool had someone on it. And when I did my first show proper, it was standing room only. So don't act like you were doing me a favor. I did *you* a favor."

Leslie's face darkened. "Let's get to the point. You, *Eloise Ankins*, violated our contract when you ran off with that Watkins girl. The question is, will you still be in violation? Or have you come to your senses?"

El inwardly flinched at the use of her birth name. The

name she didn't choose and still doesn't. She felt her smile dim a wattage or two, but to her credit, she kept it up.

"That all depends on what you have to say about this." She reached into her inside pocket and brought out the papers Madam Watkins had given her. She laid them on top of Les's desk.

He gestured to them. "What's that?"

"A new agreement. Drawn up by the one and only Madam Watkins."

El watched as he picked up the papers and started paging through them.

"You'll find an entire financial analysis on the money you, Mr. Charles, will be making on my farewell performances."

"Farewell? Now hold on—"

"I won't be taking a single cent. It's all profit. All for you."

His eyes remained on the pages. "In exchange for what?"

"Releasing me from my contract."

"She's trying to buy me out. Out of the question. I will not concede to that woman. Absolutely not. Over my dead body."

If only that could be arranged.

"Look," she said, her voice softening. "I get it. You've got a reputation to uphold. An image to protect."

"Damn right."

"And think of how your reputation is going to soar by hosting *the* biggest event of the year. Do you know how many people—how many *white* people—are gonna show up to this thing? They can't get into the Watkins Hotel! I don't mean to badmouth her, but Madam Watkins is getting the losing end of this deal."

That white lie got his interest.

She kept going. "Her audience will be half of yours. No. A *quarter*."

"Why can't I have that for the rest of the year? The rest of next year too?"

"Supply and demand," El replied, repeating what she'd heard Madam Watkins say a few times before. "If I'm always here, why do people have to rush to get inside? They can just wait until the next night or the next week or the next month." She held up a finger. "But if I'm here for only two more weekends, good Lord, Les, you'll be beating 'em off with a stick! You'd have lines out the door for ages. People stacked on top of each other. And if you play it right, reporters and photographers capturing you and your club in all its glory."

"My club? Don't play me for a fool. The story is you."

"It starts as me," she said, "but it doesn't have to finish that way. I can wax poetic about this place. On stage. In my interviews. Talk about how the Oyster House is *the* club to find Harlem's hottest, newest talent. The brightest stars. And you, Mr. Charles, you will be known as the star-maker."

He lifted his chin. His faraway eyes picturing what she described. The fame. The fortune. She had him now. She knew it.

"A star-maker," he said, his voice dreamy before hardening back to reality. "But who's my next star? 'Cause it ain't my worthless nephew out there."

For damn sure not.

"You'll find someone," El said, her voice going higher like when people talk to babies. "You have a knack for picking out the shiniest, sharpest needle in the haystack."

"Don't blow smoke, El. I need a new act. I need a guaranteed winner before I can even agree to this." He handed the pages back to her. "Tell Madam Watkins I like the numbers. I need the next step. I need the next act. By this Friday."

El's smile fully dropped now. "You want me to find my replacement? In a few days?!"

"You find it. Or she does. I want a name. Friday. Non-negotiable. Otherwise, I'll see you on my stage next weekend."

El thought of several responses but said none. Instead, she turned on her heel and left the office, slamming the door in the process.

Les's nephew, who was butchering a Ma Rainey song, stopped abruptly, causing his mama—and Les's sister, presumably named Aurora—to squawk yet another objection.

El said, "Sorry about that."

Aurora replied, "This is *most* outrageous."

"I agree. What's even more outrageous is that Les—excuse me, Mr. Charles—isn't going to give your boy the chance he so deserves."

Aurora raised her hackles. "What do you mean?"

"Well, Aurora—it's Aurora, isn't it?—well, Mr. Charles is forcing me back into the spotlight so Junior there isn't going to be headlining the club anytime soon."

Aurora smacked the table with her palm. "That little shit. He promised my boy, he promised!"

El held up her hands. "I know how you feel. I too think it's just *so* unfair. I already had my break into the business, and it's time for others to have their shot. And with Leslie trying to take away opportunities from such a talented young man like your son? Why, I think it's downright immoral."

Aurora stood up, fists clenched at her sides. "If he thinks he's going to ruin my boy's dream, he's got another think coming!"

She stormed off towards the office.

As she passed the stage, she said, "Keep playin', baby," to her son. She reached the office door and barged in without knocking.

"Aurora!" Les shouted. "You gotta learn to give a man his peace."

"I'm not giving you nothing! What the hell do you think you're doing, Les?!" she said before slamming the door closed behind her.

Muffled shouts followed.

The boy on stage didn't know what to do. His eyes slid from the office door to El.

She gestured at him. "You heard your Mama. Keep playing, child."

***

El fumed all the way back home. Goddamn that Leslie. Madam Watkins made him a helluva offer and he tossed it aside because he doesn't want to do the simple legwork of finding a new act? Wasn't that his job?

No, his job is collecting sugar while other people do the work.

What do they call this? Oh yeah: management.

The initial shockwave of offense gave way to a tired dread. How was she gonna find a new act that Les would *like*, much less approve of? When she also had to save Alice from an extortionist fiancé?

The thought of Alice reignited her concern from this

morning. Why wasn't anybody at the townhouse answering?

She found her usual telephone booth on the corner of 134th and Lenox and asked the operator, for the third time today, to connect her with the Holloway extension.

The line rang and rang. No answer.

"Want me to try again?" the operator asked in a nasally voice.

"If you would, please."

The line rang again to no avail.

"One more time, if you'd be so kind," El said, ignoring the pulse hammering against her temples.

This time, the line was picked up.

A harried voice said, "Holloway residence."

"Hullo. This is Miriam King. I was hoping to speak with Miss Alice Holloway. Is she available?"

A slight pause followed by a hiccup. Or was that cough, maybe? "Umm, uh. I don't—I can't—" This poor maid, young by the sound of her, was clearly struggling to handle this simple request.

"It's alright, child. Slow down. Now. Tell me, is Miss Alice Holloway around?"

Another noise jostled El's ear. This time, there was no mistaking it. An escaped sob. "I'm sorry," the voice said tearfully. "I regret to inform you that Miss Alice Holloway is dead."

El didn't understand. "Dead?"

"Yes. She was found last night outside the factory entrance. Those grimy strikers—"

"I'm sorry, there must be some mistake."

"That's where the police found her, Miss King. I heard them say so, I'm certain of it. They've been here all night and all morning questioning—"

Suddenly the maid's voice disappeared and a man's voice—Rich's voice—cut in. "Who is this?"

El's mouth dried out. "Miriam King," she managed to say.

"Who?"

"From the Ladies' Auxiliary."

"Oh. Housewives with hobbies."

"Mr. Holloway—"

"I must apologize for my staff. They've been speaking out of turn and not practicing the discretion I demand."

A brief hope filled her chest. "So Miss Holloway isn't dead?"

"That is none of your goddamn business."

"I'm her friend, Mr. Holloway. As her friend, I'm entitled to know if anything has happened to her."

"You're not *entitled* to anything."

El squeezed her eyes shut. "Please, Mr. Holloway," she said, trying hard to keep the tears from her voice. "*Did* something happen to her?"

Dear God, please let this be a mistake. Please. Please!

She heard Rich sigh over the line.

"Yes," he said. "Alright? Yes. Alice is . . . she's dead."

BEFORE THE ARREST

14

El found the first newsstand she could find on her street. None of the papers mentioned Alice Holloway's death. But these were the morning editions; the evening editions hadn't yet been released.

Until then, what? She glanced at her wristwatch. Only a little past three o'clock.

It's not true. What Rich said is not true.

But what if it is? asked another voice.

No, no, no. Don't you start! Alice isn't dead.

El went to another newsstand on her block. They told her the same as the last place, that the evening papers would be coming later. Though they gave her a time: around five o'clock.

"Well, what the hell am I supposed to do until then?" she barked.

"I don't know, ma'am," replied the newsstand owner.

"Don't call me ma'am!"

She couldn't breathe. Couldn't think. Could barely see. Her heart hammered in her chest like a bass drum.

"You okay?" the newsstand owner asked. "You need help getting home?"

Home was the last place El wanted to go. Flo was there, and Flo would ask what was wrong the moment she saw El's face. Once the words left El's mouth, they'd make this horrible thing true.

It is true, El.

No, it isn't!

"Ma'am?"

El whirled around and glared at him. "I said, don't call me ma'am."

He cleared his throat. "Pardon me. You don't mind my saying so, you look like you could use a drink."

"Now that—" She stopped. "That, sir, is a great idea. Thank you. You got a place in mind?"

He directed her to one nearby underneath a hardware store. There, she sipped whiskey in a darkened corner and told herself this was all some big mistake. A cruel joke put on by Rich and the staff. Or maybe Alice faked her death to get away from Lucien. Though why wouldn't she tell El?

She's gone. You know she is.

No, she's not! Now shut up!

Hours passed in that fever dream state where it felt like forever but also felt like five seconds. Soon enough, her wristwatch said a quarter to five.

She returned to the newsstand she'd left, ready to be there when the truck arrived.

"You're early," the owner said.

"I intended to be."

El lit up a cigar and puffed, a highly transgressive act. Women weren't supposed to smoke in public.

Huh, we women aren't supposed to do a lot of things, according to men.

The newsstand owner shook his head at her but thankfully didn't comment. She smoked, watching the sun slip behind the buildings and beneath the asphalt horizon of the streets.

At about ten minutes past five, the larger headlights of a truck loomed in the distance. El's eyes fixed on it, willing it to be the delayed newspaper delivery. It took its sweet time but eventually pulled to the curb. El's heart leapt at the company name painted on the side of the hull: HARLEM DAILY NEWS.

The back door opened, and a man jumped out. She went straight to him.

"Excuse me, sir, I need your latest paper."

He turned, adjusting his cap on his head. He was older, about forty, his brow flecked with gray. "Now hold on there. I need to deliver these to the newsboys."

"I understand that but there's something I need—I have to know."

"Another two minutes isn't going to kill you."

Yes, it damn well will!

El didn't back down. "Have you taken a look at the headlines?"

He bent down and picked up the first large stack of papers. "I have." He leaned his head back and whistled at the boys at the newsstand. "C'mon now, hot off the presses!" The boys advanced forward.

"Was there anything in there about the Holloways?"

The boys pushed their way in between her and the man, their greedy hands reaching for the stacks he tossed their way.

"There's always something about the Holloways ever since that strike," the man replied. "Today's no different."

The boys took the stacks and ran back over to the news-stand. Excited chatter quickly followed.

El asked, "Was there anything about Alice Holloway?"

The man stopped what he was doing and placed a hand on his hip. "You trying to get a story for free?"

El reached into her pocket and pulled out two pennies. "They're yours if you'll tell me if there's anything in there about her."

The man gave her a curious look. Shaking his head at himself, he took the two pennies and handed her one copy of the paper. "On page two."

El's heart sank as she took it, the pages still warm from the presses. "What happened?"

The man replied, "Someone shot her at the factory last night."

El's body went numb as she read the story in the same diner from this morning. A coffee cooled beside her, untouched, as she went over the details again and again.

The body of Alice Holloway, age 25, was discovered at 3:34 A.M. this morning when an anonymous call came into the precinct at about 3:15 A.M. The caller said they'd heard shots fired at the Holloway Paper Box Factory. When the police arrived, they found Alice Holloway sprawled at the entrance. She'd been shot once in the chest. The body had been sent to Bellevue for further examination. The police's only comment was their condolences to the Holloway family and their vow to find the killer and bring him to justice.

El's mind couldn't stop picturing what could've happened. Alice at the factory in the dark, trying to get away. The killer standing in front of her, blocking her exit. The gun in the killer's hand. Raising it up. Aiming it. And firing.

El winced at the imagined sound of the shot. Was Alice scared? Did it hurt? Did she know she was dying?

I knew something bad was gonna happen. I knew it!

This damnable strike. Her damnable brother. And that snake Lucien Laurent. All of them received her wrath equally. As far she was concerned, she would burn each and every one of their worlds *down*.

A fresh wave of fury filled her entire body. She barely made it to the WC before she vomited for a full minute while tears poured down her face. Her chest heaved, working overtime but unable to keep up with the level of crying that had now overtaken her.

When everything finally ebbed, she sniffed, her vision clearing. A gentle knock on the door roused her.

"Miss?" a small voice asked. "Miss, are you okay in there?"

The waitress.

"I'm copacetic, baby," she replied. "I'll be, uh, I'll be out in a minute."

She went to the sink to wash out her mouth and splash water on her face. A strange calm descended upon her and with it, a cool detachment and a startling clarity. Someone killed Alice. The police likely won't catch who did it— they'd be too busy framing the easiest patsy they could find. Not to mention they didn't know about Alice's involvement in the strike nor Lucien's extortion. No, if Alice's killer was to be caught, El had to be the one to catch them.

Back in the diner, she reread the newspaper again, this time slower and with more attention to detail. Alice's whereabouts prior to the anonymous telephone call were unaccounted for after 11:00 p.m. when the household staff saw her leave the townhouse. (El, of course, knew she went to Augusta Wilde's for the emergency meeting with the union strike leads.) Rich spent the evening alone in his office where he was on the telephone with several business associates before retiring to bed at close to 1:00 a.m. By 4:00 a.m., he'd been woken up by the police and told the news.

The newshawk speculated several theories for the crime without landing on a single one. Some of the evidence suggested this was a robbery gone wrong, since her purse had been emptied and her blue velour overcoat with fur collar and lining, (*which always looked so damn good on her*), was missing. Of course, there was the factory strike to contend with and the newshawk wondered if one or more of the strikers was responsible. Rich certainly seemed to think so in his one statement to the press. Lastly, the French aristocrat and Alice's fiancé Lucien Laurent got a mention, the newshawk pondering if the couple had a falling out, though Mr. Laurent could not be reached for comment.

The one detail about the crime scene that struck El as odd was Alice being called "unarmed." That didn't make sense. She told El she was carrying her Colt .32 with her that night, so where was it?

The killer must've taken it, El answered herself.

But why?

I don't know.

She signaled the waitress for her check.

The waitress objected. "But you didn't touch your coffee."

"I'll pay for it all the same."

The waitress shrugged and took El's coin, thankfully giving her no further argument. El needed to move, to get out of here, to go someplace.

And where are you going?

You know where I'm going.

You sure that's a good idea?

Probably not but what else do I have to lose? I've already lost everything.

When El stepped back out onto the street, night time had fully arrived. The streets were drenched in charcoal and punctuated by the round white lights of automobiles ratting and humming up and down the avenue. The sky above was a dark navy blue. No stars yet and only a sliver of a moon. It was Wednesday night, her one night off from performing at Chez J.A. Which meant she had all evening to get some answers.

She lit up a cigar to wash the foul taste of her sick out of her mouth and started walking uptown. Since their biggest financial benefactor would no longer be writing their checks, she figured there'd be another emergency meeting of the Holloway Paper Box Factory union strike leads.

And El figured it was high time she met them.

15

When El arrived at Augusta Wilde's building, she found the front door propped open. Not very security-minded, these tenants. She entered and traversed the hallway and stairs until she arrived at Augusta's studio door. She paused, listening. Muffled voices murmured behind the door. Good. They were here.

She knocked loudly and the murmuring abruptly stopped. Silence stretched like a held breath. Eventually, she heard shuffling feet and the familiar rattling of the security chain. The locks turned. Once again, Augusta opened the door just a crack, her freckled face peering out.

"El? What are you doing here?"

"Evening, Mrs. Wilde. Apologies for barging in like this, but I, uh, I assume you've heard about Alice Holloway."

"Oh. Your friend. I am so sorry. It's just terrible. She was a nice person. Had a good heart."

"Thank you. I appreciate that." El swallowed the large lump in her throat that threatened to suffocate her.

Come on, now. Get to it!

"Mrs. Wilde, I need to have a conversation with the union leads."

"I'm sorry, but you must be mistaken—"

"I know they're in there. I heard them through the door. Now I'm not here to make trouble"—*unless one of them killed her*—"and I'm not connected with Alice's brother Rich in any way. But I need to know what happened during and after last night's meeting. For my own peace of mind."

Augusta studied her through the crack in the door. "She was a good friend?"

Tears threatened to well up in her eyes, but El blinked them down. "The best," she said, the tightness of her voice betraying her.

Augusta nodded and closed the door. El heard the rattle of the chain being undone. The door opened again and this time, El saw all of Augusta Wilde. A modest woman. Her hands were stained with red clay but she'd somehow managed not to leave rusty fingerprints over the plain white housedress she wore. Her hair was tied back and secured with several pins. Everything about her was practical for the purposes of her art, not vanity.

"Come in, please," Augusta said.

El thanked her and entered the studio.

Augusta stepped out of the way and El jolted at the sight of a giant plaster bust of a Black man's head. He stared at El, his blank eyes opened as wide as his mouth. The facial features were still being formed—the outline of his nose, the bridge of his brow, and the curve of his cheek—but they lacked definition. All except that mouth, which, to El, looked like it was frozen in mid-scream.

Augusta closed the front door, securing it again. She said over her shoulder, "You don't have to be afraid of Darius."

El inched away from the silent, screaming man. "Who, this?"

"Yes," Augusta replied, turning to face El. "I name all my models while I work on them. Not necessarily the names of the men or women who pose for me, mind you. Sometimes it works out that way, but as I mold them, their spirits reveal themselves to me and whisper their true names." Augusta pointed to Darius. "The man who posed was named Theo but that didn't feel right to me. While I was shaping his eyes, I heard a voice whisper to me 'Darius.' I said the name aloud, and it fit. Then I said, 'Nice to meet you, Darius,' and the two of us have been friends ever since."

"I hear you about the names. The one I was born with didn't feel right to me either until I said out loud 'El Train.'"

"Names are a powerful thing. To name a thing, even oneself—perhaps *especially* oneself—is to reclaim that power. To own it and shape it."

"You speak the truth, Mrs. Wilde."

El took in their surroundings. Only one source of light burned ahead of them, leaving the entry way in varying shades of shadow. The wood floor was covered with stained tarpaulins. Wooden crates and boards braced dozens of works-in-progress. Bust after bust, sculpture after sculpture, many of them El's height or taller. Men, women, children in various poses in various stages of completion. Sometimes only the limbs were done, disembodied arms and legs thrashing about. El felt certain that in the daylight hours, this room would be beautiful. Inspiring, even. But tonight, when she had to question people about the murder of her wife, the sculptures were grotesque, ghoulish. Haunting.

"Mrs. Wilde," El said. "Last night after the meeting ended, did you see Miss Holloway leave with anybody?"

"They all left at the same time, and I didn't follow them up to the street. Once they passed through this door, I couldn't say one way or the other what happened."

"Did Miss Holloway mention anything to you in passing?"

Augusta sadly shook her head. "I'm sorry, El. She only thanked me and left." She gestured to the other side of the studio where the light blazed. "I'll take you to Malek and the others."

She led El through the sculpted, nightmarish shapes until they came upon an open space lit by a bulb on a chain hanging above their heads. Four figures sat in a circle: two white men, one of whom El recognized as Malek Polowski from the picket line yesterday, a Black man, and a white woman. The three men glanced at her with interest while the woman glared.

Alice made the formal introductions: Malek, of course, followed by Ferrin Thomas (the other white man), Booker Freeman (the Black man), and Ramona Westfall (the white woman).

"El is here," Augusta explained, "because she is—was, I'm so sorry—a good, good friend to Alice Holloway."

"Alice has—had many friends," Ramona said. "Not all of them get an invitation to this meeting." She looked to El like a raven. Thick black hair tied up with black rhinestone barrettes, a sharp beak of a nose over a pointed chin, and a navy dress so dark, it might as well have been black.

"Ramona," Malek said. He still wore the flat cap and threadbare white work shirt El saw yesterday at the picket line. Up close, his face held more lines around the eyes and mouth, his skin paler, if that could've been possible, and his eyes even more dark-lidded and heavy with bags.

Augusta went on as if Ramona hadn't uttered such a

rude greeting. "If Alice felt comfortable telling El about you all, then I'm confident El is a safe person to know this secret."

"Yes," Ferrin said. "Alice was most prudent about these meetings. She wouldn't blab to just anybody." He appeared the youngest of the four and the most shy. Brown hair combed unassumingly to the side, his eyes never quite meeting hers or anyone else's. Boring gray slacks, suspenders, and tie, a white shirt with faint wrinkles. He wore circular glasses that he kept pushing up the bridge of his nose while his right knee bounced up and down.

"So we hope," Ramona countered.

El cut in. "I understand the caution, but I have no ties to her brother, nor any financial stake in the Holloway Factory. I am here because my friend is dead. Now she told me she was calling an emergency meeting last night." She looked to Malek. "Did that meeting occur, Mr. Polowski?" She already knew the answer from Augusta Wilde, but she wanted to test the truthfulness of this group.

Malek regarded her for a moment before nodding.

Ramona still had her guard up. "Why would Alice tell you about the emergency meeting?"

"Because I told her about the damage squads."

Booker smiled. "Ah, so you're the one."

El turned to him. Booker Freeman was the epitome of confidence. He sat calm, collected, still. His immaculate dark hair was pomaded down, a chin smooth as a baby's bottom, and warm brown eyes that welcomed everything they saw. Impeccably put together, his pressed brown suit held creases so sharp, they could cut steak.

"Yes, Mr. Freeman," El replied, "I'm the one."

"You caused quite a stir."

"Not my intention. It wasn't even my intention to find that information out. It sort of fell into my lap."

Augusta said, "Well, I'm sure you have much to talk about. I'll go into my bedroom and give you all some privacy. Remember, I'm out of town next week. If you intend to use my space for meetings, please use the spare keys and lock up when you leave."

Malek touched the brim of his cap. "We shall, Mrs. Wilde. We are most grateful."

They were silent until she left the room and heard the door close.

Malek focused on El. "I am truly sorry about your friend. It is an unfortunate tragedy."

"Well, now, that is the word for it, Mr. Polowski. *Unfortunate*." El put her hands on her hips. "What happened last night?"

Booker shrugged. "We held a meeting."

Ramona said, "Are we seriously going to tell her everything? We don't know who this woman is!"

"I know her. Anyone in Harlem who likes good music does."

"I don't care if she's a well-known musician, Booker, I care if she's going to sell her story to the newspapers, to the police, or worse, to Rich himself."

Ferrin adjusted his glasses. "Malek, Ramona has a point. We are in a vulnerable position right now. The last thing we need is more, uh, attention."

Malek kept his curious gaze on El. "Do you swear that you will keep the same strict confidence as Alice once did?"

Funny, El thought to herself. *Yesterday, I made a cabbie swear an oath to silence and here I am being asked to do the same damn thing.*

She held up her right hand, as if she were about to testify in a court of law. "I do."

Ramona scoffed. "I can't believe this."

"Believe it, Mrs. Westfall."

"*Miss.* A married woman isn't allowed to keep her job."

"Duly noted." El watched the four people sitting before her. "Were you all hiring damage squads?"

"Absolutely not," Malek replied. "When Alice asked us the very same question, we were outraged. We do not believe in violence of any sort."

"And did Alice believe you?"

"It took some convincing, but in the end, yes. Once we agreed to let her look at the financials so she could see for herself that there were no unauthorized payments."

Atta girl, El thought.

"And did you give her the books?"

Ferrin said, "Not yet. I was going to give them to her today, as a matter of fact."

"And you didn't cook the books, Ferrin? To hide those payments from her?"

"El," Booker said. "The union made it clear we are not to engage in any destructive tactics. It would invite bad press and give more credibility to Mr. Holloway's claims."

"Which are . . . ?"

Malek answered that one. "That unionization is a communist plot born of anti-American fanatics. He also went on to say that if unions like ours succeeded, it would lead to further attacks against men of industry, disrupt the economy, and prevent much-needed progress and growth."

Ramona added, "Don't forget destabilizing society by emboldening the poor, the immigrant, and the criminal."

El quipped, "Which, in Rich's mind, are one and the same."

Malek asked, "How did *you* find out about the damage squads?"

"From Lucien Laurent."

Ramona sneered. "Alice's fiancé? Excuse me, *former* fiancé? You're chewing gum, lady."

Malek ignored her. "How did he come to this information?"

"He *says* that he was in Saint Nicholas Park for an evening stroll and overhead a group of tough guys talking about setting the trucks on fire. And before you ask, he says he didn't overhear names or get a good look at them."

"Do you believe him?"

El had been asking herself the same question. "He definitely found out *something*. Whether it was this sabotage stuff or something else remains to be seen. Otherwise he wouldn't have been at the factory during that little ruckus with the scabs yesterday."

Ramona frowned. "How do you know he was there?"

"'Cause I stopped him from going into the factory."

"And why were *you* there?"

Booker shook his finger at El. "I *thought* I saw you through the crowds." He grinned. "You're sort of hard to miss."

Ramona said to the others, "See? I'm telling you, she's a spy. We should get her out of here—"

"I was there," El interrupted, "to stop Lucien from talking to Rich."

"Oh yeah? Why would you do that? Why would a—a night club singer care about a factory strike?"

"Because I was afraid he was going to tell Rich about Alice's involvement with it. I went there to protect her. And to protect all of you."

"Ha! Tell that to Sweeney."

Malek cleared his throat. "I take it you intercepted him there? And that's when he told you what he heard?"

El turned to him. "Yes. He said some things out loud he shouldn't have, and I had to save him from some angry picketers. I told him he owed me and that's what I would take in return."

"You forced him."

"Not . . . exactly."

Ferrin said, "But he was coerced. Coerced people often embellish or say the first thing that comes to mind to get out of the situation. This damage squad stuff, for example. Which means your first inclination might still be correct, that he found out about Alice."

Ramona groaned. "If that's true, Ferrin, then we're really in the soup. Rich will make us the prime suspects, saying we killed her for her money."

Booker muttered, "He's already suggesting that to anyone who will listen."

"Well," El said, taking advantage of the natural flow of their conversation, "let's talk about Alice's murder. Where were you all last night? You got alibis that'll get the pounders off your backs?"

Malek replied, "No, unfortunately. After the meeting ended a little after midnight, we all went home. Booker was with his wife and children. Ferrin and Ramona with their roommates."

Ferrin coughed. "And they can say we asked our wife or roommates to lie for us, so pretty flimsy."

"As for me," Malek continued, "I was by myself in the room I rent."

El said, "Great. No alibis, essentially."

Booker sighed. "That about sums it up."

Ramona pursed her lips. "I knew having Alice involved

would be trouble. Didn't I tell you all? She'd be nothing but bad news."

El looked at her. "You don't like Alice very much."

"A spoiled rich girl playing union? No, no, I don't—didn't like her. I sure as hell didn't trust her."

"What did she do to earn your distrust?"

"For one thing, she told you about us. Which says to me that she told others. I don't care what you say, Ferrin. For another thing, all she did was write checks and stupid thank-you notes." Ramona rolled her eyes. "How high-society of her."

"Thank-you notes?"

"Yup. A waste of time. We need to enact real change and she's writing debutante letters."

El looked to Malek for an explanation.

He replied, "Since the strike was going on for so long, Alice wanted to give people encouragement and hope. She wrote them letters. All one hundred of them. She sent them a week and a half ago." He focused on Ramona. "They were very well received."

Ramona averted her gaze.

Why didn't she tell me about this? El thought before answering herself: *This was right when I started working at the Watkins and she was dealing with that goddamn Lucien.*

She asked, "How'd she know who and where to send them to?"

Booker replied, "When we began the strike, she went in and copied the most recent payroll records. Even then she knew she wanted to make sure her donations matched the pay of each worker."

Ferrin muttered, "She should've come to me for them. I'm the accountant, after all."

"Uh huh," El said, wondering what to ask next. "Did

Alice say where she was going after the meeting? Did she give any indication she'd be going to the factory?"

All four shook their heads.

"Any idea why she was there?"

Not one of them knew.

Dammit.

They were either stonewalling her or they were truly as in the dark as her.

A thought. What had Alice said to her when El telephoned yesterday? That she had to meet with someone about some sort of confusion. When El asked the group this, she got more blank stares.

"Is that all?" Ramona snidely asked, once everyone finished shaking their heads to El's questions.

"For now," El replied sweetly.

"Good. Booker, kindly escort her out. We have other business to discuss that is not her concern."

16

As Booker led El through the nightmarish limbs and faces of Augusta Wilde's creations, she muttered, "Tell me something, brother. Is there anything strange going on?"

"Don't know what you mean."

"Yes, you do. That's the queerest group of people I ever saw working together."

"A cause like this makes unlikely bedfellows."

"Yeah, but there's something else. I know the negotiations haven't been going well, but tensions seem unusually high, don't they?"

Booker didn't reply.

El tried again. "Please. Alice told me about the emergency meeting and I wanted to come with her for support. She shrugged it off. And it turns out, she shouldn't have, because someone killed her that night. If I was here with her, I could've—I don't know—stopped whatever was about to happen."

They paused at the studio's front door, speaking in low tones so the others couldn't overhear.

"You feel guilty," he said.

"Wouldn't you?"

"Yeah, I suppose I would."

El asked, "Do you have any idea why she was at that factory in the middle of the night?"

"She didn't say anything about that. But . . . "

"But what? C'mon, Booker. Help a sister out."

Booker chewed on a thought or two before finally saying, "She asked me about a name."

"What was the name?"

"Alice is more than a friend to you, isn't she?"

El felt her cheeks burn. "That's neither here nor there."

"The pounders won't think that."

El made her voice steely. "You gonna blackmail me now, Booker?"

"No, not at all. I'm just trying to get a feel for what's going on here. Frankly, I don't care who does what to whom. But you coming in here like a—well—runaway locomotive, it makes me curious, is all."

"Well, your curiosity's satisfied," El said flatly. "The name, Booker. What was the name?"

Booker leaned in close. "Raymond Price."

"Raymond Price? Who's he?"

"Don't know. Never heard that name before."

Back on the street, El considered her next move. This name business was curious. Who was Raymond Price? And why was Alice asking about him?

As for the union strike leads themselves, their answers were a mixture of truth and lies, she knew that much. But how to tell which was which? She believed their denials of hiring the damage squads. The four of them didn't have the same ruthlessness as Rich (which, in her opinion, put them at a distinct disadvantage). She didn't believe, however, that they didn't have a clue as to why Alice was at the factory. To fetch something for them? To grab records? To make sure the trucks weren't being vandalized? Maybe her presence there nothing to do with them but rather her brother. Did Rich summon her there and things got out of hand? The papers mentioned Rich was home all night but he and his staff could've lied about that. And Rich had a gun and a willingness to fire it, as El witnessed herself.

How am I going to get his alibi? she wondered.

That was stickier.

What was less sticky was Lucien Laurent. He was the next suspect on her list. She walked until she found a telephone booth and asked the operator for the Hotel Eudora. The front desk said Mr. Laurent was not in for the evening. She disconnected the call, called back, and using her Miriam King voice, asked to be connected to the head porter. It wasn't Isaiah Scott—he must've clocked out by now. But by lowering her voice to a gruff gravel and pretending to be Leslie Charles wanting to know where Lucien Laurent was this very minute because that little frog owes him money, (and eventually promising the porter a free night of drinks at the Oyster House), she learned the whereabouts of the extorting fiancé.

"Gotcha, you son of a bitch," El muttered, hanging up the telephone. "Time to get some answers."

Pearlie's was running on all sixes by the time El showed up. The smacks of cue balls and the rattling of pockets filled the air, as did cigarette smoke and woodsy cologne. Conversations and laughter spiced the proceedings, giving the parlor a jovial vibe that would only get more jolly as the games—and the liquor—continued late into the night and likely into the early hours of the next morning.

At the base of the staircase to the second floor stood the griffin, arms crossed, lips locked in his usual grimace.

"I'm here to see Pearlie," El said, raising her voice to be heard over the din.

"He's busy," replied the griffin. Damn, his lips *still* didn't move when he talked.

"So am I, which is why I don't want to be kept waiting."

"Come back another night."

"No can do. The time is now. Go get him."

His brow furrowed into deep, angry lines. "You think you can boss me around?"

"Yes, as a matter of fact, I can."

They stared at one another—El, keeping her face calm and collected; the griffin, pouting and frowning. She could practically see the gears turning in his head. Should he throw her out? Should he call the pounders?

What ended their standoff was a set of stomping feet on the stairs and Pearlie's voice saying, "I'll be right back! I just gotta get something from behind the bar—El! What are you doing here? Interested in a Midnight Game?"

El slid her gaze from the griffin to Pearlie, who stood behind him dressed in a flawlessly tailored tuxedo. "As a matter of fact, I am. If you've got a certain player back there."

Pearlie's grin dimmed. "Uh huh. And who's the player?"

"Lucien Laurent."

"Who says he's here?"

"Doesn't matter. We both know he is, and we both know why I gotta talk to him."

"I don't know what the hell you're—oh. This is about—"

"Yes, it's about that."

Pearlie pulled at his lips. "I can't let you up. I can't, El," he added before she could object. "You're gonna cause trouble."

"I'm not gonna do anything but talk to him."

"Yeah, and that's how it starts. Then it ends with me cleaning up a mess."

"Why you being so difficult? Is this about those tough guys looking for him?"

"I told you, they haven't been back. And it's not about Lucien's nonsense; it's about yours."

El held up her hand, the second time she's had to swear tonight. "I promise on a stack of Bibles I will not harm a single hair on that man's head."

"I'm gonna need more than just a promise." He rubbed his finger and thumb together. Of course.

"Lucky for you," El said, "I've got a pocketful of lettuce."

"Feed me some, then."

El reached into her pocket and pulled out a dollar. She reached around the griffin and placed it into Pearlie's outstretched palm. "Here's your leaf, little rabbit."

She couldn't swear to it, what with the room being so noisy, but she thought she heard the griffin growl at her.

Pearlie pocketed the dollar and put a hand on the griffin's shoulder. "Don't let her get to you. She's all bark and no bite."

That's what you think.

Pearlie gestured to El. "Come on up."

The griffin stood aside.

El followed Pearlie up the stairs and down the hall to the second door. He opened it and said, "Good luck."

She went inside the secret game room. Pearlie didn't join her—likely wanted nothing to do with what was about to transpire—and shut the door behind her.

The room was a simple rectangle with a billiard table in the center and a glass lamp that looked like a Tiffany hanging above it. The surrounding walls were done up halfway in mahogany wood before giving way to a pale green wallpaper with a gold diamond pattern. A painting hung on the wall to her left, some still life of fruit in a bowl. A round end table stood in one corner, covered in glasses carrying varying liquid quantities. Mostly brown liquor by the looks of it. A rack of pool cues took up the main wall directly in front of El while dark leather chairs pressed up against the far walls to her right and left.

Dressed in a black tuxedo, Lucien Laurent was lining up a shot to the far corner pocket. With a smooth motion, he slid the pool cue forward, striking the cue ball. It knocked the nine ball into the pocket and gently bounced off the corner, setting up another shot.

The other player was a Creole-looking man in a flashy cake-eater suit of the bright blue persuasion. He grimaced as Lucien easily made the shot.

Lucien glanced up at El. "Ah, *Mademoiselle* El Train, isn't it? Funny meeting you here."

El shrugged, nonchalant. "I heard you were in the neighborhood."

"Heard. Is someone keeping tabs on me?" He walked around to the other side of the table.

"Yeah. Me."

"How very interesting." He gestured to the other player. "I'll be finished with him shortly and then we can talk."

The Creole man smirked.

Lucien's face was the model of concentration. He weighed his options, bent down, lined up the pool cue, and soon two more balls rocketed into the side and corner pockets respectively. All he had left was the eight ball.

"Right corner pocket," he called and proceeded to knock it in effortlessly.

The Creole man groaned and handed over a handful of dollars.

"Thank you very much, *monsieur*," Lucien said.

The man didn't say much, just downed his drink and left, closing the door behind him. Now it was only El and Lucien.

"O *mon dieu*, I think I may have ruined his evening," Lucien remarked.

"How much sugar did you take off him?"

He shrugged. "Ten dollars."

El whistled. "Hey, did you get your motorcar back unscathed?"

He groaned. "By the time I got back to the factory, someone had towed it. Now I have to figure out where to go pick it up, pay the fine. What a nuisance!"

He seems more upset about his damn car than he does Alice!

"Life is one tragedy after another, isn't it? I assume you've heard the news."

Lucien glanced away from her. "About Alice? Yes."

"You sound real broken up over it."

"Oh, I am. *Mademoiselle*, I must tell you, this is a most terrible thing."

"Especially since she died without giving you her money."

"*Oui*." He chuckled at her reaction. "What? You Americans. You're so afraid to speak the truth. You're like little children always hoping to please Mama and Papa. Why deny what is so obviously the truth?"

"Tact, for one thing."

"Tact is overrated. And it wastes so much time."

"Fine with me. 'Cause I'm real short on patience and my time is expensive."

He smirked but didn't say anything.

"How'd you find out?" she asked. "In the papers?"

"I went over to the Holloway residence to have lunch with her. When I walked up, I saw all these policemen around. The maids were crying. It was really quite dramatic. Her brother Richard was barking orders at everyone, including the police." Lucien leaned forward on his cue stick. "He even had the temerity to suggest *I* had something to do with it. Can you believe it?"

"I can, actually. Where were you when Alice was killed?"

The question surprised him. "That is what you're here about?"

"Can you think of anything better?"

"No, I suppose not. But I am curious. Why are you so interested in Alice's unfortunate death?"

"People keep throwing around the word."

"What, 'death?'"

"'Unfortunate.'"

He lifted his chin. "Who is Alice to you? Really?"

El had to tread carefully here. This man extorted at the drop of a hat and he knew Alice was a lesbian. It wouldn't take long for him to put two and two together.

She said the first lie that occurred to her. "She was an audience member of mine. Back at the Oyster House where

I used to perform. We'd chat after the show and slowly over time, we became friends."

In reality, nothing about their courtship had been slow. El walked into the Drip Dry one night for a pick-me-up and spotted Alice from across the room, dressed in a suit like El's and smoking that cigar. It took them exactly one verbal exchange for them to realize what was happening between them.

"*Careful,*" Alice had said, gesturing to El's glass. "*This whiskey is coffin varnish.*"

"*That's 'cause you don't know to ask Vi for her secret stash,*" El had replied.

"*Oh? Is it expensive?*"

"*A little, but life's too short.*"

"*Especially to put bad things on your tongue.*"

Good Lord, the gumption on that girl! "*Uh huh. Well, what say we get some of that good stuff on yours.*"

"*Is that here? Or elsewhere?*"

"*Hey, girl. You better pump the brakes before you run your car off the road.*"

Alice had then taken a drag on her cigar. "*Didn't you say life was too short? And I'd love to drive around those curves of yours . . .* "

Lucien watched El carefully. "An audience member. A —what do you Americans call 'em?—a fan? And that somehow makes you care about her death?"

"Why is caring about someone a strange act?"

"Because you Americans don't tend to do that."

"You know, if you dislike us so much, you can leave. Go back to ol' Paree."

Lucien tapped the cue stick. "I think I know why you care."

Shit.

Looked like he put two and two together and got four.

"Alright, then," she said. "Well, *I* know that you forced her into an engagement she didn't want so you can stay in this country and spend her family money."

"My, my. I didn't think you'd say that part out loud."

El gave him a mean smile. "Tact is overrated."

He chuckled. "I'll tell you what, *mademoiselle*. I'll play you for the answers to your questions."

"Say again?"

He patted the side railing of the table. "*Oui*. If you win, I'll answer where I was the night Alice died and whatever else you want to know. And if I win, you tell me all about you and Alice. Do we have a deal?"

How badly do I want to know his alibi?

Very badly. Very, very badly.

She gestured to the green felt. "Rack 'em up."

17

With an expert hand, Lucien lined up all the object balls in the triangular rack and rolled them down to the foot of the table, lining up the point to the foot string. He removed the rack from the object balls, careful not to disturb their organized pattern.

El selected her cue from the wall, weighing it in her hand. It would do. She went over to the head of the table, placing the cue ball in the center just before the head string. She chalked her cue stick.

Lucien stood at the foot of the table. "I should tell you that Pearlie just had the felt replaced. The balls spin fast on it."

"Appreciate the warning," El replied as she placed her hand on the head rail and lined up her shot, aiming the cue ball at the object balls. She was in the "kitchen" of the billiard table—*huh, the only time I'm ever in a kitchen*—and got her breathing under control. That's what her Uncle Jim taught her. Always be sure to breathe. Otherwise you'll futz up the shot.

She struck the cue ball and it flew forward, smacking

into the object balls with a resounding *crack!* The balls spread out with two solid balls going into the corner pockets and a third bouncing off the foot rail and coming to rest in front of the center pocket.

Lucien arched an eyebrow. "Nice break."

"Thank you." El went over to the side rail, bent down, lined up her shot, and got the third solid into the center pocket. The next shot would be trickier, as her solids were blocked by the stripes. "By the way, did you end up telling Mr. Holloway about the damage squads?"

"I did not. He's been distracted by Alice's death."

"I think it's because he suspects you."

El knew she didn't have a clear shot, so she went to the other side of the table hoping to place the cue ball in a less hospitable place for Lucien. She knocked a solid in front of a stripe and smiled as the cue rested behind a mix of balls with no clear way to a pocket.

Lucien smirked. "Not anymore. As you said before, I don't get her money, so I do not benefit from her untimely demise."

"Unless you wanted to hock her blue velour overcoat. The one with the fur collar and lining?"

The one I gave her.

"You're reaching," he said. "A gentleman as distinguished as I would never stoop so low to petty theft. Besides, Rich now thinks it's one of the union leads."

"Why would he think that?"

"He thinks they're anarchists. Militant Robin Hoods hellbent on stealing from him, the rightful rich, and giving to the undeserving poor."

"You mean, the fortune he inherited and didn't work for?"

"The very same."

Without seeming to study the table, Lucien bent down, and shot the cue ball forward, knocking the cluster of object balls. Despite the odds, two stripes fell in.

El asked, "Was that story of you overhearing a coupla tough guys in Saint Nicholas Park bushwa? Or the Bible?"

Lucien slinked around to the other side rail at the foot of the table. "You mean, the truth or a lie? The truth." He lined up his next shot. "They said the Holloway Paper Box Factory very distinctly."

Smack!

The cue ball hit a stripe in.

"Nice shot," El said.

"*Merci.*" Lucien circled the table again. "How long have you been performing?"

"Oh, since childhood, I guess. I can't remember *not* playing."

"What do you play?"

"Piano. I also sing too."

"And you are successful?"

"Very." El held up a warning finger. "But you're not gonna get my sugar, mister."

"Sugar?"

"Money."

"Ah." Lucien struck the cue ball again and missed. "I am envious of people who work on the stage for a living."

"Most people are." El re-chalked her stick and searched for the next shot.

"You know, I dabbled on the stage for a bit in school, but I was never very good. At least, that's what the director said. As plain as that new painting over there." He gestured to the fruit still life on the wall.

"In this business, you can't listen to people. Everyone's

got an opinion about what's good and what isn't, but to survive, to make it, you only have to believe your own."

"That's what you did?"

"Damn right."

A look of respect crossed his face. "Where are you from?"

"What makes you think I'm from someplace else?"

"Because everybody is in this city. And I'm wondering how you got this—this 'can-do' attitude of yours. Is it just the American Way, as they say?"

"I wouldn't know about that, but I'm from Philadelphia, if that answers your question."

"Have you always dressed in—how shall we say— mannish dress?"

She found her shot and bent down. "Wore dresses until I was about four or five. Didn't like 'em. Didn't feel right. Every time I put on one, it felt like I was covered in ants, all stinging me. Couldn't get out of them fast enough."

Smack!

Two solids went in the pocket.

She went around to the other side of the table. "I started wearing my brothers' old clothes. Felt much more natural."

"And yet," Lucien said, "there are some people in this city who would say you're unnatural for wearing them."

"Some people need to mind their own damn business. I'm not hurting anybody. And if people are uncomfortable with me wearing a suit and tie, well, that's on them."

She lined up her stick to the cue ball and struck. Missed.

"I must say, I agree with you," Lucien said. "I do not understand Americans obsession with having only men do this and only women do this. Seems . . . juvenile."

"It didn't keep you from using people's discomfort to profit yourself off an innocent woman."

"Ah, well, what can I say? It is the American Way."

El hooted a bitter laugh. "You're not wrong there, mister, not wrong."

Lucien got two more stripes in before scratching on the third. They were now even, both having knocked in five balls each.

As El took the cue back to the kitchen, she asked, "Why'd you leave Paris?"

"Got sick of all that war and death."

"Heard it was pretty bad over there." El smacked the cue ball down to the foot of the table, knocking in a stripe by accident. "But what's the real reason you left?"

Lucien went to the cue ball. "What do you mean?"

"I *mean,* yeah, the war was bad. And I can understand why you didn't like it over there, but you obviously don't like it over here."

"Buyer's remorse?"

"Hmm, maybe." As Lucien brought back his stick for his shot, she decided to bluff. "I think you did something or took something and *had* to leave the city you were in. Probably why some tough guys are after you."

His stick missed the cue ball entirely, causing him to glare in her direction. "That was a dirty trick, *mademoiselle.*"

"It's New York, baby. Dirty tricks are how you survive. You've seen them around lately?"

"No," he replied darkly. "Not lately."

"They weren't the damage squad fellas you saw in Saint Nicholas Park, were they?" It occurred to her perhaps he *followed* them there, instead of just being out on a *highly* coincidental midnight stroll.

"You're very interested in my past."

She smiled. "You've got secrets, *monsieur*?"

"We all have secrets." His look became shrewd. "What about you? What in *your* past caused you to run to New York?"

Her smile faltered. "What happens to a lot of people like me. My family thought I'd grow out of wearing my brothers' clothes. When I didn't, they forbade me from doing it. It wasn't that they hated me—they liked me a lot. Or at least I think they did. They just didn't know how to protect me from busybody neighbors and shitty pounders. Policemen," she clarified for Lucien's benefit. "When it was clear I was going to keep on wearing what I wanted, they said they were going to take me to a preacher who promised to cure my 'sickness.'"

"Oh? And how did he expect to cure it?"

"I don't know. I left before they could send me to him." She took a shot, sinking one more solid before missing the follow-up. Tied up again; six-six.

Lucien chalked his stick. "It seems we both know when it's time to leave, non? Is that when you moved to New York?"

"Not quite. I bounced around Philadelphia before eventually getting the money from my Uncle Jim to come here. Said I'd be safer in Harlem. He heard of clubs that welcomed people like me." She gave a brief smile. "Truth be told, I think Uncle John and I had something in common. Maybe that's why he helped me. Giving me the freedom he couldn't have for himself."

"How noble."

El ignored the sarcasm.

Lucien gained some ground, knocking in another stripe, leaving only the eight ball.

Dammit! I'm gonna lose to this extorting son of a bitch!

And when she'd already lost so much today.

She drummed her fingers on the rail of the table. "What about you? Think it's time for you to leave again?"

"Not when they are investigating her murder. That would look suspicious, don't you think?"

"Just a little bit," she said. "Any idea why Alice was at the factory that night?"

"If I was a betting man—and I am—I'd say she was searching for something and she did not want her brother to know she was looking for it."

"You don't have any idea what that could've been?"

"*Non.*" He pointed with the cue stick to the center pocket for the eight ball.

She held her breath, her Uncle be damned, as Lucien struck the cue ball. It cracked into the eight ball, which went into the center pocket . . . and so did the cue ball.

Lucien scratched. An automatic loss.

His face deflated, his self-congratulatory expression quickly falling into a dark anger.

"Damn!" he said, before pointing the cue stick at El. "That wasn't a proper win."

"A loss is still a loss," El replied. "And that means *you* get to answer my questions. All of my questions."

"No. You did not beat me. I lost. There's a difference." He tightly gripped the cue stick. "Let's play again."

"I don't have time for that, I'm afraid."

"Then I'm not going to answer your questions. And you can't make me."

Oh little boy, you do not want to try me.

El looked at the table, measuring the distance of her remaining solid plus the eight ball. She gestured to them. "What if I sink both of them with one shot?"

Lucien studied the table and the angles. "That's an impossible shot."

"Then you don't have to worry, now do you?"

Lucien's mouth twitched. *"Bon."*

El retrieved the scratched cue ball and the eight ball, placing the eight ball in the center, and set up her shot. It was gonna be a close one, no doubt about it. She had to line it up perfect and get the right speed on the cue ball. Otherwise, she'd scratch like Lucien did.

She eyeballed the distances and the angles, bent down, her eye on the cue ball, her breathing slow and low. She brought the cue stick back—paused—and then slid it forward.

Crack!

The cue ball surged forward, hitting the solid, which slid easily into the far corner pocket. The cue ball bounced off the corner and rolled forward towards the eight ball. It hit the side of the eight ball, sending it towards the near right corner pocket. She could tell from the angle that it was going in. The ball sunk into the pocket and now both of their eyes watched the cue ball heading towards the near left corner pocket. It was slowing down but not fast enough. One roll. Two rolls. Three.

Stop. Stop! Goddammit, stop!

Lucien smiled. "As I was saying, it's an impossible—"

The cue ball got up to the pocket and then, miraculously, ceased rolling. It perched on the edge of the pocket but didn't drop in.

Neither one of them breathed.

They watched, mesmerized.

When the cue ball didn't fall, El smiled. "Pay up."

Lucien tossed the cue stick onto the table causing the cue ball to drop into the pocket. Didn't matter. El still won.

"Careful," she said. "You don't want to scratch Pearlie's new felt."

Lucien grumbled a bit more before finally relenting. "*D'accord.* Alright. I was at my room in the Hotel."

"The Eudora? Convenient. Anybody vouch for that?"

"*Oui.* The head porter. What is his name? Isaiah Scott."

"Bushwa. He doesn't work the night shift."

"Someone called out and he covered for him. I must say, I like *Monsieur* Scott much better than the other one. He tells me where to go for the most fun. Like here."

"And how can Mr. Scott account for your whereabouts? He watching you the whole time?"

Lucien's grin was smug. "There was a leak in my bathroom. From the floor above. He was there watching the maintenance man fix the damage. Once they were done, I went to bed."

"What time was that?"

"You're playing detective, aren't you? First, you played spiritualist in the taxi we shared. Now, you're being Hercule Poirot."

"Answer the damn question."

"More Pinkerton, I think. I called *Monsieur* Scott at around two-thirty in the morning when I discovered the leak, and they went away about an hour later."

"So three-thirty."

"Exactly. When the telephone call to the police came reporting the gun shots." His smile widened. "As you can see, I am in the clear, *n'est-ce pas?*"

Damn.

Amused by her disappointment, he said, "I am sorry, *mademoiselle.* I am not her killer."

"That remains to be seen," she retorted before taking a deep breath. She wasn't ready to give up on interrogating him. "The last few days, did Alice mention a name? A Raymond Price?"

"*Non*. Who is he?"

"I don't know."

"Ah, perhaps our little Alice kept a secret from you."

She sent him a warning look. "Don't push it."

"Don't be offended. We all keep secrets at one time or another from those we love. I wouldn't take it personally."

"You know," she said. "I don't get it. You're staying at the Hotel Eudora, which is one of the most expensive hotels in Harlem. You bought a brand new maroon Chrysler coupe with magenta pleated and and buttoned mohair seats."

"Alice told you a lot, didn't she?"

"Don't bother trying to blackmail me, mister. I told her to drop you into the East River. She was kind-hearted. I am not."

He chuckled. "What's your question?"

"Why did you need her family money? You spent all of yours?"

"I think I have answered enough of your questions." He stared at her with those those queer blue and green eyes of his, the luminous colors turning dark, like the ocean before a storm. "But, *mademoiselle,* if you find whoever did this, please don't keep that secret. I would very much like to know."

"Why? So you can extort them too?"

"*Non*," he said. "You aren't the only one here who lost something valuable . . . "

18

The goddamned elevator was *still* out of service.

El banged on the metal cage, shouting, "What the hell am I paying rent for?!" Her voice and her banging echoed up the elevator shaft, but no one answered in return.

She squared her shoulders and began walking all the way up to the top floor. By the time she arrived, her lungs were on fire, her breath short, and her face slicked with sweat. She paused at the landing hoping to slow her heart rate down before she passed out.

Trudging down the hallway, she pulled out her apartment keys, but before she could slide them into the lock, her front door opened and there stood Flo.

"Oh, thank God!" she said, rushing across the threshold and embracing El in a tight hug.

"Flo? What are you still doing here?"

"I've been looking all over town for you, but figured you'd come home eventually." Flo pulled away and scowled. "Do you have any idea what time it is?"

"What are you, my mother?"

"*Some*one's gotta be." Flo pulled El inside and shut the

door behind them. She turned and faced El. "I saw the newspapers."

The concerned look on Flo's face undid El. Her eyes blurred with tears. Before she could stop herself, she was crying onto Flo's shoulder, muttering incomprehensible words while Flo held her, saying to let it out, let it out.

When the spasm passed, El released her friend and frantically searched for her handkerchief. "It's been awful, Flo. I can't believe it. Sometimes I think it's a mistake. That she's gonna meet me at our favorite club, smoking that damn cigar of hers. How can she be gone? How?!"

"Some bastard with a gun, that's how."

"I'm so angry, Flo, so unbelievably angry. I want to—I want to yell, I want to scream, but I just don't know at who. That's the hell of it. Who am I gonna be mad at? Huh? I don't know who killed her. Could've been her brother, could've been one of the union strike leaders. Could've been that extorting conman fiancé of hers, though he told me he has an iron-clad alibi."

"Say what now?"

"How am I supposed to get this—this feeling outta me when I don't know who to place it on?"

Flo held up a hand. "Wait a moment. When you say Lucien told you he had an alibi, does that mean you talked to him?"

"I've been talking to everybody I can."

"Why on *earth* are you doing that?"

"Because I'm going to find out who killed her, that's why! And when I do, I'm going to make them pay and trust me, they won't be able to handle the number on *my* tab."

A voice behind her said, "Revenge won't patch together the break in your heart."

El whirled around to see Madam Watkins standing in the doorway between the front room and the kitchen.

"Madam. I—I—I didn't realize you were here."

Flo said, "When I couldn't find you, I went to Madam Watkins and told her about Alice's murder. I told her everything."

"Everything?"

"I'm sorry, El. I figured she needed to know."

Madam Watkins stepped forward. "I am so sorry, El. Please accept my deepest condolences."

The dam of tears threatened to burst once again, but El held them in check. "Thank you, Madam. I appreciate that. I didn't mean to keep that from you. I just didn't know how to tell you."

Madam Watkins gave her a kind smile. "It's alright, El. Sometimes we don't know who we can trust with something about ourselves that others don't, or won't, understand. I certainly know firsthand about that."

"You do?"

"I most certainly do. You remember Mac the Parrot? Well, he belongs to a man I love. Leonard Frazier."

El stared at her. "Leonard Frazier? You mean the millionaire who's been in the news lately?"

Even Flo was shocked. "The *white* millionaire whose daughter was murdered?"

Madam Watkins replied, "That's the one. So you see, El, I do understand what it's like to be in a relationship that can be dangerous for the wrong people to know about."

El nodded. "Thank you. Thank you for telling me."

Flo waited a beat before saying, "Now that we've got that settled, let's get back to you running around town talking to people like you're some kind of detective. What in the world are you thinking?"

El snapped her head towards Flo. "I'm thinking the pounders aren't gonna find who did it and her killer is gonna get away scot-free."

"Are you crazy? The only thing keeping you safe right now is that nobody knows about you and Alice. And you asking questions and acting like a bull in a china shop is painting a giant target on your back."

El put her hands on her hips. "Well, you know me, Flo. I put the *bull* in *bulldagger*."

"Please. You put the *bull* in *bullshit*."

"Ladies!" Madam Watkins stepped into the front room and into El's line of vision. "Your friend is correct, El. The NYPD will want to wrap up their case as quickly as possible. A wealthy white woman dead? The public outcry is already immense and will only grow with time. Rich is facing a public relations disaster because of a strike that's going on six months with no end in sight. He will want this solved. He will want someone to blame."

Flo added, "And he's gonna lean on the police and we all know the police bend to the will of white folks. Especially *rich* white folks."

El waved her off. "I know that. You think I was born yesterday?"

"The way you've been acting, I'd say so."

"Now listen here, Flo—"

Madam Watkins raised both her hands. "Arguing will do us no good." She focused on El. "I know why you want to do this. If someone I loved were murdered, I'd be tearing this town apart until I find them and I would administer a little justice of my own. But you must admit, El, this is dangerous. We are your friends. We want you to stay safe."

Flo agreed with every word Madam Watkins said. "She's right, El. You best lay low for a while."

El shook her head. "You know I can't do that."

"El—"

"Don't 'El' me, sis. You know I've got to do this. I've *got* to." El looked at the two women standing before her. "I don't have a choice. My world? It's gone. The future I thought I was gonna have with her was taken away from me. *Stolen* from me." She gestured helplessly, her voice cracking. "I've got nothing left—"

"You have us," Flo said.

Madam Watkins stepped forward and put a hand on El's shoulder. "We're gonna see you through this. You're not alone."

El closed her eyes. She pictured the last time she saw Alice, climbing through her window and looking up at her.

"Hey, El? You know?"

"I know," El said out loud. She opened her eyes. "I'm not gonna stop."

Madam Watkins and Flo looked at each other for a long moment.

"Alright, then," Madam Watkins eventually said, turning back to El. "We'll need to do this smart." She released El's shoulder and gestured towards the sofa and chairs. "Let's sit down and work out a plan to find Alice's killer."

———

"You sure he's gonna be here?" Flo asked the next morning.

They were walking down 143rd Street towards Jordi's Barber Shop, hoping to catch Isaiah Scott before he left for his morning shift.

El said, "Pearlie said every morning without fail."

The three of them strategized until well into the early

morning hours. Madam Watkins would reach out to a contact in the police department to find out what wasn't being reported to the newspapers. ("Sergeant Harvey Williams, New York Police Department's first-ever Black sergeant. We can trust him.") El and Flo would go to Jordi's to see if Isaiah Scott could verify Lucien's alibi. El wanted to go alone, but Flo said she'd stick to her like glue, a fact El didn't like but she didn't have much say in the matter.

"It's to prevent you from doing something half-cocked," Flo had said.

"Never had much use for a full one," El had quipped, much to Flo's consternation.

Now they were hustling towards the barber shop fifteen minutes past eight, hoping against hope Isaiah was still around.

The place was emptier than El's first visit. No one was waiting their turn and only one of the barbers had a customer in their chairs. Isaiah.

They had just finished, and Isaiah was sitting up, running his hands over his cheeks.

"Good work as usual, Wyatt," he said to his barber. He turned when the shop door closed behind El and Flo. "El, isn't it? What brings you back here?" He glanced over at Flo. "And with a friend, I see. You know women aren't allowed."

Flo started to reply, but El beat her to the punch. "We'll just be a minute, Mr. Scott. I promise." She glanced to the two barbers. The one Isaiah called Wyatt was wiping off the straight razor and the other one was sitting in his barber's chair reading a newspaper. "What's good, gentlemen?"

Isaiah sighed. "Well, not a whole lot, considering your friend was killed by a striker."

Wyatt tutted, "We don't know that."

"Well, who else would be at the factory in the middle of the night? They were likely going to damage some machine or truck. All them union boys are always up to no good. And Miss Holloway caught them in the act."

The second barber reading the newspaper turned the page. "You still haven't said why *she* was there in the first place. Her brother ran things, not her."

"Alvin," Isaiah said to the second barber, "it was her family's factory. She could visit any time she wanted to. What if she got a call from that guard that he spotted someone sneaking in?"

"The guard called her and not Rich? That don't make no sense." Alvin rattled the newspaper trying to flatten the wilted pages out. "Besides, the guard said he didn't see or hear nothing all night."

Wyatt put the straight razor into the top drawer of his station. "Sounds to me like he was *paid* not to see or hear anything. How does someone get shot in the factory you's supposed to be watching and you don't hear or see nothing? Either he's the dumbest guard who ever lived or he was told to look the other way."

Isaiah countered with, "The factory's a big place. It'd be easy to miss something there. You two see conspiracy where there isn't any."

"C'mon, man," Alvin opined. "You know these factory men cover things up. Look at what they did to Sam Willing. He loses his entire *hand* in a machine, and everybody from the foreman to the lineman said it was operator error."

Wyatt agreed. "They look out for themselves over there. Everybody knows they've been scrimping on the maintenance for years."

Alvin turned another page of his paper. "That's why

they only had one guard watching at night. A Frank Nicker-son. It says here they fired him yesterday."

Wyatt said, "No shit." He cut his eyes over to El and Flo. "Excuse my language, ladies."

"No excuse, necessary," El replied. "I've said far worse."

Flo added, "Believe me, she has."

Alvin read directly from the paper. "Mr. Holloway called it a dereliction of duty letting his sister get shot like that."

Wyatt leaned on the counter of his station. "Dereliction of duty? What are the odds that man ever served in the army?"

"You already know the answer to that. Them rich boys get a free pass on everything."

"Now see? That's what I'm talking about. The wealthy in this country designed a system that perpetuates violence without ever having to experience that violence themselves. They just get to keep to all the profits from the war machine—"

Isaiah stood up. "I best be going now. Spent enough time bumping gums." He walked past El and Flo and collected his overcoat and hat on the rack by the front door. "El, good to see you. Wyatt? Alvin? I'll see you tomorrow." He shrugged into his coat, placed the hat on his head, and left the shop.

El and Flo followed him outside.

"Mr. Scott," El said, once they were out on the street. "We have a question for you."

"I'm going to be late for my shift."

"It won't take too much time, I promise."

"I was already questioned by the police all about Mr. Laurent. Where he was and what he was doing that night."

"And what are the odds the police will do anything good with what you said?"

Isaiah stopped walking and turned to face them with an exaggerated show of patience.

El spoke fast. "Mr. Laurent. Did he have a leak in his bathroom that night?"

"Now how did I know you were going to ask about that? Dare I ask how you even *know* about the leak?"

"He told me."

"Alright. Well, I'll confirm it like I confirmed it with the police. Yes, he did. Bad one too. Likely have to replace the whole ceiling."

"And what time was that?"

"About two-fifteen was when I got the call. Two-twenty-five was when we got to the room with the engineer. Two-thirty, we began work. And before you ask, it took about an hour. I oversaw the whole operation."

Flo spoke up. "Was Mr. Laurent there all night?"

Isaiah glanced at El. "Remember what I said about discretion?"

El clasped her hands together as if in prayer. "Please, Mr. Scott. Miss Holloway was my friend."

"You gotta get better friends." Isaiah pressed his lips into a disapproving line. "No, he was not. He asked me earlier in the evening for a club to attend. One with good music and good dancing. He left the hotel around eleven o'clock and came back a little past two to discover the leak."

Flo said, "And while you were overseeing the engineer fix the bathroom, did Mr. Laurent have any visitors?"

"No."

"What about telephone calls?"

El flicked her eyes over to her friend. Dang, she was good at this.

Isaiah pressed his lips into a straight line. "He might have."

"Might have?"

"Fine, he did."

"You happen to overhear what he said? Or hear who he telephoned?"

Isaiah looked around, wanting to be anywhere but here. "I didn't tell the police what he said."

El asked, "Why not?"

"Because I don't volunteer information to a bunch of white cops." He glanced at Flo. "And they weren't smart enough to ask better questions like you." He rubbed his chin again. "I didn't hear who Lucien asked to be connected to, but I did hear parts of his conversation. A bit difficult to understand him. He was slurring, his words sloppy."

"He was drunk."

"Yeah, but he didn't often get that way. Probably had something way stronger than he was used to. Maybe. I don't know, all I know is he didn't sound like himself. Sounded odd. Could barely understand him and when I did . . . " Isaiah shuddered.

"What did he say, Mr. Scott?"

"You're not going to leave me alone unless I tell you, right?"

"Right."

Isaiah grimaced. "He said, 'It was an accident. An accident. I don't care if you believe me. What's done is done.'"

19

Lucien Laurent was no longer a resident of the Hotel Eudora, said an officious voice on the telephone.

El had called the front desk from a telephone booth in the back of a coffee shop near Jordi's.

"What do you mean, 'he's no longer a resident'?" El asked in her Miriam King voice.

"He was asked to vacant the premises."

"That sounds like he couldn't pay his bill."

"He could not," the officious voice sniffed. "The Hotel Eudora is a prestige establishment. We erroneously thought Mr. Laurent was of such a pedigree. We were mistaken."

"Out of curiosity, how much does he owe?"

"I'm not disclosing that information, Mrs. King!"

"If he's a deadbeat, I need to know and to what degree. He is a donor to the Ladies' Auxiliary. We depend upon his generosity."

"I'd find someone else. He owed several weeks of rent as well as room service and charges for long-distance telephone calls. We simply couldn't abide his freeloading any longer. Good day, Mrs. King."

El hung up the telephone, frowning.

"What?" Flo asked when she saw El's face.

"Lucien was kicked out of the Hotel Eudora."

"Damn. Any ideas of where he could've gone?"

El looked around the shop. A murmuring collection of men and women having coffee or tea with little slices of cake or finger sandwiches. It reminded her to eat something soon. "Probably some fleabag motel which we'd never find in a million years. If he's still in the city, that is."

"Oh, he is. Didn't he tell you his brand new motorcar was towed? If he's broke, it's unlikely he'd be able to get it out of hock. And he certainly wouldn't leave town without it."

"Alright," El said. "Let's assume he's still in the city for now. We don't know where he'd lay his head, but we *do* know the man can't resist a billiard table. It's how he makes his sugar. Games or marks, either one."

"You want to ask around all the billiard parlors in Harlem and see if they've seen him?" Flo pointed to a table and flagged down a waitress. "We're eating first. It's gonna be a long morning."

Fortified, they started at Pearlie's, who was nonplussed to see El so soon ("I haven't seen him since last night, now leave me alone!"). From there, they hit all the billiard parlors that allowed white players: The Cue, The Pocket, Snookers, Benjamin's.

Things got interesting after lunch when they went to The Hub, a low-stakes parlor on 144th and Seventh. As they walked up, two men were leaving the joint. The first fella was big—six foot four, broad-shouldered, and barrel-chested. His square face showcased a nasty scar from his eye to his mouth, like a tear that had dug a deep groove into his skin. His charcoal suit was immaculate though, El had to give him that.

The second fella was half his size and weight. A dark mustache on an otherwise baby face. He wore a navy suit as expertly tailored as his refrigerator-built friend.

A chill descended upon El.

The two of them walked passed her and Flo, neither giving them a second look.

Flo muttered, "Do you think . . . ?"

"Let's find out."

Inside The Hub, they found a nearly empty parlor save for two men in patchwork pants playing in the far corner. An older man with gray hair and a graying mustache sat at the bar, watching the door with a guarded expression. A cigarette smoldered in between his fingers.

"Not a place for ladies," he said.

El jerked her thumb over her shoulder. "With boys like that coming out of here, you don't have to tell me twice."

"Good afternoon, then."

Flo stayed at the door, but El sauntered forward. "I want to know who they're looking for."

"What makes you think they're looking for somebody?"

El settled onto the barstool next to him. "Womanly intuition. They looking for a man with one blue eye and one green eye?"

The man took a deep drag on his cigarette. "What do *you* want with him?"

"I want to talk with him."

"That's funny. So did they."

"They say why they're looking for him?"

"No, and they didn't say who they're working for either."

El watched as one of the two men playing sunk three

solids. "You ever see them before?" she asked, bringing her attention back to the man next to her.

"Nope. They're mean though. I wouldn't mess with them. Boston folk, judging from their accent. New York boys think they're tough but I'm here to tell you, they'd lose badly in a fight with the boys from Boston."

"Careful. That's heresy right there."

The man smirked. "I'm not talking baseball." He took another drag.

"Yeah," El said. "I know."

Back outside, Flo brushed off her shoulders and arms. "Yuck. That place gave me the creeps." She looked up at El. "So Boston, huh? You have any connections up there?"

"Not a one." An idea sparked. One she didn't like but had to entertain. "But we've got a connection here."

"No, we don't. We don't know any gangsters."

El hesitated. "Actually, we do."

Flo's mouth dropped open before closing again. "No. No. Absolutely not."

"If someone were on her turf, she'd know."

"El. We *can't!*"

"How else are we going to find out who's after Lucien?"

Flo muttered under her breath some more before relenting. "Shit. Fine. Where do we find her?"

"At her usual place, of course."

———

The Hot Cha, an infamous speak, shimmied and shook in a brick building on 133rd Street and Seventh Avenue. Usually. But here in the afternoon, it sat empty. Barren. The air smelled of decaying cigarettes. The stage missed its music; the floor mourned its missing dancers. Tables longed for their patrons, while the bar stood stoic as a solitary man counted glasses and stacked bottles.

The only other person in the place, besides El, was one of the most powerful women in all of Harlem. The Baroness of Business.

Zora Mae.

Lithe figure. Unblemished, smooth skin. An ingenue's face with a delicate, upturned nose. Her hair had been cut into a straight flapper's bob with nary a curl or a wave. She'd lined her eyes in black and brushed shimmering turquoise from her lids to her eyebrows. Her cheeks blushed with a rose-tinged rouge, and she'd painted her lips dark red, which, to some, might've been a salacious invite, like Morse code beeping across the room.

The dress she'd donned was a beaded number in royal blue that left her shoulders uncovered. A turquoise ribbon tied around her neck before flowing down her front and cinching together with another ribbon tied around her waist. The beads, also in turquoise, formed a paisley pattern that shimmered in the pale light of the club. El couldn't see her shoes, but she imagined they were just as ornate as the dress above them.

Zora sat at an empty table smoking a cigarette placed in a long black holder. A mink coat lay folded on the chair next to her, topped with a wide-brim hat in complementary colors to the dress. She took a deep, long drag before slowly blowing out a narrow, steady stream of smoke.

"The indomitable El Train," she said. "To what do I owe the pleasure?"

"Afternoon, Baroness. Thank you for seeing me on such short notice."

El had arrived at the Hot Cha with Flo about a half hour before. They had to do a little haggling with the guard, who kept watch behind a metal door that, to outsiders, looked more like a delivery door than an entrance. After fews and twos were exchanged, he let them stand in the long hallway that led to the club until the Baroness declared for El—and only El—to enter.

Flo didn't like it, but she didn't have a choice. No one disobeyed the Baroness.

Now Zora studied El with those cobra eyes of hers. A shiver formed at the base of El's spine as they evaluated her, like a predator determining if she was worthy of being prey.

"I must admit I'm surprised to see you," Zora said. "What with you and Leslie having your little lover's spat."

El had forgotten all about that. Didn't she owe him an act by the end of the week? Goddammit, was that tomorrow?

When it rains, it pours.

"Baroness," El said, "I know Mr. Charles is your friend—"

"More of an acquaintance. He's less of a disappointment that way. And for what it's worth, I think Leslie is being obtuse. He couldn't really expect you, a star of your incandescence, to sing in his decrepit little dive forever, could he?"

"If he did, he should've paid me more."

"And he can't be this naïve to think you'd turn down a woman like Madam Watkins. I thought Leslie was a bit more worldly than that. But apparently he's as common as corruption."

Which you know a thing or two about.

See, Zora Mae wasn't an actual Baroness. Not in the traditional sense of the word. She'd worked her way up the Harlem Numbers racket before going into rum-running, liquor-stealing and -selling, and eventually throwing lavish parties. Some of those parties satiated darker appetites. The so-called "degenerate" wantings the preachers and anti-vicers warned about. El heard of one such party where Zora's main attraction was a man who stripped off all his clothes, stood on the apartment's dining room table, and sat down to make a candlestick disappear. They called him "The Snuffer."

El liked the profane. Loved it, even. And if that's where Zora Mae stopped, she might've been less wary of the woman. But the Baroness also had a dangerous side, and rumor had it she'd made several men and women perma-nently disappear for missing payments, cheating her, reneging on a promise, or, God forbid, telling the police about her activities.

Then there was her girlfriend, a crazy woman with even crazier eyes named Sonya Sanders who believed every man and woman was conspiring to steal Zora away from her. El looked around. Sonya wasn't anywhere to be found. Odd. She usually skulked in the shadows.

"Well, you know Les," El said. "He always has to have the last word. Usually at his own expense."

Zora chuckled low in her throat. "My, my, you have him pegged. You always were a great study of people, El. I think it's one of the things you and I have in common. We know humanity. And the dark little crevices of their hearts where the secrets lie."

"Don't butter me up now."

"I'm not. I don't flatter, El. It's too time-consuming and frankly, it's too male. Too much how men do busi-ness. Slathering all that butter on the bread until it's soaked through, and then no one can tell what the hell the sandwich is supposed to be. Least of all the men selling it."

"They're just covering up the fact that it's a shit sandwich they're serving you."

Zora leaned back her head and laughed. "Oh, El! I do enjoy your humor. You know, I really did love you playing at my Dante's Inferno Party in August."

Wish I could say the same. You forced me to do that gig.

"I'm all Madam Watkins's now," El replied. "But she might lend me out for a night or two."

"Let's see if the favor you want from me warrants that." Zora pointed to the empty chair at her table. "Have a seat."

Before El sat down, she glanced around once more for Sonya.

Zora caught her look. "Miss Sanders is on a little vacation."

"Oh? I didn't think she could stand being away from you for very long."

"I simply explained to her that it was for her own good. She argued for a bit, but you know me, El. I always get what I want."

El's hands went numb. "Did you—?"

"I didn't kill her. I simply *persuaded* her. Now. Enough about Miss Sanders. How can I, the Baroness of Business, help you, the infamous El Train?"

Here, El had to be careful. A favor from Zora meant granting her one in return. And Zora charged a high price for anything she gave.

"There's a Frenchman in town that's being looked for by a couple of tough guys from Boston. I want to know if you've heard of anyone seeking out this Frenchmen and if so, what they want with him."

"Boston, you say? Strange for them to be going after a Frenchman. Isn't it all Irish up there?" Zora thought for a moment. "There's a lot of torpedoes looking for people in this town. You're going to need to be more specific. Like some names."

"I don't know theirs, but I know the man they're looking for. Lucien Laurent."

"What's your interest in this?"

"Lucien may have inadvertently led these men to a friend of mine, and they may be responsible for her death."

Zora leaned forward. "Are we talking friend? Or *friend*?"

"I don't see how that pertains."

"Oh, but it does. It lets me know how badly you want to know this information. So . . . friend? Or *friend*?"

Goddammit.

"A very, very good friend."

"Hmmm," Zora hummed. "What's the relation to this Lucien Laurent?"

"Mr. Laurent, excuse me, *Monsieur* Laurent, is an opportunist who, shall we say, insisted upon a marriage my *friend* does not—did not—want."

"Why didn't your friend tell him no? Oh," Zora said. "She couldn't. Because he knew, didn't he? About who graces her bedchambers. And he threatened to tell?"

"That's the short of the long of it."

"Did he kill her?"

"I haven't ruled him out, though motive is a bit murky. He wanted her money. Now he gets none."

"And you think he has a past, or a present, that is unsavory."

"That's the suspicion," El said.

"More like hope. The more unsavory, the better your chances of nailing him for murder. Or exacting revenge." Zora took another long drag on her cigarette. "Like I said, we both know humanity and what they desire."

"Can you find out for me who might be after this Laurent fellow?"

"There's not much that happens in Harlem that I don't know about. The question is how much *you* are willing to offer for the information."

Here it was. The favor.

"Reasonably willing," El replied.

Zora shook her head. "Not good enough."

El sighed. "Alright, fine, *very* willing."

"See? That wasn't so hard." Zora turned her attention to smoothing out imaginary wrinkles in her dress. "When I find something out, I'll let you know what you can do in return for me." She looked up at El, those cobra eyes twinkling. "I'll be in touch."

20

"Are you crazy?" Flo said, when El told her about the deal with Zora Mae. They were walking down the street away from the Hot Cha. "We both know what the Baroness is capable of!"

"I am aware, Flo. But how else are going to find out who those tough guys are and who they're working for?"

"I don't know why you're so keen on making a deal with the devil."

"She's not the devil. She's a powerful, albeit dangerous, woman."

"And *you* are not thinking straight."

El ignored the charge and said, "I think for the time being, we have the Lucien Problem taken care of. For now. Where do we go from here?"

"Maybe we ought to visit this Frank Nickerson."

"The guard?"

Flo shrugged. "Why not? He might've seen or heard something that night."

"The papers said he didn't."

"But maybe like Isaiah Scott, he did and just won't say."

"Or wasn't asked." El considered this. "They did just fire him. Might loosen his tongue some. But how are we going find him?"

"Do you know someone who's got a list of addresses for Holloway Factory employees?"

El felt herself smile. "I actually might. I just hope he's where he's supposed to be."

———

The Holloway Paper Box Factory had even more picketers than the first time El was here.

Flo marveled at the marching men, women, and children holding their signs and shouting their mantras. "Look at them," she said. "There's so many."

"About a hundred strong, give or take."

"They're taking on a lot of risk."

"Yeah, but we know better than anyone that if you don't stand up for your own rights, nobody's going to do it for you."

"Preach, sis." Flo turned to look at El. "What's your plan?"

"Asking Ferrin Thomas for Frank Nickerson's address."

"That's it?"

"Sometimes it can be simple."

"Alright, but how are we going to find him that picket line?"

"We ask. C'mon."

And ask they did. Took about three attempts, but eventually one of the picketers, a fellow Black woman, directed them to the other side of the picket march.

Ferrin Thomas was dressed in a pale brown suit and

blue tie and held up a sign that said: "*PAY US WHAT WE'RE WORTH!*"

El she gave an appreciative nod to Ferrin's sign. "Mr. Thomas. I like what you're saying there."

"Oh," he replied, immediately pushing his glasses up the bridge of his nose. "El Train, right? Yes. It's one of the items we're fighting for. Fair wages. The people on those factory floors work very hard and receive very meager incomes. Hardly enough to cover their rents and other expenses."

"I feel that," Flo muttered.

"Meanwhile, Holloway Boxes is making piles upon piles of money. I know this for a fact, because I saw it first-hand."

"As the accountant," El said.

"Correct. There's not much I don't know about the Holloway business."

"Including their employees."

"That is . . . that is true."

El smiled. "Wonderful. We're trying to find one of them."

"Oh?" Ferrin swallowed. "Who?"

Lord, this boy is a Nervous Nellie.

"Don't worry," she said. "We're not going to cause trouble or futz up your strike here."

Flo added, "There's a man we need to speak to. Who was working the night Alice—well, you know."

"Right," he said. "The guard. Frank Nickerson, was it?"

El nodded. "That's the one. You wouldn't happen to know where he lives, do you?"

"I, uh, I. Not off hand."

"Any way you can look it up?"

Ferrin pushed up his glasses again. "I'd have to ask

someone. Accountants deal with numbers, but Personnel deals with people."

"Anyone from that department striking with you now?"

"Only one. A junior associate. Farther down the flagpole, as they say, but perhaps she might know."

"Wonderful news! Can you ask her now?"

Ferrin's glasses almost slipped off his nose. He pushed them back hard. "N-n-now?"

"No time like the present."

Ferrin looked around. "I-I can't leave the picket line. You know. Solidarity and all that."

"C'mon now, Mr. Thomas. We've got a murder to solve."

"*We?*"

A sharp female voice interrupted them. "What are you doing here?"

Both El and Flo turned to see Ramona Westfall in a plain navy blue wool dress glaring at them.

El tried to smile, though it likely looked like barring teeth. "Chatting with Mr. Thomas about Frank Nickerson."

Ramona crossed her arms over her chest. "And what do you want with him?"

Ferrin tried to reply. "They want to ask him some questions about that night—"

"Ferrin, stay out of this. Ladies? Or lady and gentleman, whichever you prefer. Frank Nickerson, as well as this strike, are *none* of your business. And if I see you on these grounds again, I'm getting the police involved. Do you understand?"

El and Flo flicked looks at one another before El said, "You've made your point."

Ramona smiled cruelly. "Good."

El stepped forward, causing Ramona to shrink back a

little, which pleased El to no end. "And let me make *my* point: I'm going to find who killed Alice Holloway. You hear me? And you better pray it's not one of you, because hell hath no fury like mine. Do *you* understand?" She held Ramona's gaze for a few seconds before turning and walking away.

Flo caught up with her. "That didn't go well."

"We'll find it some other way."

"How?"

"You heard Ferrin. Employee addresses are with Personnel."

"You want to go inside and ask them?" Flo gestured to the picketers marching in front. "If we cross this picket line, they'll tear us to pieces."

El remembered what the men almost did to Lucien Laurent when he tried to speak with Rich. "You're right. Let me think of something."

While she did, she spied two familiar figures in the distance on the other end of the picket line. She squinted. Malek Polowski and Booker Freemen. They were having an argument. A big one, from the looks of it. Lots of arm gestures from Booker. A loud voice too, though she couldn't make out his words. Malek stood stoic, his hands on his hips. Once Booker finished whatever point he wanted to make, Malek responded with that cool, detached manner of his his, which set Booker off. Malek tried to calm him down, but only earned a: "No, man! No!"

Booker stormed off.

"You know them?" Flo said, breaking El's concentration.

"Yeah. That's Malek and Booker."

"What were they fighting about?"

El watched Booker go around the corner. "I don't

know," she replied. She then snapped her gaze over to Malek, who frowned to himself before rejoining the picket line.

"Any bright ideas about finding Frank Nickerson? El? *El.*"

She roused herself. "Sorry. Um, yeah, yeah I think so. We need a telephone. Time for Miriam King to ask for a reference.

The block of 119th between Sixth and Seventh Avenues was filled with buildings that had seen far better days. Front stoops cracked and slanted. A few windows boarded up. Trash strewn about like New Year's confetti.

El and Flo were on the receiving end of many a wary look from people—all white—walking on the sidewalk or staring out the windows. They didn't belong here. Not only because they were Black, but because they had significantly more sugar in their bowls than the entire block put together.

"You got your pistol?" murmured El.

"My two-shot Derringer. You got your Browning?"

"You know I do." She counted the numbers on the buildings. "We're almost there."

"How are we going to get this Mr. Nickerson to talk to us anyway?"

"You've got a piece of paper or a notebook or something in that purse?"

Flo gave El a curious look. "A little notebook with my shopping list. Why?"

"You'll see."

They got to the address Personnel gave them and rang the buzzer to no avail.

"Think he's avoiding the newshawks?" Flo asked.

El rang the buzzer again and still no answer. "Maybe he's drowning his sorrows somewhere. He did just get fired."

"I am not going speak-hopping around here. If the outsides of this block are this rough, I certainly don't want to see what's behind these walls."

A scrape of shoes turned their heads. A white man built like a rich man's safe walked towards them.

El subtly slipped her hand into her pocket to touch the comforting handle of her Browning. "Excuse me, mister? We're looking for Mr. Frank Nickerson."

The man frowned. "That's me. Who are you?"

El removed her hand from her pocket and clasped her hands in front like a Sunday school teacher. "I'm Miriam King and this is my assistant Mercy Baker. We're both from the *Harlem Daily News*."

El glanced at Flo, who picked up on her cue. Flo reached into her purse and pulled out her notepad and pencil.

El continued. "And we're here to talk with you about Miss Alice Holloway's tragic death."

Frank held up a hand. "I'm not talking to no reporters. I don't know anything anyways. It's why I got fired, in case you didn't know."

El gave a sympathetic pout. "We're aware of your disappointing employment situation, Mr. Nickerson."

"Then you'll understand if I don't say nothing. Excuse me."

Flo held up her pencil. "Mr. Nickerson, we're very much interested in your side of the story."

El nodded. "And we think the factory moved with too much haste."

"Why, it wasn't *your* fault the crime occurred."

"How could you know such a terrible thing would happen that night?"

"No one could know."

"And the factory is a big place," El said, repeating what she heard at Jordi's earlier. "How could they expect only one man to cover that much ground by himself?"

Frank rocked back on his heels. The need for privacy didn't stand a chance against his bruised ego's need to set the story straight. "I've been a loyal employee of theirs for years. And this is how they treat me?"

"It's such a shame what's happened to that place," El commiserated. "We've spoken with other employees and learned how the current Mr. Holloway has been running the factory."

"Oh, yeah? What do they say?"

Flo replied, "Well, we wouldn't want to speak out of turn before our article comes out. But let's just say it hasn't been a ringing endorsement of Mr. Rich Holloway."

"You gonna go after Rich? You're playing with fire, ladies, if you don't mind my saying so. And why does a Black paper care so much about the Holloway Factory?"

"The Holloway family employed people of all races," El said, smoothly. "We too have a stake in what's happening there."

Flo tapped her notebook with her pencil. "And we've also been covering the strike, which is why people are talking to us about Mr. Holloway and his policies."

Frank seemed to think for a moment. "I see." He jerked his thumb over his shoulder. "There's a speak at the end of the street that lets you people—I mean, Black people—I mean, *anyone* sit there." He blushed before recovering. "You want to buy me a beer?"

21

Frank Nickerson led them to a speak behind, of all places, a book shop. Both El and Flo kept a hand near their pockets that held their respective pistols. El didn't get a dangerous vibe from Frank, but she'd been fooled once before and she wasn't about to be fooled again.

Quinn's Books sat on the corner of 119th and Seventh, with windows so dirty, El could hardly see inside. The front door needed paint, the hinges needed oil. Inside, the shelves specialized in pulp magazines and cheap novels with a few tabloids thrown in for good measure.

The salesclerk was a white man in his sixties, his face wrinkled, his head bald and covered in liver spots. Tiny glasses perched on the end of his nose while he read the newspaper. His thick fingers held a cigarette burnt down practically to the nub.

He didn't even glance up, just said, "Hello, Frank. They said here you got fired."

"It's bullshit, Q. 'Cuse my language, ladies," Frank added to El and Flo.

"Ladies ain't allowed in here," said the man El presumed to be Quinn. Q for short, evidently.

"Q, give me a break. It's been a helluva week and these reporters are gonna buy me a drink and let me tell my story."

"What story you gonna tell? You fell asleep on the job?"

Frank gave a self-conscious glance to El and Flo before replying, "That didn't happen that night. Or any night. I take my job seriously, Q."

"As do I. Menfolk don't like to drink with womenfolk."

"Is there anybody back there?"

Quinn kept silent.

"Ah ha! That's what I thought. C'mon, Q. Just a little drink? A little drink for two?" he sang, referencing a popular radio tune the white folks loved.

Quinn finally looked up from his newspaper and studied El and Flo. "You ladies sure you wanna go back there?"

El replied, "We can take care of ourselves."

"I can tell. Alright, Frank, it's your funeral. One drink apiece. That'll be six cents."

El pulled out a nickel and a penny from her pocket and placed them on the counter in front of Quinn. He quietly palmed it and looked back down at his newspaper.

Frank said them, "Follow me."

He walked around the counter to a bookcase directly behind Quinn. He pulled, but didn't take, a book from the middle shelf, and El heard a click. The bookcase swung inward. Somehow the book Frank grabbed acted like a doorknob.

He led them inside a dirty room that doubled as a cleaning closet. There were two tables, a shoddily built bar with no bartender, and one table lamp for light. He clicked it on and went to the bar, grabbing a bottle and three glasses.

"Sit anywhere you like," he said over his shoulder.

"Such choices," Flo muttered. "Wanna sit next to the broom or next to the mop."

"Hush up, sis," El muttered back. "And get your notebook out."

Once they settled in next to the mop, Frank held up his glass in a toast.

El and Flo glanced at each other before awkwardly raising their glasses.

"To Holloway Boxes," he said. "May they get what's coming to them." He downed his drink.

El and Flo took a sip each and grimaced. Bathtub gin.

El suppressed a shudder and said, "So, Mr. Nickerson, what can you tell us about that night?"

He poured himself another drink. "Don't tell Q."

"We'll be the soul of discretion."

This time, he only took a sip, licking his lips before replying, "It was an ordinary night. I clocked in at eleven o'clock, taking over for the guard working the afternoon-to-night shift. The picketers had gone home by that point."

Flo scribbled in her notebook.

El asked, "What about the scabs?"

Frank gave her a curious look. "You know about them? Yeah, the scabs—the additional workers, as Mr. Holloway calls them—had been sent home before I got there."

"Do you know where Mr. Holloway found these additional workers?"

"No idea, but it's not too hard to find somebody in this city who will do a job. Rent's so high, who can afford to say no to whatever a man asks you?" He blushed again. "I didn't

mean it like that. I meant—well, you know what I meant."
Another sip.

"Mr. Nickerson, where do you stand guard?"

"There's a little office just inside the front gate. Beside
the gate, there's a door for workers to enter and leave.
Behind me is the garage where the trucks come in and out."

"There's no back entrance?"

"No, ma'am."

"And no way for someone to sneak in past your office?"

"If they broke a window on the ground floor, maybe, but
even the police didn't find any tampering with them. Which
is why Mr. Holloway blamed me personally for what
happened," he added, his face darkening.

Flo spoke up. "Do you ever leave your post during your
shift?"

"I do rounds to make sure nobody snuck in or stayed in
when they should've clocked out. Doing the sweeps, we call
it. Used to be, we'd do them every hour on the hour, but the
last few days, Mr. Holloway changed it to be every two
hours."

"Why's that?"

"He said he wanted us to keep watch out front more.
He was convinced the strikers are going to sabotage his
machines or his trucks, and he doesn't want them coming in.
So of course, when Miss Holloway was found by the garage
entrance, I was on a sweep doing what I was told to do
when I'm told to do it. Yet somehow it's *my* fault I didn't see
who shot her."

Flo made more pencil scratches into her notebook. "Did
you see anything odd that night? Arguments? A motorcar
idling nearby for long periods of time? Someone watching
the factory?"

Frank closed his eyes, trying to remember. "Arguments?

No. Didn't see any swarthy characters or the like." He opened his eyes. "There was a motorcar parked for a while near the corner, but it looked empty to me."

"Can you remember what it looked like? Color? Make and model?"

"Miss, I don't know one motorcar from another. They all look the same to me."

"Fair enough. And the color?"

"I—it was too dark."

El said, "Any guesses?"

He shook his head.

Something gnawed at her. His eyes kept glancing away, looking everywhere but her face. Could've been uncomfortable sitting with her and Flo, but given his banter with Q, he came often to this non-segregated speak. Which meant he had to have *some* level of ease with Black folks. And he'd just downed a gin followed by sipping another. That should've settled any remaining nerves.

He's lying . . . but about what?

She leaned forward. "Mr. Nickerson, if you want us to print your side of the story, we need the truth."

"I *am* telling the truth."

"No, you lied to us just now. About the color of the motorcar."

His mouth set in a determined line. "I am not lying."

El gestured to Flo. "Alright, pack it up. Let's go." She made a move to get up.

"Wait," he said. He blew out a breath. "You can't print this. You must promise me you won't print this. I've already got it bad enough with being fired for 'dereliction of duty,' or whatever the bushwa reason Rich gave. I'll never get another job if this particular thing gets out."

El settled back into her chair. She folded her hands and placed them onto the table. "Well?"

Frank glanced off to the side, embarrassed. "I can't see color," he mumbled.

El cocked her head. "Excuse me?"

Frank squirmed in his chair and faced her. "My eyes. They don't see color. I mean, they see blacks, grays, and whites, but reds, greens, blues?" He shrugged. "I couldn't tell you what they look like. So the motorcar I saw was gray but it could've been—"

"Any color," El finished for him.

"Exactly." Frank averted his eyes, obviously ashamed of his inability.

El waited a beat before asking, "And the shots?"

"Now that, I know. Ain't nothing wrong with my ears. I don't care what those coppers said. No one fired a gun that night. And trust me, living in this city, I know what a gunshot sounds like." He tapped his finger on the table, looking at Flo and her notebook. "Make sure you get that."

Flo nodded. "Duly noted."

El said, "And where were you at around three o'clock that morning? Which floor?"

"On the ground floor checking the machines and making sure there wasn't any funny business."

"And a half hour past that?"

"Still on the ground floor. There's lots of nooks and crannies there, plus I checked all the trucks."

Flo said, "You were being thorough."

"Damn right, I was. And that's how I know there were no shots. I would've heard 'em at that hour. The city's actually quiet in the middle of the night, and you can hear everything."

El knew that to be true given all the times she came home well past midnight and just before dawn.

Flo continued making notes while El pondered her next question.

"Mr. Nickerson," she said. "We have heard rumors of some men looking to destroy the delivery trucks."

"Oh yeah?"

"'Damage squads,' I believe they're called. The union denies it, but a source says they overheard talk of vandalizing factory property."

Frank rubbed the bottom of his chin. "If it isn't the union, who else could it be?"

"We don't know. Do you have any ideas?"

Frank sat back in his chair, causing it to creak and pop. "Honestly, I'd say it was Rich Holloway himself."

Flo looked up from her notebook. "Why would Mr. Holloway sabotage his own factory? Doesn't he have enough with this strike to deal with?"

"Think about it. The strike's been going for six months. He looks like a weak man for not getting it resolved. Public opinion's mixed, but it's not shifting overwhelmingly in his favor. He's losing customers and he's losing money. And I heard Mr. Holloway spends far more than he makes."

"He'd be desperate."

"That's the word I'd use," Frank said. "Vandalizing his own property would give him the ammunition he needs to discredit the union, get more people to side with him, and upset future negotiations. Especially if he gets law enforcement involved. Then he gets to use the might of the law to put pressure on the union."

"He'd do that?"

Before El could stop herself, she said, "Of course, he

would! I saw him fire a gun into the air to get people to do what he wanted."

Frank laughed and pointed at her. "You know Rich pretty well."

"I, uh, well, do enough interviews with people and you get a decent sketch of a man. A few more questions, if you don't mind."

"Fire away."

"Did Miss Holloway ever come to the factory after hours? We know that she'd been banned from the premises after an argument with her brother."

"Oh, you heard about that? Pretty good reporting skills, ladies. Yeah, it was a bad one. About the maintenance he was scrimping on. Just after Sam Willing lost his hand in the machine. Let me tell you, she was *furious*. But if you're asking if I ever saw her after that? No, I never did."

"What about Lucien Laurent?"

"Her fiancé?"

El described Lucien—not the eye color, since Frank wouldn't register it, but Lucien's general appearance—but Frank said he hadn't seen him.

"What about the name Raymond Price?" she asked. "Does that mean anything to you?"

"Raymond Price, Raymond Price." Frank gave a sad smile. "Sorry, miss. Name means nothing to me."

Something gnawed at El, something about Frank's candidness. Sure, he was a bitter employee unjustly fired, but there was something else, something that didn't quite make sense.

"Mr. Nickerson, it's clear from this interview that you don't approve of how Mr. Holloway is running his business. I'm curious: why didn't *you* join the strike?"

He paused for a moment. "Well," he said. "It comes down to rent. I couldn't risk not paying it."

"I'm told the union is covering people's expenses."

"Yeah, but for how long? It's only a matter of time before Rich and his cronies wait it out. And I wasn't about to be thrown onto the streets. But you're right, Miss King. I don't like the way that place is run." He suddenly turned somber. "Those union folks better be careful. If these so-called damage squads are getting involved? No matter who hired them, there's gonna be violence. And someone else may get killed."

22

"Alright, now," El called from the stage at Chez J.A. "This one comes from our Mother of the Blues, Miss Ma Rainey. I hear she's going to record her version of 'Black Bottom.' And let me tell you, she knows a thing or two about bottoms."

"I'd love to see yours!" yelled a male audience member.

El scoffed. "I love how menfolk think that they can ask for something and get it with no questions asked. Can I get an 'amen' from the sisters out there?"

"Amen!" the women in the audience replied.

The man, however, wouldn't give up. "I can take you to church and themsome! I got me a big ol' gospel pipe!"

"Baby, I can guarantee it doesn't hold a candle to the size of mine. But let me sing Ma's song and clear something up for you. And for the rest of you fellas. You all know Ma Rainey?"

"Yeah!" replied the crowd.

"I *said*, do you all know Ma Rainey?!"

"Hell, yeah!"

"Let's get to it." El cracked her knuckles and with a trill and a vamp, she set off on another bluesy adventure.

Went out last night, had a great big fight
Everything seemed to go on wrong
I looked up, to my surprise
The gal I was with was gone

Where she went, I don't know
I mean to follow everywhere she goes
Folks said I'm crooked, I didn't know where she took it
I want the whole world to know

El pointed in the direction of the male voice cat-calling her. "Here's the part you need to pay attention to."

They say I do it, ain't nobody caught me
Sure got to prove it on me
Went out last night with a crowd of my friends
They must've been women, 'cause I don't like no men

At that last line, the whole place erupted into cheers and applause.

It's true, I wear a collar and a tie
Makes the wind blow all the while
Don't you say I do it, ain't nobody caught me
You sure got to prove it on me!

El finished the song to her usual rousing applause and paused to take a bow. She leapt off the stage and returned to her dressing room, filled with the crackling energy only a good crowd can bring.

Earlier that night, El and Flo had shared with Madam Watkins everything they'd learned or set in motion that day. In turn, they learned Madam Watkins was still waiting on

Sergeant Williams, although he did tell her the pounders were searching pawn shops for Alice's blue velour coat. So far, no one had tried to pawn it. And no one had found Alice's .32 Colt pistol at the Holloway townhouse.

After that discussion, they tried to keep El from going on stage.

"It's quite understandable," Madam Watkins had said, "given the circumstances."

El had been adamant. "I can't let you down."

"You won't be letting me down. You've had one of the worst things happen to you that can happen to a person. You lost the love of your—"

"I *said* I'm going on."

Flo attempted to intervene. "El, you're in no state to get on that stage tonight."

"But I'm in the state to play detective?" El bit her lip. "Look, I appreciate your concern. Both of yours. But I need this. I need to sing. I need to laugh. I need to hear other people sing and laugh. Alice is—was—my life, but so is music. I've lost Alice. I can't lose music too."

They hadn't been persuaded.

El tried a different tack. "If we're trying to keep suspicion off me, then I can't all of sudden disappear from the spotlight, now can I? There's not much else we can do tonight to solve her murder. And selfishly, I've *got* to do something."

She then played her trump card. "Flo, you've got to perform tonight, so you can't stick to me like glue. Madam, you've got responsibilities of your own to tend to. If I'm on stage, I'm staying out of trouble."

They eventually, but reluctantly, agreed.

And the show went well, though El skipped over the more sad songs and focused purely on the raunchy blues.

She'd just taken off her stage outfit and settled into her silk robe when there was a knock on her dressing room door.

"Who is it?" she called, checking her reflection in the mirror.

A muffled male voice said through the door, "Someone wants to meet you, Miss El."

"I told you before, it's just El! And have them wait by the stage door!"

"They're most insistent."

"Means they slipped you a bill or three," she muttered to herself. She made sure her robe was good and tied shut and called out, "Come on in!"

The door opened. One of the waiters, who at least had the good grace to look sheepish. Behind him was a man of average height and weight dressed in a chocolate-brown pinstriped suit with a cream-colored shirt, a hunter-green tie, and a matching handkerchief peeking out from his front breast pocket. He held a dark brown trilby in his hands, exposing thick but short black hair flecked with gray. A dark brown overcoat was draped over his forearm.

Standing next to him was a woman with posture so straight, her spine must've been a steel rod. The severity continued with a narrow triangle of a face unadorned of any face paint. A slight lift of her pointed chin gave the appearance of her gazing down her nose at everyone and everything. Plain brown hat, high ruffled collar, a brown coat draped over a shapeless pink dress that would've gone past the ankles had the floor not been there to stop it.

"Miss El—err, El," the waiter said. "Maybe I present to you Reverend Elijah Blackburn and his wife Constance."

At first, the name didn't register. Then it did. Reverend Blackburn. The up-and-coming preacher passing out flyers demanding that the "good, righteous citizens of Harlem" boycott shows like El's. She felt her stomach drop.

"Reverend and Mrs. Blackburn," she said through a forced smile. "What an unexpected surprise. I hope you don't mind my not getting up. I just finished a set and I need to rest for a little bit."

Reverend Blackburn's smile was big and toothy as he entered the room. "I understand. And don't worry, neither Constance nor I stand on ceremony."

Constance entered much more reticently, her eyes scanning the area as if masked bandits would come flying out of the woodwork.

The waiter bowed slightly to the Reverend. "I'll leave you be, then. Reverend. Mrs. Blackburn."

Reverend Blackburn clasped the man's hand into his own. "Thank you, my son."

El didn't doubt another bill had just been slipped into the waiter's palm.

The door soon closed and it was only the three of them.

Reverend Blackburn said, "A pleasure finally meeting you, Miss . . . "

"Call me El, if you don't mind."

Constance interrupted. "But that's not your Christian name. I thought it was Eloise Ankins."

El gazed warily at her. "My name is El." She turned back to Reverend Blackburn. "Reverend, what's good?"

"God," he replied. "God is good. And God is wonderful, as is this part of the city we are making our own."

"No argument here."

Reverend Blackburn glanced around. "You have a wonderful setup here."

"All thanks to Madam Watkins."

"We saw your show this evening. I must say, it was—well, it was quite the experience."

Constance muttered, "Nothing but blasphemy."

Reverend Blackburn shot his wife a warning look. "I do, however, agree with my wife. It toed the line in several places, which I don't mind at all. But then, you crossed it and crossed it with glee. That number about the bluenoses, well." He laughed self-consciously. "As a bluenose, I suppose you'd call me, I must take offense."

El replied, "It's only offensive if you're a hypocrite. See, Reverend, that's what the song is about. Those who claim to be high and mighty but then act quite differently behind closed doors."

"I don't see how that's very Christian of you."

"Oh, I disagree, Reverend. I think it's quite Christian of me. If I recall from my Bible-school days, Jesus himself didn't react well to the hypocrites. Had a good old-fashioned temper tantrum in a temple about it."

Constance glared at her. "Insolent. How dare you speak of our savior that way—"

Reverend Blackburn held up a hand. "I don't see a need to get angry with one another."

El nodded. "I agree. I get the sense you want to say your piece, so the floor is yours, Reverend."

Reverend Blackburn gestured with the trilby in his hand. "This is a great time for us. A wondrous opportunity. I don't go in for all the so-called artistic-ness of some of these youngsters, like Hughes and Wallace, but I do appreciate what they're trying to achieve. Reclaiming our identity, defining who we really are, outside of our history being enslaved."

El placed a hand behind her ear. "I hear a 'but' coming."

Reverend Blackburn gave another toothy smile,

although this one was of a parent indulging a precocious child. "*But* I must advise you, as a sister in our community, that the days of jazz and liquor will soon come to an end."

"Not from where I'm sitting. The clubs are as packed as ever."

Constance's voice dipped a few temperatures below freezing. "Just because something is popular doesn't mean it's right. And it doesn't mean it can't be erased."

"Constance," murmured Reverend Blackburn.

She dipped her chin and bowed her head in deference to her husband.

He turned to El and said, "Though my wife spoke out of turn, she does speak the truth. It's never too late to turn your heart towards the Lord."

"Hearts are fragile things, Reverend," El replied. "I tend to be very careful who I give mine too."

"With Jesus, it's in good hands."

"Yeah, but is Jesus in good hands with the church?"

He bit his lip. "I see we may be at an impasse. For now. Come on, Constance." He started towards the door, but stopped. "I am building a coalition to stop the promotion of perversion, on stage and off. I would hate for you to become a target of that coalition."

El crossed her arms over her chest. "Is that a threat, Reverend?"

"Not at all. Consider it a . . . warning. Have a good evening."

As they turned to leave her dressing room, Constance shot one more look of daggers El's way.

23

"How is it that you *still* managed to step in it with your good shoes on?" Flo said the next morning in El's apartment. "'I'll be on stage,' you said. 'I can't possibly get into trouble,' you said."

"Relax, Flo. I handled them just right."

"No, you didn't! You practically declared war on the most powerful preacher in Harlem!"

El shrugged as she went about dressing. "I got them to leave my dressing room and that is good enough for me."

"El—"

She waved Flo off. "The Reverend and his sourpuss of a wife are tomorrow's problem. We need to focus on today's problem. Speaking of which, what *is* today?"

"Friday."

El felt a surge of panic. "Friday? Oh shit. Flo. I forgot all about it. I'm supposed to give that no-good Les a replacement act by today or else he's holding me to my contract!"

"Madam Watkins and her team of lawyers couldn't break it?"

"No, but she made a counteroffer that he refused to sign

unless I give him another act. What am I gonna do, Flo? I can't find Alice's killer and bring him to justice *and* play talent agent?"

Flo placed both hands on El's shoulders. "What we're going to do," she said in a calm voice, "is tell Les you're getting an extension."

"We can't ask that!"

"Listen to the words I'm saying, sis. We're not asking him. We're *telling* him. What time does that fancy wristwatch say?"

El glanced down at it. "Uh, it's a little past eleven. Les has been auditioning acts during the afternoon. Acts. Huh. More like talentless family members."

"Then that's when we'll go. Now. Let's grab some lunch. I'm starved. And you can't meet with Les on an empty stomach."

Once they were both dressed, they hoofed it down the stairs.

"They ever going to fix this thing?" Flo said, pointing to the out-of-service elevator.

Outside, they headed to a corner cafe, holding onto their hats so the vicious November wind didn't snatch them off their heads. Winter felt like it was coming early this year, and El was not ready for it.

Fed and fortified with coffee, they exited the cafe, the wind calmer now.

"Hold on," El said. "There's something I gotta do first."

"What?"

"My numbers."

Flo rolled her eyes. "Are you serious? We've got too much to do."

"It'll only take a second." El was already charging towards her usual street corner. To her dismay, she saw

Terrence giving Lucky's son Lenny more unnecessary grief.

She marched over to them and yelled, "Terrence!"

The old man whirled around, causing his too-big trilby to slip down his forehead. He pushed it back with annoyance. "What the—El?"

"What did I say about going after a defenseless little boy?" She got up close to Terrence and placed her hands on her hips, ready to do battle.

"Now listen to me and listen to me good," Terrence fired back. "You ain't gonna tell a man how to feel and what to do. I know what I know and I know this boy and his no-good father are pocketing my winnings."

"You got no proof!" Lenny yelled back.

Both Terrence and El looked at the boy with surprise.

"Alright," El said. "I see someone's brave enough to stand up to a bitter, crazy old man."

"I ain't crazy," Terrence replied. "And I ain't old, either."

"Check your mirror. What number did you put in yesterday?"

"Forty-six. See, I had a dream that I was on a ship going to the Argentine. I was dressed all fine in this white linen suit, straw hat, and cane. I looked like a million dollars. And when I went to my cabin, it was number—"

"Forty-six, yeah, I get that."

Terrence frowned at her but continued. "So I put in a combo of four and six."

El feigned patience she certainly didn't feel. "And what was the number?"

Lenny answered, "Three-hundred and sixty-seven."

"Alright, so you won some with the six. What's your problem?"

Terrence sputtered indignantly. "But I should've won more! The dream, El. Cabin forty-six and I'm a millionaire heading to South America!"

"You and your damned dreams. Don't you know they don't mean nothing!"

Terrence lifted his chin piously. "Not according to Freud."

"Oh come off it, Terrence. You don't read Freud."

"No, but I know what he's about and he's about dreams having meaning."

"He's also about all of us wanting to do something nasty with our mothers. What's your point?"

"My *point* is that I should've won the whole pot!"

El said to Lenny, "Next time Terrence gives you grief, kick him in the chins."

Terrence pointed a threatening finger at the small boy. "You do that, I'll drop-kick you into the street."

"That's it." El grabbed the old man by the forearm and practically carried him away from Lenny, the motion almost causing Terrence to lose his ridiculously big trilby. A small crowd had gathered watching the two of them, including Flo, but El didn't care.

Once they were far enough away from Lenny, she said through clenched teeth, "Listen to me. You need to stop putting so much stock into these dreams. They're not visions. They're not premonitions. They're the result of too much—" She sniffed his breath. "—cheap gin by the smell of it."

Terrence straightened the trilby on his head. "You gotta learn to respect a man, El."

"No, you gotta learn to respect *me*. I told you if you threatened that boy one more time—"

"Yeah, yeah, alright, you'd change the way I walk permanently. Now let go of me."

She waited a moment before releasing her grip.

Terrence rubbed his arm, wincing. "You probably bruised me, El."

"Serves you right. You know, instead of you chasing these nonsense dreams, you could be making an honest living."

"I did that."

"And?"

"Kept getting fired," he mumbled.

"Well, you gotta do something. How else you going to pay your rent?"

"Maybe I outta throw myself a rent party like that Sam Willing is."

This surprised El. "Say what again? And how do you know Sam?"

"I don't, but I saw a flyer for the party. They're raising money on account of the strike ain't resolved and the Willings are going to be evicted. Ain't fair. He lost his hand and now he's gonna lose his home."

"When's the rent party?"

"Tonight. I've got the flyer here, if you wanna see it."

"I do."

A sly grin spread his lips. "I'll give it to ya only if you let me put in my numbers."

El grit her teeth. "Fine. But you better place your bet and leave. No more harassing Lenny."

"I won't, I won't. I promise." Terrence reached into his coat pocket and pulled out a small rectangular piece of paper. "Here you go. Should be one hummer of a party. They got Tubs Walker playing."

"Tubs? No kidding. I used to play the circuit with him."

El took the flyer from Terrence, scanning the details, including the times (9:30 UNTIL LATE) and the address.

Terrence whined, "Can I place my numbers now?"

"Yeah, yeah, sure."

Terrence scampered off towards Lenny. El watched to make sure he gave his number without incident, which thankfully he did.

Flo walked up to El, frowning with concern.

"What?" El said. "He was being a bearcat and I needed to tame him a little."

"You don't need to be causing public scenes right now. You need to be laying low."

"Well, it wasn't all for nothing." El held up the flyer. "Tonight, we have a golden opportunity to question all the union leads." She chuckled to herself as she folded the paper and placed it into her pocket. "I think our luck maybe changing."

"Let's hope that luck extends to Les."

"Nope. Absolutely not."

Leslie Charles preened in his cake-eater suit, one arm leaning on his bar, the other on his hip. The light gray fabric and white shirt with turquoise tie brought out the sapphire of his eyes. They sparkled now, knowing he had the upper hand on El.

They were standing next to the bar in the Oyster House while an older man with gray hair and an even grayer mustache plucked out keys on the out-of-tune piano.

Les had a drink in front of him. He didn't offer any to El or Flo. Flo stood just behind El, squeezing her hand to let her know she saw this bushwa as well.

"Look," El said. "It's been a hard week for me, and I don't have anyone worthy of my replacement. *Yet.*"

"Uh huh. I think you're stuck with me and I can call off this audition."

The music—which El could describe as a-tonal at best— abruptly stopped in the background. An indignant male voice said, "What was that now?"

El called out to the piano player, "You're doing great."

Les rolled his eyes. "He is *not* doing great," he hissed before clearing his throat and trying to calm down. "I have suffered through every jalopy piano player this side of Harlem. Every set of hands can't find the notes in the right time. Or hell, in *any* time. And if they sing? Good Lord, they sound like braying donkeys or caterwauling cats in heat. My ears have run out of blood, they've been bleeding for so long."

"Then you know how hard it is to find somebody decent, much less transcendent, like me."

"Or," Les said, "I can just keep you. Which is what I intend to do."

Flo cut in. "Les. You're giving her another week."

Les scoffed. "And if I don't?"

Flo stepped forward. "If you don't, I place a telephone call to the anti-vice folks every day until they decide to raid this place. Drinking. Dancing without a license. Maybe even . . . cocaine being snorted in the back."

Les's eyes widened. "You wouldn't."

Flo placed a hand on her cocked hip. "Wouldn't I?"

Les and Flo stared each other down.

El's head swiveled from one to the other.

The old man at the piano called, "Should I keep playing or what?"

Les blinked first, muttering a curse under his breath.

El smiled. "Keep it going, my brother!" she replied back to the player. The horrendous music started up again.

Les closed his eyes. "Alright, El. Another week. But no more. I mean it. I can't bear any more of this shit."

As they left the Oyster House, El murmured to Flo, "Thank you, sis."

"Any time."

They stepped out into the light, giving a quick goodbye to Horace.

"He give you more time?" he asked.

"Yeah, he did." El glanced back at the Oyster House. "Not sure if I'm gonna make that deadline either. Your brother Ambrose doesn't play, does he?"

"Shoot. He can barely play sweeper at that LeHane place. Though they've got him cleaning every inch of it. A big-time funeral coming through this weekend."

Flo asked, "Who?"

"That Holloway girl."

El froze.

Her funeral. It's this weekend. And I'm not even going to be able to say goodbye.

Horace noticed the change that came over her. "You alright, El?"

"Yeah. No. No, I'm not alright, Horace." She took a deep breath. "I'm gonna tell you something, but you can't tell anyone. Promise?"

"Of course, El."

"I'm not kidding. No chin music about this. To anyone."

Horace pursed his lips. "Don't insult me now. I meant what I said. I've kept plenty of secrets in my time, and I'm gonna keep yours."

And so, El told Horace about Alice. Not everything, of

course, but enough for him to understand why she asked him what she eventually asked him.

"Think you can do that for me?" she said.

Horace nodded. "I'll make it happen."

"Thank you, Horace."

"Don't mention it. And sis? I'm so sorry."

"Now what?" Flo asked.

"I don't know. We've got some time to kill before the Willings' rent party." El blew out an exasperated breath. "Something we're not seeing, Flo. I can feel it. But dammit, it's just out of reach."

Flo patted her shoulder. "It'll come."

"Yeah, but we don't have enough time to wait around for epiphanies." Which was, of course, when she had one. "Oh goodness me. How could I forget that?"

"Forget what?"

"Saint Nicholas Park. Lucien was walking through it the night he overhead the damage squad making their plans."

"He was walking through that place in the middle of the night? Is he crazy? That's one way to end up in the morgue fast."

"He said it's the best way to clear his head, but I think he's lying about that. I think it's the best way to do something criminal."

"Meet up with another extortion victim?"

"Possibly," El said. "But that's a different thought for another day. There's gotta be people in the park who might've overheard the same thing as Lucien."

"People . . . as in the tramps?"

El shrugged. "It's worth a shot, don't you think?"

Flo frowned. "That's one helluva long shot, El."

"You got any better ideas?"

Flo sighed. "Nope."

The rest of the afternoon passed slowly. It reminded El of the billiard games in Pearlie's Parlor, the irregular cadence that fell into a numbing routine: the crack of the cue ball, the impact into the object balls, and either the sweet sound of making the shot or the frustrated groan of a miss. Although in the case of El and Flo, they were missing every single shot.

Every tramp they stumbled across in Saint Nicholas Park hadn't seen or heard of a group of men planning something for the Holloway Paper Box Factory. Those that spoke to them, that is. El couldn't blame them. The best way to survive New York was to mind your business. Still, she hoped someone would sing a little chin music for a nickel or two.

"Lucien might've been lying," Flo said as they walked down another winding path.

"Don't think the thought hasn't crossed my mind."

After a few more silent stares or "no ma'am, I don't know a thing about that," Flo suggested they leave the park and grab a drink or two. El certainly needed a whiskey or three by now.

It was when the sun started to set and they reached a little clearing, home to a cluster of wooden benches, that things began turning around.

A man with a dark beard, wrapped in several overcoats and a crumpled, torn fedora was rearranging his possessions on one of the benches. Trousers, suit jackets, a couple of pairs of shoes, a few beat-up books, and a stack of discarded newspapers standing at least one foot tall.

"Excuse me, sir?" El said.

The man paid them no attention.

"Sir? Can we talk to you for a minute?"

The man held up a pair of trousers, eyeballing the waist and the length.

El pointed to them. "Those will look good on you. Might need to pin up the cuffs a bit, but I can show ya how to do that."

Now, the man looked up, interested. "Oh, yeah? I can never get 'em to stay put."

El held out her hand. "You got a needle? Or a hat pin?"

The man nodded.

"I'll teach you the trick."

The man narrowed his eyes. "These are mine."

"I know that. I'm not gonna take 'em."

"These are mine," he repeated. "Remember that." He looked over at Flo. "You's a witness."

Flo replied, "I'll swear to it in court."

The man hesitated for a minute before reluctantly relinquishing his hold over the trousers.

El turned them upside down so the cuffs were eye level. "See, what you do is fold it like so, making sure it's even all the way around liiiiike that," she said, doing the actions she described. She gestured to the man. "Pin?"

The man went rummaging through his stuff on the bench, coming up with what looked like a dozen pins.

"Got quite a stash," El said. She selected a ladies' hat pin and held it up. "What you do is take one and gently pin the folded-up part . . ." Once that was done, she asked for another pin and worked on the other cuff. She handed the trousers back to the man. "There. That should hold. You won't be able to go dancing in that, but you can walk around for a bit."

Flo gave El an appreciatively nod at her handiwork. "How'd you learn how to do that?"

"My oldest brother was the tallest, even taller than me. So when I wore his trousers after he outgrew them, they dragged the ground. My Mama sure wasn't going to help me fix them, so I had to figure it out for myself."

The man turned the trousers over right side up and studied the length again. "Yeah," he said, pleased with the result. "Yeah, this'll work. Thank you, sis, thank you."

"You're welcome. I'm El, by the way. This is my friend Flo."

Flo said, "Hello, sir."

The man tipped his hat to both of them. "Afternoon, ladies. My name's Ennis."

El smiled. "A pleasure to meet you Ennis." She waited a beat. "Ennis, can I ask you if you stay here at night?"

"Sure do. Safest part of the city. The streets are too dangerous. Gangsters running around shooting each other." Ennis shuddered. "Give me the park anytime. Only people here at night are folks getting some fresh air, maybe some sweethearts looking for a little privacy."

"Were you here a couple of nights ago?"

"Sure was."

"Did you see or overhear a group of fellas talking about the Holloway Factory?"

Ennis hesitated. "I might have."

El and Flo glanced at one another.

"I promise you, we're not gonna get you in trouble," El said. "We just want to know if they mentioned something about the trucks."

"The trucks," Ennis repeated.

"Yeah. The Holloway Factory trucks."

Ennis worked his tongue over his blackened teeth. "I might have."

Keep it steady now, El told herself.

She asked, "Did they say anybody's name?"

"Name?"

"Yeah. Like Rich or Malek or Ferrin. Ramona, Booker."

They watched each other for a moment.

"Girl's name," he mumbled.

"What was that?"

"They said a girl's name first."

"Who? Ramona?"

He shook his head. "Alice."

The name caught El by surprise. "Wha—what did they say about Alice?"

"One fella said, 'You gonna keep your sister in line?' Another fella said, 'I'll worry about Alice, don't you worry.'"

Your sister.

Goddammit. It was Rich who was here that night.

Ennis continued. "A third fella said, 'Alice is a soft touch. We set some fires and crack some skulls, she might side with the union.' The second fella said again, much meaner this time, 'I said, I'll worry about Alice.'"

Ennis went back to his bench, sorting through his stack of newspapers.

El looked up at the sky streaked with pink and orange. So Frank's theory proved to be right. Rich *was* trying to discredit the union by vandalizing his own property. After El told Alice about the damage squad, did she assume the same as well? Did she confront him? And did he kill her to keep her quiet?

Now if what Ennis said was true—and instinct told her it was—then Lucien must've recognized Rich's voice. Which meant he didn't just *happen* to be here and overhear the conversation. The extorting bastard followed his future brother-in-law here. And El would bet all the sugar in her bowl that Lucien didn't come to the factory that day she saved him from the picketers to warn Rich. He was going there to blackmail him.

She lowered her gaze, watching Ennis open one newspaper and scan the pages. Wait a moment. There was something else in what he said.

"Excuse me, Ennis? Sorry, I don't mean to interrupt. I know you're busy, but you told us they 'said a girl's name first.'"

"Yes, miss." Ennis turned the page.

El stepped forward. "What other names did they say?"

"Just one more." He turned the page again, his eyes never leaving the newspaper.

"And that was . . . ?"

He closed the newspaper and folded it. "I'm hungry."

"Same, baby."

"No. I mean, *I'm hungry.*"

El understood. She reached into her trouser pocket and pulled out a nickel. She held it up for him. "This should get you something."

He licked his lips. "Mmmhmm." He held out his hand.

She placed the coin in his palm. "There you go, Ennis. Now. What was the second name they said?"

24

To El and Flo's surprise, Madam Watkins insisted that she go with them to Sam Willings's rent party. Especially when they told her the name Ennis said he overheard: "Malek."

"Yeah," Ennis had said. "The mean fella told them, 'Malek will play ball, because if he doesn't, it's over for him.'"

Ennis didn't know what it meant, but El had a fair idea.

So did Madam Watkins. "You and Flo are walking into a room with a potential murderer surrounded by people who will protect him. I'd like to even out those odds."

"You got something to protect yourself with," Flo asked.

Madam Watkins replied by showing the Smith & Wesson in her purse. "What time should we meet there?"

They'd agreed on ten o'clock.

Madam Watkins picked them up from El's apartment in a black limousine, one of the most impressive motorcars El had the privilege to ride in. ("It's a Daimler. Danish. I saw it when I visited Copenhagen and knew I had to have it. Made order to spec, on account of the steering wheel needed to be put on the left side instead of the right.")

There were shiny black leather seats in front with a wood panel console and a giant steering wheel. The back interior sported light blue leather and teak wood underneath the windows. Madam Watkins and Flo sat in two swivel chairs made of grey cloth while El perched on the long bench behind them.

Their chauffeur dropped them off in front of the Willings' building on 150th Street, a four-story walk-up in faded brick, with chipped doorways and uneven floors and walls. By the time they reached the top floor, the party was hitting on all sixes. El felt the vibration of the music and dancing and heard the laughter and shouted conversations before they even reached the front door. When it opened, she barely heard the fella manning the door—a tall, lanky specimen in suspenders—tell them the price to get in.

They paid their two cents each and entered the mêlée.

The entrance hall held the couples that had peeled off from the main room. Men and women leaned against the white plaster walls in pairs, faces close, bodies closer, lips moving in murmured conversations, eyes only on each other. Some were a few paragraphs from leaving the place and beginning stories of their own.

El led Flo and Madam Watkins forward and found the living room jammed so full of people, she couldn't see beyond the first few feet. A rollicking piano played from somewhere—Tubs—its notes shouting over their heads and flying around the air. The floorboards beneath her shook. She couldn't see the people dancing, but she could hear those standing on the sidelines cheering them on.

Flo shouted in her ear, "Where are the union leads?"

El glanced around the smoky space. Nothing but working people who had survived the week and were ready to cut loose. Hotel and townhouse maids, railroad porters, shoeshine boys, laundry workers, truck drivers, kitchen chefs, corner butchers. All were done up in whatever glad rags they could find with drinks in their hands and smiles on their faces. Several sported cigarettes, adding to the cloud that hung over the room.

But of all the people she spied, none of them were Malek, Booker, Ferrin, or Ramona.

"I don't see them!" she shouted in Flo's ear.

Madam Watkins gestured to them, and they leaned their heads in. "I'll check the bedrooms. Miss Russell, you check the kitchen and the dining room. El, see if you can make it through this living room."

They dispersed, El watching as Flo and Madam Watkins disappeared into the crowd. She turned, squared her shoulders, and pushed her way through the throng, eventually finding the dance floor in the center. She saw a few women doing the Black Bottom, several men doing the Mess Around. One fella dropped to the floor and did the Fish Tail. Sweat tinged with sweet perfume and cedar cologne filled the air. The piano, tucked into the far corner, was commanded by a giant man in a flashy yellow pinstripe suit, his body almost as wide as the piano bench.

Tubs Walker.

He played fast and furious, as if he had to get the notes out before the world ended. He always played like that. Drank and smoked and—rumor had it—loved that way too. Like there was no tomorrow and he might as well suck up all that life had to offer in one night. Considering how the world almost ended a few years ago, with that "War to End All Wars" and the newspapers declaring that "God is Dead," El saw Tubs's point. Peace and freedom were on loan, and they could be recalled at any time.

Tubs chatted with a gaggle of girls while he played. Itty

bitty things leaning on the side of the piano. He was all smiles, his big, bushy brows bounced over his sparkling eyes, causing them to giggle. His gaze flicked over to El causing him to do a double take and grin even wider. Without missing a note, he raised one hand and gestured her over.

She pushed her way through and stood next to him.

"El!" Tubs called over his playing. "What are you doing here?"

"Doing my civic duty and helping out workers who want a fair shake. What are you doing?"

"Making money, baby."

"It's a fundraiser, Tubs!"

He shrugged. "They get the door, I get the tips."

One of the girls in the gaggle gave El the once-over with a dash of poison in her smile. The jealous type.

El gestured to the girls. "Tubs, you gonna introduce me to your harem?"

"Oh, where are my manners? Belinda, this is the infamous El Train. El Train, Belinda."

Belinda held out her hand, limp as a dead fish. "Charmed, I'm sure." Her face was a long oval, eyes a bit too far apart, mouth a bit too big. The layers of makeup she piled on didn't help to disguise these facts. She wore a simple blue dress with a dropped back and a high front. The fit wasn't quite right, and El assumed it was a dress she borrowed.

"What about me?" asked girl number two. This one was dressed in metallic silver with a black shawl draped over her arms.

"Sorry, baby," Tubs replied. "Winnie, this is El. El, Winnie."

Winnie was more attractive than Belinda, in El's opinion. Rounder face, thicker arms, thicker hips.

The third girl didn't wait for Tubs's introduction. She extended her hand. "I'm Dorothy. Dot for short."

Dot was taller than all three, over six feet, El had to guess. She was stick-thin with sharp cheekbones and a pointed nose. Her eyes, though, were arresting—big and round with large lashes. Reminded El of Josephine Baker's eyes.

Belinda stared at El uneasily. "How do you and Tubs know each other?"

Winnie and Dot leaned forward, curious for the answer as well.

Tubs, oblivious to the danger hidden in plain sight, replied, "Oh, El and me go way back, don't we, El? We both rotated around the rent party circuit."

Winnie's eyes bored into El's. "Did you now? And you two are still such good friends?"

Now *this* time, Tubs didn't miss the danger. "Winnie, baby, we were never like that. Only friends."

El chimed in. "Yeah, *Winnie*, I wouldn't dream of making moves on him. He'd crush me for one."

Tubs barked a laugh. "That's rich, El, that's rich. Me crushing you. More like the other way around."

"Boy, I wouldn't smother you. I'd break you. There's a difference."

Belinda did not find any of this banter funny. "Well, he's mine now, so hands off, El Train."

El looked at her. "Child, you've got nothing to worry about."

"Yeah, Bel," Tubs said. "Nothing to worry about."

Belinda was not mollified. "Do I look like a girl who takes wooden nickels? Maybe these two," she added, pointing to Winnie and Dot, "but I'm smarter than them."

Winnie and Dot took offense to this. They started

arguing with Belinda, their dander rising up like a bunch of squawking hens.

"Ladies! Ladies!" Tubs called. "C'mon now. Bel, I only got eyes for you." He looked over to Winnie and Dot. "And you and you."

Speaking of eyes, El rolled hers.

Luckily, *Bel* wasn't looking at her. She scrunched up her face and said in a baby doll voice, "Really, Daddy?"

"Do you mean it?" Winnie rushed in.

Dot, not to be outdone, practically draped herself over the top of the piano. "Do you *really* mean it?"

"Of course, I do!" Tubs replied. "Now why don't you three go to the bar and grab us a couple of whiskeys. Think you can do that for Daddy?"

El felt something revolt in her stomach. She swallowed it—and the unbidden retort—down with a forceful swallow.

The gaggle nodded, all smiles. As they turned, El saw their lips drop and their eyes narrow as they gave each other the cold shoulder. El did *not* want to see how this was going to end.

As soon as they were gone, El and Tubs looked at each other.

"Daddy?" she said, arching an eyebrow.

He shrugged, still playing. He never once looked down at the keys, never once missed a note. "That's what they call me. And don't give me no lip, El. They're pretty and they're willing. Fits all the requirements I need."

"Except they're all not gonna fit in your bed."

He bounced those bushy eyebrows up and down. "Yeah, but we gonna have fun trying."

"Uh huh." El glanced around. "I'm hoping you can help me. I'm looking for the union leads, the folks putting on this clambake." She repeated their names. "You seen them around?"

His smile dimmed somewhat. "Yeah, and let me tell you, they've *not* been getting along. That's the problem with these kind of parties. I see and deal with all the drama under their roofs. Makes me wanna quit this shit."

"Anything to do with Malek Polowski?" El asked.

"Now how'd you know that?"

"Lucky guess. What's the word?"

"The word is he may be on his way out. The strike's been going for six months with no gains in sight. People are getting nervous. There might be a vote of no confidence. Or at least, that's the chin music I'm hearing near my piano."

Rich's words echoed in El's mind: *"Malek's gonna play ball or it'll be all over for him."*

"Where can I find him?" she asked.

Tubs looked around, his hands still pounding out chords. "He might be on the fire escape. I heard he wanted some fresh air."

El patted his shoulder. "Thanks, Tubs. Good seeing ya."

"You too, El."

She left the piano, passing by the gaggle of girls carrying Tubs's drinks. They gave her death stares, which amused her to no end.

The next room held the food and the bar. Oily smells of fried fish, boiled greens, and steaming chitterlings mixed with the pungent sweetness of whiskey, gin, and beer. A long table had been set up near the wall where a line of folks waited for their plates. On the other side of the room was the bar—or rather, an end table stacked with bottles. A man stood behind it, serving up cocktails as fast as he could.

The crowd here flicked her curious glances. Some whispered to each other and smiled. She heard her name bandied about and felt her chest warm with pride.

She continued walking to the back corner of the room and found a window opened a crack. She peered outside and saw Booker and Malek leaning against the railing of the fire escape, engaged in an intense conversation.

She pushed up the sash and leaned her head out. "Mind if I join you?"

Booker took one look at El and glanced away, muttering.

Malek was more polite. "Good evening, El." He offered her a hand as she navigated her way through the window.

"Whoo!" she said once she steadied herself. "Thank you, Mr. Polowski."

"Please, call me Malek."

"I will then. So," she said, "what are we talking about?"

Booker replied, "With all due respect, El—and you know I deeply, deeply respect you—our conversation is none of your business."

"Well, then. I guess I'll just take what I learned about Malek and Richard Holloway and go to the police with it. Or better yet, maybe to a reporter. I hear they pay good money for sources now."

Malek frowned.

Booker tilted his head in surprise. "What is this? What are you talking about?" He looked at Malek. "What is she talking about?"

"Nothing," Malek replied.

El put her fists on her hips. "It's not nothing. I've got a witness who overheard Rich say to a damage squad that you're gonna play ball or you're out."

Malek's voice stayed eerily calm. "What's that supposed to mean?"

"I suppose it means he either has something on you, or

will, or you're already in his back pocket. Which is it, Malek?"

Booker held up his hands. "Now wait just a minute. You can't waltz out here and accuse people—"

"What do you think, Malek?" El said, running right over Booker's words. "You desperate for a deal? Word around the party is that you haven't been able to get anything done for six months. Desperate men do desperate things—even make deals with the Devil."

Booker sent a beseeching look to Malek. "Tell me this isn't true."

Malek tugged at his bottom lip, the first sign of nervousness El had seen in the man. "Mr. Holloway is a formidable opponent. We haven't been able to crack him. I was hoping Miss Holloway's money would keep us afloat as well as give the impression this will be a very long, very expensive strike for him. But it appears that Mr. Holloway is a stubborn man."

Almost as stubborn as Alice.

"And he is a devious man," Malek continued. "He told me last weekend that he has contacts with the government. He would get me expelled from the country unless I agreed to a deal."

El said, "He threatened to *deport* you?"

Malek paused before nodding.

Booker's mouth went slack. "What deal did you make?"

"I haven't made any deal. Not yet. The terms are—not what—not what we want them to be."

"Which are . . . ?"

Malek ran his hand over his mouth before responding. "A two-dollar raise. Monthly machine maintenance only. Shifts are still fourteen hours."

Booker's face darkened. "Malek, we can't *possibly* accept that deal!"

"I know that. But now . . ." Malek glanced over at El. "Without your friend's money, we don't have a choice."

Booker cursed under his breath. "That explains it then."

El said, "Explains what?"

Booker looked at her. "He wanted me to agree that the Black workers would earn less than the white workers." He turned back to Malek. "That was gonna be your counteroffer, wasn't it? Has a certain appeal to a man like Rich."

El gestured to the both of them. "Is that what you were fighting about at the picket line yesterday?"

"You saw that, huh?"

"Booker, I think *everybody* saw it." She focused her attention on Malek. "Did Alice know about this deal with Rich or your counteroffer?"

Malek swallowed with some difficulty. "She did."

"And what did she say?"

Malek pulled at his bottom lip again. "She refused to accept Rich's offer or my counter."

"Did you listen to her?"

"I—I know there are rumblings of replacing me if things do not change. My own situation aside, I needed to—"

Booker exploded. "You needed to what, Malek? If you were a liability, you needed to step aside. What about the workers? The people who trusted you, trusted *us*? What about *them*?

"If we continue on any longer, it'll be like that factory in New Jersey. The money runs out, the people return to work only to find they've been replaced. Do you want to tell me that Mr. Holloway won't do the same thing? He's already doubled the number of scabs. Their production is almost at the level of what ours used to be. We're . . . we're out of time."

Booker didn't respond.

El cleared her throat. "Malek, did you tell Alice you were going to agree to Rich's terms?"

"I—" Malek averted his eyes, not wanting to look at either of them. "I said there was a possibility it would be the final offer. I hadn't decided then." He looked up at El. "But then you told her about the damage squads. At the meeting, it became clear to me that Rich would not only threaten deportation to me, he would commit crimes in order to end the strike. Not only would we lose our members' employment, they could possibly lose their freedom. Their lives." He turned to Booker. "I couldn't let that happen."

Booker stared at Malek for a long time. "Sometimes we have to do what's difficult. To sacrifice. That's what you told all of us. Was it just talk, Malek? Just rhetoric?"

El interrupted them. "At the emergency meeting, where Alice told you about the damage squad: Was that when you decided to go against her wishes and agree to Rich's deal?"

Malek didn't answer right away.

El waited him out.

Finally, he said, "Yes."

Booker exhaled a long breath that sounded like a hiss.

El leaned towards Malek. "And now she's dead. Quite a coincidence, don't you think?"

"I didn't kill her."

El dropped her voice, anger torching her words to ash. "You better pray to the good Lord that's true. Because of it isn't . . . ?"

She left the threat unspoken and returned to the apartment.

25

Inside, the party had become even louder than from when El first arrived. Voices ricocheted like gangsters' bullets off the walls and the ceiling. No one here had any idea that their strike leader Malek Polowski had agreed to sell them out for relative pennies compared to what men like Rich Holloway were making.

Lord, I need a drink after hearing all that.

She went to the bar line and ran smack dab into Ramona Westfall.

Ramona's eyes widened. "You!" she said.

"That's right! Me!"

"What are you doing here?"

El cupped a hand behind her ear, even though she heard what the woman said.

Ramona raised her voice. "I said, what are you doing here?"

El gestured to the room around them. "I can't hear you! Where's a quiet place?"

Ramona looked aghast. "I'm not going anywhere with you!"

"What?!"

"I said I'm—oh for goddsakes. Come with me!"

It was exactly what El wanted to happen. She kept the smirk off her face as Ramona led her to a tiny hallway just off to the side of the bar and food room. A line of three people—two men, one woman—leaned against the wall. This must've been where the WC was.

The noise level here dropped by half.

"Alright," Ramona said, turning around to face El. "What is it you want?"

"You know, we gotta work on your manners."

"I don't have time for this—"

"I hear Malek's getting ousted. You know anything about that?"

Ramona bit her lip. "I'm not discussing union business with you."

"Who started the groundswell to get him removed? Was it you?"

"Me? Why on earth would it?"

"Because you haven't gotten results and you disapprove of the way Malek runs things. That was clear as day the night I first met you. And after all, it was *his* idea to bring in Alice, wasn't it? Which has put the union in a precarious position in light of her murder."

"Seems to me those are all good reasons to have the man removed."

Wait until she hears that he was going to make a deal with Rich.

El asked, "Who's going to take his place?"

"There are a few contenders."

"One of them you?"

Ramona scoffed. "Please. A woman's not allowed to lead an entire union section."

"Why not?"

"Because the men won't let us. Anyway, this doesn't concern you."

"That night after the emergency meeting, did you chat with Alice at all?"

"Like I told you and I told the police, I went home."

"You did say that, yeah, but I'm wondering if you simply *forgot* a little meeting afterwards."

"What meeting? Oh, that thing you mentioned. Something about a confusion she needed clearing up."

El pointed to her. "That's the one. That confusion wasn't something to do with you, was it?"

"Like I said the other night, I have no idea what you're talking about."

"What about the name Raymond Price?"

"Who?"

"Raymond Price. Alice asked Booker about him and he didn't know anyone by that name."

"Well, add me to the list, because I haven't the foggiest idea who that man is."

"Not one of the strikers?"

"Nope."

"And you haven't heard it mentioned by anyone else."

A slight hesitation. "No, I haven't."

El grinned. "Oh, Miss Westfall. You lied just now."

A patch of red formed at the base of her throat. "I did not!"

"Oh, yes, yes you did. Someone else mentioned it. Who was it?"

"I don't have to tell you."

"It'd be easier on you if you did. Look. I don't like talking to you anymore than you like talking to me. You give me some answers, I'll leave you alone. Especially if, as you claimed, you had nothing to do with Alice's death."

Ramona's face shut down. "I can't tell you who."

"Miss Westfall—"

"I *can't*. It's—it's too dangerous for me."

El frowned. "Dangerous? Why would that be dangerous? Did this person threaten you?"

"No," Ramona replied quickly. "No, never. But the identity of this person would cause me trouble. This person had nothing to do with Alice's death, I swear it. I swear it on my life."

"Did this person have a connection with Miss Holloway?"

The WC door suddenly opened and out stepped Ferrin.

"Oh!" he said. "Miss Westfall. And . . . El, is it?"

"Mr. Thomas. Nice to see you again."

"Likewise. Did you find the address for Mr. Nickerson?"

Ramona scowled. "What?"

El ignored her. "I did, thank you, Mr. Thomas."

"Good," he replied. "Sorry I couldn't have been more helpful. You understand why I couldn't—well—anyway." He looked over at Ramona. "Are you waiting in line?"

"No," she said darkly. "I was just leaving."

Which she did.

Ferrin looked after her while the next person in line ducked into the WC. "What's up with her?"

"I may have upset her. I have that effect on some women." El turned to Ferrin. "Mr. Thomas, what does the name Raymond Price mean to you?"

Ferrin's glasses slid down his nose and he paused to push them up. "Who is that?"

"I don't know. Alice was asking about him, but no one seems to know who he is."

"Oh, I see. I wish I could help but—" Ferrin shifted his weight from foot to foot.

"You need a drink?" El offered.

"No, no. I just—I don't like crowded spaces."

The WC door opened behind him, and he bent closer to El to let the man pass by.

"Sorry about that," Ferrin said, once he was able to back up a bit. "Are these types of parties always like this?"

"Packed like sardines? Usually. You hear Malek's out?"

Ferrin sighed. "Yeah, I heard. Shame. He's been really good and has really fine ideas, but putting them into practice proved to be more difficult."

"Especially with a man like Rich Holloway."

"Especially him."

"Ramona really led the charge against Malek?"

"She did. I know it might seem heartless of her, but she's only looking out for the union." Ferrin looked off to the spot where Ramona had disappeared into the crowd. "She's a very sweet, very lovely girl."

Intuition pricked El's ears. "Really? 'Cause she's been anything but sweet and lovely to me."

"Oh, that's just her way. You know, she hasn't had an easy life. Father used to beat her. Mother too. She worked in factories as a child, but neither of her parents did. Spent all the money she earned on drink. Eventually took up with a man who promised to marry her but never did. He also drank and, well, treated her like her parents did. That's why she's so passionate about protecting the women and children workers. She knows firsthand how vulnerable they are—both inside and outside the factory."

"She's built up a lot of walls, I suppose."

"Yeah," Ferrin said. "And topped them with barbed wire. But once you get past all that, she's—she's—well, she's special."

"You sweet on her?"

Ferrin blushed. "Hard not to be when you know her, I mean, really know her."

"She feel the same for you?" El knew the answer already—if Ramona had any feelings for Ferrin, they were either locked up behind that wall with barbed wire, or they didn't exist.

He sighed. "I'm hoping to change her mind. She's made it quite clear she doesn't want to stop working and earning money. Factory rules: Once she's married, she's fired. And she told me she doesn't want to be dependent on anyone ever again."

"I hear that. That's my philosophy too."

"She wants to go to a university, get out of the factory life. Doesn't have the money yet. Sometimes I think . . . maybe I could . . ." He trailed off.

"Pay her tuition?"

He gave her a shy smile. "It's silly, isn't it?"

"Not silly. Maybe misguided. If you don't mind my saying so, Mr. Thomas, if Ramona wants to be independent, that means she won't be beholden to a benefactor. She'd want to earn the tuition herself."

"Maybe. But in the end, how likely is it she won't need a husband who can provide for her? I could do that. I can't, yet, but I've been saving up for the day."

"I still think it's a fool's errand."

He bounced on his heels again, that nervous energy back. "I think I need some air."

"Fire escape," El replied. "Straight ahead that way."

"Thank you. And it was nice—nice seeing you again."

El followed after him as far as the food and drink room before returning to the main area where Tubs played. She paused to say goodbye to him, earning more hateful glares from his little harem.

A sudden hush quieted the crowd. An intrusive wariness blanketed the room followed by a volatile mix of fear and indignation. Even Tubs, who normally kept playing during police raids, knew better than to continue on. The last chords he played reverberated through the air before disappearing into silence.

Footsteps clicked their way towards them.

The crowd parted.

There stood Rich Holloway.

He glanced around, his beady eyes looking but not seeing. Finally, he said, "Where are Mr. and Mrs. Sam Willing?"

No one moved. No one talked.

"I have something for them. Something they'll want."

The crowd murmured, not knowing what to make of this. Finally, a tiny woman and a tall, lanky man missing one hand stepped forward.

"Good evening, Mr. Holloway, sir," the man said. "I'm Samuel Willing. This is my wife Ruth."

Rich pretended to smile. "Good evening." He reached into his inside coat pocket and brought out an envelope. He held it up, like a magician at the start of a trick, turning in a slow circle so that everyone could see what was in his hand.

"This is a check for the next six months' rent," he said.

A shocked gasp breathed its way around the room.

What's the catch? El wondered.

"But," Rich went on, "I will only part with this if the Willings agree to stop supporting the strike."

And there it is, El thought ruefully.

"You have misplaced your trust in Malek Polowski as well as his cohorts Ferrin Thomas, Booker Freeman, and Ramona Westfall. They have done nothing for you except keep you out of work. I don't wish that for you. I'm willing to agree to some of your terms. But this pro-Socialist, anti-American nonsense stops now."

El saw the room starting to divide between those who stood firm in their convictions, and those who wavered.

Still holding the envelope aloft, he said, "This offer for the Willings goes when I leave this apartment."

Sam and Ruth looked at one another, having a wordless conversation with their eyes. The money was tempting. It would solve many of their problems, as money often did. But a union, a community, a people were only strong if they kept together.

Sam tilted his head. Ruth nodded. He returned his attention to Rich. "The offer is most generous, Mr. Holloway. Lord knows we could definitely use it. But we respectfully decline."

The crowd murmured even louder.

Rich's face reddened but he kept his temper in check. "I see. I regret to inform you that you've made a very, very foolish decision." He tucked the envelope back into his inside coat pocket. "A very foolish decision, indeed." His eyes glittered with fury. He turned on his heel and slowly walked back through the crowd towards the front door.

Tubs tutted behind El.

She turned around. "What's that?"

"That's the beginning of a war," he replied. "And it's gonna get ugly."

"No doubt about that."

Once Rich crossed the threshold of the apartment and the front door closed, the entire place cheered. Several people went up and congratulated Sam and Ruth for staying steadfast with the union. Tubs started a jaunty tune, trying to right-size the party after Rich Holloway had almost capsized it.

Madam Watkins and Flo appeared at her side.

"What the hell was that?" Flo asked. "The nerve of him walking in here, making that kind of offer!"

"He's a very dangerous man," Madam Watkins summed up. "He believes he owns everyone and everything around him. He likely thinks he owns this apartment, despite the Willings' name being on the lease."

Flo muttered a few choice words about Rich before asking El, "You find the union leads? What'd you find out?"

"Nothing good," El replied. "Apparently, Rich has doubled the number of scabs working the factory, so his output is inching up closer to what it was before the strike."

"Damn. That's going to undermine the effect of the picket line."

Madam Watkins said, "I learned that Rich has been working with the landlords in Harlem. Coincidentally, every striker on the picket line has been notified of a sudden rent increase come December."

El rubbed her brow. "Right in time for Christmas. What a son of a bitch that man is. Excuse my language, Madam. On top of that, Malek is as good as gone as their leader. And none of them know who this Raymond Price is or why he's important."

Flo amended, "*If* they're telling the truth."

"Right." El gestured to the front door. "Come on, let's get outta here." She glanced at her wristwatch. "We're gonna be late for Horace."

26

The Lehane Family Mortuary, where Horace's brother Ambrose worked the night shift, was in a three-story building, with the first two floors dedicated to the mortuary and the third being the Lehanes' apartment. All the windows were dark.

Sitting on the front stoop was Horace, smoking a cigarette. When he saw them, he slowly stood, unfolding his large frame. He stamped out the cigarette.

"How you holding up?" he asked El.

She sighed. "I don't know. I've been running all over town, so I'm not certain how I feel." She glanced up at the Mortuary, a sorrow building up in her chest. "How am I going to get through this?"

"With us," Madam Watkins replied.

Flo reached out for El's hand, giving it a reassuring squeeze. "You're not alone, sis."

El squeezed the hand back. "Alright," she said. "Let's go see her."

Horace turned and knocked softly on the door. "Ambrose is already inside," he said over his shoulder.

The door opened and they stepped into darkness. El made out the shadowy shapes of chairs and couches for the grieving to sit. A counter separated the front room from the back. They went around the counter, Horace opening a side door that led them to a staircase.

Up top was a man half the size of Horace but with the same square-shaped face.

"Really appreciate this, brother," Horace told him.

"Just don't take too long in there. I gotta get everything dusted up."

Horace gave him a hard look. "We'll take as long as we need to." He held up a finger. "Remember, we weren't here. You don't know nothing."

"And I don't." Ambrose opened the door and gestured them inside. "Stay quiet. They're light sleepers." He pointed to the ceiling above, meaning the Lehanes.

Horace went in first, followed by Flo and Madam Watkins. When it was El's turn, she hesitated.

Go on now. Let's do this.

She inhaled and entered the room and immediately stopped at the sight before her.

Coffins.

Row after row of coffins.

The sight alone was enough to freeze even the bravest soldier in their tracks. But there was something else. A stillness that felt . . . oh, what would be the word? Reverent? Not quite. It didn't remind her of her younger days when she actually went to church and prayed with the congregation. All those heads bowed, all those eyes closed, lips murmuring, offering up thanks or pleas, sometimes both to a mystical force no one could explain, yet everyone understood.

Then she grew up. And the awe was replaced by confusion followed swiftly by disappointment. So, no. The stillness here wasn't reverence.

Eventually the word came to her: permanence.

Death was permanent, no matter what the preachers all said. No one ever came back. Certainly no one that El ever knew who died. Not her grandmother from old age. Not her brother from tuberculosis. Not her childhood best friend who went swimming in the river and got caught in the current.

But maybe Alice will.

Dimly lit hope. That's all it was. Just dimly lit hope.

The door closed behind her. Must've been Ambrose giving her some privacy. For that, she was grateful. She didn't need a stranger to see her like this. Not with her hands clammy and nausea swirling in her throat. She took deeper breaths, grateful for the ability to do so. These poor souls laid out before them would never draw breath ever again.

Flo cleared her throat. "Please tell me they say who's in what box. I don't want to open them all up."

Horace replied, "There should be tags somewhere."

Madam Watkins looked over the first coffin. A piece of paper rested on top of the lid. She picked it up and read it.

"Shay Little," she read aloud. "Not our Alice."

El turned to Horace. "Do they—I mean, do they fix them up? They don't leave them like they found them, do they?" She didn't want to see the look of pain and panic on Alice's face, the bloodstains, the marks of violence.

Horace said, "Don't worry. They make them look good, my brother says. Look peaceful."

The floorboards creaked under Flo's weight as she carefully threaded her way through the line of coffins, checking the names on the tags. After three, she paused. She looked over at El.

"Alice Holloway," she said in a quiet voice.

El swallowed. Her legs felt as heavy as lead. She concentrated on lifting one, then the other. One foot down, one foot up until she arrived at Alice's coffin. She ran her hands along the wood, feeling the buffed and polished grain underneath her fingers. Unbidden tears spilled from her eyes and slid down her face. She made no move to wipe them away, to sniff them back, to swallow them down. What was the point?

Flo came over to El's left side, Madam Watkins to her right. Horace stayed in the background, giving them space.

Surrounded by her two friends, El's hands shakily gripped the lid and lifted it up.

Her heart stopped at the sight of Alice's still face. The eyes and mouth were closed. Makeup had been applied to her cheeks, but it looked all wrong. The skin didn't glow as it normally would have. Alice looked pale, almost ghostly. The lips were painted but not with her usual ruby red, but rather, a muted burgundy. It wasn't her style, wasn't her personality. Alice *burned* with brightness. She sparkled like a sequin. Here, she was sanitized into a stately sainthood that was completely at odds with the rebellious, cursing, smoking, drinking soul she was.

The makeup wasn't the only thing wrong. They put her in a dress, some frilly frock she'd have mocked on sight. A demure beige that made her powdered skin even more alabaster. Likely Rich's idea.

At least her hair was more or less correct. That brown still luscious and thick. Only the curls had been straightened and flattened, the kinks erased.

El felt herself step back. It was Alice—and yet, it wasn't.

All the so-called "offensive" parts of her had been smoothed out for public social consumption.

Without realizing it, El's trembling hand reached out and gently brushed Alice's cheek. The skin was cold, almost waxy to the touch. Not human. Not her. El felt the inexplicable urge to grab both of Alice's shoulders and shake her awake.

Instead, she withdrew her hand, noticing a little of the funeral home's makeup had transferred itself to her skin. She brushed it off.

Madam Watkins said softly, "Shall we say a few words?"

El glanced over at Flo, who gave her a small but reassuring nod. "I'm not sure what to say."

"Say whatever you want," Flo replied. "This is your chance to say goodbye."

El flinched at the word. She gritted her teeth, willing herself to stay strong. "Alice." Her voice caught on the name, and she had to clear her throat. "Alice," she said, her voice stronger this time. "I, uh . . . I never intended to fall in love with you." A little laugh burst its way through. "It's true. I didn't want it. I just wanted to have my fun and to go on my merry way. And God knows, you *were* fun. Up for anything. You saw life as a great big adventure, one incredible wonder after another. Turns out you felt the same about a lifetime love."

El glanced up at the ceiling. "To be honest, babe, I—I didn't think that was possible for people like us. Making promises to each other and keeping them. Seems like everybody in this world wants to make sure we can't."

She dropped her eyes back down to Alice's face. "But you. You said those bluenoses with those pearls they clutched every hour on the hour could go f—I mean, could do something to themselves. It was the two of us against the world. And we were gonna win."

She lightly tapped the edge of the opened coffin. "I never met anybody as stubborn as me. 'Cause I felt the same, babe. Nobody was gonna tell me what I could and couldn't do. So when I knew you had to be my wife, I didn't hesitate. Just asked you right then and there at the goddamn Drip Dry."

She smiled at the memory. "It wasn't often I could shock you but Lord, I did that night! Your jaw dropped open, your eyes got all big. I thought you were gonna faint and had to remind you to breathe. Then you said, 'We can't do that. Nobody would marry us.' I told you, 'We're not doing it in a church. We don't need them. We just need us, a reverend substitute, and a witness. We don't even need a ring,' though I thought about getting you one. Maybe for when you'd finally leave that townhouse with all them busybodies around, Rich included. Maybe when you lived with me."

Which is never going to happen now.

She brushed the thought aside and continued. "Well, we got the reverend substitute. Vi from the Drip Dry. She predicted we'd end up like that from the beginning, the wise old crone." She flicked her gaze over to Flo. "And, of course, we got Flo here as our witness. Vi closed down the Dry for us, and we stood in the place where we met, dressed in our finest tuxes, and promised to always be there for one another. No matter what happens. Sickness, health. Richness, poorness. With you, my life was complete."

She took a shaky breath. "I don't know how I'm going to live without you, babe. I honestly don't. I'm incomplete again and I can't—"

A sudden flash of anger hit her. "Goddammit. You just

had to get yourself involved in this bullshit. You wouldn't listen to me. You never did. And now, because your dumb heart had to be so big, you couldn't let this mess with the strikers go. Why'd did you have to be so selfish? Why couldn't you walk away? From the strike, from the Sam Willings of the world, from . . ."

She trailed off, lost in her grief before she found her way back again. Wanting to ask, to say out loud, the question that kept coming back to her again and again and again. "Why wasn't I enough? Huh? Why wasn't building our life together enough? You're helping so many people, putting your life on the line. What about *our* life?"

She stared at Alice's face, memorizing it, hoping she'd never, ever forget it. "I didn't mean that," she said. "I didn't. I—I love you for thinking of others. For wanting better for others. And if you weren't this way, I don't know if I would've been so in love with you. Shit."

Her hands gripped the edge of the coffin. "I'm gonna find out who did this to you, babe. I am. I won't rest until I know who took you away from me, who took the other half of my heart."

Alice's face remained still.

El's mouth curled into a trembling smile. "Hey. You know?"

Come on, Alice. Come on. Sit up. Sit up and tell me you know. Do it!

But Alice remained frozen in time.

After a moment, El pulled herself together and replied for her: "I know."

Madam Watkins dropped them off at El's apartment. For once, El listened and decided not to go on stage tonight. They stopped at a telephone booth so Flo could call in sick to Connie's—over El's objections, but Flo held firm, saying El shouldn't be alone tonight.

"Are you sure you're okay?" Madam Watkins asked as El got out of the Daimler.

El turned and said, "I'm not sure of much anymore, but it's time to turn in. And I've got my friend with me."

Flo nodded, resolutely. "Damn right."

Madam Watkins looked up at them. "We'll meet tomorrow and discuss the rent party as well as everything else."

The chauffeur shut the passenger door and returned to his place behind the steering wheel. With a click and a wrench of gears, the Daimler moved forward, leaving El and Flo behind.

"You're certain you don't want to be on stage?" El asked Flo. "I don't want you to lose your spot over me."

"Quit that. You've been through hell tonight." Flo gestured to the building's entrance. "Let's get on up. I think we could both use a drink."

They turned and entered her building where, of course, the elevator was still out of order. Did *anything* get fixed in this city?

Once inside the apartment, El poured them both whiskeys. She lit up a cigar, and they chatted for an hour and a half about anything other than Alice's death. Naturally, the conversation turned to Flo and her career prospects.

"I asked them for a raise," Flo said.

"The Connie Brothers? What did they say?"

"They don't have the money."

"Bushwa. They got it. They just don't want to share it." El puffed on her cigar. "Those cheap bastards. You're the best damned dancer they've ever had. They wouldn't have *half* the audience they've got without you."

"They don't see it that way." Flo paused to take a sip of whiskey. "You know, maybe it's a sign. Maybe I've outgrown Connie's. Maybe it's time to go someplace else. Like you did going from the Oyster House to Madam Watkins's place."

"Well, if I get my big show off the ground, I'm gonna hire you first thing. 'Cause I've decided: I want it all. A big band. Dancers." El grinned. "You'd be perfect for it."

"I don't know about that."

"Yes, you will, and don't you argue with me. You can choreograph the show and dance the lead."

A faint smile spread Flo's lips. "Yeah. That would be fun working together."

"It'd be the best time."

Flo raised her glass. "To the best times yet to come."

Their glasses clinked.

That was when they heard thudding shoes in the stairwell. Both El and Flo looked up at her front door. The footsteps came down the hallway and stopped right in front of El's apartment.

Somehow El knew who they were.

An angry fist pounded on the door.

"Police! Open up! We're here to arrest Eloise Ankins for the murder of Alice Holloway!"

BEFORE THE TRIAL

27

El watched as the newshawks faded into a blur of streetlights and headlights. Her grip on the bars tightened, as did the fist inside her chest. The wagon turned this way, then that, going from Lenox to a side street to another avenue. A few newshawks had jumped into their respective motorcars and were following them. El gave them a baleful glare. The paddy wagon hit a giant pothole that rattled her teeth and almost caused her to fall.

"Jesus Christ!" said a male voice behind her. "Can they ever fix anything in this goddamn city?"

The voice startled El almost as much as the pothole did. She thought she was alone.

She slowly turned around, expecting to see a man. What she saw instead sitting on one of the two benches was a figure with pale brown skin all done up in black and silver fringe and furs.

A female impersonator.

Blond hair showcased a small, round face, smooth save for a few wrinkles around the eyes and mouth. Their lipstick might've been red but in the darkness of the paddy wagon, it appeared dark cherry.

They leaned forward, their manner concerned. "You okay, miss? Or is it mister?"

"Just El," El said, her voice still tight. She didn't like that. Made her sound weak.

"Well, Just El, you better sit down. We'll likely hit another one of those potholes from hell. Lord knows, they never fix anything in this city unless it's a street a Rockefeller or a Vanderbilt lives on."

To demonstrate her point, the wagon hit another one, not quite as deep as the last one, but still enough to almost take El's feet out from under her. Putting one hand on the ceiling and the other on the side wall, El slowly lowered herself onto the bench opposite the female impersonator.

"Where are we going?" El asked.

"At this hour? Probably the Fifth District Prison at the Harlem Courthouse. They got temporary cells and I hear the Jefferson Prison is full up at the moment, what with all the men complaining about independent women these days." The impersonator's eyes turned inquisitive. "You look shaken up. You ever been arrested before?"

"Can't say that I have."

"First time, huh? Well, I am impressed. Dressed like you, I'd have thought for sure one cop would've gotten his dander up and thrown you in the clink. They certainly get angry when they see me. God knows why. I'd brighten up their day if they stopped being so high-and-mighty." The impersonator smirked. "Bluenoses. Life would be so much better without them. Anyway, we're lucky. Only the two of us tonight."

The wagon made a sharp turn, pushing El forward. Her hands gripped the edge of the bench, trying to stop herself from being thrown onto the floor. Whoever was behind the wheel didn't know how to drive worth a damn.

"You got a name?" El asked, when she recovered.

"Depends. In the daytime, I'm Eugene; a name that, like the suit I have to wear to work, is a crime against the soul. But at night, I become *Mona Sinclair*." They struck a glamorous pose. "What do you think?"

"Beautiful," El replied and meaning it. "Both the name and the dress."

"Why, thank you! Mona suits me, as do the four F's: feathers, furs, and fringe."

"That's only three F's. What's the fourth?"

"If you have to ask . . ."

El held up a hand. "I got it."

"What about you? I assume it's not Just El."

El chuckled. "You're right. It's El Train."

"El Train." Mona's eyes lit up. "Wait a minute. I think I heard about you. You're a singer, right? At the Clam House?"

"Oyster House, although now I'm at the Watkins Hotel."

Mona raised their brows. "Woo! Too rich for my blood. I think one drink there costs as much as my rent." They tapped their chin. "But weren't you playing down in the Village recently?"

"Yeah, as a favor for a friend. Played Mischief Night."

Mona snapped their fingers. "That's it! That's how I *really* know your name. Do you know a bass player named Vernon? He plays down at this speak called Pinstripes. It's owned by what's-his-name? Dash Parker!"

"Hold up. You're seeing *Vern*?"

Mona grinned. "Indeed, I am. I'm a dancer and perform at the Siamese Cat Club. Tonight was my off night and I promised Vern I wouldn't get into any trouble, but then . . ." They gestured to the wagon around them. "Here I am, courtesy of Officer Ugly and Officer Uglier."

"What did you do?"

"It's too humiliating for words. I need a ciggy to tell this story." Mona reached into their purse and pulled out a cigarette and some matches. They placed the cigarette between their lips, struck the match, and cupped their hands around it. Once lit, they tossed their head back, taking in the initial puff with a satisfied moan. "Oh, that's much, much better."

An angry fist pounded the wall of the wagon separating them from the coppers. "I said no smoking back there!" a muffled male voice yelled. Sounded like Morton, the pockmarked pounder who'd sneered at El in the stairwell.

Mona yelled back, "How long do you want me to go without a ciggy, huh? You said we'd be at the jail by now!"

"You'll get there when I'm good and ready!"

"That what you say to all the girls?" Mona smiled, pleased with herself, and took another drag. They tilted their head at the wall separating them from the coppers. "That's Officer Uglier. I hope for the girl's sake he takes 'em from behind. At least that way, they don't have to look at his face."

"Sis, you gotta be more careful," El said. "They'll likely pop you in the mouth talking like that."

Mona waved her off with the cigarette in hand, drawing curlicues in the air. "They're all talk. They wouldn't dream of bruising their knuckles. Not to mention, I'd kick their behinds until hell won't have 'em again. I've learned to defend myself against men." They raised a finger. "But not against Vern. I never have to worry with Vern. He's—he's different. Treats me like a queen, like I can do no wrong. It's so strange, I can hardly believe it. That another person can love, I mean *really* love someone like me, you know?"

"Yeah," El said, thinking of Alice. "I know exactly what you mean."

"So." Mona leaned back against the wall. "You wanted to know how I ended up in here, right? Wanted me to tell my humiliating story?" They took another drag and said with a mouthful of smoke, "Vern's working tonight, so I was out getting myself a cocktail (or three). A gentleman comes by and sits next to me, striking up a conversation. I chat him up—I didn't want to appear rude, you understand—but I also mentioned I was seeing someone." They leaned forward for emphasis. "As was he. He had one of these on." They pointed to their ring finger. "Anyway, we've having a good time, but then I feel his hand on my thigh. I told him I was flattered but he really needed to remove it."

"Let me guess," El said. "He didn't."

"He kept inching his hand higher and higher until . . . well . . . let's just say he found out something he'd rather not have known. He runs out of the bar and I thought that was that. I finish my drink, pay my tab, and walk outside. And there he is, talking to a cop. When he sees me, I watch him, clear as day, slip a five-note to Officer Uglier and point me out. Next thing I know, I'm in here for hooking. Hooking?! The nerve."

"He was probably worried you'd tell his wife."

"More like he got excited and got scared of his own feelings. God deliver us from men who are afraid of themselves." Mona shrugged. "That's my story. What about you? What are you doing here? Did the tux finally do it?"

"I wish it did."

"Oooh, is it something big? I bet it's something juicy. When we were driving to wherever they picked you up, I overheard them talking." Mona pointed their cigarette towards the wall. "They were excited, let me tell you!"

"They were, huh?"

"Mmmhmm. Officer Ugly actually modulated his pitch up and down, if you can believe that. Now. Tell Mona. What's the story? What's the scoop? What's that sweet, sweet chin music?"

El couldn't see the harm in telling Mona. Hell, by the time they got to the jail and were processed for their crimes, Mona would find out anyway.

"Alright," she said, and then looked Mona dead in the eyes. "Murder. They arrested me for murder."

Mona froze, the cigarette halfway to their mouth. The ash on the end of it threatened to topple over and fall to the wagon floor. When it eventually did, it snapped Mona out of their trance.

"Wow," they said. They lowered their voice. "Did you?"

"Did I what?"

"Did you do it?"

"Of course not!"

"That's good! That's exactly what you say to the judge magistrate."

"I'm not lying, Mona. I really didn't do it."

Mona sighed. "I wish I could say that mattered, but you and I both know it doesn't." They lowered their voice again. "Who'd you kill?"

"I said—"

"Sorry, sorry. Who do *they* say you killed?"

"I—I can't say."

"C'mon, El, you can trust me. I'm a female impersonator sleeping with a man. Who's a *bass player*. In a band that plays in a speakeasy catering to homosexuals. Dancing. Degeneracy. Liquor. I'd be locked up for longer than any member of Harding's original cabinet, provided our judges weren't bought and paid for. Who am I gonna tell? And who's gonna listen to me anyway?"

Mona had a point. Still, El held a finger to her lips. "You can't breathe a word of this to anyone." She gestured to the wagon wall. "I don't think *they* know the connection. At least, I hope not."

Mona proved to be no dumb Dora. "Your lover?"

"My wife," El whispered.

"Oh."

"My . . . white . . . wife."

Mona's mouth dropped open. "You are just full of surprises, El. Oh my goodness. That's—that's—" They recovered and said soberly, "I'm so sorry for your loss." They extended their hand with the cigarette. "Want a drag?"

"Butt me, please." El gratefully took it and inhaled the tarry, yet sweet smoke into her lungs. She needed that. Relief immediately flooded her body. She took another deep drag and handed it back to Mona.

They asked, "What's the evidence against you?"

El shrugged. "No one would tell me. I'm still trying to figure out how they even got to me."

"Well that, I know. Or part of it, at any rate. Like I said, I overheard 'em before we picked you up. They threw me back in here, drove for a bit, and then stopped somewhere's to make a telephone call. Check in with the precinct or something like that, I suppose. Officer Ugly, the big fat one? He comes back, sounding excited, which for him is slightly less bored. 'Hey,' he says, 'we gotta go. Someone called into the station and it's a doozy of a collar.'"

"A doozy of a collar? He said that?"

"Word for word. They crank up the wagon and we're

flying even more than we are now. You know what that says to me?"

"Anonymous tip," El replied.

Mona pointed their cigarette at her. "Smart cookie. Who do you think dropped the call on ya?"

"The real person who killed her."

"And do you know who that is?"

El felt her eyes narrow, her jaw tighten. "Not yet," she replied, her voice darkening. "But I got a few ideas."

28

The Harlem Courthouse for the Fifth District looked like a Moorish castle. Or at least that's how Mona described it. Turned out they were big into architecture. They said the building was designed in the Romanesque Revival style with some Victorian Gothic touches.

El took their word for it. To her, the roofline was nothing more than a bunch of jagged points with some ornamentation resembling Catholic crosses. A turret blessed one corner whose rounded curves at the bottom gave way to even more sharply angled points and triangles at the very top. It impressed Mona, but El? Not so much. The building looked imposing and oppressive. The end of the line for most.

But not me, dammit, she thought. *It will* not *be the end of the line for me.*

The two arresting pounders—the pockmarked-face Officer Morton and his partner, whom El learned named Officer Daggett—marched them towards the side entrance for prisoners. The few newshawks who followed them popped out of their motorcars, voices yelling more questions.

El couldn't help herself; she looked over her shoulder. At the buildings surrounding the courthouse and jail. At the newshawks. At the night sky.

Will I ever see this sky again?

A set of hands pushed her forward.

Inside, she saw brick walls, austere and solid; the smell dank and musky, like old cellars. They walked to an admitting area. Across the way was a giant metal door. El's heart jumped into her throat at the sight of it. On either side of it stood two officers. To El's left sat a canceled stamp in glasses. In front of him was a desk piled with papers.

Without looking up, he asked them, in a toneless voice, a bunch of questions: name, date of birth, address. Mona went first and gave their impersonator name. Inspired by that, El gave hers as El Train. She'd be damned if she was gonna be booked as Eloise Ankins. Officers Morton and Daggett provided the crimes. For Mona, Officer Daggett said soliciting a married man for prostitution. Surprising El, he said nothing about Mona being a man in a dress. The married man with wandering hands didn't want to admit too much, apparently.

Morton, the pockmarked weasel, was all too thrilled to say "murder" when it was El's turn. Grinning like a bigtimer.

His partner Daggett corrected him. "Suspicion of murder."

El glanced at him with interest. Stickler for details and protocol, this one.

The man filling in the forms slowly glanced up at El. If he was shocked to see a woman in a man's suit, he didn't show it. Instead, he adjusted his glasses and said, "I see. Don't think she should share a cell with Mona then."

El felt a stab of panic. In the short while they spent in the back of the wagon, she'd grown attached to the garrulous, irreverent, architecture-loving Mona. She'd felt less scared, less hopeless. Less alone. Now, the thought of being separated revived all those feelings again.

Mona piped up. "Actually, I don't mind."

The canceled stamp tilted his head. "You sure, Miss Sinclair? She could be dangerous."

"I'll have you know, mister, I can take care of myself."

"Your funeral." The canceled stamp tilted his head towards Morton and Daggett. "And what are your names?"

Morton smirked. "You mean you don't know us, Steve?"

"All you flatfoots look the same to me. And I need them for my records, so if you don't mind, officers."

Daggett cleared his throat. "Officer Morton Kelly and Officer Stanley Daggett."

Morton sneered, "Do you need us to spell it for ya?"

Steve arched his brows. "Do I need to spell out 'insubordinate' to you? Oh. I suppose I do."

"Now you listen here—"

"Morton!" Daggett glared at him. "Knock it off. You got your collar, now simmer down."

Yeah, Morton, El thought to herself. *Simmer down.*

Morton turned on that ugly smile again. "I apologize, Steve. I'm just thrilled we got a murderer off the streets."

"Suspected," Steve said, printing in very neat letters Morton's and Daggett's names.

"What?"

"Suspected. Officer Daggett here said she was *suspected* of murder."

Morton leaned on the desk. "Same thing, isn't it?"

Steve finished filling out his forms. "Alright, officers. You're free to go. We've got it from here."

Morton flicked another ugly look to El. "See ya at the chair, *El Train*." He snickered, pounded Steve's table with his fist, and then said to Daggett, "C'mon. Let's go talk to the chief and celebrate."

Daggett rolled his eyes, whispered an apology to Steve for his partner, and then left.

Mona crept over to El and murmured, "Don't listen to him. He's just peacocking."

El replied, "A bird's a bird, Mona. And they do nothing but shit on people's heads."

"Language," Steve said, though his monotone never changed. "Ladies, please empty your pockets."

El took out her cigars and lighter along with some fews and twos, a handkerchief, and some other odds and ends. She also gave them her wristwatch and she hoped to heaven the pounders wouldn't steal it for themselves. Mona contributed their cigarettes, lipstick, eye shadow, eyeliner, rouge, a few coins, and a slightly bent picture of a man. El looked closely. It was of Vernon taken at one of those photo booths at Coney Island.

Steve took them all without comment. "Both of you, please go with Officer Abbott."

A rustle of movement caught El's ear and she turned. One of the officers El saw when they first came in snapped-to and left his post next to the closed metal door. He gently grabbed Mona and her by the arms.

"Let's go," Abbott said.

The large metal door squealed open and she and Mona entered the dimly lit hallway with Officer Abbott. The other officer closed the door behind them, the clang echoing loudly throughout this horrid place. At the end of the hallway, they came to a set of stairs leading down to the cells in the basement. The clicks of their shoes on the limestone steps sounded like two pebbles knocking into one another. Or two billiard balls. Like the ones El sunk to win the game against Lucien Laurent.

Did you squeal on me? Was I getting too close to you?

The pathway they walked down was narrow and surrounded by brick. Rounded archways announced each cell, their whispering occupants bathed in shadow. When El looked in, all she saw were multiple sets of eyes staring out at her. It looked to be two, three, four people per cell. What truly creeped El out were the whispers from the dark.

"Hey, new blood!"

"What did ya do?"

"Did you do it? I didn't do it."

"Hey, I didn't do it either. Tell 'em I didn't do it."

A matter-of-fact voice said, "Better pay that guard if you want a mattress. Nothing for free in here."

Officer Abbott replied through clenched teeth, "Be quiet!"

Above it all, one woman yelled, and kept yelling nonstop: "I don't belong here! Get me out of here! Somebody, please! Get. Me. Outta here!"

The air down here was stale and slightly sour, that damp mold rising up from the ground and seeping through the brick.

Officer Abbott stopped.

El and Mona did as well and turned. They were at their cell. A metal door with a barred, rectangular window at the top greeted them. Officer Abbott unlocked it with a heavy set of keys. More clanging and banging followed by an ear-piercing squeal as the caged door swung open.

"In there," Officer Abbott said.

Mona went in first. El took a deep breath and followed after them. The door shut behind her, the deadbolt sliding in with a reverberating slam. Determined clicks of Officer Abbott's shoes faded away as he returned to his post.

"Well," Mona said. "I suppose we both outta get some sleep."

Mona went in first. El took a deep breath and followed after them. The door shut behind her, the deadbolt sliding in with a reverberating slam. Determined clicks of Officer Abbott's shoes faded away as he returned to his post.

A clang of metal jolted El awake.

"Hey, you!" a voice bellowed. "Outta bed."

She groaned, sitting up slowly, the muscles cramped and stiff. Sleeping on this bed was like sleeping on a hard wooden board. She blinked. The room was still heavy with darkness. She didn't have a window to tell her what time of night, or day, it was. She looked over to where the voice rudely resided. The shape of a guard, tall and mean, stood there with his hands on his hips.

"Outta bed," he repeated. "You got a visitor."

The bed creaked underneath as she slid her legs over the side and shifted her body into a sitting position. Damn, her neck hurt. She glanced over to the other side of the cell where Mona slept. Either they were the soundest of sleepers or they were pretending to be asleep so the guard wouldn't pick on them.

"I'm not going to repeat it a third time."

El stood up, her knees and ankles protesting all the way. The guard came over and slapped a pair of metal cuffs on her wrists. He grabbed her arms and roughly pulled her out of the cell, locking it behind them. She didn't ask any questions, didn't demand who was seeing her. She'd know in due time, and it wasn't like he'd tell her anyway.

They walked the narrow hall between the cells, the

guard's metal keys jangling and clanking against his hip. Voices whispered from the dark as they passed.

"Where they taking you?"

"Can I come with you?"

"I'm not supposed to be here."

"I'm innocent."

"Hey, me too, I'm innocent. Can I leave?"

"Shut it!" the guard said before reaching the end of the walkway. There was a door with several locks. Another guard opened them from the other side.

Next thing El knew, she was sitting at a table under a harsh light. How did she get here? She couldn't recall. Her body, her mind both moved so slow, like she was stuck in molasses and trying to run, yet couldn't. Where was she?

She glanced around. A meeting area of sorts.

Another door squealed open. Slow, deliberate footsteps followed. A silhouette appeared at the farthest edge of her vision. Her eyes couldn't focus. The light was too bright, the pain in her neck too sharp. The silhouette sat down in front of her. Realization slowly broke like the morning dawn.

El squinted and sat forward, not believing her eyes. "Zora Mae?"

29

The Baroness of Business herself smiled that Cheshire grin of hers. "Good evening, El."

El stared at her in disbelief. She wore a stunning blue chiffon dress cut high in the front and low in the back. A white fox coat draped over her shoulders and giant pearls adorned her neck. Such formal attire to wear to a jail.

El managed to say, "What are you doing here?"

Zora shrugged. "I came to see how you were faring."

It was such a ridiculous thing to say. How she was faring? How the hell did Zora *think* El was faring?

Zora chuckled. "Oh, I see I've awakened your tempestuous nature. Good. I need you to be at your best. A place like this can make even the strongest person weak. And one thing you aren't, El, is weak."

El swallowed. She didn't feel strong right now. She felt broken.

Alice is gone. My freedom is gone. And soon, so will my life.

"El," Zora said, her voice sharp.

El focused her attention onto the powerful woman sitting in front of her.

Zora measured her inch by inch, taking her sweet time in doing it. Once her inspection was complete, she said, "Did you kill Alice Holloway?"

"Of course not! Why in hell would I—"

Zora held up a hand. "I believe you. You've got a bail hearing coming up on Monday. Since they arrested you on a Friday, you're going to have to spend two more nights in here." She leaned forward and lowered her voice. "How badly do you want to get out?"

It was a trick question. Had to be.

El squinted at her. "What are you asking me?"

"I thought the question was straightforward."

"No. With you, it's never the question you ask; it's the one in between the lines."

Zora's smile was bemused. "You're a Black woman—a Black lesbian woman—accused of killing a wealthy white girl. What are the odds you'll get a fair trial, much less make bail?

El's heart sank. She knew the answer. How could she not? "Zero," she said.

"Exactly. What I'm *really* asking you is, how badly do you want to stay alive?"

"What do you want in return?"

Zora clicked her tongue in disapproval. "Always business with you."

"Now ain't that the pot calling the kettle. And speaking of business, weren't you looking into someone for me? Remember? Lucien Laurent and who was after him? Been a while since I asked for that information."

"It's taken a minute to find the answers."

El sat up straighter. "Does that mean you have it?"

Zora's face betrayed nothing.

"What is it?" El asked. "And can it get me outta here?"

Zora pretended to pick a piece of lint from the shoulder of her dress. "You do realize that you already owe me one favor."

"Uh huh, and with whatever this other thing is you're about to propose will make it two."

Which is two too many.

"I don't think you're in much position to argue," Zora said. "Or negotiate. You need me, El. Don't bother denying it."

They stared at one another.

Finally, El asked, "What is it you want?"

Zora absent-mindedly began drawing circles on the tabletop with her fingertip. "I want a meeting with Madam Watkins."

"A meeting? That's it?"

"You know it's not."

"You're right. I do. What do you want with Madam Watkins?"

"Oh, my. You're quite taken with her, I see. The big, strong El protecting her mentor."

"Cut the bushwa, Zora. We don't have much time."

"I have all the time in the world. In case you didn't notice, I'm here well after—or before, depending on your point of view—visiting hours. I got a guard to roust you out of your cell and to treat you relatively kindly. All these things happened because of me."

"You got people on the inside?"

Zora stopped her fingertip, her gaze hardening with intensity. "I have people everywhere. And not just in this jail. In the courtroom you'll be appearing in. Do you see what I'm prepared to offer you? Now all I'm asking in return is for you to set up a little meet-and-greet with the great Madam Watkins."

El watched her warily. "If I do that, then what?"

"I'll get you out of here."

"How? As you said, I'm a Black woman—a Black *lesbian* woman—accused of murdering a wealthy white girl. How could you possibly free me?"

"Ye of little faith." Zora extended her hand. "Do we have a deal?"

"Will you also tell me what you found out about Lucien?"

"I am a woman of my word."

El worked her jaw as she considered the cobra-like woman in front of her. "What's this meeting about with Madam Watkins?"

"I wouldn't concern yourself with it."

"I don't want to involve her in something criminal."

"With all due respect, of the two of us, it's *you* who's involved her in something criminal."

"Low blow, Zora."

"Live in my world and see how far taking the high road gets you," she replied. "Not that it's any of your concern, but what I want with Madam Watkins is a simple business proposal."

"I know what kind of business you're in. Madam Watkins does too, and she won't agree to it."

Zora shrugged. "Too bad. I so would've enjoyed seeing your shows." She stood up. "If you change your mind, there's a sign you can give. A signal, if you will."

"Not interested. Madam Watkins is gonna come through for me."

"Perhaps. Perhaps not. Like I said, time is not on your side. Do you know what these guards would love to do to you? They all think the reason you are who you are is because you've never had a gospel pipe as big as theirs."

"Stop it."

"Saying that won't stop them."

"I *mean* it."

Zora reached into her purse and pulled out a blue silk handkerchief. "If you want my help, tie this to the bars at the top of your door after lights-out." She set it directly in front of El.

El made no move to take it.

"El," Zora said sharply. "Don't be stubborn. Take it. It doesn't hurt to have an insurance policy—especially in a place like this."

Sighing, El snatched it up.

"Good girl. Hide it somewhere so a guard can't take it away from you."

El hesitated for a moment, then tucked it into her shirt, sliding it in between her breasts.

Zora turned and started walking away. Over her shoulder, she added, "I hope you'll see reason sooner rather than later."

And like a shadow at dawn, she disappeared.

The guard materialized again and roughly led her back to her cell. Once she was lying on the cot, Mona's voice whispered, "You okay? He didn't do nothing to ya, did he?"

"No," El replied, "he didn't."

"Thank goodness. I'm sorry I'm such a sound sleeper. I had a few too many at the speak. I'll try and keep a better eye out for ya."

"Thank you, Mona. Good night."

"Good night."

El laid on her back, staring up at the ceiling. Well, what

she supposed was the ceiling. With the lights out, it was pitch-dark in here. She saw nothing.

Would death be like this? Just never-ending nothingness?

The silk handkerchief rustled against her skin.

The next day, a guard came and sprung Mona from the cell.

"It's Vern. I knew he'd come!" They looked over at El. "You gonna be alright?"

"I'll be fine. You get outta here while you still can."

Mona's cot was given to a Black woman skinny as a bird. Reminded her of Flo. This girl's name was Imogene.

"What'd you do to get yourself in here?" El asked.

Imogene bit her lip. "Stabbed my husband."

"Huh. Why'd you do that?"

"'Cause he threatened to put me in Bellevue. Said I was acting crazy. But I wasn't. He was cheating on me and giving this other woman all our money. We wasn't going to make rent. I tried to make it up with my hair business, but there was only so many girls I could fit in my kitchen."

"You a kitchen beautician?" El meant those women who weren't technically licensed by the city to do hair but did it anyway.

Imogene smiled with pride. "Yes, I am. And I'm one of the best. Imogene Harper on 143rd. I do nearly every woman's hair on that block."

El whistled. "God bless you kitchen beauticians. You're doing the Lord's work."

"Yeah, well. While I was doing the Lord's work, Maurice was doing Miss Betty on 144th. And Miss Betty had all sorts of problems. She couldn't afford her groceries, she couldn't pay the doctor's bills, and there's my Maury, putting my hard-earned sugar into her hand. I told him to stop. He said I was paranoid, that I was imagining things."

"So what happened?"

"I went over there to have a talk with Miss Betty. And you should've seen her place! All done up satins and silks, the newest radio and phonograph on display, the newest furniture I've ever seen."

"Doesn't sound like she was on hard times."

Imogene scoffed. "Ain't that the truth. I also find my Maury in her bed, relaxing on her nice pillows, sipping brandy, and smoking some real expensive cigarettes. Meanwhile I'm in hand-me-downs and bumming the cheapest ciggies off my customers. I still had the scissors in my hand from a job and, well, the next thing I know, the handles are sticking out of his gut."

El winced. "Did he die?"

"No, but his cheating ass had to have surgery. And Miss Betty, she told the police I was a crazy lunatic running around with those scissors, threatening to kill everybody. Such bushwa. I only said I'd kill *him*. And in the end, I couldn't even do that."

"Do you have a lawyer?"

"Nope. I can't afford it and Maury certain isn't gonna pop for one on my behalf. Certainly not Miss Take-All-My-Sugar Betty."

"I've got a friend who may know someone," El said, thinking of Madam Watkins. "I'll tell her about you. Seems to me, you can make a case for temporary insanity."

"I said I'm not crazy."

"Not saying you are. Just that your man drove you to a state."

Imogene shook her head. "Did he ever."

The rest of the day and the night was spent lying on the cot. Imogene slept. El did some thinking.

Who wanted her out of the way? What did she know—or what did they *think* she knew—that caused them to make that anonymous tip. And was the tip enough to land someone in the clink?

Don't be naïve; of course, it is.

If only El knew what the anonymous caller'd said. *I saw El Train shoot Alice Holloway?*

This line of thinking led to a dead end. Better to focus on the facts she'd compiled. A few hypotheses for Alice's murder came to mind:

1. The tough guys after Lucien. Maybe they found him somehow—it wasn't like the boy was being careful, going to every billiard hall in town—and they saw him with Alice. They followed her and tried to get Lucien's location out of her. Alice refused, they argued, and a gun goes off.
2. Malek Polowksi. He'd admitted he was losing control of the strike, both the union's trust and any negotiating power with Rich. Plus there was Rich's deportation threat. Had Alice found out what Malek was going to do? And did Malek shoot her to protect the deal?
3. Rich Holloway. If he'd had an inkling of what Alice was doing with the family money, he wouldn't even blink pulling the trigger. But what if it was something different? What if Alice had confronted him about the damage squad? Alice was smart; once she learned the union strike leads weren't involved, it wouldn't

take her long to zero-in on Rich. Maybe she
threatened to expose him, and he silenced her.

4. Frank Nickerson. He was on duty the night she
   died. He claimed he'd left his post to "check on
   the delivery trucks" for a good half hour and
   swore that he didn't hear any shots. But what if
   everything Frank said was a lie? What if he was
   caught sabotaging the trucks? Alice, looking to
   check out the factory, perhaps exonerate the
   union strike leads and satisfy her curiosity, saw
   Frank, confronted him, and he shot her. Bad
   luck for him someone heard the shots and called
   the police. The best lie he could come up with
   was "see no evil, hear no evil."

Some of these theories ranged from solid to shaky, and
all of them depended upon timing and luck, either good
or bad.

Her mind went to the other union leads, who puzzled
her.

For starters, there was something off about Ramona.
Not only was she unnecessarily hostile towards, and about,
Alice, but she had the nasty superiority of a woman who
knew something she shouldn't. Something powerful. But
what? And did Alice find out about it?

There there was Ferrin, the Nervous Nellie who
couldn't keep his glasses on his face. No motive that El
could see and she didn't see him being a murderous master-
mind. Covering up for someone, though. She could easily
picture that—especially if that someone was Ramona.

And then there was Booker. She sincerely didn't want a
brother to be a part of this, but she couldn't discount him.
She only had his word that he never heard the name

Raymond Price. Perhaps he did and when Alice mentioned it to him, she inadvertently put herself in danger.

But who the hell was Raymond Price? He was a phantom, a ghost. Who was he to Alice? And why was he important? Was he the confusion Alice claimed she needed to clear up?

A baton banging on the door jerked her awake. She hadn't realized she'd fallen asleep and rubbed her eyes, hoping against hope that it wasn't the middle of the night and a lonely guard wanted attention.

She blinked. "What day is it?" she asked Imogene.

"It's Sunday. Morning, if you wanna know the time."

"Stand back!" a muffled male voice yelled on the other side. The door swung open, revealing a guard who pointed his baton at El. "You," he said. "You've got a visitor."

El stood up. "Another one?"

"Yeah. Your lawyer."

30

El knew that Madam Watkins would come through for her. What she didn't expect, however, was the white woman with black hair cut short like a man's, wearing a pinstripe suit.

"Good morning, El," she said, her lavender eyes sparkling with intelligence. "My name is Prudence Meyers. I'm a criminal attorney."

El took her seat, bewildered. They were in the same room as when she spoke with Zora Mae. Different circumstances. Different women. Different time of day. It made her head spin.

"Did Madam Watkins hire you?" she asked.

"I'm part of the legal defense team she's putting together. There are two other attorneys working with me—Black attorneys, if that helps." Pru took her seat, bringing up a brown leather briefcase and setting it onto the table between them.

"And how does Madam Watkins know you, Miss Meyers?"

"She doesn't. I'm here because a friend of yours contacted me. And you can call me Pru."

"A friend," El repeated. "You mean Flo?"

"Dash Parker."

"*Dash*? How did he hear about this? The papers?"

Pru shook her head. "His band."

"Mona," El said. "Mona must've told Vernon, who passed it on."

"Please. We don't have much time." Pru reached into her briefcase for a file folder, opened it up, and began relaying the facts. "You're being charged with murder in the first degree. The evidence they have is, admittedly, pretty scant, but considering your race and your preferred style of dress, the district attorney unfortunately doesn't need much for the charge to stick."

"How'd they get to me?"

"An anonymous telephone call to the precinct Friday evening."

Right after the rent party, where she confronted all four union strike leads.

Pru continued. "The caller stated that you were seen having an argument with Alice Holloway in front of the factory. You pulled out a pistol and shot her."

"That's ridiculous! I'd never—"

Pru held up a hand. "Please. Let me finish this. You were on stage at the Watkins Hotel until 11:30 P.M. and the police have interviewed your neighbors who did not see you or hear you that evening, so you don't have—"

"—an alibi for the murder."

Pru looked up from the file folder. "Where were you?"

"I stayed after the show to talk with Madam Watkins about a contract. Then I stopped off to—to check on a friend." *If only I'd gotten to Augusta Wilde's earlier, maybe Alice would still be alive.* El swallowed the lump in her throat. "And then I went home. Swear to God."

"Why wouldn't your neighbors vouch for you?"

"Most of 'em are asleep after midnight. A lotta day workers."

"And the others?"

El shifted in her seat. "They don't see or hear anything that doesn't concern them."

"I see."

"There is one thing you need to know about Alice. But if I tell you, that's, what? Attorney-client privilege, yes?"

"That is correct. And before you say anything—especially anything here," Pru added, cutting her eyes to the guards who stood in the corners. She lowered her voice. "I already know."

Mona again.

El said, "That complicates things, doesn't it?"

"Most certainly. But the detectives don't know this information yet. And I must say, we must do everything within our power to ensure that doesn't happen."

"Believe me, I know."

"The district attorney's story is that you saw a random white woman on the street, tried to rob her, and panicked when she refused. In her refusal, you shot her and ran off with her money and her fur coat."

"Right. 'Cause we Black folks are nothing but violent robbers," El scoffed. "This makes no damn sense. I'm paid with Madam Watkins's money. From a bonafide millionaire working in *the* finest hotel in Harlem. Why would I need to steal from a, according to them, random white girl? Lemme ask you: Did they find her fur coat in my apartment? Huh?"

Pru pressed her lips into a straight line. "No, they didn't. Like I said, it's not a very strong case. The coroner stated the caliber bullet found in Alice's chest is a .32."

".32? Shit. Like what's in my Browning."

"Correct. That's the one strong piece of evidence they have against you."

El massaged her temples, trying to ease the building tension in her skull. A weapon with a matching caliber? She was as good as fried.

Her mind sparked on something that she'd nearly forgot. Something that was missing in those newspaper articles about the murder.

"Wait a minute," she said. "Did the pounders on the beat ever find Alice's pistol?"

Pru frowned. "She carried one with her?"

"All the time. A Colt pocket pistol with an ivory handle. She never left home without it." El tapped the tabletop. "It's also a .32."

Pru tilted her head. "You think she was killed with her own gun?"

"Makes more sense than my Browning."

One of the guards in the corner said gruffly, "You got five more minutes."

Pru took out a pen and a notepad from the briefcase. "We need to hurry. Madam Watkins told me that she, you, and your friend Flo, is it? The three of you were conducting an investigation, of sorts. I need to know what you learned."

El wondered if it was wise to tell this white attorney anything, but this Prudence Meyers had been sent by her friend Dash. Now Dash was a lot of things—naïve, privileged, stubborn (like her)—but he also wasn't stupid. If he trusted this woman, and Madam Watkins also trusted her enough to put her on El's defense team, then El could give her the benefit of her considerable doubts.

She spilled it all while Pru took notes in a neat, organized hand.

"Seems you weren't the only one without an alibi," Pru murmured when El finished.

"Yeah, but we haven't found anything definitive against any of them."

"No leads on the tough guys after Lucien?"

"Not yet. I'm supposed to hear from a source very soon."

"A reputable source?"

"Do reputable sources know people in the underworld?"

"Fair point," Pru said. "And no idea why Alice was there that night at the factory?"

"None. The only thing I can gather is that she went there to retrieve something. But I don't know what."

"The coroner finished examining the body but requested the crime scene photographs again. Something's bothering him about it. I'm hoping to chat with him today in person. Maybe he'll come up with something that throws doubt on this accusation."

The guard made an impatient motion to the two of them. "Wrap it up."

Pru spoke quickly. "Listen, I'm not going to sugarcoat this. There's a bail hearing tomorrow and the likelihood of you being granted it is practically nothing. I'll do what I can but don't be surprised if you're staying in your cell until the trial."

"I can't do that, Miss Meyers. Prudence. Pru. I was so close to finding the answer. I know I can do it, but I've got to be free to find it."

"I don't see another outcome. I'm sorry."

The guard stepped forward. "Alright, ladies, we're done here." He roughly jerked El up from the table. "I said, we're *done* here."

"Hey!" Pru called out. "Treat that prisoner with respect."

The guard sneered at her, "You better watch your mouth, or you'll be in here, too. Dressing like a man doing a man's job. Unnatural. A sin against God. Both of ya's."

Pru made a move to speak more but El quickly shook her head. Pru would only make it worse. Thankfully, Pru took the hint and stayed quiet.

The guard took her back to the cell. As he opened the door, he whispered in her ear, "I'll see you tonight. Make a real woman outta you."

El shuddered. She sat on the cot, letting her head drop into her hands.

"Bad news from your lawyer?" Imogene said, her voice sounding so far away.

"Bad news doesn't begin to cover it," El replied, lifting her head to look at the bird-like woman.

The silk from Zora Mae scratched against her skin.

"But I might have a way out."

After lights out, she slipped the handkerchief from its hiding place and tied it to one of the bars in the door's window.

***

The bail hearing began at 9:00 A.M. on the dot. El and a whole host of other prisoners were escorted into the courthouse. The place was filled to the brim with newshawks and onlookers, all angling to get a better look at El, her wrists clasped in irons. The steam heat had been turned on full blast, turning this hallowed hall of justice into a sauna. Both men and women wiped their brows with handkerchiefs. The women fanned themselves while the men took off their hats.

They saved her for last. Every case called before hers resulted in all but one—white, of course—not making bail.

When it was finally her turn, she felt every single set of eyes on her. The district attorney, some old white man with a bald spot and sweat stains, stood up and tried to make an anonymous, unsubstantiated telephone call to a police precinct more than it was. As Pru predicted, he focused on her dress, her "obvious loose morals," and the threat she represented not only to New Yorkers' safety, but also to the very foundation of America.

The judge looked over to Pru, who made her argument about the lack of evidence—the arresting officers not finding Alice's blue velour coat with fur lining in El's apartment; the detectives not finding a single fence in Harlem who had the coat, much less identifying a woman of El's description. She focused on lack of motive—El made good money—and that a .32 caliber bullet was common in a city full of pocket pistols.

"Even the victim had one," she said before the prosecutor objected on grounds of discovery. Pru withdrew the comment, but the words were out there. Alice Holloway had a .32, which the police had not recovered.

"One last item, which we intend to enter into evidence, but is prudent to this bail hearing," Pru said. "I spoke with Charles Norris at Bellevue Hospital. He had requested from the investigating officers the crime scene photographs.

Upon his study, it is his opinion that Miss Holloway was not shot at the factory entrance, but rather, she was killed elsewhere and her body moved."

The courtroom gasped in response.

The prosecutor sputtered objections.

The judge silenced everyone. "What is his basis for this?" he asked Pru.

"Simply put, the bullet penetrated Miss Holloway's chest, striking a crucial artery that proved fatal. The arterial spray, as he calls it, would've drenched the sidewalk with blood and may have even splashed onto the iron gates at the factory's entrance."

El felt queasy.

Don't think about that. Don't picture it.

Pru continued. "When he examined the crime scene photographs, there was very little, if any, blood on on the sidewalk."

"Your Honor!" said the prosecutor. "This is most outrageous. Let the defense place this evidence into trial, which is the proper procedure, so we can interrogate this Charles Norris."

"Normally I would agree, your Honor," Pru countered. "However, the only basis for Miss Ankins's arrest is this anonymous telephone call that places Miss Ankins at the factory gates, attempting to rob and then murdering Miss Holloway. However, if Alice Holloway wasn't shot at the factory gates, then we can conclude that the anonymous caller was lying. There's no basis for the charges against Miss Ankins and the defense asks for them to be dismissed."

More shocked reactions from the courtroom gallery.

The judge banged his gavel. "Alright, that's enough!" He sat still for a moment, considering this new revelation.

El could tell by the frown on his face that he was not happy about it.

He eventually spoke, saying, "While Eloise Ankins has an unusual state of dress, and I do agree with the prosecution that it is against the morals of this country as well as the state and city of New York, I am leaning towards agreeing with the defense."

The prosecutor shot up from his chair. "Your Honor!"

The judge held up a hand. "Sit down, Fred. Your case is nothing and you know it. Your anonymous tip is being disputed by Dr. Charles Norris, whose work is unimpeachable. If he says Miss Holloway was shot elsewhere, then she was shot elsewhere."

"What if the anonymous caller saw Miss Ankins placing the body there? Made a mistake about the gunshot?"

The judge gave the prosecutor a sad look. "Fred. Your case hinges on a witness seeing Miss Ankins pull the trigger. That didn't happen. What else do you have?"

"The .32 caliber bullet."

"Which is a common enough caliber."

"But Your Honor—"

"No buts about it. Fred, all you have is a bullet that *may* have come from Miss Ankins's gun. But you didn't have that when you got a midnight warrant. You just had an anonymous tip, that's now being disputed, and the hope you'd find something. *And* you didn't find the stolen coat. Now I don't like it as much as you do, but I can't in good conscience let you proceed with the case as it is. Give me some solid evidence, and I'll give you a trial." He raised his gavel. "The charges against Eloise Ankins for the murder of Alice Holloway are dismissed."

Shouts erupted from the galley.

The judge banged his gavel again. "Quiet! Quiet in my courtroom!" Once everyone settled back down, he said, "The only charge against Miss Ankins will be that of indecency, of which she'll pay a fine of five dollars. Her two days spent in confinement will count towards the jail time served. Miss Ankins, please wear a dress next time. You're free to go."

31

"Hello, Rosie! How's tricks!"

El surprised herself by smiling at the parrot. "Good to see you too, Mac."

Mac squawked. "What the hell were you thinking? What the hell were you thinking?"

She laughed. "I guess I wasn't."

She couldn't believe it. She was standing in Madam Watkins's office free as a—well—bird. After the bail hearing, she'd spent the rest of the morning being processed. The justice system, El learned, was one big paperwork machine. By the time she got out, it was past noon.

Madam Watkins smiled as she handed El a glass of whiskey. "Here. I figured you could use this."

"You know that's right." She wanted to gulp the whole pour right then and there, but she knew she shouldn't. She had to keep her wits about her. After all, she still had Alice's killer to find.

She took a dainty sip and sighed. "Good stuff, as always, Madam."

"It's not often we get miracles in this life. We should celebrate them."

El hesitated. "About that. It wasn't exactly a miracle. It was—"

"Zora Mae, yes I know. The Baroness came to see me this morning. Said she fulfilled her end of the bargain and I'm to fulfill mine."

"Madam Watkins, I apologize profusely. It's just that—"

"No need to explain. You're free and you're safe and that's what matters." She ruefully arched an eyebrow. "I know how to handle slippery people like her. Don't you worry about me. Although speaking of the Baroness, she wants you to meet her at this address this afternoon."

El took the card Madam Watkins handed her. She glanced down at it. "CORAL'S DESIGNS?"

"That's where she said to meet her. Told me to tell you that it's about Lucien Laurent."

El felt a surge of energy. "About the people after him?"

"She didn't say any more than that," Madam Watkins replied. "I don't hold with what she does for business, but I am impressed with the results she gets."

"It helped the evidence against me wasn't really there in the first place. That, and the conclusion from the city coroner Dr. Norris."

"Indeed. While you were in jail, I paid Sergeant Williams a visit. Got tired of waiting for his reply, though I learned later what was causing the delay. Sergeant Williams told me that the lead detective, a man named Michael Gahan, thought the crime scene looked odd from the start. The officers who responded to the telephone call detailing the shots were all, according to Williams, 'too bored from the overnight shift and too excited to have something to do,' and missed several obvious clues that Detective Gahan later put in his report."

"Like the lack of—lack of blood from the scene."

Madam Watkins squeezed her shoulder. "I'm sorry, El. I know it's hard." She let a beat pass. "Now Detective Gahan already had his doubts so when Dr. Norris called to request the crime scene photographs, the two of them conferred and—"

"Determined she was killed elsewhere." El whistled. "Lucky me."

"This alone wouldn't have stopped them from burying you. But Miss Mae had something on the judge that would've ruined his career. I guarantee it. Some vice, some evidence of corruption. I know how Zora operates."

"I know it too."

Flo's voice rang out from behind El. "Everybody knows how the Baroness does her business."

El turned to see her walking into the office. "Sis!"

Flo smiled as she practically galloped over and hugged her. "They didn't hurt you any?" she murmured into her ear.

"No," El replied. "I had a guardian angel."

"Thank the Lord."

They parted.

"I've got a surprise guest," Flo said. "He was insistent on seeing you and would not take no for an answer."

The side door to Madam Watkin's office opened and in walked Dash Parker, the white owner of the Greenwich Village speak Pinstripes. He was a tall, trim man with what he called "misbehaving brown hair." It was no misnomer. The strands curled at the ears and the nape of his neck while other random hairs stuck straight up on his crown.

His sharply cheekboned face was stretched into a smile, his hazel eyes sparkling.

"Hello, El," he said.

El looked over to Madam Watkins. "How the hell did you sneak him into a Blacks-only hotel?"

Madam Watkins shrugged. "I'm the owner. I can do whatever I want, including throwing him into a trunk and having him ride up the elevator with a bunch of other luggage."

As if on cue, Dash flicked dust from the shoulders and lapels of his immaculately tailored blue pinstripe suit. "Yes," he said. "It was quite the thrill. I felt like a war spy."

El asked, "What are you doing here?"

"I had to make sure you were alright ever since I heard the news from the band."

"Yeah, well, here I am. All in one piece."

"As Finn would say, 'thank goddess.'" He glanced over to Madam Watkins. "Madam, it's good to see you again."

Madam Watkins smiled. "I thought you looked familiar. Though I must confess, it was dark in that tunnel." She lowered her voice. "Thank you for protecting Leonard."

Mac squawked, "Bitch! Bitch! Goddamn, bitch! She'll ruin us, she'll ruin us!"

Dash laughed at the bird. "Hello, Mac. Eloquent as ever, I see."

Madam Watkins groaned. "You don't know the half of it. I can't wait to return this devil bird back to Leonard."

Mac ducked his head up and down. "I'm falling, Sophie, I'm falling."

El furrowed her brow. "What are you two talking about? And how do you know about Mac, Dash?"

"Another story for another time," he said before clasping his hands together. "What can I do to help?"

"I'm not sure yet," El answered honestly. "Don't worry; you're gonna help me. I helped you plenty of times and it's high time you returned the favor." She then ran them through the thinking she'd done in her jail cell. "And now that we know Alice wasn't at the factory, then everything, and everyone, is back on the table."

Flo agreed. "This list of suspects didn't have strong alibis to begin with."

El patted her pockets, forgetting that the jail staff took her supply of cigars.

Flo, that angel of mercy, produced one from her purse.

El paused to light it and then said, "Someone moved Alice there. Why?"

"She still could've been killed at the factory," Flo offered. "Frank Nickerson says he didn't see or hear nothing, but what if he killed her *inside* the factory and moved her *outside* so he could clean up the mess. Sorry, El."

"Hmm. Seems a little sloppy. Then again, Frank isn't exactly slick. And it would explain why there wasn't enough blood by the gate, and why he spent so long in the garage."

"Will be tough to prove though," Flo admitted. "Likely no evidence left."

Dash tapped his chin. "What about your other suspects? How would they have moved her body? It's not like they could carry her blocks upon blocks without attracting attention." He blushed slightly at their inquisitive stares. "I may have, ahem, had experience with something similar."

El pointed at him with her cigar. "You never cease to surprise me. Downtowner has a point. Did the killer take a cab?"

Flo said, "A cabbie overlooks a lot of things, but a bleeding body?"

"Yeah, you're right. We're looking for someone with a motorcar."

"Or access to one. Friend, family member, etcetera."

El took a drag. "Rich Holloway owns a car. Lucien too, although he claimed it was towed. He could've been lying."

Madam Watkins offered up, "The tough guys looking for him—they must have one too. Especially if they're working for a gangster."

Dash said, "All viable options. What about the strike leads? Who are they again?"

El ticked them off one by one. "Malek, Booker, Ferrin, and Ramona. They don't own any motorcars as far as we know, but maybe we should look into that."

Dash raised his hand. "I can tackle that."

"You can't with Booker, no offense. A white man asking questions about him will get people to clam up tight."

Flo raised her hand as well. "I'll check on Booker."

Dash asked, "What about motives? Do we have a list of those?"

El nodded. "That we do. Money, sibling rivalry turned to hatred, wrong place and wrong time, as in saw something she shouldn't have or got caught in a situation outside of her control."

"Like the tough guys after Mr. Laurent."

"Exactly."

Madam Watkins leaned a hip on her desk. "Something else we should consider. Is it possible that whoever killed Alice and placed her body at the factory was trying to frame someone? Like Rich?"

Flo said, "He owns the factory. It was well-known those two didn't get along. And he did ban her from the grounds after she publicly accused him of negligence after Sam Willing lost his hand."

El tapped her cigar into an ashtray on Madam Watkins's desk. "Flip it another way. She was left there to discredit the union. Which seems to be working, going by Rich's comments to the newshawks." She took another drag. "One other clue we haven't solved: Raymond Price." She took a quick second to catch Dash up on the significance of the name. "Who is he? And why was Alice asking about him?"

Flo cleared her throat. "Actually, we solved that. The first part, at least. I telephoned the factory's Personnel department and pretended to be Miss Miriam King asking for a reference. Just like you did with Frank Nickerson. Raymond Price is a former employee that was fired when Rich did a major round of job cuts this past spring. Strange, though. Personnel said he'd been fired twice. Apparently, after the first time, around November of last year, he managed to get rehired."

"That's strange." El looked to Madam Watkins. "That isn't common, is it?"

Madam Watkins shook her head. "It's very odd."

El turned back to Flo. "Did you get an address?"

"You know I did," she replied. "I got them for all the union leads, too."

El grinned. "Good work, sis." She glanced at her wrist-watch. "I've got to see Zora Mae this afternoon about our favorite Frenchie Lucien. I'm guessing I've got to go alone?"

Madam Watkins confirmed it. "But I'll have my driver take you there and back." Her face took on a commanding severity. "One thing to keep in mind, everyone. My contact in the police department, Sergeant Williams? He says a few detectives are quite angry El got off. They're going to be watching her like a hawk, waiting for any reason to arrest her again. Jaywalking. Littering. You name it." She pointed to El. "From here on out, you're staying at the Hotel where we've got security to keep most of them out. If you go anywhere, you're sneaking out the back and you're using my private motorcar. Is that clear?"

"Yes, Madam."

"I took the liberty of grabbing some of your clothes from your apartment. I hope you don't mind."

"Not at all."

"You'll be staying with me here in the penthouse. You'll have your own room, bathroom, and so on. This is about safety, El. Not control. I promise you that."

"I know."

"Good. Now get yourself cleaned up."

Flo said, "I don't like her going to the Baroness unarmed. They didn't give back her Browning, did they?"

Madam Watkins walked over to her desk and opened her purse. "Here. She can take mine." She handed over a Smith & Wesson pistol to El.

Dash's eyes widened. "Oh, my."

"What?" El said, pocketing the gun. "You've never seen armed women before?"

"Oh, I have." He glanced at Madam Watkins again. "I know firsthand how Madam handles that thing."

Mac squawked in the background. "She'll ruin us! She'll ruin us!"

El sent Dash a suspicious look. "You're gonna need to tell me this story sometime." She took in the people around her and saw love and resolve in each of their faces. It filled her with energy and hope. They were going to solve this thing, she knew it like she knew the sky was blue. "Alright, now. Who's ready to find a killer?"

32

El had this to say for Dash: he wasn't lying when he said being crumpled up inside a trunk wasn't the easiest way to travel.

At the first major bump, El said, "Shit goddamn!"

Luckily it was only Flo pushing the cart, who muttered, "Will you keep quiet?"

"Well, what the hell is happening out there?"

"If you don't want to get caught, you gotta muzzle that mouth."

El had some retorts for that but in the spirit of friendship, she kept them to herself.

After Dash left in his own trunk, El suggested it wasn't a bad idea to use the same trick for her. While it was nice to assume no one in the hotel would blab if they saw El coming and going, a few pieces of lettuce changing hands would be all it'd take for a few staff members to bump their gums to somebody.

Madam Watkins agreed, so Flo snuck down the hall and stole an empty luggage cart. They found a giant steamer trunk for Atlantic crossings and placed it onto the cart. El climbed inside, standing up but seriously crouched down, and Flo sealed the door shut.

Since then, it'd been a dark, rattling, bumpy ride made all the worse because El was squished so tightly into that trunk, she could hardly breathe. She heard Flo talk to the elevator operator, an older man who asked why she wasn't in uniform.

"Shift's over but they told me to bring this down," El heard Flo respond.

"Maids ain't supposed to be handling the luggage," the elevator operator retorted.

"You know that and I know that, but the kid? The new one they got on this floor?"

"Young one?"

"Yes, sir."

El grinned at her friend's ingenuity. There was always a new young person on staff—and always an older one willing to disparage them.

The elevator operator hissed out a curse. "That's Clovis. I told 'em Clovis was a lazy no-account who spends all his time rolling those godawful cigarettes. And I *know* he's putting dope in 'em, though I can't prove it."

El heard Flo click her tongue. "It's a crying shame."

"You're telling me. You want me to go get him right now and tell him to do his job?"

"No, no," Flo quickly replied. "I don't want to make trouble and I desperately want to get home and put these feet up."

"You let him get away with it, he going to do it again. That's how boys like Clovis work."

Flo sighed. "I know, I know. But tonight, it's not worth it."

There was a pause, during which El imagined the operator shaking his head.

"Alright then," he said. "Let me help you get it in here."

El felt herself rattling forward and bumping over the gaps from the floor to the elevator. A squeal of the gate being closed followed by the heart-leaping lurch of the elevator car heading downwards.

The operator and Flo murmured small talk until they arrived on the first floor. He said while squealing open the gate, "You know if they see you on the floor, they're gonna ask you about this, right?"

"Let's hope nobody's paying attention tonight."

"Head to the left, girl. It's a maintenance hallway nobody uses."

"Thank you kindly."

"Don't mention it. Hey! You're a fine dinner. Want to take me out sometime?"

El rolled her eyes. Why did men assume every interaction with a woman was an invitation?

"I got a husband, mister," Flo replied.

"Aw, man! All the cute ones are married. Hey, listen. I can treat you better if he can't, if you know what I mean."

Flo laughed. "I doubt it. The man's a boxer who's over six foot and two hundred pounds, and if he knew you were trying to date his wife, he'd knock your ass out."

The operator guffawed. "Alright, now, alright. I get the point. You don't have to make up a pretend husband."

"Pretend nothing."

"Uh huh. To the left, girl, to the left. Have a good night. And don't let Clovis off the hook tomorrow."

"I won't."

El felt herself being turned and rolled on smoother floors. The cart jerked to a stop, causing her head to hit the far side of the trunk. She bit down a curse and tried to regain her purchase in this thing. How strange was it that she couldn't move a muscle and yet the stopping and going was pushing and tugging at her?

There was a creak of a door, Flo murmuring, "Excuse me," and then they were on the move again.

Another turn, then another.

A sudden stop.

Flo cussing.

Full speed ahead through another set of doors. The texture underneath the luggage cart's wheels changed from polished stone to rough concrete. The cart tilted and El felt herself going down a ramp, pitching her to the side, before leveling out again.

The cart rolled to a stop.

Flo said, "Wait a moment, El."

Through the walls of the trunk, El heard the rattling of a motor. A male voice said, "Allow me, madam."

El felt herself being lifted upwards and carried forward. Must've been Madam Watkins's chauffeur putting the trunk into the back of the Daimler. The plan was to drive away, ensure no one followed them, and then stop to let El out.

"Provided you behave," Flo had said with a smile.

El had replied with a new phrase for Mac the parrot to repeat.

She felt the trunk flip down, so that now she was on her back, and settle onto a surface. A door slammed. Some slight shaking and jostling of the motorcar as the chauffeur presumably settled into his seat. A roar followed by vibration and soon they were in motion.

Five excruciating minutes went by before they rolled to a stop. A door slam, followed by another one. The trunk was lifted and set on the ground, where they opened it. El winced as the afternoon sun blinded her. She squinted as the chauffeur helped her up.

"Lord. That's not an easy trip," El said as she brushed the wrinkles out of her suit.

"Good afternoon, ma'am," he said. "Nice to see you again." He wore a dark navy uniform complete with brass buttons and a cap, which he took off at the sight of her. Thick hair pomaded down in waves sat on top of a square face with a square chin. He was midsized with a long torso and short legs. El wondered how he reached the pedals.

She asked, "You know where we're going?"

"Yes, ma'am. Coral's Designs."

"What's your name, baby? I didn't catch it the other night."

"Abe."

"Abe. A few things. One, I'm nobody's ma'am. Two, I'm nobody's madam. I'm just El. Understand that, we'll get along just fine."

"Yes, ma—Yes, El."

"Good." El glanced at her wristwatch. "We've got a little time to spare before my meeting with the Baroness. Mind if we make a short stop on the way?"

———

Abe drove her to her usual numbers corner, where she once again saw the old man Terrence arguing with Lenny. Almost comforting, in a way, this familiar—albeit irritating —sight.

"Terrence!" El called from the motorcar window before opening her door and stepping out.

"El," said Abe. "You're supposed to wait for me to open it."

"I don't stand on ceremony, baby," she said over her shoulder before slamming the door shut. She charged towards Terrence and Lenny. "Do I need to permanently rearrange the way it hangs?"

Terrence's mouth fell open in shock. "El? You riding around in a limousine? After being in jail?"

"Yes, I am. On account of the charges being dropped and the New York Police Department issuing apologies."

Terrence didn't know what to make of that. He stopped and started many replies before returning to his favorite subject at hand. "Now, listen. I am not terrorizing him at all. I am simply trying to negotiate with this boy, but he is being right difficult."

El put a hand on her hip. "Negotiate what?"

"Giving me a hint that I'm on the right track."

"Terrence, the numbers are random. He's not gonna know what number the Exchange is gonna be the day before they announce it."

"I don't believe that for one minute." Terrence pointed to Lenny. "He knows what numbers are gonna be called. I see him with other people. They're so happy to see him and they give him their coins with big smiles on their faces. That's 'cause he gives them hints."

"Terrence, has it ever occurred to you that maybe people be smiling because they're happy? And they're happy to see Lenny, because he's a friendly boy?"

"Thank you, El," Lenny said.

"You're welcome, baby. Now, Terrence, stick with your cockamamie dreams and stop trying to cheat."

"I'm not cheating! Boy, am I cheating?"

Lenny shifted his feet. "A bit."

"Why you little shit—"

El reached out an arm and blocked his way. "Old man, walk away. Walk away while you still can."

She and him glared at one another.

"Fine," he said. "Fine. We'll stick with my dreams then." His pout turned into a cheek-spreading grin. "I had a good one too. Took a bus to San Francisco where I had a big ol' mansion. Servants and everything."

"Uh huh," El replied. "And the bus number was what?"

"Nine!" He reached into his pockets and pulled out a nickel and four pennies. He made a move towards Lenny, but El held him firm.

"You gonna behave?" she said.

"Yes." He tried to advance forward again but she refused to let him budge. "Hey, now! I said I will and I will."

"Promise?"

"Promise."

She held up a warning finger. "I'm watching you."

She let him go and he took a moment to smooth out the wrinkles caused by her grip. To his credit, he gently placed into Lenny's hand his five coins.

"I want a combo: four, three, two. You got that? Write that down, now: four, three, two." He glanced over at El. "See? I kept my word."

"That you did, Terrence. I thank you. Lenny thanks you, don't you, Lenny?"

"Thank you," the boy replied.

"The whole world thanks you, Terrence."

Terrence sniffed. "Don't know why that's so hard. Showing a man some appreciation." With his chin high and his shoulders back, he marched off, catching the brim of his trilby as it, once again, almost fell off his head.

El turned and knelt down so she was eye-level with Lenny. "Whatever you do, don't grow up to be like him."

"I won't."

She smiled. "Good." She reached into her pocket and pulled out a quarter. "Here. Take this."

"You want a combo?"

"No. We're putting it all on twenty-five."

"Risky."

She shrugged. "Maybe. But it's the age of a—" Her voice broke but she pushed through. "—the age of a good friend of mine. She was twenty-five years old."

"Was? What happened?" He must not have read the papers, or made the connection between her arrest and Alice Holloway's death.

"Well," she said. "My friend died."

Lenny, to her surprise, surged forward and hugged her. It caught her so off-guard that she almost fell backwards. It also meant she couldn't stay vigilant on the emotions bubbling up inside of her. Before she knew it, she was crying into this young boy's shoulder.

"It's okay," his muffled voice said. "It's sad. It's a sad thing."

"You're right, baby," she replied. "It *is* a sad, sad thing."

God knew what the other pedestrians thought, this tiny boy engulfed in the arms of this mannish woman. But they held each other like that for a good minute before they parted.

"Sorry about that," she said, getting out her handkerchief to wipe her cheeks.

Lenny shrugged. "Sometimes we need to cry. Daddy taught me that. We gotta get it out because if we don't, it'll always stay with us."

"Oh, yeah? Your daddy cries?"

"Every once in a while."

"That's good. More men need to cry."

Lenny studied her face. "You need to cry more, too."

She laughed. "Yeah, well. I can't right now. I've got a job to do. But once I do it, I'll cry. I'll cry until it's all outta me."

"You promise?"

Goodness, his eyes were so big and round and trusting. She nudged his chin with her knuckle. "I promise."

Back at the Daimler, Abe opened the passenger door and El ducked inside. "Alright, Abe," she said. "Let's go see the Baroness."

―――――

"Now this dress is called The Velvet Lady," said the woman at the far end of the empty room. She wore an olive-green dress with a spangled hemline and a long, flowing, dark green coat. A matching beret and veil completed the outfit.

A second woman, svelte and refined, walked in from one of the side doors and strode over to the head of the room. She posed in front of a gold velvet curtain. A baby grand piano stood to the right of her, plucking out a midtempo, jaunty little tune. The rest of the room was filled with empty white wooden chairs forming an aisle down the middle, like at a wedding.

Coral's Designs turned out to be a fashion salon, and El was gate-crashing a rehearsal of sorts. Either the Baroness had alerted the women El would be stopping by, or they were too professional to interrupt their flow.

The woman in olive green continued, gesturing towards the model. "This is a form-fitting dress in two tones of chiffon velvet with a great turban to match."

The model slowly turned to give a view of the back of

the dress while the other woman continued reading the description.

"See the uneven hemline and the bell-shaped sleeves as interesting new notes."

The model finished turning and strolled down the aisle to the other end of the salon where El stood in the corner. The model turned once more and then exited out the door El had entered.

The woman reading the descriptions—whom El assumed to be Coral—turned a page in her notebook. "Next we have a new design called Song of the Nile."

Another model stepped through the side door to parade her dress through the room. She walked over to the same spot in front of the curtains and to the right of the piano.

Coral read aloud, "Turquoise blue satin has been used to make this stylish evening gown. Please note the higher waistline in the front and the lower dipping v-neck line in the back. Very smart."

The model turned, showing off a smooth upper back. She paused before slowly completing the turn, earning an impatient look from Coral.

"That's too slow, Bea. You need to keep time with the music."

"I'm sorry, Coral," the model apologized.

Coral waved off the apology. "No need for that. Now come down the center of the room."

Bea the model did as requested and then exited.

"And now," Coral said, "our final number is called Silver and Noir."

A third model entered and posed.

"Featuring an evening wrap made of metallic fabric that practically shimmers. Underneath is a stunning spangled gown made of black and silver lace. Please note the straps that expose the shoulders and arms. Perfect for those hot summer nights."

The dress, and the model displaying it, sparkled under the salon lights. She walked down the center of the room but instead of exiting, she returned to where she posed and twirled. The two previous models appeared from the side door and joined her, each waving an ostrich feather fan and posing.

Coral motioned to the piano player, who slid his fingers down the keys for a trilled finish.

"Very nice, ladies, very nice," she said. "Now remember, it's quite alright to look at the audience while you're turning, but make sure you don't stare for too long. It makes them uncomfortable. And always keep time to the music. It should all feel seamless, like it's all one piece: the music, you ladies, and the dresses. Understand?"

The three models nodded.

"Wonderful. You can get changed. And remember to be here tomorrow at six o'clock sharp."

There were some bustling noises as the women chatted with one another and exited the room. The piano player said a few words to Coral and then left.

That was when she finally noticed El. "Oh! Pardon me. I didn't realize anyone was here."

El pointed at the entry door. "The secretary was out, and I heard the music playing. I came in to see what was happening. Lovely stuff. You design all those?"

"Why, yes. They're part of the new spring line."

"I hate to break it to you, but it's November now."

Coral gave an indulgent smile. "We have to be ahead. Get people excited about the new lines so when the season comes, they're ready to buy. Are you El, by any chance?"

"I am."

"Nice to meet you. The Baroness will be with you shortly."

"The Baroness is here," a familiar voice replied.

Walking through the doorway the models exited through, Zora Mae entered the room, done up in burgundy and mink. She smiled at the designer. "Thank you, Coral. I look forward to your show tomorrow night."

"Thank you, Baroness. Once again, I really do appreciate your support."

"Please. I love investing in new artists. And you, my dear, have a gift that the rest of Harlem—nay, the rest of the world—needs to see."

Coral's cheeks blushed slightly before she said, "Good afternoon, Miss Mae. Good afternoon, El."

El and Zora waited until Coral left.

Zora gestured to one of the many empty chairs. "Have a seat."

El glanced at those tiny chairs and decided upon the piano bench instead—a move that amused Zora. In response, Zora leaned against the body of the piano, like a chanteuse ready to sing her heart out while El accompanied her.

"How does freedom feel?" Zora asked.

"Like it's temporary."

"It is for most of us, unfortunately."

"Not for the rich white folks."

"Oh, they're already imprisoned," Zora said. "They just don't know it yet. All their rules and manners and customs and traditions and who's allowed in and who's not. High society is nothing but a high-security prison, El. What's sad is that the people inside of it have no idea they're prisoners serving a life sentence."

"Well, as poetic as that is, I'd like to avoid the very *real* jail I just came from. What did you find out about Lucien Laurent?"

"I do apologize for how long it's taken me to uncover his little secret. I wanted to make sure my sources were correct. One can never be too careful these days. Especially when the recipient of this information is bereaved."

"I don't mean to be rude, Baroness," El said, "but I've always been real short on patience and now, I'm real short on time. Those pounders are coming for me—yes, you got me out of there with your voodoo magic, but that doesn't mean you can keep me out and—"

Zora held up a hand, halting El's speech. "You're right. Let's get down to business. After all, that is what I am the baroness of." She tapped the sides of the piano. "Lucien Laurent is more than a conman, of that I'm certain you already knew. He's an imposter."

"How?"

"For starters, his name is not Lucien Laurent. It's Billy Sullivan."

33

"Billy Sullivan? Wait, he's Irish? Not even French?"

Zora shook her head. "Massachusetts Irish. Second generation. Born and raised in Worcester, he moved into Boston, following his high school graduation, where he became engaged to a wealthy woman. Sound familiar?"

"Very."

"This woman's name is—or I should say, *was*—Marilyn Lee. She was eighteen, he was nineteen. He presented himself as the son of a well-to-do family from Providence, which we both know is bushwa. Yet young love blossomed, likely because it was forbidden by her father Wayne Lee. As in Lee Paints, the only serious competitor to the empire that is Sherman Williams."

"Wealthy?"

"Extremely. Marilyn's father tried everything to split the couple apart. He told anyone who would listen that Billy Sullivan was a fraud, that he was not from Providence like he claimed but from a working-class neighborhood just outside of the city. Wayne's story is that he successfully convinced Marilyn to end the engagement. One afternoon, she went off with Billy for a date on the River Charles. Witnesses say they got into a sailboat and set off. What happened next is . . . up for debate."

"What do you mean?"

"Well," Zora said. "Some people at the riverside park heard splashing and a cry for help. Marilyn had fallen into the river, and the current carried her far from the boat."

"Did Lucien—excuse me, *Billy* jump into the water to rescue her?"

"He claims he can't swim. For that matter, neither could she."

"You said she *was* Marilyn Lee. She drowned, didn't she?"

"She did. And Wayne Lee was, and is still, convinced Billy killed her. He thinks she successfully broke off the engagement, and in a rage, he pushed her overboard."

"But no one saw him do that, did they?"

"No, and yet, it doesn't matter. What Wayne Lee believes is gospel. He hired a few men to, ahem, teach Mr. Sullivan a lesson. His apartment roommates alerted him to the danger, and he skipped town."

"Coming down to New York City as French aristocrat Lucien Laurent," El finished.

"Apparently, in school, he was very much into theater—"

"He mentioned that."

"—and the idea of playing such an elaborate role likely appealed to his theatrical sensibility."

"Also helped him hide." El frowned. "Except they found him somehow. Pearlie mentioned a couple of heavies asking about him."

"Mr. Sullivan, in addition to acting, is quite fond of the

billiard tables. They've been going to every billiard hall between here and Boston."

"And Pearlie's is the biggest one in Harlem." El placed her hands on the piano keys and instinctively started improvising a light, slow melody. "You think he killed that girl?"

Zora shrugged. "He could have."

"Whose idea was it to be in the sailboat?"

"Her father says it was hers."

"A woman who can't swim suggests getting in a boat with a man who also can't swim? What are the odds?"

"Coincidental, I agree, although most women aren't taught how to swim. Were you?"

"Well . . . no."

"Neither was I. I learned later on in life." A bitter arch of Zora's brow. "Don't you find it amazing how hard men work to keep us women helpless? They teach each other how to shoot, swim, add, subtract, negotiate. Even hammer nails and connect pipes so they can build skyscrapers. In short, they learn how to serve themselves. What do women learn? How to serve *men*. Cook their food. Wash their clothes. Clean their house."

"It's a bum deal, no two ways about it." El stopped playing. "If that's true, that Marilyn suggested the boat, then if Lucien—Billy—pushed her off, it was spur of the moment. Unplanned and sloppy."

Like Alice's murder.

El thought about the hasty moving of the body, the anonymous tip that could easily be disproved once the coroner did his job. As if improvised by a bad actor.

Zora said, "For all of his scheming, Billy Sullivan comes across to me as someone who embellishes rather than keeping his crimes simple. It's likely why he keeps getting caught."

"How'd you find all this out?"

"Never you mind that, although I must thank you for pointing me in the direction of Boston. And I also must thank your departed lover. Alice's telegram to the Paris police proved there wasn't a man named Lucien Laurent on record. I've got a man in the telegraph office, you see, and the Paris telegram was the final confirmation I needed."

El stood up. "Do you know where he's hiding out?"

"Not yet. Wherever he is, he's hidden good. Must mean he has a connection. A good connection." Zora tilted her head. "Does he know anyone like that?"

"I'm not sure. The only people I know he talked to regularly were his hotel porter—" El stopped.

Zora pursed her lips. "You have an idea?"

"I do. Tell me, does this place have a telephone?"

———

Pearlie Taylor was skipping down the front stoop of his building, briefcase in hand, when El called out his name from the Daimler.

He turned, shielding his eyes from the midday sun.

"El?" he said. "How'd you get out of a jail?"

"You'll read about it in the papers, Pearlie. All charges dropped."

"For now," he smirked.

"Come on over, Pearlie. We've got something to discuss."

He glanced at his wristwatch. "I've got an appointment I'm gonna be late for."

El gestured to the Daimler. "I can take you there."

"How am I gonna get back?"

"Cab. You've got sugar."

Pearlie cursed to himself and headed over to her rolled-down window. "I'll give you two minutes." That's when he noticed the fineness of the Daimler. "Say, this is a nice ride. Whose is it?"

"Madam Watkins."

"You know, El, a lotta people aren't very happy with you. You've become the example of what happens when you drink liquor and flaunt nature's laws."

"Who's been saying that bushwa?"

"Besides some newshawks and outraged letters to their editors? Reverend Blackburn. He's been dropping your name like you's a movie star."

"I swear, that man and his bluenose wife need to mind their own business."

"Their business is the morality of Harlem," Pearlie retorted. "Or so they claim."

"Don't tell me you believe their nonsense?"

"Hell, no! But I can't ignore the power they're building in this neighborhood. If I want my permits to open a second Pearlie's, I can't anger them. Which means," he said, looking from side to side, "I can't be seen consorting with a murderer."

"Suspected murderer. And I told you, the charges were dropped."

Pearlie exhaled loudly. "What do you want?"

"Where'd you stash Lucien Laurent?"

"I don't know what you're—"

"Don't play games with me. For starters, I just spoke with his favorite porter at the Hotel Eudora, a Mr. Isaiah Scott. One of your connections in your network. Well, if Mr. Scott helped Lucien find the hottest billiard hall in town, I'm sure Lucien would ask Isaiah where he could find a secret hiding place. Now, our Mr. Scott is too refined for such requests, as he made sure to let me know." She leveled her gaze at Pearlie. "But you're not. You'll do anything for a shred of lettuce. And here's the interesting thing. Lucien made his request the day they announced Alice's murder. Now that got me to thinking about a couple of things that didn't make much sense to me at the time."

"Like what?"

"Like why was he there the night I snookered him? If he were that scared of a bunch of tough guys finding him—and I know why they were after him and trust me, he had every reason to be terrified—why go back to your parlor? They'd already been there once; they could've been staking out the place to see if he returned. But if Isaiah said you'd help him find a hiding place, well, it'd be worth the risk."

"Why play billiards then? Why not just get the address and leave?"

"Oh, come on, now, Pearlie. You know the answer to that. He was using his skills to help come up with the money to pay you. The boy was broke. He blew through all his greens. Hell, the Eudora kicked his ass out."

Pearlie gave her a look of disbelief. "How did you—? Jesus. You some kind of mind-reader?"

"I'm a people reader, Pearlie. I'm also a smart woman. And now that we've established my superior intellect, tell me, Pearlie: where'd you stash him?"

Pearlie pouted before running a hand over his mouth. "If you lead them there and they kill him, it's on your head."

"Address, please. And don't even bother asking for greens this time, little rabbit."

Reluctantly, he gave her the location.

Afterwards she said, "One last thing. When the two tough guys came by, did they ask for a Lucien Laurent?"

"Nope. Asked if I saw someone with one blue eye and

one green. When I asked for a name, they said it didn't matter; he likely wasn't using his real one anyway."

"And what did you think when they said that?"

"Like I told you days ago, El. The less I know about these things, the better."

"Yeah, well, one thing you should know if you ever see our Lucien again? His real name is Billy Sullivan. The lying bastard's from Boston, where he may have killed a woman."

El wasn't gonna lie; she enjoyed watching Pearlie's smug face fall a bit.

She tapped the seat in front of her. "Let's go, Abe. We're burning daylight."

34

From across the street in the Daimler, El regarded the dilapidated wooden building, its dirty windows darkened by thick, heavy drapes. A thick layer of grime covered the bricks and the doors. Trash collected in the corners of the building's stoop, and broken bottles and their shards glittered on the sidewalk. Something had leaked from a garbage can that had been placed out front, the pink-orange slime oozing away from the stoop, as if trying to flee this den of inequity.

The block resided in a sort of no-man's-land by the Harlem River. The air was briny and slightly sour from the brown water slapping the pilings. Neighboring warehouses lined the riverfront, which wasn't nearly used as much for freight delivery as the Hudson.

"You sure it's safe, El?" Abe said.

"That's what Madam's Smith & Wesson is for."

"I can't let you go in alone."

El shrugged. "Suit yourself."

She got out and crossed the street to the building's front door with Abe fumbling to catch up behind her. The door featured four square panes of glass, one of which sported a jagged crack. She rang the buzzer to the apartment number Pearlie had given her.

No response.

She looked back at Abe. "You know how to pick a lock?"

He shook his head.

"Me neither." She searched around and found a heavy piece of brick that had fallen off the outside of the building. Well, *that* was worrisome. Still, she knew an opportunity when she saw one. She picked it up, weighing the heft in her hand, and then struck the pane of glass with the jagged edge repeatedly until she broke through.

"Ma'am!" exclaimed Abe.

She pulled out a handkerchief from her breast pocket and wrapped it around her hand to protect it from the broken glass. "I told you not to call me ma'am." She reached through the hole she made and undid the locks. The front door swung open.

"After you," she said to Abe.

Abe's eyes widened but he thankfully kept his mouth shut. He walked through the door with El following after him.

According to Pearlie, Billy was on the first floor. Apartment 1A stood to her right. Behind the door were muffled voices raised in anger. She gestured to Abe and held a finger to her lips. She pressed her ear against the door, hearing a man's voice say, "You're gonna pay for what you did, Billy."

"I didn't kill her!" Billy's voice was devoid of his French accent. He was all Worcester now.

"Ya know what? I don't care if you did. Mr. Lee thinks so and that's all that matters. Now you're coming with us."

A different man's voice said, "Now get up, you puny little shit!"

El guessed the two tough guys from Boston finally found Billy. She looked over at Abe and whispered, "You armed, Abe?"

He reached into his pocket and pulled out what looked to her like a Remington pistol.

"Jesus," she muttered. "Do we all have guns in New York?" She pulled out the Smith & Wesson and said, "Be ready." She gave an authoritative knock on the door, growling in a low voice, "Open up! It's the police!"

Silence on the other side of the door.

El knocked again. "Open it up! We know you're in there, Mr. Sullivan!" Now she pounded on the door. "We're gonna bust in there if you don't open up right this sec—"

There was a loud click of the deadbolt. The door swung inwards and there stood one of the two tough guys, the bigger one she'd seen earlier coming out of The Hub.

Hopefully they didn't get too good a look at me then.

"Who are you and what do you want Mr. Sullivan for?" the large man demanded.

"We're detectives and we're arresting him for murder."

That was when the tough guy registered El's sex. "Wait a minute. They don't got women detectives."

El acted incensed. "I ain't no woman! How dare you insult an officer of the law." She looked over at Abe. "Did you hear him insult me?"

"I sure did."

They raised their guns, both aiming them at the tough guy.

"What's your name, sir?" El demanded. When he didn't answer, she said more forcefully, "Name!"

"John Smith."

"John Smith?" El glanced over at Abe again. "This one's a regular comedian." She shouted to the rest of the building,

"Listen here, folks! This one's got jokes! Who wants a knee slapper?" She turned her attention back to this so-called "John Smith." "Perhaps we need to take you in along with Mr. Sullivan."

John Smith darted his eyes from El to Abe, trying to determine if he could take them out or if he should let this one go. "Who did he off?" he asked.

"A woman he tried to steal from. Wealthy woman from a wealthy family. We suspect he's done this kind of thing before. Our fellow detectives in the Boston area have suspicions he drowned a wealthy girl up there. That square with the man you've got in there?"

John Smith hesitated before nodding.

His shorter partner with the mustache walked up behind him. "You really gonna take him in?" he asked.

"You got a name?"

"John Smith."

"Look at that! John Smith One and John Smith Two! Or would you prefer Big John and Little John? Well, Little John, we're gonna make sure he fries in the chair. That good enough for you?"

The two John Smiths looked at one another. On one hand, their orders were to bring Billy in to Mr. Wayne Lee. On the other hand, a shoot-out with the cops would bring attention to who hired them—and a man of business like Mr. Lee would not want a bunch of pounders coming to his door asking questions. Not if he was trying to overtake Sherman Williams. A scandal like that would torpedo his efforts.

Big John shrugged, and Little John said, "You can have him." He left the doorway, disappearing momentarily from sight.

There was a struggle, and when Big John backed away,

Little John dragged Billy to the door. He'd been worked over some, judging from the split, swollen bottom lip, the bruise on his left cheek, and the trickle of blood from his nose. Recognition flashed across his face, but he had the smarts to keep it to himself. El was his savior now.

She said to Abe, "Take him."

Abe grabbed Billy by the arm and placed the Remington against his back. "One move and you're dead."

Billy smirked. "I'm dead anyway, aren't I?"

Big John said, "That's right. You are. And if we don't see your obituary in the papers, we'll be back."

"Don't worry," El replied. "If we can't nail him, he's yours. Let's go, sir." She hesitated. "How'd you find him anyway?"

Little John shrugged. "The idiot came by the impound lot to try and sneak his motorcar out of there. We figured he'd be there soon enough, so we were watching it."

El looked over at Billy. "Really? Dumb, dumb, dumb. Alright, let's go."

Together with Abe, they marched Billy to the Daimler. Crossing the street, El heard Little John say to Big John, "Hey, why aren't they cuffing him? Don't cops usually have handcuffs?"

El quietly swore.

"Hey!" Big John called. "Hey, you! Come back here!"

"Run," El murmured to Abe.

They took off in a sprint towards the Daimler, practically dragging Billy with them. El opened the back door and shoved Billy inside while Abe jumped across the hood of the car to get to the driver's side.

El jumped in after Billy when the first bullet zinged off the top of the Daimler.

"Drive!" she yelled as she slammed the door shut.

She ducked as another bullet cracked the passenger window.

Abe started the engine and took off in a roar as the two John Smiths ran after them, firing indiscriminately. Whoever taught them to shoot needed to be shot themselves. Other than a stray bullet clipping the back fender, they didn't hit anywhere close to the Daimler.

Abe squealed around one corner, then another.

El kept watch out the back window to see if the two would give chase in their motorcar. So far, the coast was clear.

Billy breathed heavily beside her. "Jesus," he said, his Boston accent a far cry from his French one. "I think this is the second time you saved me."

"Yeah, and you're gonna give me answers."

He swallowed. "About what?"

El aimed the Smith & Wesson right between his eyes. "Did you kill Alice?"

His face paled. "No! I didn't—I swear on my word."

"I'd swear on something else since every word out of your mouth has been a lie. The night Alice died. Where did you go?"

"I told you this already. There was a leak in my bathroom and it was getting fixed when she died."

"Wrong. The coroner is going to announce in either tonight's or tomorrow's papers that her body was moved. She was killed elsewhere, *Billy*, likely well before the 3:34 a.m. anonymous telephone call, so you being in your room at the Hotel Eudora means nothing. Now I'm gonna ask again: where were you?"

Billy's lips twitched with fear. "I—I was—I was in a speak. Some place Isaiah recommended."

"It got a name?"

"Uh, uh—I think—I think—"

"Think harder, Billy."

Billy's eyes remained locked on the barrel of the Smith & Wesson. "I remember, but you have to believe me, I'm not making a joke." He paused to swallow a giant lump in his throat. "The Alibi."

El stared at him. "You're joking."

"I'm not! You can ask Isaiah!"

"Oh, I intend to. And you better hope to heaven there's someone in that place who can say they saw you. When you got back to your room, who did you telephone? Not the front desk for the leak," she added quickly. "After. The second telephone call. Isaiah overheard you say, 'It was an accident. An accident. I don't care if you believe me. What's done is done.' Was that about Alice?"

"Marilyn."

"Marilyn? Wayne Lee's daughter?"

Billy closed his eyes. "When Pearlie told me they were some tough guys asking around for me, I knew that Mr. Lee had found me. I hoped my new name and identity as Lucien would throw them off the scent, but Mother Nature decided to give me one hell of a marker."

"Your eyes," El said. "Not too many people with one blue and one green."

"I thought I could shake them by going elsewhere but they were hitting on the billiard rooms. When I went to The Alibi, I had one too many and decided to call up old man Lee and see if I could persuade him to back off. It didn't work."

"Guess not. So when you said it was an accident—"

"Marilyn was deathly allergic to bee stings. It's why we often didn't picnic together—"

"—and why she suggested the boat even though she couldn't swim."

"And somehow, in a cruel twist of fate, a wasp had made a nest in it. When Marilyn saw the damn thing fly around her, she panicked and stood up, causing the boat to tip, and she—she fell out."

"Uh huh. And why didn't *you* save her?"

"I can't swim," he admitted quietly. "But I dove in. I don't care what her father says, I dove in trying to get her. I had on one of those life raft things." He glared off to the side. "I got her up once, but Marilyn—she kept slipping from my arms. The boat moved with the current, going farther and farther away, and no one else was near us. She fell back under the surface and I—I couldn't get her." He looked at El. "It was an accident, dammit, an accident!"

She studied his face, seeing frustration, fear, self-recrimination. More importantly, she saw the truth, damn him. "And Alice?" she said.

"I had nothing to do with that. Why would I kill her? I needed her money. I was about to be thrown out of the Hotel Eudora. Without her, I have no status and I'm nowhere near protected from the likes of Wayne Lee. The Eudora may be expensive but those goons couldn't get past the front desk."

"What about those 'goons.' Alice didn't get in the way of them trying to take you, did she?"

"No. I mean, not when I was around her. I—I can't swear to it if it happened any place else, but I don't think so. Alice wouldn't stick her neck out for me. In fact, I think she'd have been relieved if they approached her. And anyway, their orders are to bring me back to Boston, not kill me then and there, so she wouldn't have dove in front of the bullet for me."

El begrudgingly admitted to herself he likely wasn't the one who shot Alice, or caused her to be shot. The motive just wasn't there. And he didn't strike her as a killer. A pathetic little conman with bad luck and timing, sure. A stone-cold murderer? That was harder to picture.

"Alright," she said. "Let's change the subject. Who is Raymond Price?"

"I don't know—"

"Abe! Baby, pull over and let's dump him out. I'm sure those two lovely gentleman will be very keen to have their paws on him again."

"Okay, okay! I think he's—or maybe was—an employee at the Holloway Factory."

"What makes you say that?"

"Because of the letter."

"What letter?"

"I found it in Alice's things. One of her locked desk drawers at the townhouse."

"Why were you going through her things?" El rolled her eyes. "Never mind. You were looking for stuff to steal. Or blackmail. God knows with you."

"I was not!"

"Billy, do you really want to argue with a bereaved woman holding a Smith & Wesson?"

"No," he replied. "No, I do not." He gestured to his coat. "I'm gonna pull it out slowly. Don't—don't shoot me."

"You better not be chewing gum, Billy. I've got a hair trigger right now."

He gently slid his hands into the inside pocket and, inch by inch, pulled out an envelope. "Here," he said. "Take a look for yourself."

El kept the gun aimed at him with one hand while she took the envelope with the other. It was addressed to a Mr.

Raymond Price on 123rd Street. The return address was a post office box. Sent on Friday, October 22. Across the face of the envelope was an officious, angry stamp from the post office: RETURN TO SENDER.

With a deft hand, she opened the envelope and slid out the folded letter inside. Unfolding it, she saw typewritten words. She gasped when she realized the contents of the letter.

It was the thank-you note Ramona said Alice had written to all the Holloway Paper Box Factory strikers to boost morale. The letter reassured Mr. Price that his efforts and sacrifice would make the world a better place. It was signed the Box Factory Union.

El re-read the letter again and looked over at Billy. "What the hell is this?"

"I was hoping you'd tell me. Just my luck. I'm rummaging around in a locked drawer, thinking I was going to hit pay dirt, and I get a lousy return-to-sender."

El returned the letter to the envelope, staring at the RETURN TO SENDER stamp. Did this Raymond Price move? Did Alice have the wrong address? No, she couldn't have. She used the payroll records to find the addresses. Though it *had* been six months. And he was fired from the factory—

"Wait, he was fired from the factory," El muttered to herself. "Why would she send him a letter of support from the union?"

She looked over her shoulder. No sign of the two John Smiths following them.

"Abe," she called, turning around.

"Yes, El?"

She tapped the envelope. "We're gonna make a quick stop at 123rd Street."

35

The building looked like every other apartment building El had seen and lived in. Boxy, three stories tall, with narrow windows and a modest front stoop.

El and Abe stood on either side of Billy, with Abe keeping a very firm grip on the man's arm. They both told him no funny business, to which he responded, "Hey, you two's have the guns."

Raymond lived on the third floor and didn't answer their buzzer. El tried again.

"Maybe he's out working?" Billy said.

El pointed at the envelope in her hand. "This says he isn't here."

"So why are we ringing the buzzer?"

"Because I want to know if he ever lived here." She pressed the buzzer again, muttering, "Come on, now."

A window above them on the second story flew up, the sash banging with enough force to cause all three of them to jump. They raised their eyes upward and saw a young woman lean her head outside.

"For the love of all that is sainted and holy, please *stop* pressing that buzzer!"

An unseen infant brayed behind her.

El frowned. "Sorry? I was pressing for Apartment 3." She double-checked where her thumb was. Nope, she hadn't made a mistake.

The woman explained. "The idiot electrician screwed up the wiring when they installed the buzzers. Apartment 3 buzzes Apartment 2, which makes my life more difficult than it already is. I just got the baby to sleep and now he's up, crying like the day he was born and I've gotta start all over again laying him down."

"I'm assuming you're in Apartment 2."

Despite the sun glaring in her face, El saw the woman was young, likely in her early twenties. Her dark hair was tied away from her face by a red handkerchief. From this vantage point, all that was visible, other than her face and her forearms leaning on the windowsill, was the high neckline of a burgundy cotton dress.

The baby's brays went to full-throated cries. The woman ignored him. "Day in, day out, nothing but buzz buzz buzz! It's enough to make a sane woman mad, and a mad woman homicidal."

"I can understand that," murmured Billy.

El said, "I apologize, miss. What do I buzz for Apartment 3?"

"Apartment 1."

"The electrician *really* futzed up, didn't he?"

The woman glanced back at the crying baby, deciding he was fine, and said, "I should've known he would. When he came, he said he was the plumber but the landlords told him to do this instead of fixing the pipes."

Billy asked, "Why would they send a plumber to do an electrical job?"

The woman gave him a jaded look. "Because all land-lords are cheap bastards who'd rather check off a box on their little form that says we have buzzers, so they can jack up the rent another two, three, five dollars a month."

"Sounds about right."

El waved at the woman. "We're sorry about waking your baby. We didn't mean to."

"I know, I know. The landlords say they'll come to fix it—"

"—but they never do."

"Then you know."

"Oh, I do," El said. "Say, have you lived here long?"

"Three years."

"Long time."

"A lifetime, in this city."

"Has a Raymond Price ever lived in Apartment 3?"

The woman squinted. "Who?"

El repeated the name.

"No," the woman said. "The only person who's in Apartment 3 is some old man who's been here forever. His name is Ian Shepherd."

"You're certain?"

"Lived there since before I moved in."

"And no one named Raymond Price lives in this building?"

"Not for the last three years." She hesitated. "You know, you're the second person to ask about this fella."

"Oh, really?"

"Yeah. Didn't catch her name, though."

"Her? A woman?" El felt her heart beat a little faster. "Was she a white woman?"

"Yeah. Brown hair. Wore a suit, like you."

Alice.

El saw Billy give her an interested look, obviously curious about her reaction, but she didn't care. She was on the cusp of breaking this mystery, she felt it in her bones.

"When was this?" she asked the woman.

"Last week. Like Tuesday, maybe?"

Her last day on earth.

El said, "Thank you very much. You've been very helpful. Hopefully your little tyke will fall back to sleep."

"From your lips to the Holy Mother's ears," the woman said as she slid the window shut.

Back in the Daimler, Billy asked the obvious question. "If Raymond Price doesn't exist, why did the union have this address? And why did Alice keep it?"

An idea gently knocked in the back of El's mind. "This letter," she said. "This was found in a locked drawer, so she didn't want other people to find it. Which meant it was valuable."

"That was my assumption. It's why I took it."

"Did you hear her mention this name to anyone?"

"No. I never heard it until you told me that night you snookered me."

"Did *you* mention it to anyone else? Say to any of the union strike leads?"

Billy turned to her, offended. "Why would I waste my time with a bunch of whining strikers? Besides, I don't even know who they are." He shifted in his seat. "Why are you even asking about all this in the first place?"

Because "someone" told Ramona the name. A someone she said was "dangerous to her" if people found out who they were.

El chased it around in her head. Was it Rich? Could

Ramona be a mole? Maybe that's why the union wasn't getting anywhere with the negotiations. They were being sabotaged from within. It also might explain her attitude towards Alice. And to El, when she started coming around. A projection, of sorts. "*See? I'm telling you, she's a spy.*"

But if that were true, then she'd have told Rich about Alice's involvement the very second Alice started giving money. Yet the strike had lasted for six months with no signs of stopping. And Rich was now so desperate that he tried to bribe workers at a rent party. That didn't square with El. Rich would've nipped this in the bud if he knew.

Which left who?

Who else did you tell, Alice?

Then a better question popped into her mind.

Who else did I tell?

A moment later, she knew.

Frank Nickerson answered El's knock, surprised to see her.

"Oh. It's you," he said. "Uh . . . I'm sorry, I forgot your name."

"I'm not surprised, knocking back all that gin," El replied. She stood by herself, trusting Abe to keep Billy in the Daimler.

Frank scratched the back of his head. "Yeah, well, I—I had a hard day."

"I know about hard days."

He glanced over his shoulder, nervous, before turning his head back to her. "Look, I'm not supposed to talk to you. Alright? I made a mistake that day. So please don't turn in your article or whatever it was you were working on."

El had almost forgotten how she and Flo posed as

reporters when they first spoke with him. "Actually, I'm here to speak with your wife. Is she here by any chance?"

Frank sent another furtive glance over his shoulder. "Oh. Uh. I'm not married—"

A woman's voice called out, "Hon, forget about that bite to eat. I was supposed to leave a half ago to get to the factory."

And into the front room walked Ramona Westfall. She stopped in her tracks at the sight of El on her doorstep. "What are *you* doing here?" she demanded.

"Well, Miss Westfall, I could ask you the same damn question. Or is it Mrs. Nickerson?"

Frank frowned. "You two know each other?"

Ramona gestured at El with an exasperated hand. "This is the woman I was telling you about! She's a nosy busybody asking too many damn questions. She's not reporter; she's a night club singer." She turned her ire to El. "And she's a murderer."

"*Suspected* murderer," El corrected. "And the charges were dropped this morning."

"That means nothing."

Frank squinted. "I'm confused. What's going on here?"

Ramona crossed her arms. "So. You pretended to be a reporter to, what? Spy on me? Spy on my husband?"

"In my defense," El replied, "I didn't know he was your husband. Not until now. You gave yourself away at Sam Willing's rent party. 'It's too dangerous for me,' you said. I thought someone was threatening to harm you. But then you told me when we first met in Augusta Wilde's studio that married women can't work at the factory. And Ferrin said later that you never wanted to be dependent on anyone ever again."

"What does any of this have to do with why you're here?"

"Raymond Price. I asked your husband about the name. He must've mentioned it to you, which is why you lied to me about where you heard it. Or rather, who you heard it from." El cocked her head. "Makes me wonder why that would make you nervous."

Ramona touched Frank on the shoulder. "Honey, go down to the precinct and file a complaint. Tell them El Train is harassing us."

Frank looked very confused. "Why would I do that?"

"Just . . . do as I say!"

"Ramona," El said. "You do that, I'm gonna point the pounders right at your husband."

Ramona scoffed. "What for?"

"He was on duty when Alice's body was dropped at the entrance. Yes, dropped off. You might've been telling the truth, Mr. Nickerson. Looks like Alice was shot elsewhere."

"I knew it!" he said. "I knew I didn't hear any gunshots."

"But you didn't see who placed her body there because you were examining the trucks for a good half hour or more on Rich's orders. To make sure no one was futzing with them, isn't that right?"

"Yes, that's exactly what happened."

El feigned confusion. "Seems odd to me, though, when Rich was hiring damage squads to torch his own trucks to discredit the union. What man would be in a better position to do that than the night guard? When the factory is empty and nobody's watching."

"Why would I?"

"Why does anyone do anything?" El said. "Money. Rich would've poured a whole lotta sugar into your bowl. Only you futzed up. Alice died. Not part of the deal."

Ramona fumed. "I can't believe you'd dare to accuse my husband of such a thing."

"Oh, girl, I can't believe you're still taking this bearcat attitude with me when you're the one who's going to lose her job if this marriage comes out."

"You wouldn't."

"I would *like* not to," El clarified. "Despite the disrespect you continue to show me, I actually think withholding jobs from married women is bushwa. Just another way for men to keep us down. I *want* you to stay in your job, Miss Westfall or Mrs. Nickerson. I want you to keep making that money." She pointed at Frank. "But I want to know what he was really doing there that night. It was clear from our 'interview' that he disapproved of Rich almost as much as you do. Hell, as much as Alice did. So what's the story, Frank?"

He and Ramona shared a look.

"I'm waiting," El said, tapping her foot.

Ramona sighed. "He was searching for proof of negligence."

That was unexpected. "He was helping the union then?"

Frank nodded. "The union needed to prove that Mr. Holloway's actions were not just dangerous but illegal. Even though there's not many protections against harming workers, there are some."

El filled in the blanks. "And if you found that Mr. Holloway was purposefully funneling funds from fixing the machines to, say, his own bank account, that would further help illustrate the selfishness of management."

"That was the idea."

"And when Alice's body was dumped out front, you

weren't actually in the garage checking the trucks. You were in the offices looking through the files."

"It's why I kept my job while Ramona here went on strike," he said. "To have someone on the inside."

"Did Alice know?" El asked.

Ramona replied, "I didn't trust her with this. No offense to her."

"I can understand why you had reservations about her, I do. But she truly believed in the cause. And trust me when I say, she had no love for the way her brother was running that place. Should've been her in charge, if her father wasn't so damn traditional." El tipped her hat to the both of them. "Appreciate your honesty. Mrs. . . . ?"

"Nickerson, please," Ramona said.

"Mrs. Nickerson." El turned to go but stopped herself. "Hey, do you need a ride to the factory?"

36

When Ramona stepped into the Daimler, she pointed to Billy, who sat in one of the swivel seats. "Who's this?"

"A loose end we're trying up," El replied.

"Hey," Billy said. "I'm offended by that."

"Good."

Ramona wanted to ask more questions but decided against it. She took the swivel chair next to Billy, as El had already settled onto the back bench.

They rode in silence for a few blocks while El turned the matter of Raymond Price over and over in her head. His being fired twice, yet his name still showing up in the employee records that Alice copied from the factory before the strike.

She should've come to me for them, a voice in El's head said. *I'm the accountant, after all.*

"Mrs. Nickerson," she said. "What's the story about Mr. Thomas?"

"Hmm? Ferrin?" Ramona looked over her shoulder and frowned. "There's not much story to him. He joined the factory six years ago as one of the accountants. Didn't move up very far. Doesn't have the stomach for the politics you have to play, especially when Rich came onto the scene. You've met him. He's a Nervous Nellie who can't keep his glasses on his face."

And who's hopelessly infatuated with you, El thought.

"So mid-management level."

"That would be an overstatement. A step above a junior account but not much further."

"Never got a promotion or a raise?"

"Under Old Man Holloway, he likely got something. But under Rich? Likely a demotion."

"I see." El thought some more. "And the young Mr. Holloway took over three years ago? Is that right?"

"Much to our detriment, yes he did."

Around, or shortly thereafter, the non-existent employee Raymond Price pops up on the books.

El saw Billy pretend to remove specks of dust from his trousers."Mr. Sullivan. You're a connoisseur of the con. Why would someone create a worker who doesn't exist?"

"Embezzlement," he replied without hesitation. "You set up that person in a job, hopefully in a big company in a crowded department—low stakes, low visibility—then find a way to collect the paychecks. Simple. Easy. Very lucrative if you do it right."

"You don't say?"

Billy's voice took on more excitement. "Oh, yeah. The hard part is setting it up—making sure you've got all the paperwork to get the worker on the payroll. Then, of course, picking up the paycheck, but you can swing that easy enough. Pretend to be a pal. Or hell, pretend to be the person yourself. These payroll folks don't get paid much and they don't care who takes the money, as long as they get the stub to show proof of disbursement. Now, if you're stupid, you'd deposit the money in your own bank account. Bad move. Someone tracks you, you're dead. But set up a separate account in a different bank? Harder to discover. Or at least it slows investigators down and gives you time to escape." Billy sent El a curious look. "You think that's what this Raymond Price is? A fake employee?"

Ramona sat up straighter. "What are you two talking about?"

El felt the Daimler slow to a stop and heard Abe announce they've arrived. She looked out the window and saw the Holloway building and the familiar sight of pick-eters carrying their signs and pacing back and forth in front of the entryway to the factory. Their loud chants penetrated the windows of the Daimler: "Keep workers safe! No more Sam Willings! Keep workers safe! No more Sam Willings!"

The rent party from Friday night must've been in the forefront of the union's mind.

"Thank you for the ride," Ramona said as she got out of the Daimler. "And nice meeting you, Mr. Sullivan."

"Nice meeting you too, Mrs. Nickerson," Billy replied.

Ramona had already started walking towards the pick-eters, her attention elsewhere.

As was El's. She searched the picket line for Ferrin Thomas, not quite believing he was the killer but not disbelieving it either.

Billy cleared his throat. "Is Ferrin Thomas your—what do the detectives call 'em—prime suspect?"

El ignored him while she still scanned the crowd. On one of her visual sweeps, she saw Ramona pick up a sign and began marching with the women and children. El had this say about her: she was dedicated. Given her personal history with abusive, manipulating men, El started to have some begrudging respect for Ramona Westfall aka Nickerson.

Still rude as hell, though.

Like last time, a crowd had gathered across the street to watch, half of whom condemned the picketers, based on their glares and headshakes, while the other half supported them.

"El?" asked Abe. "Where are we going next?"

"Just a minute, Abe." She found Malek marching with the Eastern European fraction of the workforce. A few feet down, she saw the Black workers led by Booker.

Billy turned in his seat to face her. "You think Alice found out about it, huh? That's why she was killed?"

"Shh!"

Billy started chuckling. "Oh, oh that's too good. That's too good. The accountant did it."

"I don't know anything, and neither do you."

Come on, Ferrin. Where the hell are ya?

Billy smirked, "If you say so." He stared out the window, searching the crowd like El was doing. He pointed. "That who you're looking for? The meek one with the glasses that keep sliding down his nose?"

"Where?" El followed Billy's gaze and sure enough, there he was, dressed in another plain, boring brown suit, tapping his foot incessantly, pausing to slide those glasses up every thirty seconds.

"Doesn't look like much of a killer," Billy remarked.

"And you'd know how?"

A loud engine turned everybody's heads, El's and Billy's included. Rich's black motorcar arrived, gliding through 125th Street like a shark moving through still waters. A black wagon followed it. Was he bringing in more scabs?

The motorcar and the wagon stopped. Rich stepped out and walked towards Malek. The picketers slowed their walking. The feel of the air shifted, like a storm about to start.

Without being conscious of it, El opened the door and stepped out onto the sidewalk.

Abe said, "El?"

"Keep an eye on Billy." She shut the door behind her.

Rich's words rang out, loud and clear. "This has gone on long enough!"

Malek replied, "You have the power to end this. You can renegotiate with us in good faith."

Rich scowled. "Good faith? I made you an offer, which you said that you would accept."

"I said I would *consider*."

"That's as good as accept in my world, you little shit."

Malek shrugged. "Perhaps your world needs to re-evaluate how you use words."

Rich scoffed out a laugh. "Oh, I see we have a vaudevillian here. Let's see how funny you find this." He placed two fingers between his lips and whistled.

The back door of the wagon opened up, but instead of younger Black girls like last time, a gang of men holding billy clubs jumped out. Once their feet hit the pavement, they raised their weapons and started attacking the picketers indiscriminately. It didn't matter if it was a man, woman, or child. Down came the clubs in rapid, savage arcs. Everyone started shouting, an incomprehensible roar.

Many of the bystanders by El gasped.

A woman said, "Oh my god. Oh my *god*! Somebody help them!"

A man shushed her. "They asked for this!"

A second man said, "They did not!"

An argument ensued behind El, but she didn't hear the rest of it. Her eyes remained glued to the fighting men across the street. Rich's men with the billy clubs struck the picketers every which way: torsos, backs, arms, shoulders, and, once they were down on the ground, their heads.

The picketers fought back with clubs of their own. Some of them used sawed off table legs, others rusted lead pipes. They swung their weapons back at Rich's men.

El watched in horror as one picketer's lead pipe connected with the jaw of one of Rich's men. Teeth flew from the man's mouth followed by a spray of blood. Before he could react, the picketer struck his neck and shoulder and then beat his lower back until the man dropped to the ground.

Behind the picketer, another of Rich's men raised his club and smacked the picketer in the back of the head. He went down as well. Rich's man kicked him savagely in the ribs before moving onto his next target.

Abe got out of the Daimler and implored El to get inside. Her eyes darted back and forth, looking for Malek, Ferrin, Booker, and Ramona, who were lost in the fray. She stood up on her tiptoes trying to get a view.

She caught flashes of Malek defending himself with a table leg. He aimed for stomachs to double his attackers over and then smacked their hands so they'd drop their weapons. If the attackers kept advancing, wanting to engage in a fist fight, only then would Malek aim for their heads or faces.

Down a few feet from Malek was Booker, who led a group of Black picketers. They formed a tight circle facing out with their backs to each other. Smart. That way, no one could sneak up behind any one of them.

"Please, El," Abe said. "I'm begging you. Get inside the Daimler before you get hurt."

"Hush up!'

Similar to Booker, Ramona had gathered the women, who, to El's admiration, didn't back down or run. They had makeshift weapons of their own, and gave as good as they got.

Darting in and out of the ruckus was Ferrin. He reached down and pulled men from the ground, dragging them to the side and out of harm's way. A thin line of blood trickled down Ferrin's face, his mouth set in a thin line of grim determination.

Damn, El thought. *I didn't think that boy had any strength in him.*

Instinctually, she listened for the wailing sounds of sirens. Surely the pounders would be here soon to break it up. She saw that Rich hadn't moved from his place behind the black motorcar, using it as a shield of sorts. He watched with an evil grin on his face. He was loving this. This chaos, this violence.

The fray moved to the middle of the street, effectively blocking traffic. Bodies started piling on the sidewalk. Moaning men and women and crying children bled profusely from their heads, faces, and hands. Those who didn't moan or cry laid still. El hoped to God they were only unconscious.

The street became the fighting arena, and the group of bystanders surrounding El nervously backed up. The savagery of the men and the scale of the fight itself took her breath away. Everywhere she looked, she saw people—who all looked from the same economic class, as best as El could tell—beat each other senseless.

It was vicious.

It was cruel.

It was . . . *senseless.*

Before she could stop herself, El raised her voice: "You all stop it now! Stop! You're gonna kill somebody!"

She lost sight of Malek. Ferrin too.

"Booker," she muttered to herself. "Where's Booker?"

She couldn't find him either. Or Ramona.

Rich. He was missing too. Had he retreated to the safety of his motorcar? The back passenger door was still open. Had a picketer pushed him in there? Was he being beaten like everyone else?

Sirens wailed faintly in the distance, getting louder by the second. A police truck rounded the curve with squealing tires, a bunch of pounders standing on the footrests on both sides of the vehicle, holding onto the door-frames, earning their moniker of "Elephant Ears."

Abe came up to El. "You can't be here! Remember what Madam Watkins said!"

She saw Ferrin and Ramona take off. Malek stared at the people fighting for a moment longer before he joined them, Booker at his heels.

"Come on, El!"

El followed Abe back to the Daimler, where the back door stood open. Billy Sullivan was nowhere in sight.

"Shit!" she yelled. The little bastard took off when Abe wasn't looking. But that was a problem for a different time. They needed to leave before more pounders came and blocked off the streets.

She slammed the back doors shut while Abe jumped behind the wheel.

They got the hell out of there.

37

"Bitch! Bitch! Goddamn, bitch!"

"My sentiments exactly, Mac," El replied.

She was sitting in the Watkins Hotel office once again with Madam Watkins and Flo. She'd just gone through everything she learned: about Lucien Laurent being a fraud, how Billy Sullivan was his real name, his alleged crime in Boston, and the letter he found in Alice's desk. (El also apologized for the crack in the Daimler's window from the tough guys' stray bullet.)

She ended with how Ferrin Thomas might've been embezzling from the factory and that Alice might've found out about it.

Flo listened intently to everything El said while Madam Watkins stared out the large window overlooking the city. The sun had set and night had moved in.

"That solves the mystery of the name Raymond Price," Flo said when El finished. "And why Alice was asking about him."

"It does," El agreed. "Alice did that letter-writing campaign using the payroll records she copied from the factory office to determine how much money to donate to the cause. Everything went fine for six months but then she wrote the letters."

"And one of them gets returned."

"That's what she meant when she told me on the telephone that there was something confusing. She probably assumed the first thing I did, that this Raymond Price moved or left the city. But she goes and checks out the address and discovers no one by that name ever lived there."

Madam Watkins said, "Alice puts two and two together and realizes something's fishy."

"Right. She goes to the meeting to discuss whether or not the union is hiring damage squads. And then Malek volunteers the books to ease her suspicions."

Flo hummed low in her throat. "And there's Ferrin Thomas, knowing he's about to get caught."

El let out a breath. "Ferrin Thomas. I can't believe such a—such a *canceled stamp* murdered my Alice."

"You really think it's him?"

Madam Watkins turned around. "Anybody is capable of committing a crime. Even the shy and the meek. But it's a good question. Why do you think it's him?"

"Who else would be in position to set it up? Lucien—Billy—he said the hardest part was getting the fake employee on the books. Once that's done, it's easy."

Flo countered, "Malek, Booker, and Ramona were all in management positions. They could've 'hired' this Raymond Price."

"Yes, but how do you explain Raymond Price being fired, then rehired again?"

Flo shrugged. "They're managers. Maybe they said they made a mistake."

"And Rich let them? No, it had to be someone deft with

paperwork. Someone who could literally keep the employee on the books."

"Ferrin," Madam Watkins said. "El, didn't you say he was in love with Ramona and wanted to be her provider?"

"That's where he went wrong. She didn't want someone taking care of her."

"But what did he *say*? Think back. Something about money."

El closed her eyes, picturing her and Ferrin at the Willings's rent party, standing outside the WC. "He mentioned he wanted to pay for her tuition. I told him it was unlikely given how independent Ramona wanted to remain. And he said . . . he said . . . oh! 'How likely is it she won't need a husband who can provide for her? I could do that. I can't, yet, but I've been saving up for the day.'"

Madam Watkins snapped her fingers. "That's it! Saving up for the day."

"With his embezzlement."

"It would seem to suggest that."

El opened her eyes and started laughing. "Oh my Lord. Oh, sweet Jesus. Ah! It's so obvious. Raymond Price. Do you get it? *Ramona's Price.*"

Madam Watkins stared at her. "You've got to be kidding."

Mac trilled in his cage before squawking, "What the hell were you thinking? What the hell were you thinking?"

Flo held up her hands. "Hold up, hold up. I grant you, this all makes some sense. But how did that canceled stamp move Alice's body? And where did he shoot her? Not his place. He's got roommates, I hear."

"That, I don't know," El admitted.

"Unless we answer those questions, we don't have nearly anything to go to the police with."

Madam Watkins volunteered, "Perhaps one of the other union leads? Miss Russell, what did you find out about Mr. Freeman? Did he have a motorcar?"

"Nope, and there's no way that man could—he's got six children and one on the way. He's drowning in bills and diapers, so he doesn't have a cent to spare." Flo held up a finger. "But he does a cousin who drives a hack, and he wasn't working the night Alice died."

"Damn," El said. "I really don't want it to be him, even if as just an accomplice. What about that others? Did Dash come through on those?"

A knock on the door turned their heads. One of Madam Watkins's assistants let in Dash Parker, as if right on cue.

"Evening, ladies," he said.

"Hello, Rosie!" Mac replied. "How's tricks?"

Dash chuckled. "Evening, Mac." His expression turned serious. "El, have you seen the picketers out front?"

That took El by surprise. "No, I came through the back." She squinted at him. "There's picketers?"

"I saw some of them before I was put into the trunk."

El looked over to Madam Watkins. "What's going on?"

Madam Watkins sighed. "It's Reverend Blackburn. He's protesting the hotel hiring and protecting a degenerate murderer. His words, not mine."

El remembered what Pearlie Taylor had said earlier, that she was becoming a representation of what the Reverend and his followers stood against. "I'm so sorry, Madam. I didn't mean to cause you this trouble."

"We will handle it when the time comes. But for right now, we need to bring the real killer to the police. Mr. Parker, what did you find out?"

Dash held up several pieces of paper, his face excited.

"For starters, Miss Westfall is in a common-law marriage with Frank Nickerson, the guard on duty the night—"

Flo waved him off. "We know that already. Skip to the motorcar stuff."

Dash's face fell a little. "Oh, I see. Well, uh, as far as motorcar ownership, nothing registered with the city under Westfall or Nickerson." He flipped through another page. "As for Ferrin Thomas, I'm afraid the same for him."

El felt herself getting frustrated. "Shit, how did Ferrin move her body?"

"I'm sorry?" Dash said. "The killer is Ferrin Thomas? The accountant?"

"Yeah," Flo replied. "He set up that fake employee Raymond Price to try to woo Ramona not knowing she was already married. Keep up."

Dash frowned to himself. "Well, for what it's worth, I looked up Raymond Price and struck out again. No motorcar ownership for 'him,' either."

Silence fell upon the room.

El spoke first. "Alright. Our next avenue is figuring out where she was killed. We know that, we likely can prove Ferrin Thomas is our killer."

Flo pinched her brow. "That's gonna take time we don't have."

"I know, sis. And whoever did it has had plenty of time to scrub up the floors and replace the rugs—" El stopped. A moving image like one of those cinema films played in her head. She ran it back and forth, stopping on the crucial bit of dialogue in the scene. Could that be it?

Flo said, "El?"

"Shh! I'm thinking." El played out the scenario a few times. Yeah, yeah that was likely it. And goddamn, it made her angry. Angry and sad. "I think . . . I think I know where she was killed."

Madam Watkins stepped forward. "You do?"

"Uh huh. And to tell you the truth, it makes me quite miserable."

Dash said, "What do we do next?"

El gestured to the women in the room. "*We* are going to confront this person. *You,* however, are going to stay here. If we don't return in an hour or if you don't hear from us, please telephone the pounders."

"Are you certain I can't join you? I meant what I said that I'd like to help in any way I can."

"Baby, do you even know how to shoot a gun?"

He blushed. "I—no, not really. Or rather, not very well."

"Get that Irish bartender to teach you." She sent him a friendly smile to take out the sting. "Don't you worry now. You can help us by being our fail safe. A lookout man, of sorts. Though the three of us can more than take care of ourselves."

Madam Watkins picked up her telephone. "I'll call up Abe."

El and Flo began gathering their things.

"Wait," Dash said. "What address am I giving the police in case you don't return?"

When El told him, Flo looked up sharply at El. "You serious?"

El replied gravely, "I am. Now you see why I'm miserable about it?"

38

El burst open the office door, surprising Pearlie at his desk. "Pearlie Taylor. The day of judgment has arrived." She crossed the office floor in a flash with the Smith & Wesson in her hand. She whipped around his desk, turned his swivel chair until they were facing each other, and aimed the barrel at his forehead.

Pearlie's eyes widened so big, they were like the cue balls on his billiard tables. "El? What are you doing? What are you–?"

"*Don't* lie to me, Pearlie. I swear to heaven, I will blow a hole clean through your head if you utter one—and I mean *one*—false word to me. You understand me? Nod if you understand me."

Pearlie did, his pupils never wavering in their vigilant watch of the gun. "W-w-where is Gerald?"

"Who?"

"My—my—my guard."

The griffin? "His name is Gerald? Lord. His mother must've hated him too. No, he's being held downstairs by two women with enough firepower to blow him to heaven and back. Don't worry. They were discreet about it, so no one in your bushwa billiard parlor knows what's happening. And they won't know, if you behave. Now let's back to the subject at hand." El leaned in close until her face was mere inches away from Pearlie's. "I know she was killed here."

"Wh-Wh–"

"Don't ask who. *You know who*. Alice. *My* Alice. She was in your secret parlor, wasn't she? The place for your Midnight Game. She often used it for private meetings, especially if they were of a sensitive business nature. And this one, Pearlie, I gotta tell ya, it was sensitive. More than she knew."

And if she had known that, then she would still be alive.

Sweat beaded on Pearlie's forehead before sliding down his cheeks.

"I'd answer my questions, if I were you," El replied in a bored voice.

"Yes, she was. But I didn't—"

"And she was shot in your secret parlor, wasn't she?"

Pearlie's lips trembled but his voice stayed in the basement of his throat. "How—how did you know?"

"The felt. You had it replaced the day after her death. Lucien Laurent—otherwise known as Billy Sullivan, a grifter from Boston—warned me about it when I beat his ass at a game. Now, felt being replaced at a billiard hall? Not that strange. But if we assume someone was shot there, then that new felt takes on a more ominous meaning, doesn't it?" El's voice turned savage with rage. "She bled out on your billiard table, didn't she? *Didn't she?!*"

Pearlie blinked back the beads of sweat sliding into his eyes. Or were those tears?

"And then there was the painting. Some boring still life. At first, I thought it was you showing off how well you were doing. Even Lucien—sorry, Billy—remarked on it. But, and this is just a guess here, that was to cover up a bullet hole in the wall. Because the man who fired the pistol is the nervous sort and likely missed one or two rounds. How am I doing so far?"

"I didn't—I wasn't—"

"The coroner reported the body was moved. Moving a body is a difficult, dangerous thing. *But!* If you have a motor-car, it makes it a lot easier. This killer, this *Ferrin Thomas*. He doesn't own one. But you do, Pearlie. You couldn't help but brag about it when I was here in your office. How the silver just catches the light. Remember?"

Pearlie's voice finally climbed up the rickety stairs of his throat and clambered onto his tongue. "Listen, El. I swear on my Momma's grave, I didn't know what was gonna happen that night. I'll—I'll tell you. I'll tell you everything, just get that gun off my face. Please, El. *Please.*"

She gave a theatrical sigh. "I am too understanding for my own good." She removed the barrel from his forehead, but she kept the pistol aimed at him. "Start talking. And fast. I don't have much time to waste."

Pearlie swallowed. "Alice was here. She set up a meeting with that Ferrin Thomas—I didn't know who he was at the time—in my private parlor, like you said. I asked if it was an illegal act, what she was doing, and she said no."

"Illegal act. You never used that phrase."

"Fine," he said through gritted teeth. "I said, 'this better not bring trouble to my door.' You satisfied?"

"That sounds more like you, Pearlie. Keep talking."

"It all happened so fast. I put them in the room. I shut the door. I was at my desk working and then—and then—" He shuddered. "All a sudden, I hear them arguing, followed by Alice saying, 'Get off me!' Then I heard the shots. One, then another one."

"Two shots. You certain about that?"

"Yeah. I ran out of here and opened the door to the parlor and saw her—saw her on the—the—"

"On your goddamn billiard table."

"I couldn't believe it! Thank god it was a slow night and everyone downstairs thought it was a car backfiring, or I'd have had real problems."

"You *do* have real problems. Me being first among them." El worked to control her temper—and her trigger finger. "What happened next? Whose idea was it to dump her body at the factory?"

"His. He said there was a strike happening over there. A lot of tension and fighting. This Ferrin fella thought the detectives would look at her brother, on account they didn't get along."

"Oh my God. Pearlie. You were dealing with an amateur killer! Pounders *never* look at powerful men as suspects. There was not a chance in hell they'd suspect, much less charge, Rich Holloway."

"He wasn't thinking straight." Pearlie looked up at her with pitiful eyes. "Neither of us were."

El stared at this pathetic, whimpering man. "Alright, I get his reasoning. But what about yours? To keep the pounders away from your parlor?"

"I didn't do anything wrong! Why should I lose my place of business because of someone else's bullshit?"

"That someone else's *bullshit* was the death of *my wife*, you asshole! That they arrested me for!"

Pearlie immediately looked contrite, a look that didn't fit him, like a suit that had shrunk. "I'm sorry. I apologize. I had nothing to do with your arrest. Okay? I swear it. Nothing. It was all his idea. You were coming around, asking questions, so he panics. Makes the second anonymous call saying he saw you shoot Alice at the factory gates and that's that. I—I swear, El. I didn't know any of this was going to happen. I didn't!"

El lowered the pistol. "You know what hurts about all this, Pearlie? I come to your billiard hall, heartbroken, and you didn't say anything. *Any*thing. You know who killed the love of my life and you just sat silent."

"He threatened me, El! What was I supposed to do? He shot a white girl and told me to get rid of the body and her coat and to tell no one, I mean no one, what happened here."

"What'd you do with her coat?"

"Her what?"

"Her *coat*! The one I gave her. Blue velour. Fur collar and lining. Ringing any bells?"

Pearlie's voice was hoarse and raspy. "I—I burned it. I had to! I'm Black, same as you. I had to get rid of all the evidence. You said it yourself. It's why I replaced the felt. You think the police would've believed my story if I told them *any* of this?"

"Hell, Pearlie, *I* barely believe your story." Another moving image entered El's mind—Pearlie coming out of his building with a briefcase. "What was your appointment?"

"Hmm?"

"Earlier today. What was your appointment? The one you didn't want me to drive you to. You claimed it was because you didn't want to be seen with me, but I think, Pearlie, that was bushwa. I think you didn't want me to see who you were meeting."

Pearlie's eyes widened.

"What was in that briefcase? Was it money? Were you being blackmailed?"

"He said he needed some cabbage on account of you being released."

"He was in the courthouse?" El thought about that packed galley. She didn't pay attention to any of the faces—too focused on her own fate—but it made sense. Ferrin had to make sure she stayed in jail. When that didn't happen . . .

"He said this was my insurance. Pay him and he'd stay quiet until he figured out what to do. That man is unlucky."

"No, he's not the unlucky one. And neither are you, Mr. Taylor. It was my Alice. My Alice and me." She gestured to the telephone sitting on his desk. "You mind?" She picked up the receiver without waiting for a response, asking the operator to connect her with the Watkins Hotel. "Hello, Dash? Everything's good." She eyed Pearlie. "We have a few more stops to make, though. Give us another two hours." She hung up the receiver.

Pearlie sniffed back more tears. "What are you going do?"

"I'm gonna get justice, that's what I'm gonna do." She pointed the pistol at him. "And you, Pearlie, are gonna come with me. We're going for a ride."

39

After forcing Pearlie into the front seat of the Daimler, Madam Watkins had Abe tie up Pearlie's wrists and ankles so he couldn't move.

"This is some serious bushwa!" Pearlie complained.

Flo looked at El. "Should we gag him?"

Madam Watkins opened her purse. "I think I've got an old handkerchief in here we can shove into his mouth."

Pearlie cursed before saying, "Alright, alright! I'll stay quiet."

"Good," El said. "Last thing we need is a man bumping his gums all night."

They left Pearlie's and Abe drove them to the address Flo got form the factory Personnel office. Ferrin Thomas's apartment was on West 117th Street. When they got there, he wasn't home, much to El's consternation. But it turned out that he hadn't been lying about having a roommate; he only lied about his roommate being able to vouch for his whereabouts the night Alice died. Apparently, the man—a mid-20s traveling salesman named Caleb Morganson—had been out that week for work.

"Any idea where Mr. Thomas is?" Madam Watkins asked.

Caleb scratched his head. "I overheard him talking with this other gent. Queer-looking chap. His two eyes are different colors. Never seen anything like it."

El cut in. "One blue and one green?"

"That's the one! Ferrin got home, all bloodied and bruised from a brawl at the factory." Caleb's tone sobered. "I told him it was dangerous getting mixed up in a strike. The bosses will do anything, even murder, to keep their position. Anyway, he comes home and I'm helping him nurse his wounds when this man shows up. Says they need to talk. I excuse myself, go into my room, give them some privacy."

Flo asked, "You wouldn't happen to have overheard what they talked about?"

Caleb shrugged. "I didn't hear much. I only heard that Ferrin needed to stop by the bank and then they'd go some-place wild. I suppose Ferrin and him were going to have a night on the town."

El thanked the man. "One more thing: When did Mr. Thomas leave for his night on the town?"

"Not more than fifteen minutes ago. You just missed him, matter of fact."

The three women glanced at one another before they walked briskly towards the Daimler.

"You thinking what I'm thinking?" Flo muttered.

"I am," El replied as they settled into the back. "A black-mail payment. At Augusta Wilde's."

The door to Augusta Wilde's studio had been left open just a crack. As if someone didn't want it to close behind them, alerting whoever else was here that an intruder had breached the locks. No lights on. No sounds inside.

"This isn't good," Flo said.

"Understatement of the year," El replied.

They left Abe at the Daimler to keep an eye on Pearlie, so it was only the three of them.

Flo pointed at the door. "You sure Mrs. Wilde isn't in any danger?"

"She's out of town this week. I heard her tell the union leads that."

Madam Watkins said softly but forcefully, "Ladies, arm yourselves."

They pulled out their pistols and cocked the hammers back.

"We go in quietly," Madam Watkins said. "Nobody say a word unless you absolutely have to. Understood?"

El and Flo nodded.

"Alright, El, you've been to this place before. You lead the way."

Heart hammering in her throat, El eased open the door, thanking the good Lord above that Augusta had oiled the hinges. She stepped into the darkened space. Thin shafts of light from the street lights outside streamed in from the narrow windows up top. Everything else was dark, dark, dark. And quiet. Unnervingly quiet. Either they beat Ferrin and Billy here, or it was already too late.

She turned and almost ran smack-dab into a screaming Black man. She almost cried out, "Sweet Jesus!" but luckily stopped herself in time.

It was Darius.

Augusta Wilde had added more detail to his features.

His eyes shone bright. His mouth had teeth. His brow wrinkled from the effort of screaming. More likely, he was singing, but tonight, it looked like he was wailing in agony.

She lowered her weapon and looked over her shoulder. Her eyes had adjusted to the dark and she could see that Madam Watkins remained the epitome of calm. Flo's face, however, said what El felt about the disembodied limbs and heads strewn about the studio. It looked like she was in the pits of hell surrounded by poor souls damned to an eternity of weeping and gnashing of teeth.

El turned around, sweeping her gaze across the room, her mind playing tricks on her as she saw all those ungodly clay shapes. She forced herself forward and stepped around Darius, searching for anything or anyone out of place. Impossible to do with all these faces perched on top of wooden crates and staring at her. Men. Women. Some with defined eyes and mouths, like Darius; others blank or malformed. Human. Inhuman. Otherworldly. Dear God, how was she going to know what was real in this damnable place?

Someone tugged at her coat, causing her to whirl around. Yet no one was directly behind her. Flo and Madam Watkins were still a few paces away. They gave her questioning looks. El glanced down. The tail of her coat had caught on one of the outstretched hands resting on a crate. She rolled her eyes and tugged her coat free.

She turned herself around and went up the crooked aisle. Her eyes glanced from left to right, right to left. A foot kicked out from the shadows. She braced herself for the impact. Nope. Just another limb fashioned by the gifted hands of Augusta Wilde.

I hope I never have to come back here again.

How long until she reached the clearing where the

strikers held their meetings? When Augusta led her through it, they only spent half a minute going through this nightmarish place. Now it felt like hours.

She thought she spotted the beginning of the studio's clearing. The familiar chair setup—four chairs for the union strike leads—slowly came into view. She stepped over another hand threatening to trip her and carefully exited the body-part maze. Here, the light from the windows lit the clearing like moonlight. She slowly circled the space. Another hand tried to grab her ankle and she deftly stepped over it. She was getting used to this now. Like a dance step. One-two-leap. One-two-swerve.

Some ancient, inner part of herself started clanging out a warning. The hairs on the back of her neck stood at attention. She slowly turned around and went back to the hand that tried to trip her. Something was odd about it. The color. The rest of the outstretched limbs, torsos, and screaming heads were made of that dark red clay. This hand was white.

A low moan rumbled in the base of El's throat.

She stepped forward, tracing the hand to the wrist to the dark sleeve of a coat. The sleeve ended at a shoulder which led to a neck holding up a face. A mouth opened in a scream like Augusta Wilde's "children." Eyes wide with surprise, though the pupils refused to sparkle. The skin slack, relaxed, pale-looking like Alice's had been.

"Oh, shit," El muttered.

She was looking at the corpse of Billy Sullivan.

El whirled around, her pistol raised. Was Ferrin still in here? Her eyes darted to the four corners of the room, then scanned the mess of limbs and heads leading to the door.

"Psst!" she whispered. "Flo. Madam. Over here."

She heard two sets of feet creep their way over to the clearing.

Flo gasped when she arrived. "Well, damn."

Madam Watkins came into the clearing and saw Billy's body. "Who is that?"

"Billy Sullivan," El replied. "Formerly known as Lucien Laurent."

"We need to determine if anyone else is here."

El searched for the light bulb overhead. Time to get out of these shadows. From what she remembered, the chain should be above their heads. There! Gleaming in the beams of light from the windows. She reached up and gave it a yank. Light flooded into the clearing area. The sudden loss of darkness caused all three of them to wince. She blinked several times, trying to adjust to the change, before she started scanning the far corners of the studio.

No one there.

She eyed the unfinished works of Augusta Wilde. The busts still cast shadows. She kept her breathing and her fear in check. Torso, head, torso with head, arm, arm, leg, hand, waist, head, torso—

She paused.

Her eyes slowly went back to the waist. That was odd. Augusta either did full torsos or heads or limbs in isolation. Never just a waist.

El narrowed her eyes. The waist wasn't quite the same color as the sculptures neither. A tan versus a rusted-out red.

Ferrin!

She took one step forward and the waist moved. Fast. She heard footsteps stamp on the wooden floor.

"Hey!" she yelled as she charged forward. "He's still here!"

She heard the studio door being ripped open and someone bang up the stairs. She ran down the crooked aisle, adrenaline pumping. She was almost to the studio door when her ankle got caught on something and she went down. Hard.

As soon as she hit the floor, her shoulders made contact with some of the wooden crates. Suddenly, limbs and heads rained down on her. She screamed when one of the heads rested in front of her face, malformed eyes and mouth grinning at her. She leapt up, shouting, "Shit, shit, shit, goddamn, motherfucker, get off of me!"

"El!" Flo called. "El, are you alright?"

El tried to step over and away from the mess but threatened to trip again. Her hands reached out and grabbed the shoulders of Darius. He threatened to go down with her but was heavy enough to stabilize himself and her. Still holding onto him, she got her feet and ankles free from the knocked-over body parts.

"Fuck!" she yelled. Then she took stock of herself and the situation and said over her shoulder, "I'm copacetic. I think." She took in more air. "I just had a bunch of body parts fall all over me."

"Did you lose him?"

El sighed her disappointment. "Unfortunately, I did."

Abe's voice cut through the air. "Fortunately, I found him." The chauffeur stepped through the door keeping a firm grip on a squirming, cussing Ferrin, whose arms were held behind his back. He looked the worse for wear. Caleb, his roommate, hadn't exaggerated; the factory brawl left Ferrin more than a little battered and bruised.

"Let go of me!" he shouted at Abe. "I say, let go of me right this instance! Or I'll—" He stopped when he saw El standing there.

"You'll what? Call the precinct, get some pounders over here?" she said. "Oh, I dare, I *dare* you to do that." She heard footsteps behind her.

"El," Flo said. "Keep it steady now."

"Don't worry, Flo. Thanks to Augusta's creations, they took my gun away from me. A good thing too, because Ferrin, I'd love nothing more than to put a bullet in you like you put a bullet in Alice."

His eyes widened. "W-what?"

"You gonna play stammering fool like Pearlie Taylor did?" El wagged her finger at him. "Nah, we're not doing that."

Madam Watkins said, "Let's check him for weapons."

"Already did, Madam," Abe replied. "Found a Colt .32. Recently fired too. Barrel's still warm. I used a handkerchief to keep my prints off it."

"Good work, Abe."

El pointed at Ferrin. "Alice's missing gun. You took it off her when you scuffled in Pearlie's back room and killed her with it. And it looks like you killed Lucien Laurent, otherwise known as Billy Sullivan. You're on a real roll, Ferrin. Who'd you plan to shoot next?"

Ferrin's mouth opened and closed a few times before he said defiantly, "I'm not saying anything until I speak with my lawyer."

"Won't help. There's the gun with your fingerprints over it. There's the books with your fake employee taking checks from the Holloways. Oh, and this." El pulled out Alice's letter addressed to Raymond Price, the envelope stamped RETURN TO SENDER. "My guess is you fought with Alice, because you wanted this back. Too bad for you she locked it in a drawer for safekeeping."

"Son," Madam Watkins added. "It's going to be a lot better for you if you turn yourself in and confess."

Ferrin aimed for smugness. "They won't believe you. Three Black women and a Black man? They'll listen to me over you any day of the week."

El ran her tongue over her teeth. "That is true, what you say there, Ferrin. Absolutely true. What's also true is that you killed a man that a very powerful businessman with mobster connections—Wayne Lee, founder of Lee Paints, a giant corporate enterprise—was hoping to bring back to Boston. Because Mr. Lee blamed the man you killed for the death of his daughter. And now *you*, Ferrin Thomas, on West 117th Street, Apartment D, roommate Caleb Morganson, took that chance away from him. And he's bereaved. And angry. And vengeful. What do you think he's going to do with the likes of you?" She gestured towards the clearing where Billy's lifeless body laid. "Did you get a chance to see what Wayne Lee's associates did to Billy's face? And I interrupted their time together." El lowered her voice for maximum effect. "But no one—listen to me now— no one is going to interrupt your session with the men Wayne Lee will hire to work you over. The question is, will he kill you slow? Or *very* slow?"

Ferrin's fear was so palpable, El could almost taste it. He swallowed. "I tried to reason with her. I did. But she wouldn't listen. I told her it was only a few bucks. Sure, it was a lot over time—"

"Three years."

"Right. But don't tell me that upper management doesn't do that. Her own brother does, for God's sakes! I've seen it with my own eyes!"

"That may be. Life isn't fair, I hate to tell you. But it does balance out in the end, and here's how you're going to right-size the scales you tipped over with your criminal actions. You're gonna write a confession. You're gonna give it to Madam Watkins here, who's going to give it to the detectives and to every newshawk in town."

"I can't!"

"Oh, you can and you will. 'Cause if you don't, Wayne Lee will make what's left of your life a living hell."

Flo said, "I'd take her advice."

Madam Watkins agreed. "You'll be safer in a jail cell than out on the streets."

Ferrin stubbornly shook his head.

El laughed, though it was without mirth. The nerve of this guy. "Still thinking you can get away with it and run off with Ramona? Well." She looked over at Flo and Madam Watkins, who watched her with concern. She gave them a reassuring smile and turned back to Ferrin. "I've got my trump card. You can't marry Ramona."

"You don't know that—"

"You can't, because she's already married."

"Lies!"

"Oh, she is. To Frank Nickerson, the guard. You don't have a chance with her, Ferrin, and you never, ever did."

Ferrin glared at her, his eyes welling with tears. "How can she be married? She can't work—"

"It's why she hid it."

His eyes darted back and forth in their sockets. "But that means . . . that means I did all this . . . for nothing?" His face fell like a curtain descending upon a darkened stage. And he started to weep.

Madam Watkins cleared her throat. "Abe, let's get him into the Daimler. We're paying Sergeant Williams a visit."

That was then El remembered something important. "Oh, shit. Abe, where's Pearlie?"

Abe replied, "Tied up in the front seat. Should still be there."

She ran out of the studio and up the stairs to find out he wasn't. Somehow he'd managed to open the passenger door and fling himself from the Daimler. Fortunately, because his wrists and ankles were tied, Pearlie had been forced to do an impersonation of a worm, inching his way slowly across the concrete sidewalk. He'd only gotten half a block before El intercepted him.

"And where the hell do you think you're going?" she demanded as she stood right in front of him.

Pearlie craned his neck upwards. "Oh, hi, El. I was just —you know—taking a little stroll."

El crossed her arms. "Uh huh. Well, good news. We've got your best friend dead to rights. Mr. Ferrin Thomas is distraught and ready to confess."

Pearlie cursed and closed his eyes.

El reached down to help Pearlie up. Once he was off the ground, she said, "If I were you, baby, I'd be the first canary to sing."

EPILOGUE

JANUARY 1927

Gabriels squealed Armstrongs from their trumpets while the hide-beater pounded the skins of his drums. The crowd roared with laughter and applause. El finished up her tune dedicated to Alice Roosevelt's blue gown with a grand flourish. While at the Oyster House, she'd gotten the brilliant idea to combine the sweet little ditty "Alice Blue Gown" with "Sweet Georgia Brown" and make it a stomping, swearing blues about—well—"backdoor loving." (El had been inspired to put the two songs together by her then newfound relationship with Alice. Alice, of course, loved the obscenity of the revised lyrics and laughed the loudest at its first performance.) The song still killed every single time. Almost her signature tune—next to the one she wrote about bluenoses, that was. Except instead of just playing it on the piano, she now had a full band behind her—drums, bass, horn section, guitar, banjo. And a set of dancers, choreographed by Flo, who acted out the raunchy lyrics to the song.

Tonight was the grand opening weekend of The Club Car. *Her* club. She marveled at how she got here.

After that horrific scene at Augusta Wilde's studio, Madam Watkins hand delivered Ferrin Thomas and Pearlie Taylor to Sergeant Harvey Williams. Pearlie heeded El's advice and started singing as soon as he entered the precinct. He confessed to hearing the shots in his secret parlor and being coerced by Ferrin into moving Alice's body. Ferrin confessed to the murders of Alice Holloway and Billy Sullivan. Sergeant Williams took both confessions along with Alice's pistol and the Raymond Price letter and envelope. An accounting audit found the fake employee in the Holloway books. Later, the coroner matched the bullet in Alice's body as coming from her Colt .32 by using a newfound technique called "ballistics." El didn't quite understand it, but the way Sergeant Williams explained it, a gun can leave distinctive, microscopic marks on a bullet. So the coroner fired Alice's gun, examined the bullet, and compared it to the one they found in her body. Similar markings. Conclusive evidence Alice was killed with her own gun.

A jury indicted Ferrin Thomas for first-degree murder of both Alice Holloway and Billy Sullivan with an additional charge of embezzlement.

Initially arrested for accessory after the fact, Pearlie Taylor received a plea-bargain for testifying against Ferrin. He'd serve a few months of hard labor before returning to his billiard parlor. Last El heard, the griffin Gerald was running things for now.

As for Wayne Lee, Madam Watkins contacted Leonard Frazier (her secret lover and fellow millionaire) and asked him to telephone Mr. Lee. They had a chat, rich man to rich man, mourner to mourner. (Leonard had also lost his daughter recently to horrible circumstances.) Whatever he said caused Mr. Lee to call off Big John and Little John. According to Zora Mae, they'd left the city.

Madam Watkins never did tell El what Zora Mae wanted, but El noticed the bottles of liquor in the Watkins Hotel were different. New supplier, according to the bartenders. El had an inkling who it was.

The press finally admitted that El was innocent of Alice's murder. Unfortunately, her exoneration didn't stop Reverend Blackburn's protest. For days after Ferrin's arrest, a picket line three people deep paced in front of the Watkins Hotel. She saw one sign that said: "NO SINNERS ON STAGE!" And another that proclaimed: "MEN SHALL BE MEN, WOMEN SHALL BE WOMEN!"

Reverend Blackburn and his followers weren't going anywhere, it seemed.

Dread lay heavy on her chest. She'd wanted this gig at Chez J.A. so badly, wanted to make herself proud, make Madam Watkins proud. Instead, she'd dragged the Watkins name through the mud. Suspected murderer. Degenerate performer.

How long until I'm fired from this gig?

One night, she ducked around the back way, sneaking through the rear entrance of the lobby, and sprinted to the private elevator. A few people saw her—some fans, some protestors—and they called her name before she said to the elevator operator, "Go, go, go!"

The doors closed just as the throng of people arrived.

The elevator operator looked over at her. "You El Train?"

"Depends on who's asking."

"Huh. You gone and made a name for yourself."

"That I did."

"Not sure that's a good thing."

El replied ruefully, "I'm not so sure either."

They got to the top and El knocked on Madam Watkins's door.

"Come in!" she said.

As soon as El entered, Mac the parrot squawked, "Hello, Rosie! How's tricks?"

"Pretty lousy, Mac. Pretty lousy."

Madam Watkins looked up from her newspaper. "El. Nice to see you." She gestured to the pages in front of her. "I see you're fully in the clear with Pearlie's testimony and Ferrin's confession."

"Yes, Madam. Thanks to you."

"No, you did it, El. You saved yourself."

El waffled her hand from side to side. "Eh, I had a little help."

"We always have help. None of us can do life alone. But without your bravery, Alice's killer wouldn't have been caught." Madam Watkins folded up the newspaper. "Have a seat."

El did.

"I suppose you've seen the picketers outside."

El's heart sank. Here it came.

"I have, Madam," she said. "I completely understand why you can't keep me on as an act. I'd be too much of a disruption, too much of a distraction for your business."

"That is true. I have met with Reverend Blackburn, and he is unmovable in his position. And though I enjoy the irreverence you bring to my establishment, as a hotel, I can't have guests crossing a picket line."

"Just as well," El said. "I can go back to the Oyster House. I never did find a replacement act for Les."

"Oh, I don't think you have to do that." Madam

Watkins reached into her desk and pulled out an envelope, tossing it onto the desk. "Open that."

El looked at her with curiosity but did as she suggested. "What's this?"

"It's a lease. A new performance space on 131st Street and Seventh Avenue. And a check for any refurbishments and embellishments you'd like to make."

"Wha—? I don't understand."

"I hate to lose you, but I'd rather lose you to your own club than to Leslie Charles."

"You . . . you bought me a club?"

"I certainly did. It's an investment in the community. And an irreverent speakeasy being protested by a prominent Reverend is actually good publicity. Don't you think?"

El struggled to grasp what was happening. "I have my own club?"

Madam Watkins grinned. "Yes, El. Yes, you do."

El started laughing and crying at the same time. "I don't know how to thank you."

"Invite me to your opening night. I'll be in the front row."

El wiped her face. "I can't believe this." She looked up at Madam Watkins. "What about Les? I've got to give him someone. He'll never let me go otherwise."

Mac squawked behind her, "Bitch! Bitch! Goddamn bitch!"

Madam Watkins sighed. "That's it. Mac, I'm putting you in the tub and scrubbing that beak until it shines."

"Tub?" El felt herself light up. "Tubs! Of course! I can get Tubs Walker! He told me at the Willings's rent party that he wanted out of the circuit." She started laughing again and turned back to look at the parrot. "Mac, I could kiss you!"

Mac ruffled his feathers before saying, "She'll ruin us! She'll ruin us!"

To her utter amazement, Leslie Charlies agreed to having Tubs Walker take her place. She'd done the farewell shows that Madam Watkins proposed and, as she predicted, the money Leslie Charles earned made him so happy, he actually hugged El when she left the Oyster House for the final time.

And true to her word, tonight, Madam Watkins was in the front row on this opening night, cheering El on.

The Club Car's stage, though not the size of Chez J.A., could still hold a dozen people. Plus there was the dance floor they sometimes used to get closer to the folks seated in the back. Abstract paintings of trains, done by Madam Watkins's artist friend Richard Bruce Nugent, decorated the walls. Conductor's lanterns hung from the ceilings while cocktails were served at two black granite bars on either side of the space.

In honor of Alice's commitment to the working class, El gave discounts to Pullman porters and their wives, girl-friends, (or secret boyfriends), seeing how they unionized around the same time all that mess with the Holloway Factory went down. A portion of the profits would also go to the Paper Box Union.

As for the Holloway strike itself, a deal had been struck. Infinitely better than what Malek was originally going to agree to, likely driven by the fact that it came out Rich Holloway conspired to sabotage his own factory. (One of the strike busters squealed when he was arrested at the factory brawl El witnessed.) But it was not as good as they all had hoped. Still, they had to start somewhere. El hoped her contributions would move them closer to where those workers ought to be.

El stood up from her piano bench and waited for a lull in the rapturous applause before holding up her hands. "Alright, now. Alright. After an evening of 'shoving it up her brown,' poor little Alice needs to sit down."

"If she can!" called out a high-pitched male voice from the audience. That earned more laughter and applause.

El put her hands on her hips. "Oh, really? Well, I can tell by the highness of your voice, baby, that you know plenty about sitting down on things. In fact, where's your date? Maybe it's time to let him out. Boy needs to breathe sometime."

She returned to the piano and plucked out an improvised chord progression as she talked. "Now, before I leave here tonight, I want you to know that it's all fun and games, but in the end, what we're all looking for is love. Some of us have found it, some not yet. And others found and lost it." She paused. "It's—it's the hardest thing in the world to lose love. It's precious, like a rare diamond found buried under the hardest rock in the deepest dirt. To lose something like that more than breaks your heart. It can . . . it can break your spirit. 'Cause you might think you'll never find it again—heaven knows, I sometimes think that myself. But love . . . love always comes back to us. Just in mysterious ways."

Then she started singing:

> *Lonely days are long, twilight sings this song*
> *Of the happiness that used to be*
> *Soon my eyes will close, soon I'll find repose*
> *And in dreams you're always near to me*

She could already hear the tears in her voice, feel them bubbling up in her eyes, but she didn't care. Like she promised little Lenny, she'd cry it out. And even though it'd been two months, she still had tears left in her. Only now, she set them to music.

She launched into the chorus:

> *I'll see you in my dreams*
> *And I'll hold you in my dreams*
> *Someone took you right out of my arms*
> *Still I feel the thrill of your charms*

She closed her eyes and saw Alice, laughing as she snookered another man at the billiard table; dancing to the scratchy record on the Victrola in one of the many secret hotel rooms they met at, her hands motioning for El to join her; smoking that damned cigar and looking like the finest dinner there ever was while doing it.

> *Lips that once were mine*
> *Tender eyes that shine*
> *They will light my way tonight*
> *I'll see you in my dreams*

> *Oh, someone took you right out of my arms—*

The music stopped.

El's hands wouldn't budge.

Her voice refused to leap from her throat.

She opened her eyes. The stage lights, normally a comforting glow, burned. She felt hot, stifled. The tuxedo felt like those dresses her Mama made her wear: itchy, awful, and wrong. She reached up and wiped her face, which was wet with tears.

A cough in the distance.

Suddenly, she became aware of the audience. She turned. So many silhouettes staring at her.

A woman's voice—Madam Watkins's—asked, "Are you alright, El?"

Panic flooded El's chest. Every nerve in her body, every voice in her head demanded that she leave this stage right now.

She tried to speak but failed. She swallowed and tried again. "I'm sorry, y'all," she said. "I guess—I guess this one cuts a little too close tonight."

Another woman's voice called, "You got this!"

"Come on now!" a man's voice echoed.

More shouts of encouragement followed.

"Keep going now!"

"Tell that truth!"

"Take your time!"

"Yeah, take your time!"

El laughed, not because it was funny, but because she needed relief. Release. And all these voices lifting her up made her feel like when her Uncle John raised her above his head when she was young. The surprise, the joy, the love. She laughed then too.

She wiped her face once more and willed her hands to move.

They did.

And then her voice, strong and steady, sang:

Lips that once were mine
Tender eyes that shine
They will light my way tonight
I'll see you in my dreams

She finished the song and turned to the adoring crowd,

who stood on their chairs, cheering and whistling. Glancing off to the side, El saw a familiar silhouette. She could've sworn she saw the outline of Alice's black tuxedo, the shape of her brown hair curled at the ear.

El mouthed, *I love you, baby*, before taking a bow.

When she finished, she turned back to the side. Alice's silhouette was gone—if it had ever been there in the first place.

Trick of the light, El told herself. *Or maybe . . . maybe her spirit saying goodbye one last time.*

She liked that.

Backstage, she saw Flo, who had just completed a quick change into a spangled fringe number in pale pinks and contrasting burgundies, come running out of the dressing room.

"Lay down that iron, sis!" she told her.

"You know it!" Flo called over her shoulder as she ran towards the stage.

The band and the dancers would do a few numbers while El changed into a different tuxedo for the ending set.

In her dressing room, all done up in bordello red and dark wood, she dried herself off, changed into her black tuxedo, and sat on a chaise lounge, sipping some whiskey. She had about ten minutes to herself before she needed to get back to work.

She opened the paper, reading through various news. More of the same, really. Crooked politicians. Crooked businessmen. Sales on radios, motorcars, and steam liners.

One story caught her attention for two reasons: the first, it involved a landlord that wasn't a crooked son of a bitch. "The Patron Saint of Village Artists," as he was called, would often accept works of art—paintings, sculptures, even music—if a tenant couldn't make his rent.

This Patron Saint had been missing for several days, causing many members of the Greenwich Village art scene to be concerned.

That concern had intensified with today's discovery of a dead judge lying in the landlord's living room. The judge had multiple stab wounds, though the coroner's full report was still outstanding. The Patron Saint's defenders were quoted that he'd never, in a million years, harm anyone, much less stab someone repeatedly. The pounders, to no one's surprise, declared him the primary suspect.

Now, a murder—in this town?—that wasn't much to capture El's eye.

But a name was. Specifically a name she thought she recognized. It appeared the judge was involved with a property company that not only was looking to purchase the Patron Saint's building (for which he refused countless offers), but whose president was Maximilian Parker.

El read the name again.

Maximilian Parker.

Hey now, wasn't that—? Wasn't that Dash Parker's *brother?*

"Weeeellllllll shit," she muttered.

DASH AND THE BOYS RETURN IN
HIDDEN GOTHAM 5

AFTERWORD

This book was made possible by the following sources: *Bulldaggers, Pansies, and Chocolate Babies: Performance, Race, and Sexuality in the Harlem Renaissance* by James F. Hamilton; the National Museum of African American History & Culture; The Metropolitan Museum and their fabulous Harlem Renaissance exhibit; the New York State Museum; the New York Public Library and its newspaper archives; Henry Louis Gates's 1993 essay, "The Black Man's Burden," in which he writes that the Harlem Renaissance was "surely as gay as it was Black"; Eric Garber's essay "T'ain't Nobody's Business: Homosexuality in 1920's Harlem"; the website CrimeLibrary.org and its chapter on Harlem Numbers; the brilliant novel *Jazz* by Toni Morrison; Cab Calloway's *Hepster Dictionary*; and the website QueerMusicHeritage.com for its history on Queer blues singers.

El Train is a fictionalized take on the incredible Gladys Bentley, one of Harlem's most famous Queer performers. She openly paraded her lesbianism, walking the streets in suits, tuxedos, and other forms of "mannish dress." She even married her white girlfriend in Atlantic City in the early 1930s—wearing a tux, of course. Gladys would eventually open her own club and perform in front of a chorus of drag queens for the showstopper "Nothing Perplexes Like The Sexes, 'Cause When They Switch, You Don't Know Which is Which."

Madam J.A. Watkins is a fictional mashup of Madam C.J. Walker, who became a millionaire making hair products for Black women in the late 1800s/early 1900s, Madam Walker's daughter A'leia Walker, who ran the poshest and most successful beauty parlor in Harlem called The Dark Tower, and Elizabeth A. Gloucester, who started off as a domestic servant and through saving and investing, became one of the richest Black women in New York City in the mid-1800s.

The Watkins Hotel is loosely based on the Hotel Olga on West 145th Street and Lenox Avenue. The Hotel Eudora is loosely based on the Hotel Theresa on Seventh Avenue between 124th and 125th Streets.

Augusta Wilde is loosely based on Augusta Savage, who was a talented sculptor during the 1920s and 1930s. She created a stunning piece for the 1939 World's Fair called "Lift Every Voice and Sing," a reference to the poem and song.

Zora Mae is loosely based on Stephanie St. Clair, a famous numbers racketeer in the 20s and 30s who was also an activist for the Black community. She spoke out against both the police *and* the Mafia, and she managed to remain an independent operator until the end of Prohibition.

Speaking of which, the Harlem Numbers was a multimillion dollar industry that was solely Black-owned and Black-operated. There were an estimated 800 numbers-runners working each day.

Tubs Walker is a fictionalized take on Fats Waller, a piano virtuoso with a huge personality who was famous in the 1920s and 30s.

The Sergeant Harvey Williams character references the real Sergeant Samuel Battle, who was one of New York City's first Black police officers in 1911 and became New York City's first Black police sergeant in 1926.

Richard Bruce Nugent was one of the few figures of the Harlem Renaissance who was "out" about his homosexuality. Check out his artwork—it's breathtakingly beautiful.

Connie's Inn operated in the 1920s and 1930s and was owned by three brothers from Latvia. Like the Cotton Club, it only allowed white audiences—though eventually they added a late show for Black audiences.

The Hot Cha was a real after hours club, although I've fictionalized what the inside looks like.

Mac the Parrot is based on a real life bird owned by my husband's great-great grandmother. The parrot originally lived on the docks and cussed like a sailor.

And lastly, there was a paper box factory strike throughout New York City during November of 1926. The protest signs are pulled from photographs of similar strikes in the time period, and the concept of damage squads and corporate-funded violence against picket lines are both based on historical facts. Powerful men do anything to stay dominant, as we are witnessing yet again.

—*Chris Holcombe*

JOIN THE EMAIL LIST AND PATREON

If you want to learn more about the Hidden Gotham world, please sign up for my email list at:

https://www.chrisholcombe.com

If you want exclusive updates including sneak peeks into the upcoming Hidden Gotham novels, please join my Patreon:

https://www.patreon.com/ChrisHolcombeAuthor

Thank you so much for your support!

ABOUT THE AUTHOR

Chris Holcombe is the author of the Hidden Gotham series, LGBTQIA+ noir that readers call, "Honest-to-goodness pulp fiction at its gayest and most glamorous!" Set in the Queer clubs of 1920s NYC, Hidden Gotham exposes and explores that fabulous yet gritty life during The Decade That Roared. He is currently hard at work on his next book, and he asks that you send gin and chocolate for encouragement.